D0776355

HISTORY OF THE SECOND WORLD WAR

B. H. Liddell Hart

HISTORY OF
THE SECOND
WORLD WAR

Volume I

Capricorn Books
G. P. Putnam's Sons
New York

FIRST AMERICAN EDITION 1971

CAPRICORN BOOK EDITION 1972

Library of Congress Catalog
Card Number: 79-136796
SBN: 399-50253-X

Second Impression

PRINTED IN THE UNITED STATES OF AMERICA

FOREWORD

by

Lady Liddell Hart

Some months ago, when I was asked by the publishers to write the Foreword to my husband's *History of the Second World War*, I very soon realised that to thank all those who have helped in its preparation, acknowledgements should properly be given to hundreds of people, from field-marshals to privates, professors, students, and friends, with whom Basil had had contact during his active, enquiring life. In the Foreword to his *Memoirs*, he wrote that 'Memoirs are, on their happiest side, a record of friendships—and in these I have been very fortunate.' This *History* has also benefited from such friendships.

As a small boy Basil developed a love of games and the tactics of games, and he kept records and newspaper cuttings about them, as he did about the early days of aviation, when pilots were his schoolboy heroes. This habit he kept throughout his life and for all his ever-widening interests, so that at the time of his death he left hundreds of thousands of cuttings, letters, memoranda, pamphlets and the like on subjects which ranged from armoured warfare to fashions in clothes. Later, in diary form, or what he called 'Talk Notes', he recorded discussions he had about subjects that especially interested him, as soon as possible after they had taken place.

His first post-war book was *The Other Side of the Hill*, the record of his talks with a number of the German Generals who were prisoners-of-war in England. Many had been readers of his pre-war books and were eager to discuss their campaigns with him. In December 1963, looking back, he wrote 'A note on why and how I wrote this book' which explains why he attached so much value to this kind of record:

> When exploring the events of the First World War, in the 1920s and 1930s, I came to realise how much history was handicapped because no independent and historically minded enquirer had been able to ascertain and record what the military chiefs were actually thinking at the time—as a check on their subsequent recollections. For it became very evident that the memories of the participants in dramatic events are apt to become coloured or twisted in retrospect, and increasingly as the years pass. Moreover official documents often fail to reveal their real views and aims, while sometimes even drafted to conceal them.

So during the Second World War, when visiting the British and Allied commanders, I made extensive 'notes for history' of the discussions I had with them, recording particularly their current views—as a supplement to the documentary records and a means of checking memories and accounts written in later years.

At the end of the war I was given an early opportunity of interrogating the German commanders who were then prisoners-of-war, and had many long discussions with them about the operations in which they were concerned and about wider matters. While this investigation naturally could not be quite so contemporaneous, as a light on what they had been thinking before a particular event or decision, it came at any rate *before* memories had become hazy with the passage of time, while their accounts could be cross-checked with those of other witnesses, as well as by the documentary records.

Readers of this *History* will see from the footnote references to these talks how they have stood up to the test of the 'passing of time'—and to Basil's continued cross-checking over the years.

Early in 1946 the Colonels-Commandant of the Royal Tank Regiment asked Basil to write the history of the Regiment and its predecessors, covering the two World Wars and the years between the wars. It was an immense task which took many years, and the book was not published by Cassell until 1958. But the research needed for *The Tanks* was a great help when Basil came to write this *History*, for he had come to know personally many of the younger commanders who had fought on both sides, while he had also had many long discussions with such old and valued friends as Field-Marshal Montgomery, Field-Marshal Alexander, and Field-Marshal Auchinleck, as well as his 'tank people' and many of the German Generals 'on the other side of the hill'.

After the 1946 War of Independence, Israeli officers of all ranks came to see Basil to consult him about the formation of their Army. Among them was Yigal Allon, who became a close friend—and it was Yigal who inscribed his photograph in the library at States House with the now much-quoted words 'To the Captain who teaches Generals'. In 1961 Basil was asked to visit Israel and lecture to the armed forces and universities. Many tributes have been paid to Basil's teachings by the Israelis, and Basil often said, somewhat ruefully, that rather than his own countrymen, the Germans and the Israelis were his 'best pupils'.

In 1951 Frau Rommel asked him if he would edit her husband's papers. He agreed and a warm relationship developed between us and Field-Marshal Rommel's widow, his son Manfred, and with General Bayerlein, who had been Rommel's Chief of Staff; and also with Mark Bonham Carter of Collins, who was the very able publisher's editor.

In 1952 Basil lectured at War Colleges in Canada and the United States. These were exhausting months, but rewarding, and he was able to meet wartime friends from both countries and to make new ones. Among the honours he received that gave him most pleasure was his honorary membership of the U.S. Marine Corps, and until he died he daily wore the gold tie clip presented to him on that occasion.

In 1965 he was asked to be Visiting Professor of History at the University of California, Davis: so at the age of seventy he became a Professor and lectured and taught on the two World Wars. This was a stimulating experience which he thoroughly enjoyed, but unfortunately our stay was cut short by several months as he had to return to England for a major operation. At the time of his death he was looking forward—against his doctor's advice—to returning to America in April 1970 at the invitation of the U.S. Naval War College to give a series of lectures on strategy.

Travel was an essential part of Basil's life, and he accepted many invitations to visit European countries and to lecture at Staff Colleges. He was a brilliant map reader and his vivid accounts of Sherman's battles in the American Civil War were written with the aid of an intensive study of large-scale maps, long before he visited the battlefields of the Southern States. After the last war we made almost yearly visits to Western Europe to study battlefields and landing beaches, to visit old friends, and, maps in hand, to check data for this *History*. He loved beautiful country, cathedrals, and good food, so for our tours the *Guide Michelin*, battlefield maps and tourists' guides were always put in the car together, and careful daily notes about terrain, food, and church architecture were dictated to me for subsequent filing in the ever-growing records at home.

Basil had been critical of the Official Historians of the First World War, saying that sometimes the word 'Official' cancelled out the word 'History', but he had a high opinion of most of those who wrote about the Second World War, and his files are full of correspondence with many of them in this country, the Commonwealth, and America. Friendships with historians —the younger historians particularly—and students from all over the world enriched his life and he spent a great deal of time reading and criticising the drafts of their theses and books, to the neglect of his own work but to his infinite pleasure. As one of them, Ronald Lewin, wrote: '... he praised only where on his terms praise was due, and [gave] you hell if he thought you were wrong in fact or opinion.' Young scholars, academics, authors, journalists—and older ones—came to work in the library and to examine the books and papers which were all made available to them. 'Tutorials' would be given at any time of the day or night, over meals and during walks in the garden. Correlli Barnett, General André Beaufre, Colonel Henri Bernard, Brian Bond, Alan Clark, Colonel A. Goutard, Alastair Horne, Michael Howard, Robert O'Neill, Peter Paret, Barrie Pitt, W. R. Thompson, Michael Williams, are but some of the best known among the many contemporary historians who came first for discussion and work, became regular correspondents, and to our great happiness returned again and again as our friends. Many others, such as Jay Luvaas and Don Schurman, who with their families became our devoted friends, came from America and Canada.

To all these people therefore, and to the hundreds in all those many spheres other than strategy and defence in which Basil's far-ranging interests lay whose names I have not given and who will, I trust, forgive me for that, this *History* owes much. Nobody believed more than did Basil that a teacher will be 'taught by his pupils', and his pupils and friends were among the most stimulating it was possible to have. While writing the *History*, Basil had some very able assistants. Christopher Hart, then Peter Simkins, now at the Imperial War Museum, Paul Kennedy who did some valuable work on the Pacific Campaign, and Peter Bradley who helped with the chapters on Air.

Many secretaries worked with great efficiency over the years and their interest and patience in typing and re-typing the successive drafts of the *History* made the task easier for Basil. Miss Myra Thomson (now Mrs Slater) was with us for eight years during the time we lived at Wolverton Park. Later, here at States House, Mrs Daphne Bosanquet and Mrs Edna Robinson were helpful in every possible way, and in the last stages of the preparation of the *History*, Mrs Wendy Smith, Mrs Pamela Byrnes and Mrs Margaret Haws did valuable work.

Among the countless other people to be thanked are the directors and staff of Cassell's, the publishers of the British edition of the *History*. Desmond Flower commissioned the book in 1947 and has waited patiently for it to be finished. Thanks are also due to David Higham, not only as the literary agent for many of Basil's books, but for his friendship over the years.

The publishers and I are especially grateful to the following who so generously read various chapters or the whole of the *History* before or after Basil's death and gave him the benefit of their criticisms: G. R. Atkinson, Brian Bond, Dr Noble Frankland, Vice-Admiral Sir Peter Gretton, Adrian Liddell Hart, Malcolm Mackintosh, Captain Stephen Roskill, Vice-Admiral Brian Schofield, Lieut.-Colonel Albert Seaton, Major-General Sir Kenneth Strong, and Dr M. J. Williams. Some of them have generously allowed Basil to make quotations from their own books—Colonel Seaton before his was even published.

We would like also to thank Ann Fern and Richard Natkiel for their work in respectively researching and drawing the maps; and once again thanks are due to Miss Hebe Jerrold, who has produced a first-class index, though having to work under much pressure.

Of the many people who have helped, I know that we all are most indebted to Kenneth Parker of Cassell's, Basil's editor and friend, who has had the heavy task of organizing the *History* for publication after Basil's death. Without him, the book would have been delayed even longer. Basil said, in the Foreword to his *Memoirs*, that he had 'been blessed ... with a most stimulating, knowledgeable and exacting editor with whom it has been a delight to work.' To those words I would like to add my special gratitude for his work on the *History*.

Basil had small private means, so research for the *History* was always slowed down as he had to earn a living by his journalism and by writing other, more quickly produced books. He was helped during the years 1965–67 by a grant from the Wolfson Foundation and he appreciated the special interest that Mr Leonard Wolfson showed in the *History*. Help came from another direction in 1961, when King's College, London, where Michael Howard was then Director of Military Studies, generously made possible the conversion of the stables of States House into a Library, and a small flat was built in the barn for the use of visiting historians. This greatly added to our working space and to the comfort of the scholars. Also the Inland Revenue authorities in the three different districts where we lived during these years, by their understanding of the nature and the problems of Basil's work, made it possible for us to live and work in England. Without this, we would have been forced to live abroad and the *History*, as well as much else of Basil's writing and teaching, would have suffered.

To 'all who helped', therefore, named and unnamed in this Foreword, I would like to dedicate this book.

KATHLEEN LIDDELL HART

States House,
Medmenham,
Bucks., England
July 1970

CONTENTS

CONTENTS

PART IV

THE SPREAD
(1941)

PART V

THE TURN
(1942)

PART I

THE PRELUDE

CHAPTER 1

HOW WAR WAS PRECIPITATED

On April 1, 1939, the world's Press carried the news that Mr Neville Chamberlain's Cabinet, reversing its policy of appeasement and detachment, had pledged Britain to defend Poland against any threat from Germany, with the aim of ensuring peace in Europe.

On September 1, however, Hitler marched across the Polish frontier. Two days later, after vainly demanding his withdrawal, Britain and France entered the fight. Another European War had started—and it developed into a second World War.

The Western Allies entered that war with a two-fold object. The immediate purpose was to fulfil their promise to preserve the independence of Poland. The ultimate purpose was to remove a potential menace to themselves, and thus ensure their own security. In the outcome, they failed in both purposes. Not only did they fail to prevent Poland from being overcome in the first place, and partitioned between Germany and Russia, but after six years of war which ended in apparent victory they were forced to acquiesce in Russia's domination of Poland—abandoning their pledges to the Poles who had fought on their side.

At the same time all the effort that was put into the destruction of Hitlerite Germany resulted in a Europe so devastated and weakened in the process that its power of resistance was much reduced in the face of a fresh and greater menace—and Britain, in common with her European neighbours, had become a poor dependant of the United States.

These are the hard facts underlying the victory that was so hopefully pursued and so painfully achieved—after the colossal weight of both Russia and America had been drawn into the scales against Germany. The outcome dispelled the persistent popular illusion that 'victory' spelt peace. It confirmed the warning of past experience that victory is a 'mirage in the desert'—the desert that a long war creates, when waged with modern weapons and unlimited methods.

It is worthwhile to take stock of the consequences of the war before

Europe at the Outbreak of War

Copyright © Cassell & Co. Ltd 1970

dealing with its causation. A realisation of what the war brought may clear the way for a more realistic examination of how the war was produced. It sufficed for the purposes of the Nuremberg Trials to assume that the outbreak of war, and all its extensions, were purely due to Hitler's aggression. But that is too simple and shallow an explanation.

The last thing that Hitler wanted to produce was another great war. His people, and particularly his generals, were profoundly fearful of any such risk—the experiences of World War I had scarred their minds. To emphasise the basic facts is not to whitewash Hitler's inherent aggressiveness, nor that of many Germans who eagerly followed his lead. But Hitler, though utterly unscrupulous, was for long cautious in pursuing his aims. The military chiefs were still more cautious and anxious about any step that might provoke a general conflict.

A large part of the German archives were captured after the war, and have thus been available for examination. They reveal an extraordinary degree of trepidation and deep-seated distrust of Germany's capacity to wage a great war.

When, in 1936, Hitler moved to re-occupy the demilitarised zone of the Rhineland, his generals were alarmed at his decision and the reactions it might provoke from the French. As a result of their protests only a few token units were sent in at first, as 'straws in the wind'. When he wished to send troops to help Franco in the Spanish Civil War they made fresh protests about the risks involved, and he agreed to restrict his aid. But he disregarded their apprehensions about the march into Austria, in March 1938.

When, shortly afterwards, Hitler disclosed his intention of putting the screw on Czecho-Slovakia for the return of the Sudetenland, the Chief of the General Staff, General Beck, drafted a memorandum in which he argued that Hitler's aggressively expansionist programme was bound to produce a world-wide catastrophe and Germany's ruin. This was read out at a conference of the leading generals, and, with their general approval, sent to Hitler. As Hitler showed no sign of changing his policy, the Chief of the General Staff resigned from office. Hitler assured the other generals that France and Britain would not fight for Czecho-Slovakia, but they were so far from being reassured that they plotted a military revolt, to avert the risk of war by arresting Hitler and the other Nazi leaders.

The bottom was knocked out of their counter-plan, however, when Chamberlain acceded to Hitler's crippling demands upon Czecho-Slovakia, and in concert with the French agreed to stand aside while that unhappy country was stripped of both territory and defences.

For Chamberlain, the Munich Agreement spelt 'peace for our time'. For

Hitler, it spelt a further and greater triumph not only over his foreign opponents but also over his generals. After their warnings had been so repeatedly refuted by his unchallenged and bloodless successes, they naturally lost confidence, and influence. Naturally, too, Hitler himself became overweeningly confident of a continued run of easy success. Even when he came to see that further ventures might entail a war he felt that it would be only a small one, and a short one. His moments of doubt were drowned by the cumulative effect of intoxicating success.

If he had really contemplated a general war, involving Britain, he would have put every possible effort into building a Navy capable of challenging Britain's command of the sea. But, in fact, he did not even build up his Navy to the limited scale visualised in the Anglo-German Naval Treaty of 1935. He constantly assured his admirals that they could discount any risk of war with Britain. After Munich he told them that they need not anticipate a conflict with Britain within the next six years at least. Even in the summer of 1939, and as late as August 22, he repeated such assurances—if with waning conviction.

How, then, did it come about that he became involved in the major war that he had been so anxious to avoid? The answer is to be found not merely, nor most, in Hitler's aggressiveness, but in the encouragement he had long received from the complaisant attitude of the Western Powers coupled with their sudden turn-about in the spring of 1939. That reversal was so abrupt and unexpected as to make war inevitable.

If you allow anyone to stoke up a boiler until the steam-pressure rises beyond danger-point, the real responsibility for any resultant explosion will lie with you. That truth of physical science applies equally to political science—especially to the conduct of international affairs.

Ever since Hitler's entry into power, in 1933, the British and French Governments had conceded to this dangerous autocrat immeasurably more than they had been willing to concede to Germany's previous democratic Governments. At every turn they showed a disposition to avoid trouble and shelve awkward problems—to preserve their present comfort at the expense of the future.

Hitler, on the other hand, was thinking out his problems all too logically. The course of his policy came to be guided by the ideas formulated in a 'testament' which he expounded in November 1937—a version of which has been preserved in the so-called 'Hossbach Memorandum'. It was based on the conviction of Germany's vital need for more *lebensraum*—living space—for her expanding population if there was to be any chance of maintaining their living standards. In his view Germany could not hope to make herself self-sufficient, especially in food-supply. Nor by buying it abroad could she obtain what was needed, since that meant spending more foreign exchange than she could afford. The prospects of her obtaining an increased share in world trade and industry were too limited, because of other nations' tariff walls and her own financial stringency. Moreover the method of indirect supply would make her dependent on foreign nations, and liable to starvation in case of war.

His conclusion was that Germany must obtain more 'agriculturally useful space'—in the thinly populated areas of Eastern Europe. It would be vain to hope that this would be willingly conceded her. 'The history of all times—Roman Empire, British Empire—has proved that every space expansion can be effected only by breaking resistance and taking risks. . . . Neither in former times nor today has space been found without an owner.' The problem would have to be solved by 1945 at the latest—'after this we can only expect a change for the worse'. Possible outlets would be blocked while a food crisis would be imminent.

While these ideas went much farther than Hitler's initial desire to recover the territory that had been taken from Germany after World War I, it is not true that Western statesmen were as unaware of them as they later pretended. In 1937-8 many of them were frankly realistic in private discussion, though not on public platforms, and many arguments were set forth in British governing circles for allowing Germany to expand eastwards, and thus divert danger from the West. They showed much sympathy with Hitler's desire for *lebensraum*—and let him know it. But they shirked thinking out the problem of how the owners could be induced to yield it except to threat of superior force.

The German documents reveal that Hitler derived special encouragement from Lord Halifax's visit in November 1937. Halifax was then Lord President of the Council, ranking second in the Cabinet to the Prime Minister. According to the documentary record of the interview, he gave Hitler to understand that Britain would allow him a free hand in Eastern Europe. Halifax may not have meant as much, but that was the impression he conveyed—and it proved of crucial importance.

Then, in February 1938, Mr Anthony Eden was driven to resign as Foreign Minister after repeated disagreements with Chamberlain—who in response to one of his protests had told him to 'go home and take an aspirin'. Halifax was appointed to succeed him at the Foreign Office. A few days later the British Ambassador in Berlin, Sir Nevile Henderson, called on Hitler for a confidential talk, in continuation of Halifax's November conversation, and conveyed that the British Government was much in sympathy with Hitler's desire for 'changes in Europe' to Germany's benefit—'the present British Government had a keen sense of reality'.

As the documents show, these events precipitated Hitler's action. He thought that the lights had changed to green, allowing him to proceed eastward. It was a very natural conclusion.

Hitler was further encouraged by the accommodating way that the British and French Governments accepted his march into Austria and incorporation of that country in the German Reich. (The only hitch in that easy coup was the way many of his tanks broke down on the road to Vienna.) Still more encouragement came when he heard that Chamberlain and Halifax had rejected Russian proposals, after that coup, to confer on a collective insurance plan against the German advance.

Here it should be added that when the threat to the Czechs came to a head in September 1938, the Russian Government again made known, publicly and privately, its willingness to combine with France and Britain in measures to defend Czecho-Slovakia. That offer was ignored. Moreover, Russia was ostentatiously excluded from the Munich conference at which Czecho-Slovakia's fate was settled. This 'cold-shouldering' had fatal consequences the following year.

After the way that the British Government had appeared to acquiesce in his eastward move, Hitler was unpleasantly surprised by their strong reaction, and the partial mobilisation, which developed when he 'put the heat' on Czecho-Slovakia in September. But when Chamberlain yielded to his demands, and actively helped him to impose his terms on Czecho-Slovakia, he felt that the momentary threat of resistance had been in the nature of a face-saving operation—to meet the objections of the large body of British opinion, headed by Mr Winston Churchill, which opposed the governmental policy of conciliation and concession. He was no less encouraged by the passivity of the French. As they had so readily abandoned their Czech ally, which had possessed the most efficient Army of all the smaller Powers, it seemed unlikely that they would go to war in defence of any remnant of their former chain of allies in East and Central Europe.

Thus Hitler felt that he could safely complete the elimination of Czecho-Slovakia at an early moment, and then expand his eastward advance.

At first he did not think of moving against Poland—even though she possessed the largest stretch of territory carved out of Germany after World War I. Poland, like Hungary, had been helpful to him in threatening Czecho-Slovakia's rear, and thus inducing her to surrender to his demands—Poland, incidentally, had exploited the chance to seize a slice of Czech territory. Hitler was inclined to accept Poland as a junior partner for the time being, on condition that she handed back the German port of Danzig and granted Germany a free route to East Prussia through the Polish 'Corridor'. On Hitler's part, it was a remarkably moderate demand in the circumstances. But in successive discussions that winter, Hitler found that the Poles were obstinately disinclined to make any such concession, and also had an inflated idea of their own strength. Even so, he continued to hope that they would come round after further negotiation. As late as March 25 he told his Army Commander-in-Chief that he 'did not wish to solve the Danzig problem by the use of force'. But a change of mind was produced by an unexpected British step that followed on a fresh step on his part in a different direction.

In the early months of 1939, the heads of the British Government were feeling happier than they had for a long time past. They lulled themselves into the belief that their accelerated rearmament measures, America's rearmament programme and Germany's economic difficulties were diminishing the danger of the situation. On March 10 Chamberlain privately expressed the view that the prospects of peace were better than ever, and spoke of his hopes that a new disarmament conference would be arranged before the end of the year. Next day Sir Samuel Hoare—Eden's predecessor as Foreign Secretary and now Home Secretary—hopefully suggested in a speech that the world was entering 'a Golden Age'. Ministers assured friends and critics that Germany's economic plight made her incapable of going to war, and that she was bound to comply with the British Government's conditions in return for the help that it was offering her in the form of a commercial treaty. Two ministers, Mr Oliver Stanley and Mr Robert Hudson, were going to Berlin to arrange it.

That same week *Punch* came out with a cartoon which showed 'John Bull' awaking with relief from a nightmare, while the recent 'war scare' was flying out of the window. Never was there such a spell of absurdly optimistic illusions as during the week leading up to the 'Ides of March', 1939.

Meantime the Nazis had been fostering separatist movements in Czecho-Slovakia, to produce its breakdown from within. On March 12 the Slovaks declared their independence, after their leader, Father Tiso, had visited Hitler in Berlin. More blindly, Poland's Foreign Minister, Colonel Beck, publicly expressed his full sympathy with the Slovaks. On the 15th, German troops marched into Prague, after the Czech President had yielded to Hitler's demand to establish a 'Protectorate' over Bohemia and to occupy the country accordingly.

The previous autumn, when the Munich agreement was made, the British Government had pledged itself to guarantee Czecho-Slovakia against aggression. But Chamberlain told the House of Commons that he considered that Slovakia's break-away had annulled the guarantee, and that he did not feel bound by this obligation. While expressing regret at what had happened, he conveyed to the House that he saw no reason why it should 'deflect' British policy.

Within a few days, however, Chamberlain made a complete 'about-turn'—so sudden and far-reaching that it amazed the world. He jumped to a decision to block any following move of Hitler's and on March 29 sent Poland an offer to support her against 'any action which threatened Polish independence, and which the Polish Government accordingly considered it vital to resist'.

It is impossible to gauge what was the predominant influence on his impulse—the pressure of public indignation, or his own indignation, or his anger at having been fooled by Hitler, or his humiliation at having been made to look a fool in the eyes of his own people.

Most of those in Britain who had supported and applauded his previous appeasement policy underwent a similarly violent reaction—sharpened by the reproaches of the 'other half' of the nation, which had distrusted the policy. The breach was cemented, and the nation reunited, by a general surge of exasperation.

The unqualified terms of the guarantee placed Britain's destiny in the hands of Poland's rulers, men of very dubious and unstable judgement. Moreover, the guarantee was impossible to fulfil except with Russia's help, yet no preliminary steps were taken to find out whether Russia would give, or Poland would accept, such aid.

The Cabinet, when asked to approve the guarantee, was not even shown the actual report of the Chiefs of Staff Committee—which would have made clear how impossible it was, in a practical sense, to give any effective protection to Poland.* It is doubtful, however, whether this would have made any difference in face of the prevailing mood.

When the guarantee was discussed in Parliament it was welcomed on all sides. Mr Lloyd George's was a solitary voice when he warned the House that it was suicidal folly to undertake such a far-stretched commitment without first making sure of Russia's backing. The Polish Guarantee was the surest way to produce an early explosion, and a world war. It combined the maximum temptation with manifest provocation. It incited Hitler to demonstrate the futility of such a guarantee to a country out of reach from

* I was told this soon afterwards by Mr Hore-Belisha, then Secretary of State for War, and also by Lord Beaverbrook, who had heard about the matter from other members of the Government.

the West, while making the stiff-necked Poles even less inclined to consider any concession to him, and at the same time making it impossible for him to draw back without 'losing face'.

Why did Poland's rulers accept such a fatal offer? Partly because they had an absurdly exaggerated idea of the power of their out of date forces—they boastfully talked of a 'cavalry ride to Berlin'. Partly because of personal factors: Colonel Beck, shortly afterwards, said that he made up his mind to accept the British offer between 'two flicks of the ash' off the cigarette he was smoking. He went on to explain that at his meeting with Hitler in January he had found it hard to swallow Hitler's remark that Danzig 'must' be handed back, and that when the British offer was communicated to him he saw it, and seized it, as a chance to give Hitler a slap in the face. This impulse was only too typical of the ways in which the fate of peoples is often decided.

The only chance of avoiding war now lay in securing the support of Russia—the only power that could give Poland direct support and thus provide a deterrent to Hitler. But, despite the urgency of the situation, the British Government's steps were dilatory and half-hearted. Chamberlain had a strong dislike of Soviet Russia and Halifax an intense religious antipathy, while both underrated her strength as much as they overrated Poland's. If they now recognised the desirability of a defensive arrangement with Russia they wanted it on their own terms, and failed to realise that by their precipitate guarantee to Poland they had placed themselves in a position where they would have to sue for it on her terms—as was obvious to Stalin, if not to them.

But beyond their own hesitations were the objections of the Polish Government, and the other small powers in eastern Europe, to accepting military support from Russia—since these feared that reinforcement by her armies would be equivalent to invasion. So the pace of the Anglo-Russian negotiations became as slow as a funeral march.

Very different was Hitler's response to the new situation. Britain's violent reaction and redoubled armament measures shook him, but the effect was opposite to that intended. Feeling that the British were becoming opposed to German expansion eastward, and fearful of being blocked if he tarried, he drew the conclusion that he must accelerate his steps towards *lebensraum*. But how could he do it without bringing on a general war? His solution was coloured by his historically derived picture of the British. Regarding them as cool-headed and rational, with their emotions controlled by their head, he felt that they would not dream of entering a war on behalf of Poland unless they could obtain Russia's support. So, swallowing his hatred and fear of 'Bolshevism', he bent his efforts and energies towards conciliating Russia and securing her abstention. It was a turn-about even more startling than Chamberlain's—and as fatal in its consequences.

Hitler's courting approach to Russia was eased because Stalin was already looking on the West from a new slant. The Russians' natural resentment of the way they had been cold-shouldered by Chamberlain and Halifax in 1938 was increased when, after Hitler's march into Prague, their fresh proposal for a joint defensive alliance had a tepid reception, while the British Government rushed into an independent arrangement with Poland. Nothing could have been more certain to deepen doubt and heighten suspicion.

On May 3 a warning, unmistakable except to the blind, was conveyed in the news that Litvinov, Russia's Foreign Commissar, had been 'released' from office. He had long been the chief advocate of co-operation with the Western Powers in resistance to Nazi Germany. To his post was appointed Molotov, who was reported to prefer dealing with dictators to dealing with liberal democracies.

Tentative moves towards a Soviet-Nazi *entente* began in April, but were conducted on both sides with extreme wariness—for mutual distrust was profound, and each side suspected that the other might be merely trying to hinder it reaching an agreement with the Western Powers. But the slow progress of the Anglo-Russian negotiations encouraged the Germans to exploit the opportunity, quicken their pace, and press their suit. Molotov remained non-committal, however, until the middle of August. Then a decisive change took place. It may have been prompted by the Germans' willingness, in contrast to British hesitations and reservations, to concede Stalin's exacting conditions, especially a free hand with the Baltic States. It may also have been connected with the obvious fact that Hitler could not afford to postpone action in Poland beyond early September, lest the weather might bog him down, so that the postponement of the Soviet-German agreement until late in August ensured that there would not be time for Hitler and the Western Powers to reach another 'Munich agreement'— which might spell danger for Russia.

On August 23 Ribbentrop flew to Moscow, and the pact was signed. It was accompanied by a secret agreement under which Poland was to be partitioned between Germany and Russia.

This pact made war certain, and all the more so because of the lateness of the timing. Hitler could not draw back on the Polish issue without serious loss of face in Moscow. Moreover, his belief that the British Government would not venture on an obviously futile struggle to preserve Poland, and did not really wish to bring in Russia, had been freshly fostered by the way that Chamberlain had, in late July, started private negotiations with him through his trusted adviser, Sir Horace Wilson, for an Anglo-German pact.

But the Soviet-German Pact, coming so late, did not have the effect on the British that Hitler had reckoned. On the contrary, it aroused the 'bull-dog' spirit—of blind determination, regardless of the consequences. In that state of feeling, Chamberlain could not stand aside without both loss of face and breach of promise.

Stalin had been only too well aware that the Western Powers had long been disposed to let Hitler expand eastward—in Russia's direction. It is probable that he saw the Soviet-German Pact as a convenient device by which he could divert Hitler's aggressive dynamism in the opposite direction. In other words, by this nimble side-step he would let his immediate and potential opponents crash into one another. At the least this should produce a diminution of the threat to Soviet Russia, and might well result in such common exhaustion on their part as to ensure Russia's post-war ascendancy.

The Pact meant the removal of Poland as a buffer between Germany and Russia—but the Russians had always felt that the Poles were more likely to serve as a spearhead for a German invasion of Russia than as a barricade against it. By collaborating in Hitler's conquest of Poland, and dividing it with him, they would not only be taking an easy way of regaining their pre-1914 property but be able to convert eastern Poland into a barrier space which, though narrower, would be held by their own forces. That seemed a more reliable buffer than an independent Poland. The Pact also paved the way for Russia's occupation of the Baltic States and Bessarabia, as a wider extension of the buffer.

In 1941, after Hitler had swept into Russia, Stalin's 1939 side-step looked a fatally short-sighted shift. It is likely that Stalin overestimated the Western nations' capacity for resisting, and thus exhausting, Germany's power. It is likely, too, that he also overestimated the initial resisting power of his own forces. Nevertheless, surveying the European situation in later years, it does not seem so certain as in 1941 that his side-step proved to Soviet Russia's disadvantage.

For the West, on the other hand, it brought immeasurable harm. The primary blame for that lies with those who were responsible for the successive policies of procrastination and precipitation—in face of a palpably explosive situation.

Dealing with Britain's entry into the war—after describing how she allowed Germany to re-arm and then to swallow Austria and

Czecho-Slovakia, while at the same time spurning Russia's proposals for joint action—Churchill says:

> ...when every one of these aids and advantages has been squandered and thrown away, Great Britain advances, leading France by the hand, to guarantee the integrity of Poland—of that very Poland which with hyena appetite had only six months before joined in the pillage and destruction of the Czechoslovak State. There was sense in fighting for Czechoslovakia in 1938, when the German Army could scarcely put half a dozen trained divisions on the Western Front, when the French with nearly sixty or seventy divisions could most certainly have rolled forward across the Rhine or into the Ruhr. But this had been judged unreasonable, rash, below the level of modern intellectual thought and morality. Yet now at last the two Western democracies declared themselves ready to stake their lives upon the territorial integrity of Poland. History, which, we are told, is mainly the record of the crimes, follies, and miseries of mankind, may be scoured and ransacked to find a parallel to this sudden and complete reversal of five or six years' policy of easy-going placatory appeasement, and its transformation almost overnight into a readiness to accept an obviously imminent war on far worse conditions and on the greatest scale. . . .
>
> Here was decision at last, taken at the worst possible moment and on the least satisfactory ground, which must surely lead to the slaughter of tens of millions of people.*

It is a striking verdict on Chamberlain's folly, written in hindsight. For Churchill himself had, in the heat of the moment, supported Chamberlain's pressing offer of Britain's guarantee to Poland. It is only too evident that in 1939 he, like most of Britain's leaders, acted on a hot-headed impulse—instead of with the cool-headed judgement that was once characteristic of British statesmanship.

---

* Churchill: *The Second World War*, vol. I, pp. 311–12. Full bibliographical details of all books referred to in the text can be found on p. 715.

CHAPTER 2

THE OPPOSING FORCES AT THE
OUTBREAK

On Friday September 1, 1939, the German armies invaded Poland. On Sunday, the 3rd, the British Government declared war on Germany, in fulfilment of the guarantee it had earlier given to Poland. Six hours later the French Government, more hesitantly, followed the British lead.

In making his fateful announcement to the British Parliament the seventy-year old Prime Minister, Mr Chamberlain, finished by saying: 'I trust I may live to see the day when Hitlerism has been destroyed and a liberated Europe has been re-established.' Within less than a month Poland had been overrun. Within nine months most of Western Europe had been submerged by the spreading flood of war. And although Hitler was ultimately overthrown, a liberated Europe was not re-established.

In welcoming the declaration of war, Mr Arthur Greenwood, speaking for the Labour Party, expressed his relief that 'the intolerable agony of suspense from which all of us have suffered is over. We now know the worst.' From the volume of cheers it was clear that he was expressing the general feeling of the House. He ended: 'May the war be swift and short, and may the peace which follows stand proudly for ever on the shattered ruin of an evil name.'

No reasonable calculation of the respective forces and resources provided any ground for believing that the war could be 'swift and short', or even for hoping that France and Britain alone would be able to overcome Germany—however long the war continued. Even more foolish was the assumption that 'We now know the worst'.

There were illusions about the strength of Poland. Lord Halifax—who, as Foreign Minister, ought to have been well-informed—believed that Poland was of more military value than Russia, and preferred to secure her as an ally. That was what he conveyed to the American Ambassador on March 24, a few days before the sudden decision to offer the British guarantee to Poland.

In July, the Inspector-General of the Forces, General Ironside, visited the Polish Army and on his return gave what Mr Churchill described as 'most favourable' reports.*

There were still greater illusions about the French Army. Churchill himself had described it as 'the most perfectly trained and faithful mobile force in Europe'.† When he saw General Georges, the Commander-in-Chief of the French field armies, a few days before the war, and saw the comparative figures of French and German strength, he was so favourably impressed as to say: 'But you are the masters.'‡

This may have increased the eagerness with which he joined in pressing the French to hasten to declare war in support of Poland—the French Ambassador's dispatch said: 'One of the most excited was Mr Winston Churchill; bursts of his voice made the telephone vibrate.' In March, too, Churchill had declared himself 'in the most complete agreement with the Prime Minister' over the offer to guarantee Poland. Along with almost all Britain's political leaders he had dwelt on its value as a means of preserving peace. Mr Lloyd George had been alone in pointing out its impracticability and danger—and his warning was described by *The Times* as 'an outburst of inconsolable pessimism from Mr Lloyd George, who now seems to inhabit an odd and remote world of his own.'

For balance, it should be mentioned that these illusions about the prospects were not shared in the more sober military circles.§ But in general the prevailing mood of the moment was supercharged with emotions that drowned the sense of immediate realities, and obscured the long view.

Could Poland have held out longer? Could France and Britain have done more than they did to take the German pressure off Poland? On the face of the figures of armed strength, as now known, the answer to both questions would at first sight seem to be 'Yes'. In *numbers* of men Poland had sufficient to check the German forces on her front, and at the least impose a long delay on their advance. It is equally apparent, on the figures, that the French should have been able to defeat the German forces left to oppose them in the West.

The Polish Army consisted of thirty active divisions and ten reserve divisions. It had also no less than twelve large cavalry brigades—although only one of them was motorised. Its potential strength in numbers was even

* Churchill: *The Second World War*, vol. I, p. 357.
† April 14, 1938.
‡ Churchill: *The Second World War*, vol. I, p. 357.
§ My own strategic appreciation written at the outbreak of war, forecasting the early defeat of Poland and the likelihood that France would not long continue the fight, epitomised the situation in its conclusion: 'In sum, by making our stand on ground that was strategically unsound we have got into a very bad hole—perhaps the worst in our history.'

larger than the total figure of divisions conveys—for Poland had nearly 2,500,000 'trained men' available to mobilise.

France mobilised the equivalent of 110 divisions, of which no less than sixty-five were active divisions. They included five cavalry divisions, two mechanised divisions, and one armoured division that was in process of being formed—the rest being infantry. Of the grand total, even after providing for the defence of southern France and North Africa against a possible threat from Italy, the French Command were able to concentrate eighty-five divisions on their northern front facing Germany. Moreover, they could mobilise 5,000,000 trained men.

Britain had promised to send four Regular divisions to France at the outset of war—besides providing for the defence of the Middle East and the Far East—and actually sent the equivalent of five divisions. Because of the problem of sea transport, however, and the circuitous route considered necessary to avoid air attack, this initial contingent could not arrive until late in September.

Besides her small but high quality Regular Army, Britain was just in the process of forming and equipping a Territorial field army of twenty-six divisions, and on the outbreak of war the Government had made plans for expanding the total to fifty-five divisions. But the first contingent of this new force would not be ready to enter the field until 1940. Meantime, Britain's main contribution could only be in the traditional form of naval power exercising a sea blockade—a form of pressure that was inherently slow to take effect.

Britain had a bomber force of just over 600—double that of France, though considerably less than half that of Germany—but in view of the limited size and range of the machines then in service, it could exert no serious effect by direct attack on Germany.

Germany mobilised ninety-eight divisions, of which fifty-two were active divisions (including six Austrian). Of the remaining forty-six divisions, however, only ten were fit for action on mobilisation and even in these the bulk of the men were recruits who had only been serving about a month. The other thirty-six divisions consisted mainly of veterans of World War I, forty-year-olds who had little acquaintance with modern weapons and tactics. They were very short of artillery and other weapons. It took a long time to get these divisions organised and trained collectively to operate as such—longer even than had been reckoned by the German Command, which was much alarmed at the slowness of the process.

The German Army was not ready for war in 1939—a war which its chiefs did not expect, relying on Hitler's assurance. They had consented unwillingly to Hitler's desire to expand the army quickly, as they preferred a gradual process of building up thoroughly trained cadres, but Hitler had repeatedly told them that there would be plenty of time for such training, as he had no intention of risking a major war before 1944 at the earliest. Equipment, too, was still very short compared with the scale of the army.

Yet after the event it came to be assumed generally that Germany's sweeping victories in the early stages of the war were due to an overwhelming superiority of weapons, as well as of numbers.

The second illusion was slow to fade. Even in his war memoirs, Churchill said that the Germans had at least a thousand 'heavy tanks' in 1940. The fact is that they had then no heavy tanks at all. At the start of the war they had only a handful of medium tanks, weighing barely 20 tons. Most of the tanks they used in Poland were of very light weight and thin armour.*

Casting up the balance sheet, it can be seen that the Poles and French together had the equivalent of 130 divisions against a German total of ninety-eight divisions, of which thirty-six were virtually untrained, and unorganised. In numbers of 'trained soldiers' the balance against the Germans was much larger still. What could be weighed against this adverse numerical balance was that the weightier combination was widely separated—divided into two parts by Germany's central position. The Germans were able to attack the weaker of the two partners, while the French had to attack the Germans' prepared defence if they were to bring relief to their ally.

Even so, on a quantitative reckoning, the Poles had large enough forces to *hold up* the striking force launched against them—which consisted of forty-eight active divisions. These were followed up by some half dozen of the reserve divisions that were mobilised, but the campaign ended before they came into action.

On the surface, it would appear that the French had ample superiority to crush the German forces in the West, and break through to the Rhine. The German generals were astonished, and relieved, that they did not do so. For most of them still tended to think in 1918 terms, while overrating the French Army as much as the British did.

But whether Poland could have held out, and France been more effective in helping her, looks very different when examined more closely—with clearer understanding of the inherent handicaps and of the new technique of warfare that was first put into practice in 1939. From this modern viewpoint it seemed impossible, even before the event, that the course of events could be altered.

* Liddell Hart: *The Tanks*, vol. II, Appendix V.

Describing the collapse of Poland in his war memoirs, Churchill said:

> Neither in France nor in Britain had there been any effective comprehension of the consequences of the new fact that armoured vehicles could be made capable of withstanding artillery fire, and could advance a hundred miles a day.*

That statement is only too true, in so far as it applies to the bulk of the senior soldiers and statesmen of both countries. But it was in Britain, first of all, that these new potentialities had been visualised and explained, publicly and unceasingly, by a small band of progressive military thinkers.

In his second volume, dealing with the collapse of France in 1940, Churchill made the notable, if qualified, admission:

> Not having had access to official information for so many years, I did not comprehend the violence of the revolution effected since the last war by the incursion of a mass of fast-moving heavy armour. I knew about it, but it had not altered my inward convictions as it should have done.†

It was a remarkable statement, coming from the man who had played so great a part in sponsoring the tank in World War I. The admission was honourable in its frankness. But he had been Chancellor of the Exchequer up to 1929, while the Experimental Armoured Force, the first in the world, had been formed on Salisbury Plain in 1927 to try out the new theories which the exponents of high speed tank warfare had been preaching for several years. He was fully acquainted with their ideas, and had visited the Experimental Force at work, while he continued to meet them in subsequent years.

The incomprehension of the new idea of warfare, and official resistance to it, was even greater in France than in England. And greater in Poland than in France. That incomprehension was the root of the failure of both armies in 1939, and of the French again, more disastrously, in 1940.

The Poles were antiquated in their ruling military ideas, and also to a large extent in the pattern of their forces. They had no armoured or motorised divisions, and their old-type formations were very short of anti-tank and anti-aircraft guns. Moreover, Poland's leaders still pinned their trust to the value of a large mass of horsed cavalry, and cherished a pathetic belief in the possibility of carrying out cavalry charges.‡ In that respect, it might truly be said that their ideas were eighty years out of date, since the futility of cavalry

---

* Churchill: *The Second World War*, vol. I, p. 425.

† *ibid*, p. 39.

‡ It is grimly ironical to recall that when, in my book *The Defence of Britain*, published shortly before the war, I expressed anxiety about the way that the Polish military chiefs continued to put faith in cavalry charges against modern arms (pp. 95–7), the Polish Foreign Office was spurred by them to make an official protest against such a reflection on their judgement.

charges had been shown as far back as the American Civil War—although horse-minded soldiers continued to shut their eyes to the lesson. The maintenance of great masses of horsed cavalry by all armies during World War I, in the hope of the opening that never came, had been the supreme farce of that static war.

The French, on the other hand, had many of the ingredients of an up-to-date army, but they had not organised them into such—because their military ideas at the top were twenty years out of date. Contrary to the legends that arose after their defeat, they had more tanks than the Germans had built by the time the war came—many of them bigger and more thickly armoured than any of the German tanks, though rather slower.* But the French High Command still regarded tanks through 1918 eyes—as servants of the infantry, or else as reconnaissance troops to supplement cavalry. Under the spell of this old-fashioned way of thought they had delayed organising their tanks in armoured divisions—unlike the Germans—and were still inclined to employ them in penny packets.

The weakness of the French, and still more of the Poles, in new-style ground forces was made all the worse by their lack of airpower to cover and support their armies. With the Poles that was due partly to lack of manufacturing resources, but the French had no such excuse. In both cases the needs of airpower had been subordinated to the building up of large armies —because the voice of the generals was dominant in the distribution of the military budget, and the generals naturally tended to favour the kind of force with which they were familiar. They were far from realising the extent to which the effectiveness of ground forces was now dependent on adequate air cover.

The downfall of both armies may be traced to a fatal degree of self-satisfaction at the top. In the case of the French it had been fostered by the victory of World War I and the way that their partners had always deferred to their assumption of superior military knowledge. In the case of the Poles it had been nourished by their defeat of the Russians in 1920. The military leaders in both cases had long shown themselves arrogantly complacent about their armies and military technique. It is only fair to say that some of the younger French soldiers, such as Colonel de Gaulle, showed a keen interest in the new ideas of tank warfare that were being preached in England. But the higher French generals paid little attention to these British-born 'theories'—in marked contrast to the way the new school of German generals studied them.*

Even so, the German Army was still far from being a really efficient and modernly designed force. Not only was it unready for war as a whole, but

* Liddell Hart: *The Tanks*, vol. II, pp. 5–6.

the bulk of the active divisions were out of date in pattern, while the conceptions of the higher command still tended to run in old grooves. But it had created a small number of new-type formations by the time war broke out—six armoured and four 'light' (mechanised) divisions, as well as four motorised infantry divisions to back them up. It was a small proportion of the total, but it counted for more than all the rest of the German Army.

At the same time the German High Command had, rather hesitatingly, recognised the new theory of high-speed warfare, and was willing to give it a trial. That was due, above all, to the enthusiastic advocacy of General Heinz Guderian and a few others, and the way that their arguments appealed to Hitler—who favoured any idea that promised a quick solution. In sum, the German Army achieved its amazing run of victories, not because it was overwhelming in strength or thoroughly modern in form, but because it was a few vital degrees more advanced than its opponents.

The European situation in 1939 gave fresh emphasis, and a new turn, to that much quoted remark of Clemenceau's in the last great conflict of nations: 'War is too serious a business to be left to soldiers.' For it could not now be left to soldiers even if there had been the most complete trust in their judgement. The power to maintain war, if not to launch it, had passed out of the military sphere of the soldier into that of economics. As machine-power gained a growing domination over manpower on the battlefield, so, in a realistic view, did industry and economic resources push the armies at the front into the background of grand strategy. Unless the supplies from the factories and oilfields could be maintained without interruption they would be no more then inert masses. Impressive as the marching columns might look to the awed civilian spectator, in the eyes of the modern war scientist they were but marionettes on a conveyor-belt. And in that aspect was presented the potential factor that could save civilisation.

If existing armies and armaments alone counted, the picture would have been much more gloomy. The Munich settlement had changed the strategic balance of Europe, and for a time at least made it heavily adverse to France and Britain. No acceleration of their armament programmes could be expected to offset for a long time the removal from the scales of Czecho-Slovakia's thirty-five well-armed divisions, and the accompanying release of the German divisions which they could have held in balance.

Such increase of their armaments as France and Britain had achieved by March was then more than counterbalanced by what Germany gained through her swoop into helpless Czecho-Slovakia, whose munition factories as well as military equipment she took over. In heavy artillery alone,

Germany doubled her resources at a stroke. To make the prospect worse, German and Italian help had enabled Franco to complete the overthrow of Republican Spain, thereby raising the spectre of an additional menace to the frontiers of France, and to the sea-communications of both France and Britain.

Strategically, nothing save the assurance of Russia's support could promise to redress the balance within a measurable time. Strategically, too, no time was likely to be so favourable for joining issue with the Western Powers. But the strategic scales rested on an economic base, and it was doubtful whether under the pressure of war this would long support the weight of Germany's forces.

There were some twenty basic products essential for war. Coal for general production. Petroleum for motive power. Cotton for explosives. Wool. Iron. Rubber for transport. Copper for general armament and all electrical equipment. Nickel for steel-making and ammunition. Lead for ammunition. Glycerine for dynamite. Cellulose for smokeless powders. Mercury for detonators. Aluminium for aircraft. Platinum for chemical apparatus. Antimony, manganese, etc., for steel-making and metallurgy in general. Asbestos for munitions and machinery. Mica as an insulator. Nitric acid and sulphur for explosives.

Except for coal, Britain herself lacked most of the products which were required in quantity. But so long as the use of the sea was ensured, most of them were available in the British Empire. In the case of nickel about 90 per cent of the world's supply came from Canada, and most of the remainder from the French colony of New Caledonia. The main deficiencies were in antimony, mercury, and sulphur, while the petroleum resources were insufficient for war needs.

The French Empire could not supply these particular deficiencies, and was in addition short of cotton, wool, copper, lead, manganese, rubber, and several smaller needs.

Russia had an abundant supply of most of the products; she lacked antimony, nickel, and rubber, while the supply of copper and sulphur was inadequate.

The best placed of all the powers was the United States which produced two-thirds of the world's total petroleum supply, about half the world's cotton, and nearly half the copper, while being itself dependent on outside sources only for antimony, nickel, rubber, tin and, partially, for manganese.

In striking contrast was the situation of the Berlin–Rome–Tokyo triangle. Italy had to import the bulk of her needs in nearly every product, even to coal. Japan was almost as dependent on foreign sources. Germany had no home production of cotton, rubber, tin, platinum, bauxite, mercury, and mica, while her supplies of iron-ore, copper, antimony, manganese, nickel, sulphur, wool, and petroleum were quite inadequate. By the seizure of Czecho-Slovakia she had gone some way to reduce her deficiency of iron-ore, while by her intervention in Spain she had been able to secure a further supply of it on favourable terms, and also of mercury—although its continuance depended on her use of the sea. Again, she had succeeded in meeting part of her need for wool by a new wood substitute. Likewise, though at much greater cost than the natural product, she had provided about a fifth of her rubber requirements from 'buna', and a third of her petrol needs from home-produced fuel.

Here lay the greatest weakness of all in the war-making capacity of the Axis, in times when armies had come increasingly to depend on motor-movement, and air forces had become a vital element in military power. Apart from coal-derivatives Germany obtained about half a million tons of oil from her own wells, and a trifling amount from Austria and Czecho-Slovakia. To make up her peacetime needs she had to import nearly five million tons, the main sources being Venezuela, Mexico, the Dutch Indies, the United States, Russia, and Rumania. Access to any of the first four would be impossible in wartime, and to the last two only by conquest. Moreover, it was estimated that Germany's wartime requirements would exceed twelve million tons a year. In the light of this it was hard to expect that any increase in artificial fuel could suffice. Only the capture of Rumania's oil-wells— which produced seven million tons—in an undamaged state could offer a promise of meeting the deficiency.

Italy's requirements, if she entered the war, would increase the drag, since of the probable four million tons a year which she would require in war, she could only count on providing about 2 per cent, from Albania, even in the case of her ships being willing to cross the Adriatic.

To put oneself in a possible opponent's shoes is a good check on shaking in one's own. Gloomy as the military outlook had become, there was reason for comfort in the inadequacy of German and Italian resources for sustaining a long war—if the powers opposed to them at the outbreak could withstand the early shocks and strains until help came. In any such conflict as was now on the horizon the fortunes of the Axis would turn on the chance that the war could be settled quickly.

PART II

THE OUTBREAK

1939-1940

The Tank Drive in Poland

⬭ Main Polish concentrations

▨ Polish reserves

➤ German attacks

0 Miles   80
0 Kilometres   120

◄ Partition of Poland

▨ To Germany

▨ To Russia

CHAPTER 3

THE OVERRUNNING OF POLAND

The campaign in Poland was the first demonstration, and proof, in war of the theory of mobile warfare by armoured and air forces in combination. When the theory had been originally developed, in Britain, its action had been depicted in terms of the play of 'lightning'. From now on, aptly but ironically, it came into world-wide currency under the title of 'Blitzkrieg'—the German rendering.

Poland was all too well suited for a demonstration of Blitzkrieg. Her frontiers were immensely wide—some 3,500 miles in all. The stretch of 1,250 miles adjoining German territory had recently been extended to 1,750 miles by the occupation of Czecho-Slovakia. This had also resulted in Poland's southern flank becoming exposed to invasion—as the north flank, facing East Prussia, was already. Western Poland had become a huge salient that projected between Germany's jaws.

The Polish plain offered flat and fairly easy going for a mobile invader—though not so easy as France would offer, because of the scarcity of good roads in Poland, the deep sand often met off the roads, and the frequency of lakes and forests in some areas. But the time chosen for the invasion minimised these drawbacks.

It would have been wiser for the Polish Army to assemble farther back, behind the broad river-lines of the Vistula and the San, but that would have entailed the definite abandonment of some of the most valuable parts of the country. The Silesian coalfields were close to the frontier, having belonged to pre-1918 Germany, while most of the main industrial zone, though farther back, lay west of the river-barrier. It is difficult to conceive that the Poles could have maintained their hold on the forward areas even in the most favourable circumstances. But the economic argument for making the attempt to delay the enemy's approach to the main industrial zone was heavily reinforced by national pride and military over-confidence, as well as by an exaggerated idea of what Poland's Western allies could do to relieve the pressure.

The unrealism of such an attitude was repeated in the Polish dispositions.

Approximately a third of the forces were concentrated in or near the Corridor, where they were perilously exposed to a double envelopment—from East Prussia and the west combined. This indulgence of national pride—in opposing Germany's re-entry into the piece of her pre-1918 territory for which she had been agitating—was inevitably at the expense of the forces available to cover the areas more vital to Poland's defence. For in the south, facing the main avenues of approach, the forces were thinly spread. At the same time nearly another third of Poland's forces were massed in reserve north of the central axis, between Lodz and Warsaw, under the Commander-in-Chief, Marshal Smigly-Rydz. This grouping embodied the offensive spirit, but its aim of intervening with a counterattack did not correspond to the Polish Army's limited capacity for manœuvre, even if this had not been cramped by German air attack on the rail and road routes of movement.

The Poles' forward concentration in general forfeited their chance of fighting a series of delaying actions, since their foot-marching army was unable to get back to the positions in rear, and man them, before they were overrun by the invader's mechanised columns. In the wide spaces of Poland the unmechanised state of her forces was a heavier handicap than the fact that she was caught by surprise before all her reserves had been called up. Lack of mobility was more fatal than incomplete mobilisation.

By the same token, the forty odd infantry divisions of normal pattern which the Germans employed in the invasion counted for much less than their fourteen mechanised or partially mechanised divisions made up of six armoured divisions, four light divisions (motorised infantry with two armoured units), and four motorised divisions. It was their deep and rapid thrusts that decided the issue, in conjunction with the overhead pressure of the Luftwaffe which wrecked the Polish railway system, and destroyed much of the Polish air force in the early stages of the invasion. The Luftwaffe operated in a very dispersed way, instead of in large formations, but it thereby spread a creeping paralysis over the widest possible area. Another weighty factor was the German radio bombardment, disguised as Polish transmissions, which did much to increase the confusion and demoralisation of the Polish rear. All these factors were given a multiplied effect by the way that Polish over-confidence in the power of their men to defeat machines led, on the rebound, to a disintegrating disillusionment.

The German forces had crossed the Polish frontier shortly before 6 a.m. on September 1; air attacks had begun an hour earlier. In the north, the invasion was carried out by Bock's Army Group, which comprised the 3rd Army (under Küchler) and the 4th Army (under Kluge). The former thrust southward from its flanking position in East Prussia, while the latter pushed eastward across the Polish Corridor to join it in enveloping the Poles' right flank.

The greater role was given to Rundstedt's Army Group in the south. This was nearly twice as strong in infantry, and more in armour. It comprised the 8th Army (under Blaskowitz), the 10th (under Reichenau), and the 14th (under List). Blaskowitz, on the left wing, was to push towards the great manufacturing centre of Lodz, and help to isolate the Polish forces in the Poznan salient, while covering Reichenau's flank. On the right wing, List was to push for Cracow and simultaneously turn the Poles' Carpathian flank, using Kleist's armoured corps to drive through the mountain passes. The decisive stroke, however, was to be delivered by Reichenau, in the centre, and for that purpose he was given the bulk of the armoured forces.

The success of the invasion was helped by the way that the Polish leaders, despising the defensive, had devoted little effort to the construction of defences, preferring to rely on counterattacks—which they believed that their army, despite its lack of machines, could effectively execute. Thus the mechanised invaders had little difficulty in finding and penetrating open avenues of advance, while most of the Polish counterattacks broke down under the combined effect of a repulse to their forward movement and a deepening German threat to their own rear.

By September 3—when Britain and France entered the war—Kluge's advance had cut the Corridor and reached the Lower Vistula, while Küchler's pressure from East Prussia towards the Narev was developing. What was more important, Reichenau's armoured forces had penetrated to the Warta, and forced the crossings. Meanwhile List's army was converging from both flanks on Cracow, forcing Szylling's army in that sector to abandon the city and fall back to the line of the Nida and the Dunajec.

By the 4th Reichenau's spearheads had reached and crossed the Pilica, fifty miles beyond the frontier. Two days later his left wing was well in rear of Lodz, after capturing Tomaszow, and his right wing had driven into Kielce. Thus the Polish Rommel's army covering the Lodz sector was outflanked, while Kutrzeba's army was still far forward near Poznan, and in danger of being isolated. The other German armies had all made progress in fulfilling their part in the great enveloping manœuvre planned by Halder, the Chief of the General Staff, and directed by Brauchitsch, the Commander-in-Chief. The Polish armies were splitting up into unco-ordinated fractions, some of which were retreating while others were delivering disjointed attacks on the nearest enemy columns.

The German advance might have travelled still faster but for a lingering conventional tendency to check the mobile forces from driving far ahead of the infantry masses that were backing them up. But as newly gained experience showed that such a risk was offset by the opponents' confusion, a bolder course was pursued. Exploiting an open gap between Lodz and the Pilica, one of Reichenau's armoured corps raced through to the outskirts of Warsaw on the 8th—it had covered 140 miles in the first week. By the following day the light divisions on his right wing reached the Vistula farther south, between Warsaw and Sandomierz. They then turned northward.

Meanwhile, near the Carpathians, List's mobile forces had swept across the Dunajec, Biala, Wisloka, and Wislok in turn, to the San on either flank of the famous fortress of Przemysl. In the north Guderian's armoured corps (the spearhead of Küchler's army) had pushed across the Narev and was attacking the line of the Bug, in rear of Warsaw. Thus a wider pincer-movement was strongly developing outside the inner pincers that were closing on the Polish forces in the bend of the Vistula west of Warsaw.

This stage of the invasion had seen an important variation of plan on the Germans' side. Their view of the situation was momentarily confused by the extraordinary state of confusion on the Poles' side, where columns appeared to be moving in many different directions, raising clouds of dust that befogged the aerial view. In this state of obscurity the German Supreme Command inclined to the belief that the bulk of the Polish forces in the north had already escaped across the Vistula. On that assumption, they gave orders that Reichenau's army was to cross the Vistula between Warsaw and Sandomierz, with the aim of intercepting the Poles' anticipated withdrawal into south-eastern Poland. But Rundstedt demurred, being convinced that the bulk of the Polish forces were still west of the Vistula. After some argument his view prevailed, and Reichenau's army was wheeled north to establish a blocking position along the Bzura west of Warsaw.

As a result the largest remaining part of the Polish forces was trapped before it could withdraw over the Vistula. To the advantage which the Germans had gained by their strategic penetration along the line of least resistance was now added the advantage of tactical defence. To complete their victory they had merely to hold their ground—in face of the hurried assaults of an army which was fighting in reverse, cut off from its bases, with its supplies running short, and increasingly pressed from the flank and behind by the converging eastward advance of Blaskowitz's and Kluge's armies. Although the Poles fought fiercely, with a bravery that greatly impressed their opponents, only a small proportion ultimately managed to break out, by night, and join the garrison of Warsaw.

On the 10th Marshal Smigly-Rydz had issued orders for a general retreat into south-eastern Poland, where General Sosnkowski was placed in charge, with the idea of organising a defensive position on a relatively narrow front for prolonged resistance. But this was now a vain hope. While the big encirclement west of the Vistula was being tightened the Germans were now penetrating deeply into the area east of the Vistula. Moreover, they had turned both the line of the Bug in the north and the line of the San in the south. On Küchler's front, Guderian's armoured corps drove southward in a wide outflanking thrust to Brest-Litovsk. On List's front, Kleist's armoured corps reached the city of Lwow on the 12th. Here the Germans were checked, but they spread northwards to meet Küchler's forces.

Although the invading columns were feeling the strain of their deep advances, and were running short of fuel, the Polish command-system was so badly dislocated that it could not profit either by the enemy's temporary slackening or by the stubbornness that many isolated bodies of Polish troops still showed. These dissipated their energy in random efforts while the Germans were closing up to complete the encirclement.

On September 17 the armies of Soviet Russia crossed Poland's eastern frontier. That blow in the back sealed her fate, for there were scarcely any troops left to oppose this second invasion. Next day the Polish Government and High Command crossed the Rumanian frontier—the Commander-in-Chief sending back a message to tell his troops to fight on. Perhaps it was as well that it did not reach most of them, but many gallantly fulfilled its intention in the days that followed, although their resistance collapsed bit by bit. The garrison of Warsaw held out until the 28th, despite heavy bombardment from the air and the ground, and the last considerable Polish fragment did not surrender until October 5, while guerrilla resistance continued into the winter. Some 80,000 escaped over neutral frontiers.

The German and Russian forces had met and greeted each other, as partners, on a line running south from East Prussia past Bialystok, Brest-Litovsk, and Lwow to the Carpathians. That partnership was sealed, but not cemented, by a mutual partition of Poland.

Meantime the French had merely made a small dent in Germany's western front. It looked, and was, a feeble effort to relieve the pressure on their ally. In view of the weakness of the German forces and defences it was natural to feel that they could have done more. But, here again, deeper analysis tends to correct the obvious conclusion suggested by the comparative figures of the opposing forces.

Although the French northern frontier was 500 miles long, in attempting an offensive the French were confined to the narrow ninety-mile sector from the Rhine to the Moselle—unless they violated the neutrality of Belgium and Luxembourg. The Germans were able to concentrate the best part of their available forces on this narrow sector, and they sowed the approaches to their Siegfried Line with a thick belt of minefields, thus imposing delay on the attackers.

Worse still, the French were unable to start their offensive action until about September 17—except for some preliminary probing attacks. By that date, Poland was so obviously collapsing that they had a good excuse for countermanding it. Their incapacity to strike earlier arose from their mobilisation system, which was inherently out of date. It was the fatal product of their reliance on a conscript army—which could not come effectively into action until the mass of 'trained reserves' had been called up from their civil jobs, and the formations had been made ready to operate. But the delay was increased by the French Command's persistence in old tactical ideas—particularly their view that any offensive must be prepared by a massive artillery bombardment on the lines of World War I. They still regarded heavy artillery as the essential 'tin-opener' in dealing with any defended position. But the bulk of their heavy artillery had to be brought out of storage, and could not be available until the last stage of mobilisation, the sixteenth day. That condition governed their preparations to deliver an offensive.

For several years past one of France's political leaders, Paul Reynaud, had constantly argued that these conceptions were out of date, and had urged the necessity of creating a mechanised force of professional soldiers ready for instant action, instead of relying on the old and slow-mobilising conscript mass. But his had been a voice crying in the wilderness. French statesmen, like most French soldiers, placed their trust in conscription, and numbers.

The military issue in 1939 can be summed up in two sentences. In the East a hopelessly out-of-date army was quickly disintegrated by a small tank force, in combination with a superior air force, which put into practice a novel technique. At the same time, in the West, a slow-motion army could not develop any effective pressure before it was too late.

CHAPTER 4

'THE PHONEY WAR'

'The Phoney War' was a phrase coined by the American Press. Like so many vivid Americanisms it soon came to be adopted on both sides of the Atlantic. It has become firmly established as a name for the period of the war from the collapse of Poland in September, 1939, until the opening of Hitler's Western offensive in the following spring.

Those who coined the phrase meant to convey that the war was spurious—because no great battles were being fought between the Franco-British and German forces. In reality, it was a period of ominous activity—behind the curtain. In the midst of it all a strange accident befell a German staff officer. The incident gave Hitler a fright, and in the following weeks the German military plan was completely changed. The old one would have had nothing like the same chance of success as the new one attained.

But all this was unknown to the world. The people everywhere could only see that the battlefronts remained quiet, and concluded that Mars had fallen into a slumber.

Popular explanations of this outwardly passive state differed. One was that Britain and France were not really serious in their war-making intentions, despite their declaration of war on behalf of Poland, and were waiting to negotiate peace. The other popular explanation was that they were being cunning. The American Press contained many 'reports' that the Allied High Command had deliberately adopted a subtly conceived scheme of defensive strategy, and was preparing a trap for the Germans.

There was no foundation for either of these explanations. During that autumn and winter the Allied Governments and High Command spent much time in discussing offensive plans against Germany or Germany's flanks—which they had no possibility of achieving with their resources—instead of concentrating on the preparation of an effective defence against Hitler's coming attack.

After the fall of France, the Germans captured the files of the French High Command—and published a collection of sensational documents from them.

These showed how the Allied chiefs had spent the winter in contemplating offensive plans all round the circle—for striking at Germany's rear flank through Norway, Sweden, and Finland; for striking at the Ruhr through Belgium; for striking at her remote eastern flank through Greece and the Balkans; for cutting off her loan-source of petrol supply by striking at Russia's great oilfields in the Caucasus. It was a wonderful collection of fantasies—the vain imaginings of Allied leaders, living in a dream-world until the cold douche of Hitler's own offensive awoke them.

Hitler, whose mind was always moving ahead of events, began to think of taking the offensive in the West while the Polish campaign was drawing to a close, and before he made his public proposal for a general peace conference. It is evident that he had already come to realise that any such proposal was unlikely to receive consideration by the Western Allies. For the moment, however, he allowed only his immediate entourage to know how his mind was turning. He kept the General Staff in the dark until after he had publicly made his peace offer, on October 6, and it had been publicly rebuffed.

Three days later he set out his views in a long directive* for the German Army chiefs, giving the reasons for his conviction that an offensive in the West was the only possible course left to Germany. It is a most illuminating document. In it he set forth his conclusion that a prolonged war with France and Britain would exhaust Germany's resources, and expose her to a deadly attack in the back from Russia. He feared that his pact with Russia would not ensure her neutrality a moment longer than suited her purpose. His fear urged him to force peace on France by an early offensive. He believed that once France fell out Britain would come to terms.

He reckoned that for the moment he had the strength and equipment to beat France—because Germany possessed a superiority in the new arms that mattered most:

> The tank-arm and air force have, at the present time, attained technical heights—not only as weapons of attack but also for defence—that no other power has reached. Their strategic potential for operations is ensured by their organisation and well-practised leadership, which is better than in any other country.

While recognising that the French had a superiority in the older weapons, particularly heavy artillery, he argued that 'these weapons are of no decisive significance whatsoever in mobile warfare'. With his technical superiority

* Nuremberg Documents C-62.

34

in the newer arms he could also discount the French superiority in the number of trained soldiers.

He went on to argue that if he waited, in the hope that the French would get tired of war, 'the development of British fighting power would bring to France a new fighting element that would be of great value to her, both psychologically and materially'—to buttress her defence.

> What must be prevented above all is that the enemy should make good the weakness of his own armaments, particularly in anti-tank and anti-aircraft weapons—thereby creating a balance of power. In this respect the passing of every further month represents a loss of time unfavourable to the German power of attack.

He showed anxiety about the 'will to war' of the German soldier once the exhilarating effect of the easy conquest of Poland wore off. 'His respect for himself is as great as the respect he commands from others, at present. But six months of delaying warfare and effective propaganda on the part of the enemy might cause these important qualities to weaken once more.'* Hitler felt that he must strike soon, before it was too late, saying: 'In the present situation, time may be reckoned an ally of the Western powers rather than of ours.' His memorandum wound up with the conclusion that: 'The attack is to be launched this autumn, if conditions are at all possible.'

He insisted that Belgium must be included in the area of attack, not only to obtain room for manœuvre to outflank the French Maginot Line, but also to forestall the danger of the Anglo-French forces entering Belgium and deploying on the frontier close to the Ruhr, 'thereby bringing the war near to the heart of our armaments industry'. (As the French archives reveal, that was exactly what Gamelin, the French Commander-in-Chief, had been advocating.)

The disclosure of Hitler's intentions came as a shock to Brauchitsch, the Commander-in-Chief of the Army, and Halder, the Chief of the General Staff. In common with most of the senior German generals, they did not share Hitler's belief in the power of the new arms to overcome the opponents' superiority in military trained manpower. Reckoning on customary lines in numbers of divisions, they argued that the German Army had not nearly enough strength to defeat the Western armies. They pointed out that the

---

* Events showed that Hitler's anxiety was misplaced. French morale declined more than the German in the seven months' delay that actually occurred. Allied propaganda was not effective—there was far too much talk of overthrowing Germany, and far too little attempt to distinguish between the ordinary German and the Nazi chiefs. Worse still, scant encouragement was given by the British Government to several secret approaches made by groups in Germany who wanted to overthrow Hitler and make peace if they could get satisfactory assurance as to the peace conditions that the Allies had in mind.

ninety-eight divisions which Germany had managed to mobilise were considerably fewer than the total on the other side, and that thirty-six of these divisions were badly armed and barely trained. They were apprehensive, too, that the war would spread into another world war, fearing that it would have a fatal ending for Germany.

They were so disturbed that they contemplated desperate remedies. Just as at the time of the Munich crisis, a year before, they started to consider taking action to overthrow Hitler. The idea was to despatch a picked force from the front to march on Berlin. But General Friedrich Fromm, the Commander-in-Chief of the Home Forces, declined to co-operate—and his help was essential. Fromm argued that if the troops were ordered to turn against Hitler they would not obey—because most of the ordinary soldiers put their trust in Hitler. Fromm's judgement about the troops' reaction was probably correct. It is corroborated by most of the officers who were in touch with troops and did not know what was being discussed in higher headquarters.

The mass of the troops and people, if not intoxicated by triumph, were doped by Dr Goebbels's propaganda about Hitler desiring peace while the Allies were determined on the destruction of Germany. Unfortunately, the Allied statesmen and Press furnished Goebbels with all too many quotable morsels of this kind that he could use to support his picture of the Allied wolf wanting to devour the German lamb.

While this first wartime plot against Hitler was stillborn, he did not succeed in launching his offensive in the autumn as he had hoped. Ironically, that proved fortunate for him and unfortunate for the rest of the world—including the German people.

The date provisionally fixed for the offensive was November 12. On the 5th Brauchitsch made a fresh attempt to dissuade Hitler from invading France, setting forth at much length the reasons against it. But Hitler rebuffed his arguments and rebuked him severely, while insisting that the attack must start on the 12th. On the 7th, however, the order was cancelled—when meteorologists forecast bad weather. The date was put off three days, and then postponed again and again.

While the bad and bitter weather that set in was an obvious ground for postponement, Hitler was furious at having to acquiesce, and far from satisfied that it was the only cause. He summoned all the high commanders to a conference, on November 23. Here he set out to dispel their doubts about the necessity of taking the offensive—expressing anxiety about the looming menace of Russia, while emphasising that the Western Allies would not consider his peace offers and were multiplying their armaments. 'Time is working for our adversary.' 'We have an Achilles' Heel—the Ruhr. . . . If Britain and France push through Belgium and Holland into the Ruhr, we shall be in the greatest danger.'

He went on to reproach them with faint-heartedness, and let them know that he suspected them of trying to sabotage his plans. He pointed out that they had opposed each of his steps from the re-occupation of the Rhineland onwards, that he had been justified by success each time, and that he now expected them to follow his ideas unconditionally. Brauchitsch's attempt to point out the differences and greater risks in the new venture merely drew down on his head a harder rebuke. That evening Hitler saw Brauchitsch privately and gave him a further 'dressing down'. Brauchitsch thereupon tendered his resignation, but Hitler brushed it aside, and told him to obey orders.

However, the weather proved a better saboteur than the generals, and led to a fresh series of postponements during the first half of December. Then Hitler decided to wait until the New Year, and grant Christmas leave. The weather was again bad just after Christmas but on January 10 Hitler fixed the start of the offensive for the 17th.

But the very day he took that decision the most dramatic 'intervention' took place. The story of it has been mentioned in numerous accounts, but was most succinctly put in that of General Student, the Commander-in-Chief of the German Airborne Forces:

> On January 10 a major detailed by me as liaison officer to the 2nd Air Fleet flew from Munster to Bonn to discuss some unimportant details of the plan with the Air Force. He carried with him, however, *the complete operational plan for the attack in the West.*
>
> In icy weather and a strong wind he lost his way over the frozen and snow-covered Rhine, and flew into Belgium, where he had to make a forced landing. He was unable to burn completely the vital document. Important parts of it fell into the hands of the Belgians, and consequently the outline of the German plan for the Western offensive. The German Air Attaché in the Hague reported that on the same evening the King of the Belgians had a long telephone conversation with the Queen of Holland.*

Of course, the Germans did not know at the time exactly what had happened to the papers, but they naturally feared the worst, and had to reckon with it. In that crisis Hitler kept a cool head, in contrast to others:

> It was interesting to watch the reactions of this incident on Germany's leading men. While Goering was in a rage, Hitler remained quite calm and self-possessed. . . . At first he wanted to strike immediately, but fortunately refrained—and decided to drop the original operational plan entire. This was replaced by the Manstein plan.*

* Liddell Hart: *The Other Side of the Hill,* p. 149.

General Walter Warlimont, who held a key post★ in the Supreme Command headquarters, recorded that Hitler made up his mind on January 16 to change the plan, and that 'this was chiefly due to the air accident'.†

That proved very unfortunate for the Allies, even though they were given a further four months' grace for preparation—since the German offensive was now put off indefinitely while the plan was being completely recast, and did not come until May 10. When it was launched, it threw the Allies completely off their balance and led to the speedy collapse of the French armies, while the British barely escaped by sea, from Dunkirk.

It is natural to ask whether the major's forced-landing really was an accident. It might be expected that any of the German generals involved would after the war be only too glad to put himself in a favourable light with his captors by claiming that he had arranged this warning to the Allies. Yet, in fact, none did so—and all seemed convinced that the accident was quite genuine. But we know that Admiral Canaris, the head of the German Secret Service—who was later executed—took many hidden steps to thwart Hitler's aims, and that just prior to the attacks in the spring on Norway, Holland, and Belgium, warnings were conveyed to the threatened countries—though they were not properly heeded. We know, too, that Canaris worked in mysterious ways, and was skilled in covering up his tracks. So the fateful accident of January 10 is bound to remain an open question.

No such doubt surrounds the origination of the new plan. It forms another strange episode—though strange in a different way.

The old plan, worked out by the General Staff under Halder, had been to make the main attack through central Belgium—as in 1914. It was to be carried out by Army Group 'B' under Bock, while Army Group 'A' under Rundstedt delivered a secondary attack, on the left, through the hilly and wooded Ardennes. No big results were expected here, and all the armoured divisions were allotted to Bock, as the General Staff regarded the Ardennes as far too difficult country for a tank drive.‡

The Chief of Staff of Rundstedt's Army Group was Erich von Manstein—regarded by his fellows as the ablest strategist among the younger generals.

★ He was Deputy Chief of the O.K.W. Operations Staff, under General Jodl.
† Liddell Hart: *The Other Side of the Hill*, p. 155.
‡ The French General Staff took exactly the same view. So had the British General Staff. When in November, 1933, I was consulted as to how our fast tank formations—which the War Office was just beginning to form—could best be used in a future war I had suggested that, in the event of a German invasion of France, we should deliver a tank counterstroke through the Ardennes. I was thereupon told that 'the Ardennes were impassable to tanks', to which I replied that, from personal study of the terrain, I regarded such a view as a delusion—as I had emphasised in several books between the wars.

He felt that the first plan was too obvious, and too much a repetition of the Schlieffen plan of 1914—so that it was just the kind of stroke for which the Allied High Command would be prepared. Another drawback, Manstein argued, was that it would meet the British Army, which was likely to be a tougher opponent than the French. Moreover, it would not lead to a decisive result. To quote his own words:

> We could perhaps defeat the Allied forces in Belgium. We could conquer the Channel coast. But it was probable that our offensive would be definitely stopped on the Somme. Then there would grow up a situation like 1914 . . . there would be no chance of reaching a peace.*

Reflecting on the problem, Manstein had already conceived the bold solution of shifting the main stroke to the Ardennes, feeling that this would be the line of least expectation. But there was one big question in his mind, about which he had consulted Guderian in November 1939.

Here is Guderian's own account:

> Manstein asked me if tank movements would be possible through the Ardennes in the direction of Sedan. He explained his plan of breaking through the extension of the Maginot Line near Sedan, in order to avoid the old-fashioned Schlieffen plan, familiar to the enemy and likely to be expected once more. I knew the terrain from World War I, and, after studying the map, confirmed his view. Manstein then convinced General von Rundstedt, and a memorandum was sent to O.K.H. [the Supreme Headquarters of the Army, headed by Brauchitsch and Halder]. O.K.H. refused to accept Manstein's idea. But the latter succeeded in bringing his idea to Hitler's knowledge.†

Warlimont brought Manstein's idea to the notice of Hitler's headquarters, after a talk he had with Manstein in mid-December. He mentioned it to General Alfred Jodl, Chief of O.K.W. Operations Staff, who passed it on to Hitler. But it was only after the air accident of January 10, when Hitler was looking for a new plan, that Manstein's proposal, thus brought back into his mind, began to get a hold. Even then a month passed before he swung definitely in favour of it.

The final decision was clinched in a curious way. Brauchitsch and Halder had not liked the manner in which Manstein had pressed his 'brain-wave' in opposition to their plan. So it was decided to remove him from his post, and send him to command an infantry corps—where he would be out of the main channel and not so well placed to push his ideas. But following this transfer he was summoned to see Hitler, and thus had an opportunity to explain his idea in full. This interview was arranged on the initiative of

* Liddell Hart: *The Other Side of the Hill*, p. 152.
† *ibid*, pp. 153–4.

General Schmundt, Hitler's chief aide-de-camp, who was a fervent admirer of Manstein and felt he had been badly treated.

After that, Hitler pressed the idea on Brauchitsch and Halder so hard that they gave way, and remodelled the plan on Manstein's lines. While Halder was a reluctant convert, he was an extremely able staff officer and the detailed drafting of the plan was a remarkable piece of logistical planning.

A characteristic sequel was that Hitler, once he had swung in favour of the new key-idea, was quick to assume that he had himself conceived it. All he gave Manstein was the credit of having agreed with him: 'Among all the generals I talked to about the new plan in the West, Manstein was the only one who understood me.'

If we analyse the course of events when the offensive was launched, in May, it becomes clear that the old plan would almost certainly have failed to produce the fall of France. Indeed, it might have done no more than push the Allied Armies back to the French frontier, even if it did that. For the main German advance would have run head-on into the strongest and best-equipped of the Franco-British forces, and would have had to fight its way forward through a stretch of country filled with obstacles—rivers, canals and large towns. The Ardennes might seem more difficult still, but if the Germans could race through that wooded hill-belt of southern Belgium before the French High Command awoke to the danger, the rolling plains of France would lie open to them—ideal country for a great tank drive.

Had the old plan been maintained, and come to an impasse as was probable, the whole outlook of the war would have been very different. While it is unlikely that France and Britain could ever have defeated Germany on their own, a definite check to the German offensive would have given them time to develop their armaments, particularly in aircraft and tanks, and thus establish a balance of power in these new arms. The unconcealable failure of Hitler's bid for victory would in time also have undermined the confidence of his troops and people. Thus a stalemate in the West would have given Hitler's strong group of opponents at home a good chance to gain increasing support and develop their plans for overthrowing him, as a preliminary to peace. However things had turned out after the check, it is likely that Europe would have been saved much of the ruin and misery that befell her peoples as the result of the chain of events that ensued from the collapse of France.

While Hitler benefited so much from the air accident that led him to change the plan, the Allies suffered much from it. One of the strangest features of the whole story is that they did so little to profit by the warning that had fallen into their lap. For the documents which the German staff officer was carrying were not badly burned, and copies of them were promptly passed on by the Belgians to the French and British Governments. But their military advisers were inclined to regard the documents as having been planted on them as a deception. That view hardly made sense, for it would have been a foolish kind of deception to risk putting the Belgians on their guard and driving them into closer collaboration with the French and British. They might easily have decided to open their frontier and let the Franco-British armies come in, to reinforce their defences, before the blow fell.

Even stranger was that the Allied High Command made no change in its own plans, nor took any precautions to meet the probability that if the captured plan were genuine the German High Command would almost certainly shift the weight of their attack elsewhere.

In mid-November the Allied Supreme Council had endorsed Gamelin's Plan 'D', a hazardous development—which the British Staff had at first questioned—of an earlier plan. Under Plan 'D' the reinforced left wing of the Allied Armies was to rush into Belgium as soon as Hitler started to move, and push as far eastward as possible. That played straight into Hitler's hands, as it fitted perfectly into his new plan. The farther the Allied left wing pushed into central Belgium the easier it would be for his tank drive through the Ardennes to get round behind it and cut it off.

The outcome was made all the more certain because the Allied High Command employed the bulk of its mobile forces in the advance into Belgium, and left only a thin screen of second-rate divisions to guard the hinge of its advance—facing the exits from the 'impassable Ardennes'. To make it all the worse, the defences which they had to hold were particularly weak—in the gap between the end of the Maginot Line and the beginning of the British fortified front.

Mr Churchill mentions in his memoirs that anxiety had been felt in British quarters during the autumn about that gap and says: 'Mr Hore-Belisha, the Secretary of State for War, raised the point in the War Cabinet on several occasions. . . . The Cabinet and our military leaders however were naturally shy of criticising those whose armies were ten times as strong as our own.'*
After Hore-Belisha's departure early in January, following the storm which his criticisms had aroused, there was still less inclination to press the point. There was also a dangerous growth of false confidence, in Britain as well as in France. Churchill declared, in a speech on January 27, that 'Hitler has lost his best chance'. That comforting assertion was headlined in the newspapers next day. It was the very time when the new plan was fermenting in Hitler's mind.

* Churchill: *The Second World War*, vol. II, p. 33.

The Finnish War

◄── Russian attacks
▷── Finnish counterattacks

| 0 | Miles | 100 |
| 0 | Km. | 150 |

ARCTIC OCEAN

Rybachi Peninsula
(Fisher Pen.)

Petsamo

Murmansk

Nautsi

14th ARMY

To Narvik

Gällivare

Kandalaksha

Salla

SWEDEN

Kemijarvi

Kunsamo

9th ARMY

WHITE SEA

Kemi

Luleå

RUSSIA

GULF OF BOTHNIA

Oulu

Suomussalmi

Khumo

Murmansk Railway

Repola

Vaasa

Kuopio

Porajorpi

Ilomäntsi

8th ARMY

Pori

Sortavala

Tampere

Lahti

LAKE LADOGA

Turku

Vuoksi

Viipuri

Summa

Karelian Isthmus

Helsinki

Hogland

13th ARMY

Hangö

GULF OF FINLAND

Seiskari

Leningrad

7th ARMY

Paldaski

Tallinn

MANNERHEIM LINE

ESTONIA

Copyright © Cassell & Co. Ltd 1970

CHAPTER 5

THE FINNISH WAR

Following the partition of Poland, Stalin was anxious to safeguard Russia's Baltic flank against a future threat from his temporary colleague, Hitler. Accordingly, the Soviet Government lost no time in securing strategic control of Russia's old-time buffer-territories in the Baltic. By October 10 it had concluded pacts with Estonia, Latvia, and Lithuania which enabled its forces to garrison key-points in those countries. On the 9th conversations began with Finland. On the 14th the Soviet Government formulated its demands. These were defined as having three main purposes.

First, to cover the sea approach to Leningrad, by (a) 'making it possible to block the Gulf of Finland by artillery from both coasts, to prevent enemy warships or transports entering the Gulf'; (b) 'making it possible to prevent any enemy gaining access to the islands in the Gulf of Finland situated west and north-west of the entrance to Leningrad'. For this purpose the Finns were asked to cede the islands of Hogland, Seiskari, Lavanskari, Tytarskari, and Loivisto, in exchange for other territories; also to lease the port of Hangö for thirty years so that the Russians might there establish a naval base with coastal artillery, capable, in conjunction with the naval base at Paldaski on the opposite coast, of blocking access to the Gulf of Finland.

Second, to provide better cover on the land approach to Leningrad by moving back the Finnish frontier in the Karelian Isthmus, to a line which would be out of heavy artillery range of Leningrad. The re-adjustments of the frontier would still leave intact the main defences on the Mannerheim Line.

Third, to adjust the frontier in the far north 'in the Petsamo region, where the frontier was badly and artificially drawn'. It was a straight line running through the narrow isthmus of the Rybachi peninsula and cutting off the western end of that peninsula. This re-adjustment was apparently designed to safeguard the sea approach to Murmansk by preventing an enemy establishing himself on the Rybachi peninsula.

In exchange for these re-adjustments of territory the Soviet Union offered to cede to Finland the districts of Repola and Porajorpi—an exchange which, even according to the Finnish White Book, would have given Finland an additional 2,134 square miles in compensation for the cession to Russia of areas totalling 1,066 square miles.

An objective examination of these terms suggests that they were framed on a rational basis, to provide a greater security to Russian territory without serious detriment to the security of Finland. They would, clearly, have hindered the use of Finland as a jumping-off point for any German attack on Russia. But they would not have given Russia any appreciable advantage for an attack on Finland. Indeed, the territory which Russia offered to cede to Finland would have widened Finland's uncomfortably narrow waistline.

National sentiment, however, made it hard for the Finns to agree to a settlement on these lines. While they expressed willingness to cede all the islands except Hogland, they were adamant about leaving the port of Hangö on the mainland—contending that this would be inconsistent with their policy of strict neutrality. The Russians then offered to buy this piece of territory, arguing that such a purchase would be in accord with Finland's neutrality obligations. The Finns, however, refused this offer. The discussions became acrimonious, the tone of Russian Press comment became threatening, and on November 28 the Soviet Government cancelled the non-aggression treaty of 1932. On the 30th the Russian invasion began.

The original advance ended in a check that astonished the world. A direct push from Leningrad up the Karelian Isthmus came to a halt in the forward layers of the Mannerheim Line. An advance near Lake Ladoga did not make progress. At the other end of the front the Russians cut off the small port of Petsamo on the Arctic Ocean, as a means of blocking the entry of help to Finland by that route.

Two more immediately menacing thrusts were delivered across the waist of Finland. The more northerly thrust penetrated past Salla to Kemijarvi, half way to the Gulf of Bothnia, before it was driven back by the counter-attack of a Finnish division which had been switched up by rail from the south. The southerly thrust, past Suomussalmi, was interrupted in turn by a counterstroke, early in January 1940. Circling round the invaders' flank, the Finns blocked their line of supply and retreat, waited until their troops were exhausted by cold and hunger, then attacked and broke them up.

In the West, sympathy with Finland as a fresh victim of aggression had rapidly developed into enthusiasm at the apparent success of the weak in repulsing the strong. This impression had far-reaching repercussions. It prompted the French and British Governments to consider the despatch of an expeditionary force to this new theatre of war with the object not only of aiding Finland but also of securing the Swedish iron mines at Gällivare from which Germany drew supplies, while establishing a position that threatened Germany's Baltic flank. Partly because of the objections raised by Norway and Sweden, this project did not materialise before Finland collapsed. France and Britain were thus spared entanglement in war with the U.S.S.R. as well as with Germany at a time when their own powers of defence were perilously weak. But the obvious threat of an Allied move into Scandinavia precipitated Hitler's decision to forestall it by occupying Norway.

Another effect of Finland's early successes was that it reinforced the general tendency to underrate the Soviet military strength. This view was epitomised in Winston Churchill's broadcast assertion of January 20, 1940, that Finland 'had exposed, for the world to see, the military incapacity of the Red Army'. His misjudgement was to some extent shared by Hitler—with momentous consequences the following year.

More dispassionate examination of the campaign, however, provided better reasons for the ineffectiveness of the original advance. There was no sign of proper preparations to mount a powerful offensive, furnished with large stocks of munitions and equipment from Russia's vast resources. There were clear signs that the Soviet authorities had been misled by their sources of information about the situation in Finland, and that, instead of reckoning on serious resistance, they imagined that they might have to do no more than back up a rising of the Finnish people against an unpopular Government. The country cramped an invader at every turn, being full of natural obstacles that narrowed the avenues of approach and helped the defence. Between Lake Ladoga and the Arctic Ocean the frontier appeared very wide on the map but in reality was a tangle of lakes and forests, ideal for laying traps as well as for stubborn resistance. Moreover, on the Soviet side of the frontier the rail communications consisted of the solitary line from Leningrad to Murmansk, which in its 800-mile stretch had only one branch leading to the Finnish frontier. This limitation was reflected in the fact that the 'waistline' thrusts which sounded so formidable in the highly coloured reports from Finland were made with only three divisions apiece, while four were employed in the outflanking manœuvre north of Ladoga.

Much the best approach to Finland was through the Karelian Isthmus between Lake Ladoga and the Gulf of Finland, but this was blocked by the Mannerheim Line and the Finns' six active divisions, which were concentrated there at the outset. The Russian thrusts farther north, though they fared badly, served the purpose of drawing part of the Finnish reserves thither while thorough preparations were being made, and fourteen divisions brought up, for a serious attack on the Mannerheim Line. This was launched on February 1, under the direction of General Meretskov. Its weight was concentrated on a ten-mile sector near Summa, which was pounded by a tremendous artillery bombardment. As the fortifications were pulverised, tanks and sledge-carried infantry advanced to occupy the ground, while the Soviet air force broke up attempted countermoves. After little more than a fortnight of this methodical process a breach was made through the whole depth of the Mannerheim Line. The attackers then wheeled outward to corner Finnish forces on either flank, before pushing on to Viipuri (Viborg). A wider flanking operation was carried out across the frozen Gulf of Finland by troops who advanced from the ice-bound island of Hogland and landed well in the rear of Viipuri. Although an obstinate defence was still maintained for several weeks in front of Viipuri, Finland's limited forces had been worn down in the effort to hold the Karelian Isthmus. Once a passage was forced, and their communications menaced, eventual collapse was certain. Capitulation was the only way in which it could be averted, since the proffered Franco-British expeditionary force had not arrived, though almost ready to sail.

On March 6, 1940, the Finnish Government sent a delegation to negotiate peace. Beyond the earlier Soviet conditions, Finland was now asked to cede areas in the communes of Salla and Kunsamo, the whole of the Karelian Isthmus, including Viipari, and also the Finnish part of the Fisher Peninsula. They were also asked to build a railroad from Kemijarvi to the frontier (which was not yet established) to link up to the Russian spur. On March 13 it was announced that the Soviet terms had been accepted.

In the radically changed circumstances, particularly after the disastrous collapse in the Summa sector of the Mannerheim Line on February 12, the new Soviet terms were remarkably moderate. But Field-Marshal Mannerheim, who was more of a realist than most statesmen, and rightly dubious about the pressing Franco-British offers of help, urged acceptance of the Soviet terms. In raising his requirements so little, Stalin too showed statesmanship, while evidently anxious to be quit of a commitment which had occupied more than a million of Russia's troops, as well as a high proportion of her tanks and aircraft, at a time when the crucial spring of 1940 was looming near.

Whereas conditions in Poland were more favourable to a Blitzkrieg offensive than anywhere else in Europe, Finland offered a most unsuitable theatre for such a performance, especially at the time of the year when the invasion was staged.

The geographical encirclement of the Polish frontier was intensified by the ampleness of the German communications and the scarcity of the Polish. The open nature of the country offered scope for the thrusts of mechanised forces that was guaranteed by the dry September weather. The Polish Army was even more wedded to the offensive tradition than most armies, and thus all the weaker in utilising its sparse means of defensive action.

In Finland, by contrast, the defender profited by having a much better system of internal communications, both rail and road, than the attacker possessed on his side of the frontier. The Finns had several lines of railway parallel to the frontier for the rapid lateral switching of their reserves; the Russians had only the solitary line from Leningrad to Murmansk, with its one branch to the Finnish frontier. Elsewhere, the Russians would have to advance anything from 50 to 150 miles from the railway before crossing the frontier, and considerably farther before they could threaten any point of strategic importance. That advance, moreover, had to be made through a country of lakes and forests, and over poor roads that were now deep in snow.

These difficulties set a narrow limit to the forces which the Soviet Union could move and maintain, except in a direct advance through the Karelian Isthmus against the strongly defended Mannerheim Line. This neck of land, seventy miles wide on the map, is much less in strategic reality. Half of it is barred by the broad Vuoksi River, while much of the remainder is covered by a series of lakes, with forests between them. Only near Summa is there room for deploying any considerable force.

Moreover, beyond the strategic difficulties of assembling any large forces on the apparently exposed parts of the Finnish frontier and pushing them deep into the enemy's country, lay the tactical difficulty of overcoming the resistance of defenders who knew the ground and were able to exploit its advantages. Lakes and forests tend to shepherd an invading force into narrow channels of advance where it can be swept by machine-gun fire; they offer innumerable opportunities for concealed flanking manœuvres as well as for guerrilla harassing. To penetrate into such a country in face of a skilful foe is hazardous enough in summer; it is much more difficult to attempt in the Arctic winter, when heavy columns are as clumsy as a man in clogs trying to grapple with an opponent in gym-shoes.

If Field-Marshal Mannerheim obviously took risks in keeping all his reserves in the extreme south until the Russians had shown their hand, his strategy was justified on the whole by the opportunities which the enemy's initial penetrations offered to subsequent counterstrokes—especially in that kind of country under winter conditions.

As for the Russians, it is only to be expected that plans which have been based on a false assumption should break down when put to the test of reality. But that is not of itself proof of military inefficiency throughout the army concerned. While authoritarian régimes are particularly susceptible to the kind of reports on the situation which accord with their wishes, no type of government is immune from such risks. It is wise to remember that perhaps the greatest of all false assumptions in modern history were those on which the French plans in 1914 and 1940 were based.

PART III

THE SURGE

1940

The Overrunning of Norway

Minefields laid by Royal Navy on April 8

German seaborne landings (April 9) and attacks

German airborne landings

Airfields

0 Miles 200

0 Kilometres 300

APRIL 14, 1940 BRITISH FORCES LAND

MAY 27 ALLIED FORCES RETAKE NARVIK FROM GERMANS

JUNE 7 LAST ALLIED FORCES EVACUATE NORWAY

Narvik

Gällivare (Iron Ore mines)

NORWEGIAN SEA

APRIL 16/17 BRITISH FORCES LAND, WITHDRAW ON MAY 1/2

Namsos

Trondheimfjord

Trondheim

APRIL 18 BRITISH FORCES LAND, WITHDRAW ON APRIL 30/MAY 1

Aandalsnes

Gudbrand Valley

N O R W A Y

S W E D E N

Shetland Is.

Bergen

Oslo

FORNEBU

APRIL 9 BLÜCHER SUNK

Oslofiord

Larvik

Orkney Is.

Scapa Flow

Stavanger

SOLA

APRIL 7 HOME FLEET SAILS

Kristiansand

FEB 16 ALTMARK BOARDED BY ROYAL NAVY

SKAGERRAK

KATTEGAT

Rosyth

Edinburgh

DENMARK

JUTLAND

Copenhagen

BRITAIN

NORTH SEA

BALTIC SEA

APRIL 9, 1940 GERMANY INVADES DENMARK & NORWAY

GERMANY

Copyright © Cassell & Co. Ltd 1970

CHAPTER 6

THE OVERRUNNING OF NORWAY

The six months' deceptive lull that followed the conquest of Poland ended with a sudden thunderclap. It came, not where the storm-clouds centred, but on the Scandinavian fringe. The peaceful countries of Norway and Denmark were struck by a flash of Hitlerian lightning.

Newspapers on April 9 featured the news that on the previous day, British and French naval forces had entered Norwegian waters and laid minefields there—to block them to any ships trading with Germany. Congratulatory comment on this initiative was mingled with justificatory arguments for the breach of Norway's neutrality. But the radio that morning put the newspapers out of date—for it carried the far more startling news that German forces were landing at a series of points along the coast of Norway, and had also entered Denmark.

The audacity of these German moves, in defiance of Britain's superiority in seapower, staggered the Allied leaders. When the British Prime Minister, Mr Chamberlain, made a statement in the House of Commons that afternoon he said that there had been German landings up the west coast of Norway, at Bergen and Trondheim, as well as on the south coast, and added: 'There have been some reports about a similar landing at Narvik, but I am very doubtful whether they are correct.' To the British authorities it seemed incredible that Hitler could have ventured a landing so far north, and all the more incredible since they knew that their own naval forces were present on the scene in strength—to cover the mine-laying operations and other intended steps. They thought that 'Narvik' must be a misspelling of 'Larvik', a place on the south coast.

Before the end of the day, however, it became clear that the Germans had gained possession of the capital of Norway, Oslo, and all the main ports including Narvik. Every one of their simultaneous seaborne strokes had been successful.

The British Government's quick disillusionment on this score was followed by a fresh illusion. Mr Churchill, then First Lord of the Admiralty, told the House of Commons two days later:

> In my view, which is shared by my skilled advisers, Herr Hitler has committed a grave strategic error ... we have greatly gained by what has occurred in Scandinavia. .... He has made a whole series of commitments upon the Norwegian coast for which he will now have to fight, if necessary, during the whole summer, against Powers possessing vastly superior naval forces and able to transport them to the scenes of action more easily than he can. I cannot see any counter-advantage which he has gained. .. I feel that we are greatly advantaged by ... the strategic blunder into which our mortal enemy has been provoked.*

These fine words were not followed up by deeds to match. The British countermoves were slow, hesitant, and bungled. When it came to the point of action the Admiralty, despite its pre-war disdain for airpower, became extremely cautious and shrank from risking ships at the places where their intervention could have been decisive. The troop-moves were still feebler. Although forces were landed at several places with the aim of ejecting the German invader, they were all re-embarked in barely a fortnight, except from one foothold at Narvik—and that was abandoned a month later, following the main German offensive in the West.

The dream-castles raised by Churchill had come tumbling down. They had been built on a basic misconception of the situation, and of the changes in modern warfare—particularly the effect of airpower on seapower.

There had been more reality and significance in his closing words when, after depicting Norway as a trap for Hitler, he spoke of the German invasion as a step into which Hitler had 'been provoked'. For the most startling of all post-war discoveries about the campaign has been the fact that Hitler, despite all his unscrupulousness, would have preferred to keep Norway neutral, and did not plan to invade her until he was provoked to do so by palpable signs that the Allies were planning a hostile move in that quarter.

It is fascinating to trace the sequence of events behind the scene on either side—though tragic and horrifying to see how violently offensive-minded statesmen tend to react on one another to produce explosions of destructive force. The first clear step on either side was on September 19, 1939, when Churchill (as his memoirs record) pressed on the British Cabinet the project of laying a minefield 'in Norwegian territorial waters' and thus 'stopping the Norwegian transportation of Swedish iron-ore from Narvik' to Germany. He argued that such a step would be 'of the highest importance in crippling the enemy's war industry'. According to his subsequent note to the First Sea

---

* Churchill: War Speeches, vol. I, pp. 169–70.

Lord: 'The Cabinet, including the Foreign Secretary [Lord Halifax], appeared strongly favourable to this action.'

This is rather surprising to learn, and suggests that the Cabinet were inclined to favour the end without carefully considering the means—or where they might lead. A similar project had been discussed in 1918, but on that occasion, as is stated in the Official Naval History:

> ... the Commander-in-Chief [Lord Beatty] said it would be most repugnant to the officers and men in the Grand Fleet to steam in overwhelming strength into the waters of a small but high-spirited people and coerce them. If the Norwegians resisted, as they probably would, blood would be shed; this, said the Commander-in-Chief, 'would constitute a crime as bad as any that the Germans had committed elsewhere.'

It is evident that the sailors were more scrupulous than the statesmen, or that the British Government was in a more reckless mood at the opening of war in 1939 than at the end of World War I.

The Foreign Office staff exerted a restraining influence, however, and made the Cabinet see the objections to violating Norway's neutrality as proposed. Churchill mournfully records: 'The Foreign Office arguments about neutrality were weighty, and I could not prevail. I continued ... to press my point by every means and on all occasions.'* It became a subject of discussion in widening circles, and arguments in its favour were even canvassed in the Press. That was just the way to arouse German anxiety and countermeasures.

On the German side the first point of any significance to be found in the captured records comes in early October, when the Commander-in-Chief of the Navy, Admiral Raeder, expressed fears that the Norwegians might open their ports to the British and reported to Hitler on the strategic disadvantages that a British occupation might bring. He also suggested that it would be advantageous to the German submarine campaign 'to obtain bases on the Norwegian coast—e.g. Trondheim—with the help of Russian pressure'.

But Hitler put the suggestion aside. His mind was focused on plans for an attack in the West, to compel France to make peace, and he did not want to be drawn into any extraneous operations or diversion of resources.

A fresh and much stronger incitement, to both sides, arose out of the Russian invasion of Finland at the end of November. Churchill saw in it a new possibility of striking at Germany's flank under the cloak of aid to Finland: 'I welcomed this new and favourable breeze as a means of achieving the major strategic advantage of cutting off the vital iron-ore supplies of Germany.'†

In a note of December 16 he marshalled all his arguments for this step,

* Churchill: *The Second World War*, vol. I, p. 483.
† *ibid*, p. 489.

which he described as 'a major offensive operation'. He recognised that it
was likely to drive the Germans to invade Scandinavia for, as he said: 'If
you fire at the enemy he will fire back.' But he went on to assert 'we have
more to gain than to lose by a German attack upon Norway and Sweden'.
(He omitted any consideration of what the Scandinavian peoples would
suffer from having their countries thus turned into a battleground.)

Most of the Cabinet, however, still had qualms about violating Norway's
neutrality. Despite Churchill's powerful pleading they refrained from sanc-
tioning the immediate execution of his project. But they authorised the
Chiefs of Staff to 'plan for landing a force at Narvik'—which was the
terminus of the railway leading to the Gällivare ironfields in Sweden, and
thence into Finland. While aid to Finland was the ostensible purpose of such
an expedition, the underlying and major purpose would be the domination
of the Swedish ironfields.

In the same month an important visitor came to Berlin from Norway.
This was Vidkun Quisling, a former Minister of Defence, who was head
of a small party of Nazi type that was strongly sympathetic to Germany.
He saw Admiral Raeder on arrival, and impressed on him the danger that
Britain would soon occupy Norway. He asked for money and underground
help for his own plans of organising a coup to turn out the existing Norwegian Government. He said that a number of leading Norwegian officers
were ready to back him—including, he alleged, Colonel Sundlo, the commander at Narvik. Once he had gained power he would invite the Germans
in to protect Norway, and thus forestall a British entry.

Raeder persuaded Hitler to see Quisling personally, and they met on
December 16 and 18. The record of their talk shows that Hitler said 'he
would prefer Norway, as well as the rest of Scandinavia, to remain com-
letely neutral', as he did not want to 'enlarge the theatre of war'. But 'if the
enemy were preparing to spread the war he would take steps to guard
himself against the threat'. Meantime Quisling was promised a subsidy and
given an assurance that the problem of giving him military support would
be studied.

Even so, the War Diary of the German Naval Staff shows that on January
13, a month later, they were still of the opinion that 'the most favourable
solution would be the maintenance of Norway's neutrality', although they
were becoming anxious that 'England intended to occupy Norway with the
tacit agreement of the Norwegian Government'.

What was happening on the other side of the hill? On January 15 General
Gamelin, the French Commander-in-Chief, addressed a note to Daladier, the
Prime Minister, on the importance of opening a new theatre of war in

Scandinavia. He also produced a plan for landing an Allied force at Petsamo, in the north of Finland, together with the precautionary 'seizure of ports and airfields on the west coast of Norway'. The plan further envisaged the possibility of 'extending the operation into Sweden and occupying the iron-ore mines at Gällivare'.

A broadcast by Churchill, who addressed the neutrals on their duty to join in the fight against Hitler, naturally fanned German fears.* There were all too many public hints of Allied action.

On the 27th Hitler gave explicit orders to his military advisers to prepare comprehensive plans for an invasion of Norway if necessary. The special staff formed for the purpose met for the first time on February 5.

That day the Allied Supreme War Council met in Paris, and Chamberlain took Churchill with him. At this meeting plans were approved for preparing a force of two British divisions and a slightly smaller French contingent as 'Aid to Finland'—they were to be 'camouflaged as volunteers' in an endeavour to diminish the chances of an open war with Russia. But an argument developed over the route of their despatch. The British Prime Minister emphasised the difficulties of landing at Petsamo, and the advantages of landing at Narvik—particularly 'to get control of the Gällivare ore-field'. That was to be the main object, and only a part of the force was to push on to Finland's aid. The British arguments prevailed, and it was arranged that the force should sail early in March.

A fateful incident occurred on February 16. A German vessel, the *Altmark*, which was carrying British prisoners back from the South Atlantic, was chased by British destroyers and took refuge in a Norwegian fiord. Churchill sent a direct order to Captain Vian of H.M.S. *Cossack* to push into Norwegian waters, board the *Altmark* and rescue the prisoners. Two Norwegian gunboats were on the scene, but they were overawed and the subsequent protest of the Norwegian Government about the intrusion into their waters was rebuffed.

Hitler regarded the protest as merely a gesture to hoodwink him, and was convinced that the Norwegian Government was England's willing accomplice. That belief was nourished by the passivity of the two gunboats and by

* On January 20 Mr Churchill, in a broadcast address, claimed success for the Allied navies at sea, and contrasted the losses of neutral ships to U-boat attack with the safety of Allied ships in convoy. Then, after a brief *tour d'horizon*, he asked: 'But what would happen if all these neutral nations I have mentioned—and some others I have not mentioned—were with one spontaneous impulse to do their duty in accordance with the Covenant of the League, and were to stand together with the British and French Empires against aggression and wrong?' (Churchill: *War Speeches*, vol. I, p. 137). The suggestion caused a stir, and the Belgian, Dutch, Danish, Norwegian, and Swiss Presses hastened to reject it, while in London it was announced, with some reversion to the days of appeasement, that the broadcast only represented Churchill's personal views.

the reports of Quisling that the action of the *Cossack* had been a 'pre-arranged' affair. According to the German admirals, the *Altmark* affair was decisive in swinging Hitler in favour of intervention in Norway. It was the spark that set fire to the powder trail.

Hitler felt that he could not wait for Quisling's plans to develop, especially as German observers in Norway reported that Quisling's party was making little progress, while reports from England indicated that some action in the Norwegian area was being planned, together with the assembly of troops and transports.

On the 20th Hitler sent for General von Falkenhorst and appointed him to command and prepare an expeditionary force for Norway, saying, 'I am informed that the English intend to land there, and I want to be there before them. The occupation of Norway by the British would be a strategic turning movement which would lead them into the Baltic, where we have neither troops nor coastal fortifications . . . the enemy would find himself in a position to advance on Berlin and break the backbone of our two fronts.'

On March 1, Hitler issued his directive for the complete preparation for the invasion. Denmark was to be occupied, too, as a necessary strategic stepping stone and safeguard to his lines of communication.

But even now it was not a definite decision to strike. The records of Raeder's conferences with Hitler show that Hitler was still torn between his conviction that 'the maintenance of Norway's neutrality is the best thing' for Germany and his fear of an imminent British landing there. In presenting the naval plans on March 9 he dwelt on the hazards of undertaking an operation 'contrary to all the principles of naval warfare', while at the same time saying that it was 'urgent'.

In the following week the state of anxiety on the German side became more feverish. On the 13th it was reported that British submarines were concentrated off the south coast of Norway; on the 14th the Germans intercepted a radio message which ordered Allied transports to be ready to move; on the 15th a number of French officers arrived at Bergen. The Germans felt that they were certain to be forestalled as their own expeditionary force was not yet ready.

How were things actually going on the Allied side? On February 21 Daladier urged that the *Altmark* affair should be used as a pretext for the 'immediate seizure' of the Norwegian ports 'by a sudden stroke'. Daladier argued: 'Its justification in the eyes of world opinion will be the more easy the more rapidly the operation is carried out and the more our propaganda is able to exploit the memory of the recent complicity of Norway in the *Altmark* incident'—a way of talking which was remarkably like Hitler's. The French

Government's proposal was viewed with some doubt in London, as the expeditionary forces were not ready and Chamberlain still hoped that the Norwegian and Swedish Governments would agree to the entry of Allied troops.

At the meeting of the War Cabinet on March 8, however, Churchill unfolded a scheme of arriving in force off Narvik and throwing a detachment of troops ashore immediately—on the principle of 'displaying strength in order to avoid having to use it'. At a further meeting on the 12th the Cabinet 'decided to revive the plans' for landings at Trondheim, Stavanger, and Bergen as well as at Narvik.

The force landed at Narvik was to push rapidly inland and over the Swedish frontier to the Gällivare ironfield. Everything was to be ready for putting the plans into execution on March 20.

But then the plans were upset by Finland's military collapse and her capitulation to Russia on March 13—which deprived the Allies of the primary pretext for going into Norway. In the first reaction to the cold douche, two divisions which had been allotted for the Norway force were sent to France, though the equivalent of one division remained available. Another sequel was the fall of Daladier, and his replacement as Prime Minister of France by Paul Reynaud—who came into power on the surge of a demand for a more offensive policy and quicker action. Reynaud went to London for a meeting of the Allied Supreme War Council, on March 28, determined to press for the immediate execution of the Norwegian project that Churchill had so long been urging.

But there was no need now for any such pressure—for, as Churchill has related, Chamberlain had become 'much inclined to aggressive action of some kind at this stage'. As in the spring of 1939, once he had taken his resolve he jumped in with both feet. Opening the Council, he not only argued strongly for action in Norway but also urged the adoption of Churchill's other favourite project—that of dropping by air a continuous stream of mines into the Rhine and other rivers of Germany. Reynaud expressed some doubt about the latter operation, and said he would have to obtain the agreement of the French War Committee. But he eagerly embraced the Norwegian operation.

It was settled that the mining of Norwegian waters should be carried out on April 5, and be backed by the landing of forces at Narvik, Trondheim, Bergen, and Stavanger. The first contingent of troops was to sail, for Narvik, on the 8th. But then a fresh delay arose. The French War Committee would not agree to the dropping of mines in the Rhine lest it should bring German retaliation 'which would fall upon France'. They showed no such concern about the retaliation that would fall on Norway from the other operation—and Gamelin had even emphasised that one of its aims was 'to draw the enemy into a trap by provoking him to land in Norway'. Chamberlain, however, tried to insist that both operations should be carried out, and arranged with Churchill that the latter should go over to Paris on the 4th and make a fresh effort—which did not succeed—to persuade the French to adopt his Rhine plan.

That meant a short deferment of 'Wilfred', the Norwegian plan. It is strange that Churchill was agreeable to it, for at the War Cabinet meeting the day before, reports had been presented from the War Office and Foreign Office showing that large numbers of German ships were concentrated, with troops on board, at the ports nearest to Norway. Rather absurdly it was suggested—and astonishingly, believed—that these forces were waiting in readiness to deliver a counterstroke to a British descent on Norway.

The start of the Norwegian operations was postponed three days, until the 8th. That further delay proved fatal to its prospects of success. It enabled the Germans to get into Norway just ahead of the Allies.

On April 1 Hitler had finally made up his mind and ordered the invasion of Norway and Denmark to begin at 5.15 a.m. on the 9th. His decision followed a disturbing report that Norwegian anti-aircraft and coastal batteries had been given permission to open fire without awaiting higher orders—which suggested that the Norwegian forces were being made ready for action and that if Hitler waited any longer his chances of surprise, and success, would vanish.

In the dark hours of April 9 advance detachments of German troops, mostly in warships, arrived in the chief ports of Norway, from Oslo right up to Narvik—and captured them with little difficulty. Their commanders announced to the local authorities that they had come to take Norway under German protection against an Allied invasion that was imminent—a statement that the Allied spokesmen promptly denied, and continued to deny.

As Lord Hankey, a member of the War Cabinet at the time, stated:

> . . . from the start of planning to the German invasion, both Great Britain and Germany were keeping more or less level in their plans and preparations. Britain actually started planning a little earlier . . . both plans were executed almost simultaneously, Britain being twenty-four hours ahead in the so-called act of aggression, if the term is really applicable to either side.

But Germany's final spurt was faster and more forceful. She won the race by a very short head—it was almost a 'photo-finish'.

One of the most questionable points of the Nuremberg Trials was that the planning and execution of aggression against Norway was put among the major charges against the Germans. It is hard to understand how the British and French Governments had the face to approve the inclusion of this charge, or how the official prosecutors could press for a conviction on this score. Such a course was one of the most palpable cases of hypocrisy in history.

Passing now to the course of the campaign, a surprising revelation is the smallness of the force which captured the capital and chief ports of Norway in the opening coup. It comprised two battlecruisers, a pocket battleship, seven cruisers, fourteen destroyers, twenty-eight U-boats, a number of auxiliary ships, and some 10,000 troops—the advance elements of three divisions that were used for the invasion. At no place was the initial landing made by more than 2,000 men. One parachute battalion was also employed—to seize the airfields at Oslo and Stavanger. This was the first time that parachute troops had been used in war and they proved very valuable. But the most decisive factor in the German success was the Luftwaffe; the actual strength employed in the campaign was about 800 operational planes and 250 transport planes. It overawed the Norwegian people in the first phase, and later paralysed the Allies' countermoves.

How was it that the British naval forces failed to intercept and sink the much weaker German naval forces that carried the invading detachments? The extent of the sea-space, the nature of the Norwegian coast, and the hazy weather were important handicaps. But there were other factors, and more avoidable handicaps. Gamelin records that when, on April 2, he urged Ironside, the Chief of the Imperial General Staff, to hasten the despatch of the expeditionary force, the latter replied: 'With us the Admiralty is all-powerful; it likes to organise everything methodically. It is convinced that it can prevent any German landing on the west coast of Norway.'

At 1.25 p.m. on the 7th British aircraft actually spotted 'strong German naval forces moving swiftly northward' across the mouth of the Skaggerak, towards the Norwegian coast. Churchill says: 'We found it hard at the Admiralty to believe that this force was going to Narvik'—in spite of a 'report from Copenhagen that Hitler meant to seize that port'. The British Home Fleet sailed at 7.30 p.m. from Scapa Flow, but it would seem that both the Admiralty and the admirals at sea were filled with the thought of catching the German battlecruisers. In their efforts to bring these to battle they tended to lose sight of the possibility that the enemy had a landward intention, and lost a chance of intercepting the smaller troop-carrying warships.

Since an expeditionary force was already embarked and ready to sail, why was it so slow to land and eject the German detachments before they had time to establish their grip on the Norwegian ports? The prime reason is contained in the last paragraph. When the Admiralty heard that the German battlecruisers had been spotted, they ordered the cruiser squadron at Rosyth 'to march her soldiers ashore, even without their equipment, and join the Fleet at sea'. Similar orders were sent to the ships in the Clyde that were loaded up with troops.

Why did not the Norwegians put up a better resistance against such a small invading force? Primarily, because their forces were not even mobilised. Despite warnings from their Minister in Berlin and urgings from the Chief of their General Staff, the order for mobilisation was not given until the night of April 8/9, a few hours before the invasion. That was too late, and the swift-moving invaders disrupted the process.

Moreover, as Churchill remarks, the Norwegian Government at the time was 'chiefly concerned with the activities of the British'. It was unfortunate, and also ironical, that the British mine-laying operation should have absorbed and distracted the Norwegians' attention during the crucial twenty-four hours before the Germans landed.

As for the Norwegians' chance of rallying from the opening blow, this was diminished by their lack of fighting experience and an out-of-date military organisation. In no way were they fitted to cope with a modern Blitzkreig, even on the small scale applied to their case. The weakness of the resistance was all too clearly shown by the speed with which the invaders raced along the deep valleys to overrun the country. If the resistance had been tougher, the melting snow on the valley-sides—which hampered out-flanking manœuvre—would have been a more serious impediment to the German prospects of success.

The most astonishing of the opening series of coups was that at Narvik, for this far northern port was some 1,200 miles distant from the German naval bases. Two Norwegian coast-defence ships gallantly met the attacking German destroyers, but were quickly sunk. The shore defences made no attempt at resistance—more by incompetence than treachery. Next day a British destroyer flotilla steamed up the fiord and fought a mutually damaging action with the Germans, which on the 13th were finished off by the inroad of a stronger flotilla supported by the battleship *Warspite*. But by this time the German troops were established in and around Narvik.

Farther south, Trondheim was captured with ease after the German ships had run the gauntlet of the batteries dominating the fiord—a hazard that had dismayed Allied experts who had considered the problem. By securing Trondheim, the Germans had possessed themselves of the strategic key to central Norway, though the question remained whether their handful of troops there could be reinforced from the south.

At Bergen, the Germans suffered some damage from the Norwegian warships and batteries, but had little trouble once they were ashore.

In the approach to Oslo, however, the main invading force suffered a jolt. For the cruiser *Blücher*, carrying many of the military staff, was sunk by torpedoes from the Oscarborg fortress, and the attempt to force the passage was then given up until this fortress surrendered in the afternooon, after heavy air attack. Thus the capture of Norway's capital devolved on the parachute troops who had landed on the Fornebu airfield; in the afternoon this token force staged a parade march into the city, and its bluff succeeded. But the delay at least enabled the King and Government to escape northward with a view to rallying resistance.

The capture of Copenhagen was timed to coincide with the intended arrival at Oslo. The Danish capital was easy of access from the sea, and shortly before 5 a.m. three small transports steamed into the harbour, covered by aircraft overhead. The Germans met no resistance on landing, and a battalion marched off to take the barracks by surprise. At the same time Denmark's land frontier in Jutland was invaded, but after a brief exchange of fire resistance was abandoned. The occupation of Denmark went far to ensure the Germans' control of a sheltered sea-corridor from their own ports to southern Norway, and also gave them advanced airfields from which they could support the troops there. While the Danes might have fought longer, their country was so vulnerable as to be hardly defensible against a powerful attack with modern weapons.

More prompt and resolute action might have recovered two of the key points in Norway which the Germans captured that morning. For at the time they landed, the main British fleet under Admiral Forbes was abreast of Bergen, and he thought of sending a force in to attack the German ships there. The Admiralty agreed, and suggested that a similar attack should be made at Trondheim. A little later, however, it was decided to postpone the Trondheim attack until the German battlecruisers were tracked down. Meanwhile a force of four cruisers and seven destroyers headed for Bergen, but when aircraft reported that two German cruisers were there, instead of one as earlier reported, the Admiralty was overcome with caution and cancelled the attack.

Once the Germans had established a lodgment in Norway, the best way of loosening it would have been to cut them off from supply and reinforcements. That could only be done by barring the passage of the Skaggerak, between Denmark and Norway. But it soon became clear that the Admiralty

—from fear of German air attack—was not willing to send anything except submarines into the Skaggerak. Such caution revealed a realisation of the effect of airpower on seapower that the Admiralty had never shown before the war. But it reflected badly on Churchill's judgement in seeking to spread the war to Scandinavia—for unless the Germans' route of reinforcements could be effectively blocked nothing could stop them building up their strength in southern Norway, and they were bound to gain a growing advantage.

There still appeared to be a chance of preserving central Norway if the two long mountain defiles leading north from Oslo were firmly held, and the small German force at Trondheim was quickly overcome. To this aim British efforts were now bent. A week after the German coup, British landings were made north and south of Trondheim, at Namsos and Aandalsnes respectively, as a preliminary to the main and direct attack on Trondheim.

But a strange chain of mishaps followed the decision. General Hotblack, an able soldier with modern ideas, was appointed as the military commander; but after being briefed for his task he left the Admiralty about midnight to walk back to his club, and some hours later was found unconscious on the Duke of York's Steps, having apparently had a sudden seizure. A successor was appointed next day and set off by air for Scapa but the plane suddenly dived into the ground when circling the airfield there.

Meantime a sudden change took place in the views of the Chiefs of Staff, and the Admiralty. On the 17th they had approved the plan but the next day swung round in opposition to it. The risks of the operation filled their minds. Although Churchill would have preferred to concentrate on Narvik, he was much upset at the way they had turned round.

The Chiefs of Staff now recommended, instead, that the landings at Namsos and Aandalsnes should be reinforced and developed into a pincer-move against Trondheim. On paper the chances looked good, for there were less than 2,000 German troops in that area, whereas the Allies landed 13,000. But the distance to be covered was long, the snow clogged movement, and the Allied troops proved much less capable than the Germans of overcoming the difficulties. The advance south from Namsos was upset by the threat to its rear produced by the landing of several small German parties near the top of the Trondheim fiord, supported by the one German destroyer in the area. The advance from Aandalsnes, instead of being able to swing north on Trondheim, soon turned into a defensive action against the German troops who were pushing from Oslo up the Gudbrand Valley and brushing aside the Norwegians. As the Allied troops were badly harried by air attack, and lacked air support themselves, the commanders on the spot recommended evacuation. The re-embarkation of the two forces was completed on May 1 and 2—thus leaving the Germans in complete control of both southern and central Norway.

The Allies now concentrated on gaining Narvik—more for 'face-saving' purposes than from any continued hope of reaching the Swedish iron-mines. The original British landing in this area had been made on April 14, but the extreme caution of General Mackesy hindered any speedy attack on Narvik—despite the ardent promptings of Admiral Lord Cork and Orrery, who was put in charge of the combined force in this area. Even when the land forces had been built up to 20,000 troops, their progress was still slow. On the other side 2,000 Austrian Alpine troops reinforced by as many sailors from the German destroyers, and skilfully handled by General Dietl, made the most of the defensive advantages of the difficult country. Not until May 27 were they pushed out of Narvik town. By this time the German offensive in the West had bitten deep into France, which was on the verge of collapse. So on June 7 the Allied forces at Narvik were evacuated. The King and the Government left Norway at the same time.

Over the whole Scandinavian issue the Allied Governments had shown an excessive spirit of aggressiveness coupled with a deficient sense of time—with results that brought misery on the Norwegian people. By contrast Hitler had, for once, shown a prolonged reluctance to strike. But when he eventually made up his mind to forestall the Western powers he lost no more time—and his forces operated with a swiftness and audacity that amply offset the smallness of their numbers during the critical stage.

Fall of France 1940

MAY 26/JUNE 2
ALLIED FORCES
EVACUATED FROM
DUNKIRK

HOLLAND

The Hague

Rotterdam

Dordrecht

Moerdijk

FR. 7th

MAY 10

ARMY GROUP B
(Bock)

GERMANY

ENGLAND

Dover

Dunkirk

Calais

Gravelines

St Omer

Boulogne

Aa

Aire

Lille

FR. 1st

Abbeville

MAY 20

Arras

Amiens

Somme

FRONT LINE
JUNE 5, 1940

ANTWERP

BELGIUM

BELG.
ARMY

Brussels

B.E.F.

FR.1st

FR.9th

FR.1st

Montherme

Charleville

Oise

Albert Canal

Maastricht

FT. EBEN
EMAEL

Namur

Meuse

Dinant

Givet

Ardennes

St Menges

Sedan

Aisne

XXXIX PZ.CP.
(Schmidt)

XVI PZ.CP.
(Höppner)

XV PZ.CP.
(Hoth)

ARMY GROUP A
(Rundstedt)

XLI PZ.CP.
(Reinhardt)

XIX PZ.CP.
(Guderian)

KLEIST'S
PZ. GROUP

LUXEMBOURG

FR. 2nd

MAGINOT LINE

Reims

| 0 | Miles | 100 |
| 0 | Kilometres | 150 |

German infantry and
armoured attacks

Panzer Corps attacks

Allied line and armies after forward movement of left
shoulder

British breakout attempt, May 21

German airborne landings, May 10

Front line June 5

Panzer Corps attacks

| 0 | Miles | 100 |
| 0 | Kilometres | 150 |

Calais

Brussels

BELGIUM

GERMANY

ENGLISH CHANNEL

Somme

Abbeville

XV PZ.CP.
(Hoth)

XIV & XVI-
PZ.CP.
(Kleist)

2nd & 9th ARMIES

XXXIX & XLI
PZ.CP.
(Guderian)

LUX.

Cherbourg
JUNE 19

Rouen

Amiens

Péronne

Compiègne

Creil

Château-
Thierry

Laon

Reims

Oise

Marne

Châlons

MAGINOT
LINE

Rhine

BRITTANY

Rennes
JUNE 18

Alençon

Paris
JUNE 14

Seine

Orleans

Nancy

SURROUNDED
FRENCH
FORCES

FRANCE

Loire

Langres

Nantes

Tours

Dijon
JUNE 16

Besançon

SWITZERLAND

BAY OF

BISCAY

Argenton

Vichy

Saône

Rhône

Geneva

Royan

Limoges

Angoulême
JUNE 25

Clermont
Ferrand

JUNE 25
LINE REACHED BY GERMAN FORCES

Lyons
JUNE 20

Grenoble

ITALY

CHAPTER 7

THE OVERRUNNING OF THE WEST

The course of the world in our time was changed, with far-reaching effects on the future of all peoples, when Hitler's forces broke through the defence of the West on May 10, 1940. The decisive act of the world-shaking drama began on the 13th, when Guderian's panzer corps crossed the Meuse at Sedan.

On May 10 also, Mr. Churchill, restless and dynamic, became Prime Minister of Great Britain in place of Mr. Chamberlain.

The narrow breach at Sedan was soon expanded into a vast gap. The German tanks, pouring through it, reached the Channel coast within a week, thus cutting off the Allied armies in Belgium. That disaster led on to the fall of France and the isolation of Britain. Although Britain managed to hold out behind her sea-ditch, rescue only came after a prolonged war had become a world-wide struggle. In the end Hitler was overthrown by the weight of America and Russia, but Europe was left exhausted and under the shadow of Communist domination.

After the catastrophe, the rupture of the French front was commonly viewed as inevitable, and Hitler's attack as irresistible. But appearances were very different from reality—as has now become clear.

The heads of the German Army had little faith in the prospects of the offensive, which they had unwillingly launched on Hitler's insistence. Hitler himself suffered a sudden loss of confidence at the crucial moment, and imposed a two days' halt on the advance just as his spearhead pierced the French defence and had an open path in front of it. That would have been fatal to Hitler's prospects of victory if the French had been capable of profiting from the breathing space.

But strangest of all, the man who led the spearhead—Guderian—suffered momentary removal from command as a result of his superiors' anxiety to put a brake on his pace in exploiting the breakthrough he had made. Yet but for his 'offence' in driving so fast the invasion would probably have failed—and the whole course of world events would have been different from what it has been.

Far from having the overwhelming superiority with which they were credited, Hitler's armies were actually inferior in numbers to those opposing them. Although his tank drives proved decisive, he had fewer and less powerful tanks than his opponents possessed. Only in airpower, the most vital factor, had he a superiority.

Moreover, the issue was virtually decided by a small fraction of his forces before the bulk came into action. That decisive fraction comprised ten armoured divisions, one parachute division, and one air-portable division—besides the air force—out of a total of some 135 divisions which he had assembled.

The dazzling effect of what the new elements achieved has obscured not only their relatively small scale but the narrow margin by which success was gained. Their success could easily have been prevented but for the opportunities presented to them by the Allied blunders—blunders that were largely due to the prevalence of out-of-date ideas. Even as it was, with such help from the purblind leaders on the other side, the success of the invasion turned on a lucky series of long-odds chances—and on the readiness of one man, Guderian, to make the most of those which came his way.

The Battle of France is one of history's most striking examples of the decisive effect of a new idea, carried out by a dynamic executant. Guderian has related how, before the war, his imagination was fired by the idea of deep strategic penetration by independent armoured forces—a long-range tank drive to cut the main arteries of the opposing army far back behind its front. A tank enthusiast, he grasped the potentialities of this idea, arising from that new current of military thought in Britain after the first World War, which the Royal Tank Corps had been the first to demonstrate in training practice. Most of the higher German generals were as dubious of the idea as the British and French authorities had been—regarding it as impracticable in war. But when war came Guderian seized the chance to carry it out despite the doubts of his superiors. The effect proved as decisive as other new ideas had been in earlier history—the use of the horse, the long spear, the phalanx, the flexible legion, the 'oblique order', the horse-archer, the longbow, the musket, the gun, the organisation of armies in separate and manœuvrable divisions. Indeed, it proved more immediately decisive.

The German invasion of the West opened with dramatic successes on the right flank, against key points in the defence of neutral Holland and Belgium. These strokes spearheaded by airborne troops focused the Allies' attention there in such a way as to distract them for several days from the main thrust—which was being delivered in the centre, through the hilly and wooded country of the Ardennes, towards the heart of France.

The capital of Holland, the Hague, and the hub of its communications at Rotterdam, were attacked in the early hours of May 10 by airborne forces, simultaneously with the assault on its frontier defences a hundred miles to the east. The confusion and alarm created by this double blow, in front and rear, were increased by the widespread menace of the Luftwaffe. Exploiting the disorder, German armoured forces raced through a gap in the southern flank and joined up with the airborne forces at Rotterdam on the third day. They cut through to their objective under the nose of the French Seventh Army which was just arriving to the aid of the Dutch. On the fifth day the Dutch capitulated, although their main front was still unbroken. Their surrender was accelerated by the threat of further close-quarter air attack on their crowded cities.

The German forces here were much smaller than those opposing them. Moreover the decisive thrust was delivered by merely one panzer division, the 9th—the only one that could be spared for the attack on the Dutch front. Its path of advance was intersected by canals and broad rivers that should have been easy to defend. Its chances of success depended on the effect of the airborne coup.

But this new arm was also very small—and amazingly small compared with what it achieved. In May 1940, Germany had only 4,500 trained parachute troops. Of this meagre total, 4,000 were used in the attack on Holland. They formed five battalions, and were backed up by a light infantry division, of 12,000 men, that was carried in transport aircraft.

The main points of the plan are best summarised in the words of Student, the Commander-in-Chief of the airborne forces:

> The limitations of our strength compelled us to concentrate on two objectives—the points which seemed the most essential to the success of the invasion. The main effort, under my own control, was directed against the bridges at Rotterdam, Dordrecht, and Moerdijk by which the main route from the south was carried across the mouths of the Rhine. Our task was to capture the bridges before the Dutch could blow them up, and keep them open until the arrival of our mobile ground forces. My force comprised four parachute battalions and one air-transported regiment (of three battalions). We achieved complete success, at a cost of only 180 casualties. We dared not fail, for if we did the whole invasion would have failed.*

Student himself was one of the casualties, being wounded in the head, and he was out of action for eight months.

* Liddell Hart: *The Other Side of the Hill*, pp. 160-1. Other extracts in this chapter from same source.

A secondary attack was made on the Dutch capital, The Hague. Its aim was to capture the heads of the Government and the Services in their offices, and disrupt the whole machinery of control. The force employed at The Hague was one parachute battalion and two air-transported regiments, under General Graf Sponeck. This attack was foiled, though it caused much confusion.

The invasion of Belgium also had a sensational opening. Here the ground attack was carried out by the powerful 6th Army under Reichenau (which included Höppner's 16th Panzer Corps). It had to overcome a formidable barrier before it could effectively deploy. Only 500 airborne troops were left to help this attack. They were used to capture the two bridges over the Albert Canal and the fort of Eben Emael, Belgium's most modern fort, which flanked this waterline-frontier.

That tiny detachment, however, made all the difference to the issue. For the approach to the Belgian frontier here lay across the southerly projection of Dutch territory known as the 'Maastricht Appendix', and once the German Army crossed the Dutch frontier the Belgian frontier guards on the Albert Canal would have had ample warning to blow the bridges before any invading ground forces could cross that fifteen-mile strip. Airborne troops dropping silently out of the night sky offered a new way, and the only way, of securing the key bridges intact.

The very limited scale of airborne forces used in Belgium was in extraordinary contrast to the reports at the time that German parachutists were dropping at scores of places, in numbers that cumulatively ran into thousands. Student provided the explanation—to compensate the scantiness of actual resources, and create as much confusion as possible, dummy parachutists were scattered widely over the country. This ruse certainly proved most effective, helped by the natural tendency of heated imaginations to multiply all figures.

According to Student:

The Albert Canal venture was also Hitler's own idea. It was perhaps the most original idea of this man of many brain-waves. He sent for me and asked my opinion. After a day's consideration I affirmed the possibility of such an enterprise, and was ordered to make the preparations. I used 500 men under Captain Koch. The Commander of the Sixth Army, General von Reichenau and his chief of staff General von Paulus, both capable generals, regarded the undertaking as an adventure in which they had no faith.

The surprise attack on Fort Eben Emael was carried out by a Lilliputian detachment of 78 parachute-engineers commanded by Lieutenant Witzig. Of these, only 6 men were killed. This small detachment made a completely unexpected landing on the roof of the fort, overcame the anti-aircraft personnel there, and blew up the armoured cupolas and casemates of all the guns with a new highly intensive explosive—previously kept secret. ... The surprise attack on Eben Emael was based on the use of this new weapon, which was silently transported to the objective by another new weapon—a freight-carrying glider.*

The fort was well-designed to meet every menace except the possibility of enemy troops dropping on top of it. From the roof of the fort Witzig's handful of 'sky-troopers' kept the garrison of 1,200 men in check until twenty-four hours later when the Germans' ground forces arrived on the scene.

The Belgian guards on the two key bridges were likewise taken by surprise. At one bridge they actually lit the fuse to blow up the bridge—but the crew of a glider got into the blockhouse on the heels of the sentries to extinguish it in the nick of time.

It is notable that on the whole front of the invasion the bridges were blown up everywhere by the defenders, according to plan, except where airborne attackers were used. That shows how small was the margin between success and failure on the German side—since the prospect of the invasion turned on the time-factor.

By the second morning sufficient German troops had arrived over the canal to burst through the shallow Belgian line of defence behind. Then Höppner's two panzer divisions (the 3rd and 4th) drove over the un-demolished bridges and spread over the plains beyond. Their onsweeping drive caused the Belgian forces to start a general retreat—just as the French and British were arriving to support them.

This breakthrough in Belgium was not the decisive stroke in the invasion of the West, but it had a vital effect on the issue. It not only drew the Allies' attention in the wrong direction but absorbed the most mobile part of the Allied forces in the battle that developed there, so that these mobile divisions could not be pulled out and switched south to meet the greater menace that on May 13 suddenly loomed up on the French frontier—at its weakest part, beyond the western end of the incomplete Maginot Line.

For the mechanised spearheads of Rundstedt's Army Group had mean-time been driving through Luxembourg and Belgian Luxembourg towards France. After traversing that seventy-mile stretch of the Ardennes, and brushing aside weak opposition, they crossed the French frontier and emerged on the banks of the Meuse early on the fourth day of the offensive.

It had been a bold venture to send a mass of tanks and motor-vehicles through such difficult country, which had long been regarded by conventional strategists as 'impassable' for a large-scale offensive, let alone for a

* pp. 163-4.

tank operation. But that increased the chances of surprise, while the thick woods helped to cloak the advance and conceal the strength of the blow.

It was the French High Command, however, which contributed most to Hitler's success. The shattering effect of the Ardennes stroke owed much to the design of the French plan—which fitted perfectly, from the Germans' point of view, into their own remodelled plan. What proved fatal to the French was not, as is commonly imagined, their defensive attitude or 'Maginot Line complex', but the more offensive side of their plan. By pushing into Belgium with their left shoulder forward they played into the hands of their enemy, and wedged themselves in a trap—just as had happened with their near-fatal Plan XVII of 1914. It was the more perilous this time because the opponent was more mobile, manœuvring at motor-pace instead of at foot-pace. The penalty, too, was the greater because the left shoulder push—made by three French armies and the British—comprised the most modernly equipped and mobile part of the Allied forces as a whole.

With every step forward that these armies took in their rush into Belgium, their rear became more exposed to Rundstedt's flanking drive through the Ardennes. Worse still, the hinge of the Allied advance was guarded by a few low-grade French divisions, composed of older men and scantily equipped in anti-tank and anti-aircraft guns, the two vital needs. To leave the hinge so poorly covered was the crowning blunder of the French High Command, under Gamelin and Georges.

The German advance through the Ardennes was a tricky operation, and an extraordinary feat of staffwork. Before dawn of May 10 the greatest concentration of tanks yet seen in war was massed opposite the frontier of Luxembourg. Made up of three panzer corps, these were arrayed in three blocks, or layers, with armoured divisions in the first two, and motorised infantry divisions in the third. The van was led by General Guderian, and the whole was commanded by General von Kleist.

To the right of Kleist's group lay a separate panzer corps, the 15th, under Hoth, which was to dash through the northern part of the Ardennes, to the Meuse between Givet and Dinant.

The seven armoured divisions, however, formed only a fraction of the armed mass that was drawn up along the German frontier ready to plunge into the Ardennes. Some fifty divisions were closely packed on a narrow but very deep front.

The chances of success essentially depended on the quickness with which the German panzer forces could push through the Ardennes and cross the Meuse. Only when they were across that river-barrier would the tanks have room for manœuvre. They needed to get across before the French High

Command realised what was happening and collected reserves to stop them.

The race was won, though with little margin. The result might have been different if the defending forces had been capable of profiting from the partial checks caused by demolitions that were carried out according to previous plan. It was unfortunate for the security of France that these were not backed by adequate defenders. The French had been foolish to rely on cavalry divisions to delay the invaders.

By contrast, an armoured counterstroke against the flank of the German advance at this stage would probably have paralysed that advance—by its effect on the higher commanders. Even as it was, they were momentarily shaken by the shadow of a stroke towards their left flank.

Seeing how well the advance was going, Kleist had already, on the 12th, endorsed Guderian's view that the crossing of the Meuse should be tackled without waiting for the infantry corps to arrive. But arrangements had been made for a heavy air concentration, including twelve squadrons of dive-bombers, to help in forcing a passage. These appeared on the scene early in the afternoon of the 13th, and maintained such a hail of bombs as to keep most of the French gunners down in their dug-outs until nightfall.

Guderian's attack was concentrated on a one-and-a-half-mile stretch of the river just west of Sedan. The chosen sector provided a perfect setting for forcing a passage. The river bends sharply north towards St Menges and then south again, forming a pocket-like salient. The surrounding heights on the north bank are wooded, thus providing cover for attack preparations and gun-positions as well as fine artillery observation. From near St Menges there was a wonderful panoramic view over this river-salient, and across to the wooded heights of the Bois de Marfée which form the back-curtain on the far side.

The assault was launched at 4 p.m., led by the panzer infantry in rubber boats and on rafts. Ferries were soon in operation, bringing light vehicles across. The river-salient was quickly overrun, and the attackers pressed on to capture the Bois de Marfée and the southern heights. By midnight the wedge was driven nearly five miles deep, while a bridge was completed at Glaire (between Sedan and St Menges) over which the tanks began to pour.

Even so, the German foothold was still precarious on the 14th—with only one division yet across the river, and only one bridge by which reinforcements and supplies could reach it. The bridge was heavily attacked by the Allied air forces, which enjoyed a temporary advantage as the weight of the Luftwaffe had been switched elsewhere. But the anti-aircraft artillery regiment of Guderian's corps kept a thick canopy of fire over the vital bridge, and Allied air attacks were beaten off with heavy loss.

By the afternoon all three of his panzer divisions were over the river. After beating off a belated French counterattack, he made a sudden turn westward. By the following evening he had broken through the last line of defence, and the roads to the west—to the Channel coast—lay open to him.

Yet that night was a trying one for Guderian—though not owing to the enemy:

> An order came from Panzer Group Headquarters to halt the advance and confine the troops to the bridgehead gained. I would not and could not put up with this order, as it meant forfeiting surprise and all our initial success.*

After a lively argument on the telephone with Kleist, the latter agreed 'to permit the continuation of the advance for another twenty-four hours—in order to widen the bridgehead'.

The utmost advantage was taken of this cautious permission, and full rein was given to the panzer divisions. The westward drive of Guderian's three panzer divisions converged with that of Reinhardt's two divisions from the Monthermé crossing, and also with those of Hoth's two divisions from the crossings near Dinant. It produced a spreading collapse of French resistance, and swept through an empty space.

By the night of the 16th the westward drive had gone more than fifty miles farther, towards the Channel, and reached the Oise. Yet once again the brake was applied, not by the enemy, but from above.

The higher commanders on the German side were amazed at the ease with which the Meuse had been overcome, and could hardly believe their luck. They still expected a heavy French counterstroke against their flank. Hitler shared these apprehensions. In consequence he put a curb on the advance—halting it for two days, so that the infantry corps could come up and form a flank shield along the Aisne.

After the matter had been referred to higher quarters, Guderian was reinstated, and given qualified permission to carry on strong reconnaissance. 'Strong reconnaissance' as interpreted by Guderian had an elastic meaning and enabled him to maintain a considerable degree of offensive pressure during the two days' interval before the infantry corps of the 12th Army had begun to form a strong flank shield on the Aisne and he was allowed to race all out for the Channel coast.

So much time had been gained in the preceding stages and so much dislocation had been caused on the opposing side, that the pause on the Oise had no serious effect on the German prospects. Even so, it revealed a significant difference of time-sense on the German side. The gap between the

* p. 177.

THE OVERRUNNING OF THE WEST

new school and old school there was greater than that between the Germans
and the French.

Gamelin, writing at the end of the war, said of the Germans' strategic
exploitation of the Meuse crossing:

> It was a remarkable manœuvre. But had it been entirely foreseen in advance?
> I do not believe it—any more than that Napoleon had foreseen the manœuvre
> of Jena, or Moltke that of Sedan [in 1870]. It was a perfect utilisation of
> circumstances. It showed troops and a command who knew how to manœuvre,
> who were organised to operate quickly—as tanks, aircraft, and wireless
> permitted them to do. It is perhaps the first time that a battle has been won,
> which became decisive, without having had to engage the bulk of the forces.*

According to General Georges, who was the executive Commander-in-
Chief of the battlefront, it was reckoned that the planned obstructions in
Belgian Luxembourg were likely 'to retard for at least four days' the
Germans' arrival on the Meuse. General Doumenc, the Chief of Staff, said:

> Crediting our enemies with our own procedure, we had imagined that they
> would not attempt the passage of the Meuse until after they had brought
> up ample artillery: the five or six days necessary for that would have easily
> given us time to reinforce our own dispositions.*

It is remarkable how closely these French calculations corresponded to
those made in the higher quarters on 'the other side of the hill'. It can be
seen that the French military chiefs had justification—more justification than
was apparent immediately after the event—for their basic assumptions about
the German offensive. But they had left out of the reckoning an individual
factor—Guderian. His adoption of the theory of deep strategic penetration
by armoured forces operating independently, his fervent conviction of its
practicability, and his consequent impulsion in stretching subordination
upset the calculations of the French High Command to an extent that the
German High Command would never have done of its own volition. It is
clear that Guderian and his tankmen pulled the German Army along after
them, and thereby produced the most sweeping victory in modern history.

The issue turned on the time-factor at stage after stage. French counter-
movements were repeatedly thrown out of gear because their timing was
too slow to catch up with the changing situations, and that was due to the
fact that the German van kept on moving faster than the German High
Command had contemplated.

The French had based their plans on the assumption that an assault on the
Meuse would not come before the ninth day. That was the same time-scale
the German chiefs had in mind originally, before Guderian intervened.
When it was upset, worse was to follow. The French commanders, trained

* p. 181.

73

in the slow-motion methods of 1918, were mentally unfitted to cope with panzer pace, and it produced a spreading paralysis among them.

One of the few men on the Allied side who realised the danger in time was the new French Prime Minister, M. Paul Reynaud. As an outside critic before the war, he had urged his countrymen to develop armoured forces. Understanding their effect all too clearly, he telephoned Mr Churchill early on the 15th, to say: 'We have lost the battle.'

Churchill's reply was: 'All experience shows that the offensive will come to an end after a while. I remember the 21st of March, 1918. After five or six days they have to halt for supplies and the opportunity for counter-attack is presented. I learned all this at the time from the lips of Marshal Foch himself.'* Next day he flew over to Paris, and there argued against any withdrawal of the Allied armies in Belgium. Even as it was, Gamelin was too slow in pulling them back. He now planned a deliberate counter-offensive in the 1918 way—with massed infantry divisions. Churchill continued to pin his faith to this. It was unfortunate that Gamelin's mind remained in an out-of-date groove, as he had more capacity for action than anyone in France.

That day, too, Reynaud made a move to replace Gamelin—summoning Weygand, Foch's old assistant, from Syria. Weygand did not arrive until the 19th, so that for three days the Supreme Command was in a state of suspense. On the 20th Guderian reached the Channel, cutting the communications of the Allied armies in Belgium. Moreover, Weygand was even more out-of-date than Gamelin, and continued to plan on 1918 lines. So hope of recovery faded.

In sum, the Allied leaders did things too late or did the wrong thing, and in the end did nothing effective to avert disaster.

The escape of the British Expeditionary Force in 1940 was largely due to Hitler's personal intervention. After his tanks had overrun the north of France and cut off the British army from its base, Hitler held them up just as they were about to sweep into Dunkirk—which was the last remaining port of escape left open to the British. At that moment the bulk of the B.E.F. was still many miles distant from the port. But Hitler kept his tanks halted for three days.

His action preserved the British forces when nothing else could have saved them. By making it possible for them to escape he enabled them to rally in England, continue the war, and man the coasts to defy the threat of

* Churchill: *The Second World War*, vol. II, pp. 38–9.

invasion. Thereby he produced his own ultimate downfall, and Germany's, five years later. Acutely aware of the narrowness of the escape, but ignorant of its cause, the British people spoke of 'the miracle of Dunkirk'.

How did he come to give the fateful halt order, and why? It remained a puzzle in many respects to the German generals themselves, and it will never be possible to learn for certain how he came to his decision and what his motives were. Even if Hitler had given an explanation it would hardly be reliable. Men in high position who make a fatal mistake rarely tell the truth about it afterwards, and Hitler was not one of the most truth-loving of great men. It is more likely that his evidence would confuse the trail. It is also quite likely that he could not have given a true explanation even if he had wished, because his motives were apt to be so mixed and his impulses so changeable. Moreover, all men's recollection tends to be coloured by what happens later.

In prolonged exploration of this critical event, sufficient evidence has emerged for the historian to be able to piece together not only the chain of events but what seems a reasonably probable chain of causation leading up to the fateful decision.

After cutting the lines of supply to the Allied left wing in Belgium, Guderian's panzer corps had reached the sea near Abbeville on the 20th. Then he wheeled north, heading for the Channel ports and the rear of the British Army—which was still in Belgium, facing the frontal advance of Bock's infantry forces. On Guderian's right in this northward drive was Reinhardt's panzer corps, which was also part of Kleist's group.

On the 22nd, Boulogne was isolated by his advance, and on the next day Calais. This stride brought him to Gravelines, barely ten miles from Dunkirk—the British Expeditionary Force's last remaining port of escape. Reinhardt's panzer corps also arrived on the canal line Aire–St Omer–Gravelines. But there the continuation of the drive was stopped by orders from above. The panzer leaders were told to hold their forces back behind the line of the canal. They bombarded their superiors with urgent queries and protests, but were told that it was 'the Führer's personal order'.

Before probing deeper into the roots of that saving intervention let us see what was happening on the British side, and follow the course of that grand-scale escape.

On the 16th General Lord Gort, the Commander-in-Chief, brought the B.E.F. a step back from its advanced line in front of Brussels. But before it arrived in its new position on the Scheldt, that position had been undermined by Guderian cutting the B.E.F's communications far to the south. On the 19th the Cabinet heard that Gort was 'examining a possible withdrawal towards Dunkirk if that were forced upon him'. The Cabinet, however, sent him orders to march south into France and force his way through the German net that had been flung across his rear—though they were told that he had only four days' supplies and ammunition sufficient for one battle.

These instructions accorded with the new plan which Gamelin, the French Commander-in-Chief, had belatedly made and issued that morning. In the evening Gamelin was sacked and replaced by Weygand, whose first act was to cancel Gamelin's order, while he studied the situation. After three days' further delay he produced a plan similar to his predecessor's. It proved no more than a paper plan.

Meanwhile Gort, though arguing that the Cabinet's instructions were impracticable, had tried an attack southward from Arras with two of his thirteen divisions and the only tank brigade that had been sent to France. When this counterstroke was launched on the 21st it had boiled down to an advance by two weak tank battalions followed by two infantry battalions. The tanks made some progress but were not backed up, the infantry being shaken by dive-bombing. The neighbouring French First Army was to have co-operated, with two of its thirteen divisions, but its actual contribution was slight. During these days the French were repeatedly paralysed by the moral effect of the German dive-bombers and the swift manoeuvring tanks.

It is remarkable, however, what a disturbing effect this little armoured counterstroke had on some of the German higher commanders. For a moment it led them to think of stopping the advance of their own tank spearheads. Rundstedt himself described it as 'a critical moment', saying: 'For a short time it was feared that our armoured divisions would be cut off before the infantry divisions could come up to support them.'* Such an effect showed what a vital difference to the issue might have been made if this British riposte had been made with two armoured divisions instead of merely two tank battalions.

After the flash-in-the-pan at Arras the Allied armies in the north made no further effort to break out of the trap, while the belated relief offensive from

---

* Forecasting the very situation that arose in 1940, it had been urged from 1935 on in *The Times*, and other quarters, that Britain's military effort should be concentrated on providing a stronger air force and two to three armoured divisions for a counterstroke against any German breakthrough in France, instead of sending an expeditionary force composed of infantry divisions—of which the French had plenty. This principle was accepted by the Cabinet at the end of 1937, but discarded early in 1939 in favour of building an expeditionary force of the familiar pattern. By May 1940, thirteen infantry divisions (including three 'labour' divisions) in all had been sent to France, without a single armoured division, but proved unable to do anything to save the situation.

the south that Weygand planned was so feeble as to be almost farcical. It was easily baulked by the barricade which the German motorised divisions had quickly built up along the Somme, to keep out interference while the panzer divisions drove northward to close the trap. With such slow-motion forces as Weygand commanded, his grandiloquent orders had no more chance of practical effect than Churchill's adjurations to the armies to 'cast away the idea of resisting attack behind concrete lines or natural obstacles' and regain the mastery 'by furious, unrelenting assault'.

While the highest circles continued to debate impracticable plans, the cut-off armies in the north were falling back on a slant closer to the coast. They were under increasing frontal pressure from Bock's infantry armies—though they were spared a deadly stab in the back from the panzer forces.

On the 24th Weygand bitterly complained that 'the British Army had carried out, on its own initiative, a retreat of twenty-five miles towards the ports at a time when our troops moving up from the south are gaining ground towards the north, where they were to meet their allies'. In fact, the French troops from the south had made no perceptible progress and the British were not yet retreating—Weygand's words merely showed the state of unreality in which he was living. But on the evening of the 25th Gort took the definite decision to retreat to the sea, at Dunkirk. Forty-eight hours earlier, the German panzer forces had already arrived, on the canal line only ten miles from the port. On the 26th the British Cabinet allowed the War Office to send him a telegram approving his step and 'authorised' him to carry out such a retirement. Next day a further telegram told him to evacuate his force by sea.

That same day the Belgian Army's line cracked in the centre under Bock's attack, and no reserves were left at hand to fill the gap. King Leopold had already sent repeated warnings to Churchill, through Admiral Keyes, that the situation was becoming hopeless. Now, at a stroke, it was so. Most of Belgium had already been overrun and the army had its back close to the sea, penned in a narrow strip of land that was packed with civilian refugees. So in the late afternoon the King decided to sue for an armistice —and the 'cease fire' was sounded early the next morning.

The Belgians' surrender increased the danger that the B.E.F. would be cut off before it could reach Dunkirk. Churchill had just sent King Leopold an appeal to hold on, which he privately described to Gort as 'asking them to sacrifice themselves for us'. It is understandable that the encircled Belgians, already aware that the B.E.F. was preparing to evacuate, did not see that appeal in the same light as Churchill. Nor was King Leopold willing to follow Churchill's advice that he should himself 'escape by aeroplane before too late'. The King felt that he 'must stay with his Army and people'. His decision may have been unwise in the long view, but in the circumstances of the time it was an honourable choice. Churchill's subsequent criticisms of it were hardly fair, while the violent denunciations made by the French Prime Minister and press were grossly unjust—considering the way that the Belgian downfall had been produced by the collapse of the French defence on the Meuse.

The British retreat to the coast now became a race to re-embark before the German trap closed—notwithstanding bitter French protests and reproaches. It was fortunate that preparatory measures had begun in England a week before—although on a different assumption. On the 20th Churchill had approved steps 'to assemble a large number of small vessels in readiness to proceed to ports and inlets on the French coast', with the idea that they might help in rescuing bits of the B.E.F. that might be cut off as it tried to push south into France, under the existing plan. The Admiralty lost no time in making preparations. Admiral Ramsay, commanding at Dover, had been placed in operational control on the previous day, the 19th. A number of ferry-craft, naval drifters and small coasters were at once collected for what was called 'Operation Dynamo'. From Harwich round to Weymouth sea-transport officers were directed to list all ships up to a thousand tons.

In the days that followed the situation became rapidly worse, and it was soon clear to the Admiralty that Dunkirk would be the only possible route of evacuation. 'Dynamo' was put into operation on the afternoon of the 26th—twenty-four hours before the Belgian appeal for an armistice, and also before the Cabinet had authorised the evacuation.

At first it was not expected that more than a small fraction of the B.E.F. could be saved. The Admiralty told Ramsay to aim at bringing away 45,000 within two days and that it was probable the enemy would by then have made further evacuation impossible. Actually, only 25,000 were landed in England by the night of the 28th. It was fortunate that the period of grace proved considerably longer.

For the first five days the rate of evacuation was restricted by an insufficiency of small boats to carry troops from the beaches to the ships waiting offshore. This need, though pointed out by Ramsay originally, had not been adequately met. But the Admiralty now made more extensive efforts to provide them and to man them, the naval personnel being reinforced by a host of civilian volunteers—fishermen, lifeboatmen, yachtsmen, and others who had some experience in handling boats. Ramsay recorded that one of the best performances was that of the crew of the fire-float *Massey Shaw* from the London Fire Brigade.

At first, too, there was much confusion on the beaches, owing to the dis-organised state of the troops waiting to embark—at that time largely base personnel. Ramsay considered that it was aggravated 'by the fact that Army officers' uniform is indistinguishable from that of other ranks', and found that 'the appearance of Naval officers, in their unmistakable uniforms, helped to restore order. . . . Later on, when troops of fighting formations reached the beaches these difficulties disappeared.'

The first heavy air attack came on the evening of the 29th and 'it was only by good fortune that the vital Dunkirk Harbour channel was not blocked by sinking ships at this early date'. Its preservation was the more important because the majority of the troops were embarked from the harbour and less than one-third from the beaches.

In the next three days the air attacks increased, and on June 2 daylight evacuation had to be suspended. The fighters of the R.A.F., from airfields in southern England, did their utmost to keep the Luftwaffe at bay, but, being outnumbered and unable to stay long over the area because of the distance, they could not maintain anything like adequate air cover. The oft-repeated bombing attacks were a severe strain on the troops waiting on the beaches, though the soft sand blanketed the effects. Far more material damage was done over the sea where the losses included six destroyers, eight personnel ships, and over 200 small craft—out of a total of 860 British and Allied vessels of all sizes employed in the evacuation. It was very lucky that the German Navy made very little attempt to interfere, either with U-boats or E-boats. Happily, too, the evacuation was favoured by extremely good weather.

By May 30, 126,000 troops had been evacuated, while all the rest of the B.E.F. had arrived in the Dunkirk bridgehead—except for fragments that were cut off during the retreat. The defence of the bridgehead against the enemy's encircling advance on land now became much firmer in conse-quence. The Germans had missed their opportunity.

Unhappily the French higher commanders in Belgium, still conforming to Weygand's impossible plan, had hesitated to retreat to the sea and to do so as quickly as possible along with the British. As a result of that delay nearly half of what was left of the French First Army had been cut off on the 28th near Lille, and were forced to surrender on the 31st. Their gallant three-day stand, however, helped the escape of the remainder, as well as the British.

By midnight on June 2 the British rearguard embarked and the evacuation of the B.E.F. was complete—224,000 men had been safely brought away, and only some 2,000 were lost in ships sunk en route to England. Some 95,000 Allied troops, mainly French, had also been evacuated. On the next night every effort was made to bring away the remaining Frenchmen, despite increasing difficulties, and 26,000 more were saved. Unfortunately a few thousand of the rearguard were left—and this left sore feelings in France.

By the morning of the 4th, when the operation was broken off, a total of 338,000 British and Allied troops had been landed in England. It was an amazing result compared with earlier expectations, and a grand performance on the part of the Navy.

At the same time it is evident that the preservation of the B.E.F. 'to fight another day' would have been impossible without Hitler's action in halting Kleist's panzer forces outside Dunkirk twelve days before, on May 24.

At that moment there was only one British battalion covering the twenty-mile stretch of the Aa between Gravelines and St Omer, and for a further sixty miles inland the canal line was little better defended. Many of the bridges were not yet blown up, or even prepared for demolition. Thus the German panzer troops had no difficulty in gaining bridgeheads over the canal at a number of places on May 23—and it was as Gort said in his Despatch, 'the only anti-tank obstacle on this flank'. Having crossed it, there was nothing to hold them up—and stop them establishing themselves astride the B.E.F's lines of retreat to Dunkirk—except the halt that Hitler imposed.

It is clear, however, that Hitler had been in a highly strung and jumpy state ever since the breakthrough into France. The extraordinary easiness of the advance, the lack of resistance his armies had met, had made him uneasy—it seemed too good to be true. The effects can be followed in the diary that was kept by Halder, the Chief of the General Staff. On the 17th, the day after the French defence behind the Meuse had dramatically collapsed, Halder noted: 'Rather unpleasant day. The Führer is terribly nervous. Frightened by his own success, he is afraid to take any chance and so would rather pull the reins on us.'

That was the day when Guderian was suddenly pulled up when in full stride for the sea. Next day, noted Halder: 'Every hour is precious. . . Führer HQ sees it quite differently. . . unaccountably keeps worrying about the south flank. He rages and screams that we are on the best way to ruin the whole campaign.' Not until late that evening, when Halder was able to assure him that the follow-up infantry army was wheeling into line along the Aisne as a flank shield, did Hitler agree to let the panzer forces sweep on.

Two days later these reached the coast, cutting the communications of the Allied armies in Belgium. That brilliant success seems to have temporarily drowned Hitler's doubts. But they revived as his panzer forces swung northward, especially after the momentary alarm caused by the British tank counterattack from Arras, slight as this was. His panzer forces, which he regarded as so precious, were now heading towards the zone occupied by the British, whom he looked on as particularly tough opponents. At the same time he was uneasy as to what the French in the south might be planning.

On the surface it appears to have been unlucky for Hitler that he chose to visit Rundstedt's headquarters on the morning of May 24, a crucial moment. For Rundstedt was a wary strategist, careful to take full account of unfavourable factors and avoid erring on the side of optimism. For that reason he was often a good corrective to Hitler, by providing a coolly balanced estimate—but it did not benefit German chances on this occasion. In his review of the situation he dwelt on the way that the tank strength had been reduced in the long and rapid drive, and pointed out the possibility of having to meet attacks from the north and south, particularly the latter.

Since he had, the night before, received orders from Brauchitsch, the Army Commander-in-Chief, that the completion of the encirclement in the north was to be handed over to Bock, it was the more natural that he should be thinking of the next phase in the south.

Moreover, Rundstedt's headquarters were still at Charleville, near Sedan—close behind the Aisne, and in the centre of the German front facing south. That location fostered a tendency to focus on what was in front and give less attention to what was happening on the extreme right flank, where victory seemed to be assured. Dunkirk only came into the corner of his eye.

Hitler 'agreed entirely' with Rundstedt's reservations, and went on to emphasise the paramount necessity of conserving the panzer force for future operations.

On his return to his own headquarters in the afternoon, he sent for the Commander-in-Chief. It was 'a very unpleasant interview', and ended in Hitler giving a definite halt order—Halder that evening mournfully summarised its effect in his diary:

> The left wing, consisting of armoured and motorised forces, which has no enemy before it, will thus be stopped in its tracks upon direct orders of the Führer. Finishing off the encircled enemy army is to be left to the Luftwaffe!

Was Hitler's halt order inspired by Rundstedt? If Hitler had felt that his halt order was due to Rundstedt's influence, he would almost certainly have mentioned it, after the British escape, among the excuses he gave for his decision, for he was very apt to blame others for any mistakes. Yet in this case there is no trace of his ever having mentioned, in the course of his subsequent explanations, Rundstedt's opinion as a factor. Such negative evidence is as significant as any.

It seems more likely that Hitler went to Rundstedt's headquarters in the hope of finding further justification for his own doubts and for the change of plan he wanted to impose on Brauchitsch and Halder. In so far as it was prompted by anyone else, the initial influence probably came from Keitel and Jodl, the two chief military members of his own staff. There is particular significance in the evidence of General Warlimont, who was in close touch with Jodl at the time. Astonished on hearing a rumour of the halt order, he went to ask Jodl about it:

> Jodl confirmed that the order had been given, showing himself rather impatient about my enquiries. He himself took the same stand as Hitler, emphasising that the personal experience that not only Hitler but also Keitel and himself had in Flanders during the First World War proved beyond any doubt that armour could not operate in the Flanders marshes, or at any rate not without heavy losses—and such losses could not be borne in view of the already reduced strength of the panzer corps and their tasks in the impending second stage of the offensive in France.*

Warlimont added that if the initiative for the halt order had come from Rundstedt, he and the others at O.K.W. would have heard of it; and that Jodl, who was on the defensive about the decision, 'certainly would not have failed to point to Field-Marshal von Rundstedt as the one who had initiated or at least supported that order'—as that would have silenced criticism, because of Rundstedt's 'undisputed authority in operational matters among all senior general staff officers':

> One other reason, however, for the halt order was revealed to me at the time—that Göring appeared and reassured the Führer that his air force would accomplish the rest of the encirclement by closing the sea side of the pocket from the air. He certainly overrated the effectiveness of his own branch.*

This statement of Warlimont's gains significance when related to the last sentence in Halder's diary note of the 24th, already quoted. Moreover, Guderian stated that the order came down to him from Kleist, with the words: 'Dunkirk is to be left to the Luftwaffe. If the conquest of Calais should raise difficulties that fortress likewise is to be left to the Luftwaffe.' Guderian remarked: 'I think that it was the vanity of Göring which caused that fateful decision of Hitler's.'

At the same time there is evidence that even the Luftwaffe was not used as fully or as vigorously as it could have been—and some of the air chiefs say that Hitler put the brake on again here.

* p. 197.

All this caused the higher circles to suspect a political motive behind Hitler's military reasons. Blumentritt, who was Rundstedt's operational planner, connected it with the surprising way that Hitler had talked when visiting their headquarters:

> Hitler was in very good humour, he admitted that the course of the campaign had been 'a decided miracle', and gave us the opinion that the war would be finished in six weeks. After that he wished to conclude a reasonable peace with France, and then the way would be free for an agreement with Britain.
>
> He then astonished us by speaking with admiration of the British Empire, of the necessity for its existence, and of the civilisation that Britain had brought into the world. He remarked, with a shrug of the shoulders, that the creation of its Empire had been achieved by means that were often harsh, but 'where there is planing, there are shavings flying'. He compared the British Empire with the Catholic Church—saying they were both essential elements of stability in the world. He said that all he wanted from Britain was that she should acknowledge Germany's position on the Continent. The return of Germany's lost colonies would be desirable but not essential, and he would even offer to support Britain with troops if she should be involved in any difficulties anywhere. He remarked that the colonies were primarily a matter of prestige, since they could not be held in war, and few Germans could settle in the tropics.
>
> He concluded by saying that his aim was to make peace with Britain on a basis that she would regard as compatible with her honour to accept.*

In subsequent reflection on the course of events, Blumentritt's thoughts often reverted to this conversation. He felt that the 'halt' had been called for more than military reasons, and that it was part of a political scheme to make peace easier to reach. If the B.E.F. had been captured at Dunkirk, the British might have felt that their honour had suffered a stain which they must wipe out. By letting it escape Hitler hoped to conciliate them.

Since this account comes from generals who were highly critical of Hitler, and admit that they themselves wanted to finish off the British Army, it is of the more significance. Their account of Hitler's talks at the time of Dunkirk fits in with much that he himself wrote earlier in *Mein Kampf*—and it is remarkable how closely he followed his own testament in other respects. There were elements in his make-up which suggest that he had a mixed love-hate feeling towards Britain. The trend of his talk about Britain at this time is also recorded in the diaries of Ciano and Halder.

Hitler's character was of such complexity that no simple explanation is likely to be true. It is far more probable that his decision was woven of several threads. Three are visible—his desire to conserve tank strength for the next stroke; his long-standing fear of marshy Flanders; and Göring's

* pp. 200–1.

83

claims for the Luftwaffe. But it is quite likely that some political thread was interwoven with these military ones in the mind of a man who had a bent for political strategy and so many twists in his thought.

The new French front along the Somme and the Aisne was longer than the original one, while the forces available to hold it were much diminished. The French had lost thirty of their own divisions in the first stage of the campaign, besides the help of their allies. (Only two British divisions remained in France, though two more that were not fully trained were now sent over.) In all, Weygand had collected forty-nine divisions to cover the new front, leaving seventeen to hold the Maginot Line. Not much could be done to fortify the front in the short time available, and the shortage of forces counteracted the belated attempt to apply the method of defence in depth. As most of the mechanised divisions had been lost or badly depleted there was also a lack of mobile reserves.

The Germans, by contrast, had brought their ten panzer divisions up to strength again with relays of fresh tanks, while their 130 infantry divisions were almost untouched. For the new offensive the forces were redistributed, two fresh armies (the 2nd and 9th) being inserted to increase the weight along the Aisne sector (between the Oise and the Meuse), and Guderian was given command of a group of two panzer corps that was moved to lie up in readiness there. Kleist was left with two panzer corps, to strike from the bridgeheads over the Somme at Amiens and Péronne respectively, in a pincer-move aimed to converge on the lower reach of the Oise near Creil. The remaining armoured corps, under Hoth, was to advance between Amiens and the sea.

The offensive was launched on June 5, initially on the western stretch between Laon and the sea. Resistance was stiff for the first two days, but on the 7th the most westerly armoured corps broke through on the roads to Rouen. The defence then collapsed in confusion, and the Germans met no serious resistance in crossing the Seine on the 9th. But it was not here that they intended their decisive manœuvre, so they paused, which was fortunate for the small British force, under General Alan Brooke, most of which was thus enabled to achieve a second evacuation when the French capitulated.

Kleist's pincer-stroke did not, however, go according to plan. The right pincer eventually broke through on the 8th but the left pincer, from Péronne, was hung up by tough opposition north of Compiègne. The German Supreme Command then decided to pull back Kleist's group and switch it east to back up the breakthrough that had been made in Champagne.

The offensive there did not open until the 9th, but then the collapse came quickly. As soon as the infantry masses had forced the crossings, Guderian's tanks swept through the breach towards Châlons-sur-Marne, and then eastward. By the 11th Kleist was widening the sweep and crossed the Marne at Château-Thierry. The drive continued at racing pace, over the Plateau de Langres to Besançon and the Swiss frontier—cutting off all the French forces in the Maginot Line.

As early as the 7th Weygand advised the Government to ask for an armistice without delay, and next day he announced that 'the Battle of the Somme is lost'. The Government, though divided in opinion, hesitated to yield, but on the 9th decided to leave Paris. It wavered between a choice of Brittany and Bordeaux, and then went to Tours as a compromise. At the same time Reynaud sent off an appeal to President Roosevelt for support, in which he declared: 'We shall fight in front of Paris; we shall fight behind Paris; we shall shut ourselves up in one of our provinces, and, if we should be driven out, we shall go to North Africa. . . .'

On the 10th Italy declared war. Mussolini had been belatedly offered various colonial concessions, but spurned them in the hope of improving his position with Hitler. An Italian offensive, however, was not launched until ten days later, and was then easily held in check by the weak French forces.

On the 11th Churchill flew to Tours in a vain effort to encourage the French leaders. Next day Weygand addressed the Cabinet, told them the battle was lost, blamed the British for both defeats, and then declared: 'I am obliged to say clearly that a cessation of hostilities is compulsory.' There is little doubt that he was correct in this estimate of the military situation, for the French armies were now splitting up into fragments, and most of these made little attempt to stand, but merely dissolved in a southerly flow. The Cabinet was now divided between capitulation and a continuance of the war from North Africa, but only decided to move itself to Bordeaux, while instructing Weygand to attempt a stand on the Loire.

The Germans entered Paris on the 14th and were driving deeper on the flanks. On the 16th they reached the Rhône valley. Meanwhile Weygand had continued his pressure for an armistice, backed by all the principal commanders. In a last-hour effort to avert this decision, and ensure a stand in Africa, Churchill made a far-reaching proposal for a Franco-British Union. It made little impression, except to produce irritation. A vote was taken upon it, a majority of the French Cabinet rejected it, and it turned into a decision for capitulation. Reynaud resigned, whereupon a new Cabinet was formed by Marshal Pétain, and the request for the armistice was transmitted to Hitler on the night of the 16th.

Hitler's terms were delivered to the French envoys on the 20th—in the same railway coach in the forest of Compiègne wherein the German envoys had signed the armistice of 1918. The German advance proceeded beyond the Loire while discussion continued, but on the 22nd the German terms were accepted. The armistice became effective at 1.35 a.m. on June 25, after an accompanying armistice with Italy had been arranged.

CHAPTER 8

THE BATTLE OF BRITAIN

Although the war started on September 1, 1939, with the German invasion of Poland, and this was followed two days later by the successive British and French declarations of war on Germany, it is one of the most extraordinary features of history that Hitler and the German Supreme Command had made no plans or preparations to deal with Britain's opposition. Stranger still, nothing was done during the long interval, of nearly nine months, before the great German offensive in the West was launched in May 1940. Nor were any plans made even after France was obviously crumbling and its collapse assured.

It thus becomes very clear that Hitler was counting on the British Government's agreement to a compromise peace on the favourable terms he was disposed to grant, and that for all his high ambitions he had no wish to press the conflict with Britain to a decisive conclusion. Indeed, the German generals were given to understand by Hitler that the war was over, while leave was granted and part of the Luftwaffe was shifted to other potential fronts. Moreover, on June 22 Hitler ordered the demobilisation of thirty-five divisions.

Even when Churchill's rejection of any compromise was made emphatic, and his determination to pursue the war was manifest, Hitler still clung to the belief that it was a bluff, and felt that Britain was bound to recognise 'her militarily hopeless situation'. That hope was slow to fade. It was not until July 2 that he even ordered a study of the problem of overcoming Britain by invasion, and he still sounded a note of doubt about the need when at last on July 16, two weeks later, he ordered preparation of such an invasion, christened 'Operation Sealion'. He did say, however, that the expedition must be ready by mid-August.

Even then Hitler's underlying reservations—or, at the least, his split mind— were shown in the fact that he told Halder on July 21 that he intended to turn and tackle the problem of Russia, if possible launching an attack on her that autumn. On the 29th, at O.K.W., Jodl told Warlimont that Hitler was

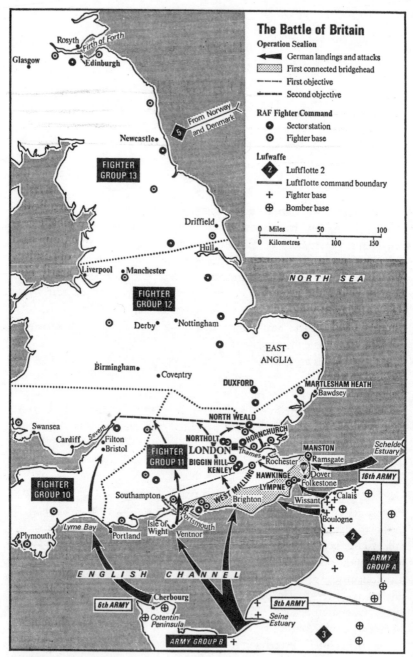

The Battle of Britain

Operation Sealion
- German landings and attacks
- First connected bridgehead
- First objective
- Second objective

RAF Fighter Command
- Sector station
- Fighter base

Lufwaffe
- 2 Luftflotte 2
- Luftflotte command boundary
- + Fighter base
- ⊕ Bomber base

Miles 0 50 100
Kilometres 0 100 150

Glasgow
Rosyth
Firth of Forth
Edinburgh

Newcastle

From Norway and Denmark

FIGHTER GROUP 13

Driffield

Hull
Liverpool
Manchester

FIGHTER GROUP 12

Derby
Nottingham

NORTH SEA

Birmingham
Coventry

EAST ANGLIA

DUXFORD
MARTLESHAM HEATH
Bawdsey

NORTH WEALD

Swansea
Cardiff
Severn
Filton
Bristol

NORTHOLT
HORNCHURCH
MANSTON
Ramsgate

FIGHTER GROUP 11

LONDON
Thames
Rochester
BIGGIN HILL
KENLEY

Dover
Folkestone
HAWKINGE
LYMPNE

Schelde Estuary

16th ARMY

WEST MALLING
Brighton
Wissant
Calais
Boulogne

FIGHTER GROUP 10

Southampton
Portsmouth
Isle of Wight
Ventnor

2

ARMY GROUP A

Plymouth
Lyme Bay
Portland

ENGLISH CHANNEL

6th ARMY
Cherbourg
Cotentin Peninsula

9th ARMY
Seine Estuary

3

ARMY GROUP B

determined on war against Russia. Several days earlier, the operational staff of Guderian's panzer group had been sent back to Berlin to prepare plans for the employment of the panzer forces in such a campaign.

When France collapsed the German Army was in no way prepared for such an undertaking as the invasion of England. The staff had not contemplated it, let alone studied it; the troops had been given no training for seaborne and landing operations; and nothing had been done to build landing-craft for the purpose. So all that could be attempted was a hurried effort to collect shipping, bring barges from Germany and the Netherlands to the Channel ports, and give the troops some practice in embarking and disembarking. It was only the temporary 'nakedness' of the British forces, after losing most of their arms and equipment in France, that offered such a hasty improvisation the possibility of success.

The main part in the operation was given to Field-Marshal von Rundstedt and his Army Group A, which was to employ the 16th Army (General Busch) on the right and the 9th Army (General Strauss) on the left. Embarking in the various harbours between the estuaries of the Scheldt and the Seine, seaborne forces were to converge on the south-east coast of England between Folkestone and Brighton, while an airborne division was to capture the cliff-covered Dover–Folkestone area. Under this 'Sealion' plan, ten divisions would be landed in the first wave over a period of four days to establish a wide bridgehead. After about a week the main advance inland would begin, its first objective being to gain the high ground along an arc from the Thames estuary to Portsmouth. In the next stage, London was to be cut off from the west.

A subsidiary operation was to be mounted by the 6th Army (Field-Marshal von Reichenau) of Army Group B, with three divisions in the first wave, to sail from Cherbourg and land in Lyme Bay west of Portland Bill for a push northward to the Severn estuary.

The second wave of the invasion would be an exploiting mobile force composed of six armoured and three motorised divisions in three corps, and this would be followed by a third wave of nine infantry divisions and a fourth wave of eight infantry divisions. Although there were no armoured divisions in the first wave, it was allotted approximately 650 tanks, all to be carried in the first of its two echelons (the leading echelon amounted to just over a third of its total strength of 250,000 troops). The cross-Channel conveyance of this two-piece first wave called for 155 transports, totalling some 700,000 tons, besides over 3,000 smaller craft—1,720 barges, 470 tugs, and 1,160 motorboats.

Preparations were only set going late in July, and the German Naval Staff declared that such a large quantity of shipping could not be assembled ready to launch 'Sealion' before the middle of September at the earliest—whereas Hitler had ordered preparations to be completed by mid-August. (Indeed, at the end of July the Naval Staff recommended that the operation should be postponed until the spring of 1941.)

But that was not the only check. The German generals were very apprehensive of the risks that their forces would run in crossing the sea. They had little confidence in the capacity of either their own navy or their air force to keep the passage clear, and urged that the invasion should be on a wide enough front (from Ramsgate to Lyme Bay) to stretch and distract the defending forces. The German admirals were even more apprehensive of what would happen when the British fleet arrived on the scene. They had little or no confidence in their own power to prevent its interference, while at the outset insisting that the Army plan for a wide front of invasion would be impossible to protect, and that the crossing must be confined to a relatively narrow mine-covered corridor, with army forces of smaller size— limitations that deepened the generals' doubts. Above all, Admiral Raeder emphasised, air superiority over the crossing area was essential.

After a discussion with Raeder on July 31, Hitler accepted the naval view that 'Sealion' could not be launched before the middle of September. But the operation was not yet definitely postponed until 1941, as Göring assured him that the Luftwaffe could check the British Navy's interference as well as drive the British out of the sky. The Navy and Army chiefs were quite willing to let him try his preliminary air offensive, which did not commit them to anything definite unless and until it proved successful.

In the event, it did not succeed, and so the struggle in the air became the principal feature—indeed, the only feature—of the decisive Battle of Britain.

The superiority of the Luftwaffe over the Royal Air Force was not so great as was generally imagined at the time. It was unable to maintain a continuous attack by wave after wave of massed bombers as the British public had feared, and the number of its fighters was not much more than that of the British.

The offensive was mainly conducted by Air Fleets (Luftflotten) 2 and 3, under Field-Marshals Albert Kesselring and Hugo Sperrle—the former based on north-east France and the Low Countries, and the latter on north and north-west France. Each air fleet was a self-contained force, of all components—an integration which had been advantageous when co-operating with the Army's advances in Poland and the West, but was less so in an all-air campaign. Each air fleet produced its own plans and submitted them separately; there was no overall plan.

On August 10, when the offensive was about to start in earnest, Air Fleets 2 and 3 had a total of 875 normal (high-level) bombers, and 316 dive-bombers. (The dive-bombers proved so vulnerable to the British fighters that they were withdrawn from the battle after August 18, and reserved for the invasion.)

In addition, Luftflotte 5 in Norway and Denmark, under General Stumpff, had 123 high-level bombers, but it took part in the battle on one day only, August 15, and its losses then proved too heavy for the distant excursion to be repeated. By its presence off stage, however, it did have a distracting effect in keeping part of the British Fighter Command's forces in the north-east of England. It also provided about a hundred bombers in the later part of August to replace losses in Luftflotten 2 and 3.

These had started the battle on August 10 with 929 fighters available. They were mostly single-engined Messerschmitt 109s, but had 227 twin-engined and relatively long-range Me 110s. The Me 109, of which the prototype had appeared in 1936, had a top-speed of over 350 m.p.h., and its high rate of climb gave it a further advantage over the British fighters. But in turning and manœuvring it was at a disadvantage in combat with them. Moreover, unlike them, most had at the outset of the battle no armour protection for the pilot, although they did have bullet-proof fuel tanks, which the British lacked.

Limited range was a decisive factor for the German single-engined fighters in this battle. The Me 109's official cruising range of 412 miles was very misleading. Its real radius of action, out and back, was little more than 100 miles, and from the Pas de Calais or the Cotentin Peninsula that could take it only just to London, allowing it scant time for fighting there. Put in another way, it had a total flight duration of barely 95 minutes, which gave it only 75–80 minutes tactical flying time. When the heavy loss in bombers, and their very palpable vulnerability, made it necessary to provide them with fighter escorts, no more than 300–400 bombers could be used on any one day even against objectives in the south of England—allowing two fighters to escort a bomber.

The Me 109, too, was difficult to handle at take-off and landing, while its undercarriage was weak, and this trouble was accentuated by the hastily improvised airfields on the French coast.

The twin-engined Me 110, despite its nominal top-speed of 340 m.p.h., proved considerably slower—often barely 300 m.p.h. or even less—and was thus easily outpaced by the Spitfire, while it was sluggish in acceleration and difficult to manœuvre. It had been intended as 'the operational flower of the

Luftwaffe's fighters' but it proved the worst technical disappointment of all—and eventually had to be escorted by Me 109s for its own protection.

But the German fighters' greatest handicap was the primitiveness of their radio equipment. Although they had radio-telephony for intercommunication during flight, theirs was poor compared with the British—and they could not be controlled from the ground.

The R.A.F. fighter strength had been rebuilt, after its loss of more than 400 in France, to a figure of some 650 by mid-July—its strength when the German offensive was launched in May. They were mostly Hurricanes and Spitfires, although still including nearly a hundred of other and older types.

That remarkable recovery owed much to the efforts of Lord Beaverbrook, who had been appointed to the new office of Minister of Aircraft Production in May on the formation of Mr Churchill's Government. His critics complained that his energetic interference had an upsetting effect on long-term progress. But Air Chief Marshal Sir Hugh Dowding, the Commander-in-Chief of Fighter Command, went on record in declaring that 'the effect of the appointment can only be described as magical'. By mid-summer even, the production of fighters had increased two and a half times, and during the whole year Britain produced 4,283 fighters compared with just over 3,000 single- and twin-engined fighters produced by Germany.

The relative situation in armament is more difficult to determine. The Hurricanes and Spitfires were armed solely with machine-guns; they had eight apiece, fixed forward in the wings. These were American Browning machine-guns—a weapon which had been chosen because it was reliable enough to be remotely controlled, while its rate of fire was high, 1,260 rounds a minute. The Me 109 fighters in general were armed with two fixed machine-guns in the cowlings and two 20-mm. cannon in the wings—a weapon developed as a result of experience in the Spanish Civil War, which had been utilised as a testing ground for the Luftwaffe—the Me 109 had been tried out there, as well as earlier types of fighters now replaced.

Adolf Galland, the German ace, had no doubt, in retrospect, that the Me 109's armament was the better. British opinion was divided, as it was considered that the high firing rate of the Brownings carried the advantage in short bursts of fire. But it was recognised that half a dozen cannon shells could do far more damage than the equivalent length of Browning bursts—and some of the British fighter pilots complained bitterly that even when sure that they were hitting an opponent 'nothing happened'. Significantly, some thirty Spitfires were equipped with two 20-mm. Hispano (Oerlikon) cannon during the course of the battle, and Hurricanes fitted with four cannon came into use from October on.

What is quite clear, and became evident at the start, was that the German bombers were too poorly armed—with a few free-traversing machine-guns—to be able to beat off the British fighters without a fighter escort of their own.

The respective situation in regard to fighter pilots was more complex, and in the earlier phases of the battle far from favourable to the British. While trained to a high standard, their shortage in number was serious. The R.A.F. flying training schools were slow in expanding, and their shortcomings largely determined the conduct of the battle. Wastage had to be kept to a minimum even if it meant some raids getting through. Men, not planes, were Dowding's main worry.

By husbanding his resources in July, Dowding managed to increase his pilot strength to 1,434 at the beginning of August—helped by a contribution, on 'loan', of sixty-eight from the Fleet Air Arm. But a month later the number was down to 840, and losses were averaging 120 a week. By contrast, no more than 260 fighter pilots were turned out by the R.A.F's Operational Training Units during the whole month. In September the scarcity became worse, as the number of highly skilled pilots shrank, while the hurriedly trained new arrivals were more vulnerable through inexperience. Fresh squadrons brought in to relieve tired ones often lost more than those they replaced. Tiredness was in numerous cases accompanied by declining morale and increasing 'nerviness'.

The Germans had no such heavy initial handicap in numbers. Despite their heavy losses on the Continent in May and June, the flying schools were turning out more pilots than could be absorbed into front-line squadrons. But morale was affected insidiously by the way Göring and others at the head of the Luftwaffe looked on, and treated, the fighter arm as merely 'defensive' and of secondary importance. Moreover it was drained of many of its best pilots to make up losses in the bomber and dive-bomber arms, while Göring kept on criticising it for lack of aggressiveness, and blamed it for the Luftwaffe's failures—largely due to his own lack of foresight and mistakes in planning. By contrast, the morale of the British fighter pilots was fortified by knowing that they were regarded and acclaimed during these critical months as Churchill's 'Few', the flower of the Royal Air Force and the heroes of the nation.

The strain on the German fighters, both pilots and planes, was multiplied by the way they were increasingly used for, and tied to, escort duties—two or three sorties a day, and sometimes as many as five. Göring would not allow rest days, or the rotation of front-line units. Thus sheer tiredness was added to the sense, and strain, of their heavy losses. Morale was becoming low by the time September came. It was deepened by a sense of doubt whether invasion was really intended, in view of the slightness, and amateurishness, of the preparations the pilots saw, so that they began more and more to wonder whether they were merely being sacrificed to maintain a façade, for an operation that was being abandoned.

The bomber crews were suffering from heavy losses, and from a sense of their vulnerability to R.A.F. fighter attack. Thus their decline in morale tended to become even more marked, gallantly as they continued to carry out orders.

In sum, while both sides were closely matched in skill and courage during the early phases of the battle, the British were helped in gaining the upper hand as it wore on by the fact, and still more the feeling, that the enemy were suffering a worse loss, and strain, than they themselves were—heavy though their own was on both counts.

A constant German handicap throughout the battle was poor Intelligence. The Luftwaffe's basic guide in conducting the offensive was a pre-war handbook, known as the 'Blue Study', which set out the available data about the situation and lay-out of industrial plant in Britain and the results of comprehensive photographic reconnaissance carried out on 'civil route proving flights'. This was inadequately supplemented by the Luftwaffe's own Intelligence department—which was headed only by a major. In a survey of the R.A.F. which this Major Schmid made in July 1940, he greatly underestimated British fighter production, allowing for only 180–300 a month—whereas it actually rose to 460–500 Hurricanes and Spitfires alone in August and September, the period of the battle, following Beaverbrook's efforts to speed up the programme. (The false impression caused by that big error was increased by reports from General Udet's production department which dwelt on the drawbacks of the Hurricane and Spitfire without pointing out their advantages.)

In Major Schmid's survey report there was no mention of the R.A.F's well-knit defence system, with its radar stations, operations rooms, and high-frequency radio network. Yet the British radar research station at Bawdsey on the Suffolk coast and the lofty lattice masts going up round the coast had been wide open to intelligent observation well before the war, and by 1939 it seemed hardly possible that the Germans could lack information of the key features in the British warning system. Although the Germans knew in 1938 that the British were experimenting with radar, and even captured a mobile radar station on the beach at Boulogne in May 1940, their scientists considered the set crude. Much fuller information about the British radar was freely available in France, owing to French carelessness over security, when the Germans overran the major part of that country, but the Germans do not seem to have profited by it. Göring himself took little account of its potential effect on the battle.

Indeed, it was not until the Germans had set up their monitoring stations along the coast of France in July that they came to realise, from the stream of signals radiating from the radar masts along the English coast, that they were faced with something new and of vital importance. Even the range and effectiveness of British radar were underrated by the Luftwaffe chiefs, and little effort was made to jam it or destroy it. Nor did the discovery that the British fighters operated under close radio control dismay them as it might have—they drew the conclusion that the system made Fighter Command inflexible, and that mass attacks would swamp the system.

The tendency to exaggerate the opponent's losses during intense air fighting was a fault common to both sides, but became more of a handicap on the German side. Initially Luftwaffe Intelligence assessed Dowding's resources, correctly, as totalling about fifty squadrons of Hurricanes and Spitfires, with an operational strength of approximately 600 aircraft, of which 400–500 at the most were in the southern part of England. But after the battle started, miscalculation and confusion developed from the combined effort of over-estimated British losses and underestimating British aircraft production, so that Luftwaffe pilots became puzzled, and then depressed, by the way the number of British fighters was maintained. Many more were reported shot down than actually existed.

Another cause of miscalculation was the habit of the Luftwaffe chiefs, when they bombed a Fighter Command base, of striking off, in red pencil, the number of the R.A.F. squadron there. That was partly due to poor photo-reconnaissance, and partly to unduly optimistic analysis of the results. For example, the Luftwaffe estimated that up to August 17 no less than eleven airfields had been 'permanently destroyed'—whereas, in fact, only one, Manston, was put out of action for any appreciable time. Moreover, effort was wasted in attacking airfields in the south-east that were not part of Fighter Command's organisation. At the same time the Luftwaffe chiefs failed to realise the vital importance of the sector stations—such as Biggin Hill, Kenley, Hornchurch—in the Fighter Command organisation, and were un-aware that their operations rooms were above ground—dangerously ex-posed. Thus the devastating attacks on sector stations that the Luftwaffe delivered at the end of August were not followed up.

Another German handicap was the weather, and that in a double sense: the weather over the English Channel was often unfavourable for the attacking side, and as it usually came from the west, the British usually knew about it first. The Germans had broken the cipher of the British radio meteorological reports from the Atlantic, but they profited little from it, and were often caught out. In particular, the timing of the rendezvous between their bombers and the fighter escorts was repeatedly upset by unexpected cloud and poor visibility. Banks of cloud over northern France and Belgium would delay the bombers, whose crews had little experience of 'blind' navigation, with the result that they arrived late at their rendezvous, and the fighters, who could not afford to waste fuel, would attach themselves to other bombers, so that one bomber formation would fly out with doubled protection and another without any escort—and suffer heavy loss. When the autumn approached, and the weather worsened, such hitches increased, with catastrophic effects.

In one respect, however, the Germans benefited by better planning. The British air-sea rescue service was at first very haphazard, and pilots who came down in the sea had to depend largely on luck for their chances of being picked up. That was the more serious because in mid-August nearly two-thirds of the air fights that had a definite issue were taking place over the sea. The Germans were better organised. They used some thirty Heinkel seaplanes for rescue work, while their fighter pilots and bomber crews were equipped with inflatable rubber dinghies, a life-jacket, a light-pistol, and a chemical that made a bright green stain on the sea round them. A fighter pilot who 'ditched' could reckon on having 40 to 60 seconds to get out before the plane sank. Without the reassurance given by these sea-rescue precautions the Luftwaffe's morale might have declined quicker than it did.

The Luftwaffe's offensive had also to face formidable opposition beyond that of the R.A.F's fighters, the anti-aircraft guns assigned for the Air Defence of Great Britain. These were provided by, and belonged to, the Army (like those which had accompanied the Expeditionary Force) although operationally linked with, and subordinate to, R.A.F. Fighter Command. If they brought down relatively few German bombers in the Battle of Britain they added much to the strain on the attackers by their upsetting effect in general, and on bombing accuracy in particular.

The G.O.C.-in-C. Anti-Aircraft Command was Lieutenant-General Sir Frederick Pile. Originally a gunner, he had transferred to the Royal Tank Corps on its permanent formation in 1923, and soon became one of the most dynamic exponents and advocates of mobile armoured forces. But in 1937, after promotion to major-general, the Army Council had appointed him to the command of the 1st Anti-Aircraft Division, which covered London and the south of England. The next year the two existing A.A. divisions were expanded into five, and then into seven. At the end of July 1939, just before the war, 'Tim' Pile was promoted to overall command of the whole, including the light batteries that were being formed for the defence of airfields and other vital points against low-flying attack.

Another valuable element in meeting that kind of attack was the balloon barrage—a string of sausage-shape balloons anchored, at heights up to 5,000 feet, by steel cables. This was provided by the R.A.F. itself, and was under separate control, although under Fighter Command.

Throughout these pre-war years, the expansion of the anti-aircraft forces for home defence had been grudgingly agreed at the best, and often strongly opposed, by the Army Council—which tended to regard them as a regrettable subtraction from the strength of the Army. So Pile's efforts to develop these anti-aircraft forces and their effectiveness met with much obstruction in the War Office, and brought him into disfavour there—with adverse effects on his prospects of re-entry, and further advancement, in the main stream of the Army. Fortunately for the country, however, he had succeeded in establishing close and harmonious relations with Dowding, a difficult personality, and they worked together remarkably well.

By the outbreak of war, at the beginning of September 1939, the approved establishment of Anti-Aircraft Command had been raised, successively, to a scale of 2,232 heavy A.A. guns—nearly double the so-called 'Ideal' plan rejected two years before—as well as 1,860 light A.A. guns, and 4,128 searchlights. But, as a result of the hesitations and delays, only 695 heavy guns and 253 light guns could be deployed when the war started—approximately one-third of the heavy guns and one-eighth of the light guns by then authorised. (That was at any rate a great improvement on the Munich Crisis a year earlier, when only 126 heavy A.A. guns were ready for action.) The searchlight situation was relatively good, as 2,700 were deployed out of an authorised scale of 4,128—more than two-thirds.

After the war began a fresh complication came from the Admiralty's demand for 255 heavy guns to defend its six Fleet anchorages—a demand that had not been made before the war when the Admiralty had shown great confidence in the unaided power of its ships to beat off air attack with their own A.A. armament. It now wanted no less than ninety-six guns to protect the anchorage at Rosyth in the Firth of Forth—as many as were then available for the whole of London, and four times as many as protected the Derby area where the vital Rolls-Royce engine works were situated.

The expedition to Norway in April 1940 brought a further large demand for, and drain upon, both heavy and light A.A. guns.

Then, after the fall of France in June, the situation of the Air Defence of

Great Britain itself was changed radically for the worse, as Britain became enveloped by a ring of enemy air bases from Norway round to Brittany.

At that time, A.A. Command's available strength had risen to 1,204 heavy guns and 581 light guns—respectively nearly double the number and over double the number at the outbreak of war. It would have been better but for the various drains upon it. During the next five weeks the fresh intake was 124 heavy and 182 light guns, but nearly half the former and a quarter of the latter had to be allocated for training purposes and for places overseas that were now endangered by Italy's entry into the war on Germany's side. At the end of July the Air Defence of Great Britain still had little more than half the scale of heavy A.A. guns, and barely one-third of the light A.A. guns, that had been considered necessary at the outbreak of war—when the strategic circumstances were far more favourable than they had become. Search-lights were more plentiful, nearly 4,000 being now available, almost up to the level of the establishment—although the changed circumstances now called for a large increase in the scale.

The preliminary phase of the Battle of Britain saw the gradual development of German air operations against British shipping and ports in the Channel, along with spasmodic efforts to lure out the British fighters. Until August 6 no precise instructions for the conduct of the offensive were sent to the chief Luftwaffe commanders, Kesselring and Sperrle—which serves to explain why the pattern of these early operations was so puzzling.*

Regular attacks on shipping started on July 3, while next day a force of eighty-seven dive-bombers, escorted by Me 109s, attacked the Naval harbour at Portland, but without much effect. On the 10th a small force of bombers, with a large escort of fighters, attacked a convoy off Dover, and the Me 110s, significantly, fared badly against the Hurricanes sent out to defend the convoy. After a heavier attack on a convoy in the same area on July 25 the Admiralty decided to send convoys through the Straits by night, and some successful attacks on destroyers led it to the decision that those stationed at Dover should withdraw to Portsmouth. The passage of another convoy in the night of August 7 was spotted by German radar from the cliffs near Wissant, and the next day it was assailed by escorted waves of dive-bombers, up to eighty at a time. They sank nearly 70,000 tons of shipping—at a cost of thirty-one aircraft.

On the 11th, in confused combats, the R.A.F. lost thirty-two fighters. Even so, during this phase from July 3 to August 11, the Germans lost 364

---

* I was sent daily charts of the raids by General Pile in the hope that I might be able to find a clue, but could perceive no clear indication of pattern or purpose.

bombers and fighters, while the R.A.F. lost 203 fighters—a loss nearly replaced by a week's output from the factories.

Following Hitler's belated order of August 1—for the Luftwaffe to 'destroy the enemy air force as soon as possible'—and Göring's discussions with his chief executives, the opening of the grand offensive was fixed for August 13. This was christened *Adlertag*—'Eagle Day'. Over-optimistic reports of Luftwaffe successes in the preliminary phase had convinced Göring that he could achieve air superiority in four days of good weather. By August 13, however, the weather had become less favourable than earlier.

Nevertheless on Eagle Day itself, the Luftwaffe launched its initial bombing attacks on British fighter airfields and radar stations in the south-east of England. The forward airfields at Manston, Hawkinge, and Lympne were badly damaged, while some of the radar stations were put out of action for several hours. The one at Ventnor in the Isle of Wight was put completely out of action, but the fact was concealed from the Germans by signals from another transmitter. The radar towers themselves tended to keep the dive-bombers away from the operations rooms at their base, and in any case the Germans mistakenly assumed that these would be safely placed underground. In this connection, tribute is due to the women radar plotters of the W.A.A.F., the Women's Auxiliary Air Force, who went on reporting raids until their own station was bombed.

The thick layer of cloud lying over south-east England caused Göring to postpone the main attack until the afternoon—but several formations failed to get the deferment signal and wasted their effort in disjointed raids. When the big attack was delivered in the afternoon it was too scattered, and its results disappointing. During that day the Luftwaffe flew 1,485 sorties, double the number of the R.A.F. For a cost of forty-five German aircraft, bombers and fighters, it only shot down thirteen R.A.F. fighters—although claiming to have destroyed seventy.

In this opening stage of the main offensive, much of the Luftwaffe effort was wasted in attacking airfields that were not those of Fighter Command— which should have been their key target and objective. It also suffered from poor co-ordination between bomber formations and their fighter escorts.

The next day, August 14, clouds helped to reduce the attack to about a third of its weight on the opening day, but when the weather cleared on the morning of the 15th, the Luftwaffe launched its biggest effort of the whole battle—a total of 1,786 sorties, in which over 500 bombers were employed.

The first attacks were against the airfields at Hawkinge and Lympne, and although the former, the more important, escaped serious damage, the latter was put out of action for two days.

Then in the early afternoon over a hundred bombers of Luftflotte 5, in two formations, flew in over the North Sea to attack airfields near Newcastle and in Yorkshire. The larger one, of some sixty-five bombers from Stavanger in Norway, was escorted by about thirty-five Me 110s, but these proved of little protective value, and the force met such stiff resistance from the R.A.F. fighters of No. 13 Group and from anti-aircraft guns that it caused no serious damage anywhere, and had fifteen planes shot down while the R.A.F. lost none. The other attacking force, of some fifty bombers from Aalborg in Denmark, had no escort, but although No. 12 Group put up three squadrons to meet it, a large part of it succeeded in getting through to the R.A.F. bomber base at Driffield in Yorkshire, where it caused a lot of damage—although it lost seven of its bombers over England and three more on the flight back.

In the south, the British defence was less successful—under a heavier and more varied series of attacks, at shorter range. Early in the afternoon a raid by thirty bombers, heavily escorted, got through to Rochester and bombed the Short aircraft factory there, while about the same time a raid by twenty-four fighter-bombers did severe damage to the R.A.F. fighter airfield at Martlesham Heath in Suffolk. The multiplicity of raids confused the radar picture, and British fighter squadrons, sent out individually, were chasing to and fro. Fortunately for the defence, Luftflotten 2 and 3 did not effectively co-ordinate their attacks, and thus lost the advantage of keeping the R.A.F. on the run. It was not until 6 p.m. that a mass of about 200 aircraft from Luftflotte 3 streamed over the Channel to attack airfields in the south-centre of England. Helped by good radar warning, Fighter Groups No. 10 and 11—the two covering the southern part of the country—put up no less than fourteen squadrons, a total of about 170 fighters, to meet this massive attack, and it achieved little. Soon afterward Luftflotte 2 attacked afresh in the south-east, with about 100 aircraft, but this likewise met prompt resistance and had little effect. Even when attacks reached their objective, they found the British fighters well dispersed and well camouflaged.

On this day, perhaps the most decisive of the battle, the actual German loss over the whole country was seventy-five aircraft, compared with thirty-four British fighters. Significantly, the Luftwaffe had employed less than half its bomber strength—a recognition, and indirect admission, of its dependence on the escort of its own fighters, almost all of which had been used. Moreover the day's operations had clearly shown the unsuitability of the

German dive-bombers, the hitherto alarming Stukas, for the tasks they were now attempting—as well as of the Me 110 fighters, on which such great hopes had been built.

It was this day which inspired Churchill to say: 'Never in the field of human conflict was so much owed by so many to so few'.

Next day however, the 16th, the Luftwaffe made another strong effort— under the delusion that the R.A.F. had lost over 100 aircraft on the 15th, and had only 300 fighters left. But although the attacks were damaging in several places, they were disappointing on the whole. On the 17th no major attacks were made despite quite good weather. On the 18th a fresh and stronger effort resulted in the German loss of seventy-one aircraft (half of them bombers) compared with an R.A.F. loss of twenty-seven fighters. From then on the attacks dwindled. In fact, hedge-hopping raids on Kenley and Biggin Hill had done considerable damage, and been difficult to counter, as they came in below the level of the radar screen. But the Germans did not realise this, and felt that their losses had been too great to continue. Bad weather then brought a lull in the battle.

Göring had called another conference of his chief executives on the 19th, and after discussion it was decided to pursue the air offensive—with a fresh effort to knock out the British fighter force.

During the two weeks following August 10 the Luftwaffe lost 167 bombers (including forty dive-bombers), and the bomber chiefs in consequence were calling for stronger and stronger fighter escorts. Tension, and friction, between the two arms was increased by Göring's tendency to side with the bombers and blame the fighters.

But there was friction also on the British side, especially between Air Vice-Marshal Keith Park, commanding No. 11 Fighter Group in the crucial south-east of England, and Air Vice-Marshal Trafford Leigh-Mallory, commanding No. 12 Fighter Group in the Midlands. Park emphasised the importance of meeting the Germans forward of their objectives and shooting down their bombers, thus driving them to use more and more of their Me 109 fighters in a close escort role for which they were not fitted. Leigh-Mallory considered that this policy put too great a strain on the R.A.F. fighter pilots, who were apt to be caught on the ground, often when re-fuelling, or before they could gain sufficient height.

There were differences as well over the tactics to be used, the 'Leigh-Mallory faction' advocating the 'big wing' theory of massive, concentrated intercepting forces, while Park held to what he believed was the more flexible policy afforded the British by their radar, feeding in interceptors as the German forces arrived—the 'diluted concentration' policy.

It was also argued that Dowding, in accord with Park, was too intent to maintain the forward airfields in the south-east, for the sake of civilian morale, when it would have been wiser to withdraw behind London, out of range of the Me 109s and their escorted bombers.

Fighter Command had lost ninety-four pilots in the period August 8–18, and sixty wounded. But there was as yet no shortage of aircraft, despite the loss of 175 fighters during the period, a further sixty-five severely damaged, and thirty aircraft destroyed on the ground.

When the weather improved on the 24th Göring launched his second bid for command of the air. This time it was better planned. Luftflotte 2, under Kesselring, usually kept some planes in the air on the French side of the Channel, and that kept Park guessing, as radar could not differentiate between bombers and fighters, or tell when aircraft would suddenly dash across the Channel. In this new phase No. 11 Group's forward airfields suffered more severely than before, and Manston had to be abandoned.

Another feature of the new plan was an intensive attack on R.A.F. stations and installations around London—and this led to the unintended dropping of bombs on London. On the night of the 24th some ten German bombers, which had lost their way *en route* to targets at Rochester and Thameshaven, dropped their loads in central London. That mistake led to an immediate reprisal raid on Berlin the next night by some eighty British bombers, and this raid was followed up by several more—leading Hitler, after threats that were ignored, to order reprisal raids on London.

Prior to the new offensive most of the Me 109 fighters with Luftflotte 3 were transferred to Luftflotte 2, so as to increase the strength of the escorts in the Pas de Calais area. That policy paid. The R.A.F's fighters had more difficulty, and lost more heavily, in penetrating the German fighter screen, while the German bombers were better able to get through to their targets. Moreover the Germans developed a new tactic of splitting up into separate raids once the mass formations had passed through the radar screen.

On the opening day, August 24, the sector stations at North Weald and Hornchurch were only saved by their A.A. gun defence. That also saved Portsmouth Dockyard in a heavy attack by Luftflotte 3, although the city itself suffered badly from the resultant scatter of bombs. After this effort Luftflotte 3 turned to night bombing, and attacked Liverpool on four successive nights from the 28th on, but many of the bombers failed to find the Merseyside area owing to their inadequate training and to British interference with German navigational beams. These raids, however, also brought out the shortcomings of British defence against night attack.

The last two days of August proved particularly bad for Fighter Command. Significantly, small formations of bombers, fifteen to twenty, had fighter escorts three times as many as themselves. On the 31st the R.A.F suffered its heaviest loss of the whole battle, having thirty-nine fighters shot down against a German loss of forty-one aircraft. The rate of loss was more than the R.A.F. could afford on its limited strength, and it was failing to deter the attackers. Most of the airfields in the south-west were by now seriously damaged, and some were so wrecked as to be unusable.

Even Dowding was considering the withdrawal of his fighting line in the south-east and bringing it back out of range of the Me 109s. He was also becoming more strongly criticised for keeping twenty fighter squadrons to protect the north, which had only been attacked once in daylight—an attack which had not been repeated. Moreover those of No. 12 Group, in East Anglia and the Midlands, were clamouring to take a more direct part in the battle—while Park complained that they did not co-operate in the way he wanted. Strained relations between Park and Leigh-Mallory, and between Dowding and Newall, the Chief of the Air Staff, did not aid a smooth solution of the problem.

During the month of August, Fighter Command lost in combat 338 Hurricanes and Spitfires, as well as having 104 badly damaged, compared with a German loss of 177 Me 109s, with twenty-four badly damaged. That was a loss of 2 for 1 in fighters. Other causes accounted for forty-two R.A.F. fighters and fifty-four Me 109s.

Thus at the beginning of September there was all too much reason for Göring to feel that he was within reach of his goal—the destruction of Britain's fighter strength and of its installations in the south-east. But he did not grasp the importance of following up the advantage he had gained.

On September 4, the Luftwaffe's concentration on Fighter Command's airfields was varied, and diluted, by a series of attacks on British aircraft factories—the Short factory at Rochester and the Vickers-Armstrong works at Brooklands. The variation was quite effective in itself, but carried with it a lowering of pressure on Fighter Command. That was the more valuable because the endurance and the nerves of pilots were strained to breaking point, and their performance had been showing a marked decline.

Dowding, with a sense of essentials, ordered maximum fighter cover for the fighter factories in the south; a fresh attack on Brooklands two days later was headed off—as well as attacks on five sector stations around London.

During the whole two weeks' period August 24 to September 6, 295

British fighters had been destroyed and 171 badly damaged—compared with a total output of 269 new and repaired fighters. The Luftwaffe's loss in Me 109s was barely half the number—although it had also lost more than a hundred bombers.

The Luftwaffe's losses, along with the call for much stronger escort of the bombers, was now seriously affecting the effort it made, or could make. Whereas it had flown about 1,500 sorties a day, and momentarily rose again to a figure of 1,300-1,400 in the last two days of August, it never reached 1,000 sorties during the first week of September. During the first two months of the battle—which had become a battle of attrition—the Luftwaffe had lost more than 800 aircraft. Kesselring's Luftflotte 2, carrying the main burden of the offensive, was now down to about 450 serviceable bombers and 530 Me 109 fighters. So at the end of this third phase of the battle the scales were at last beginning to tilt in Britain's favour. They were to do so more definitely in the fourth phase, helped by the Luftwaffe's switch of effort.

On September 3 Göring had held, at the Hague, another conference of his chief executives and this had confirmed the fateful decision to switch the daylight bombing offensive to London—as Kesselring had urged from the outset, and Hitler had now agreed. The starting date was fixed for September 7.

At the same time the 300 bombers available in Luftflotte 3 would be used for a night bombing offensive. That suited Sperrle, who had always favoured the bombing of shipping and ports, and had become increasingly sceptical about the prospect of crushing the British fighter force and knocking out its airfields.

On the afternoon of the 7th an air armada of about a thousand aircraft of Luftflotte 2—over 300 bombers escorted by 648 fighters—set out for London, watched by Göring and Kesselring from the cliffs at Cap Blanc Nez, between Calais and Wissant. It was echeloned upwards in solid layers at between 13,500 and 19,500 feet, flying in close-knit formations and in two waves. The German fighter screen adopted new tactics, one escort flying well ahead at a height of 24,000-30,000 feet, while another escort gave the bombers close cover, and on all sides, at a distance of only about 300 yards.

This new technique proved difficult to counter, but on this first occasion it was hardly needed. For at No. 11 Group Headquarters, the Controller had been expecting another attack on the inner sector stations, and such of the fighter squadrons as were airborne, four in number, were mostly concentrated north of the Thames. So the path to London was clear. The first wave flew straight to the London docks; the second flew over central London and then back over the East End and the docks. The bombing was not so accurate as the Germans thought, many of the bombers aiming short, but in the densely crowded area of the East End, that resulted in all the more loss among the population. In this first mass daylight attack on London—which was also the last—over 300 civilians were killed, and over 1,300 seriously injured.

It had been a frustrating evening for Fighter Command. But although its squadrons were mostly late on the scene, and then baffled by the new German tactics, it managed to inflict a loss of forty-one aircraft for its own loss of twenty-eight. The biggest shock to the Germans came from a particularly fierce attack by No. 303 (Polish) Squadron from Northolt.

The fires raging in the East End served as a guiding beacon for the night attack that followed, and continued from 8 p.m. until nearly 5 a.m. Göring telephoned his wife, telling her triumphantly 'London is in flames'. The lack of opposition led him, and many of his subordinates, to believe that the British fighter force was near to being exhausted. So next day he ordered an extension of the area of London that was to be bombed.

Meanwhile the assembly of invasion barges in the Channel had been growing larger day by day, and on the morning of the 7th the British Government had issued a precautionary invasion warning. After the air attack that followed so closely, the warning was inflated, with the result that a number of auxiliary units were called out and some church bells, which were to signal the invasion, were rung.

Because of the lack of suitable night fighters the defence of London, as of other cities, depended at this crucial time mainly on anti-aircraft guns and searchlights. On the night of the 7th there were only 264 guns on the spot to defend London, but thanks to Pile's prompt measures the number was doubled in the next forty-eight hours. Moreover he laid on 'the barrage' from the night of the 10th onward, telling every gun to fire as much as it could, on whatever information it had. Although the number of hits was slight, the sound of the barrage had a great tonic effect on the morale of the population, while it also had an important material effect by driving the bombers higher.

Kesselring launched his second daylight attack against London on the afternoon of the 9th. No. 11 Group was ready for it this time, with nine fighter squadrons in position, while others from No. 10 and 12 Groups co-operated. Interceptions were so successful that most of the German formations were broken up long before they reached London. Less than half the bombers got through, and hardly any of them succeeded in hitting their targets.

Much the most important effect of this new German offensive was the way it eased the strain on Fighter Command, which had been suffering so badly from the Germans' concentration on it, and was close to breaking point when the Germans switched their effort to the attack on London. The punishment that the capital and its people suffered was to be the saving factor in the preservation of the country's defence.

Moreover, the disappointing results of September 9 led Hitler once again to postpone his ten-day warning period for the invasion—this time to the 14th, for invasion on the 24th.

Deteriorating weather provided some respite for the London defences, but on the 11th and 14th a number of bombers got through, and fighter interception was so scrappy that the Luftwaffe optimistically reported that Fighter Command's resistance was beginning to collapse. So Hitler, although putting off the warning date again, postponed it only three days, to the 17th.

Kesselring launched a big new attack in the morning of Sunday the 15th. This time the fighter defence against it was better planned and timed. Although the air armada was assailed all the way from the coast by a series of single or paired squadrons, twenty-two in all, 148 bombers got through to the London area—but they were prevented from dropping their bombs accurately, and most were widely scattered. Then as the Germans wheeled for home, No. 12 Group's Duxford wing of some sixty fighters swept down from East Anglia, and although losing some of its effect through not yet having gained sufficient height, its massiveness gave the German airmen a shock. In the afternoon, cloud helped the attackers, and a large number had a clear run to London, where their bombs inflicted much damage, especially in the crowded houses of the East End. But during the day as a whole about a quarter of the bombers were put out of action and many more damaged, often with one or more of the crew being killed or wounded, to be carried back to their base, with a consequent effect on morale at those airfields.

The actual German loss that day, as established in later checking, was sixty aircraft. That was much less than one-third of the figure of 185 triumphantly announced by the British Air Ministry at the time—but it compared very well with the R.A.F. loss of twenty-six fighters (of which half the pilots were saved) and was a much more favourable balance than in recent weeks. Göring, still blaming his fighters, continued to talk optimistically, and estimated that the British fighter force would be finished off in four or five days. But neither his subordinates nor his superiors continued to share his optimism.

On the 17th Hitler, agreeing with his Naval Staff that the R.A.F. was still by no means defeated, and emphasising that a period of turbulent weather was due, postponed the invasion 'until further notice'. The following day he ordered that no more shipping was to be assembled in the Channel ports, and agreed that its dispersal might begin—12 per cent of the transports (21 out of 170), and 10 per cent of the barges (214 out of 1,918) had been sunk or damaged by British air attacks. On October 12, 'Sealion' was definitely postponed until the spring of 1941—and in January Hitler ruled that all preparations should be stopped except for a few long-term measures. His mind had now turned definitely to the East.

Göring still persisted with his daylight attacks, but the results were increasingly disappointing, despite occasional successes at out-of-the-way ports. The aircraft works at Filton, near Bristol, were severely hit on September 25, and next day the Spitfire factory near Southampton was temporarily wrecked. But a big raid on the 27th against London was a bad failure, and in the last big daylight attack on September 30 only a fraction of the aircraft reached London, while forty-seven aircraft were lost compared with twenty fighters lost by the R.A.F.

After the disappointing results in the second half of September, and his heavy bomber losses, Göring turned to the use of fighter-bombers operating at high altitude. About mid-September the German fighter formations engaged in the battle had been ordered to give up a third of their strength for conversion into fighter-bombers, and a total of about 250 was thus produced. But insufficient time was allowed to retrain the pilots and the bomb-load they could carry was not enough to do much damage, while they were instinctively inclined to jettison their bombs as soon as they were engaged.

The best that could be said for them was that their use temporarily brought a diminution of German losses while keeping up strain on the R.A.F. But by the end of October, German losses were rising again to the old ratio, while the worsening weather was multiplying the strain on the fighter-bombers' crews, who were operating from improvised and swamp-like airfields. In the month of October the Germans lost 325 aircraft, much in excess of the British loss.

The only serious harassment of Britain was now coming from night bombing by 'normal' bombers. From September 9 the 300 bombers of Sperrle's Luftflotte 3 settled down to a standard pattern, and for fifty-seven nights London was attacked, by an average force of 160 bombers.

Early in November Göring issued new orders that marked a clear change of policy. The air offensive was to be entirely concentrated on night bombing —of cities, industrial centres, and ports. With the release of Luftflotte 2's bombers, up to 750 bombers became available, although only about a third of the total were employed at a time. As they could afford to fly at a slower speed, and at a lower height, they could carry heavier bomb-loads than in daylight, and as much as 1,000 tons were dropped in a night. But the accuracy was poor.

The new offensive was launched on the night of November 14 with the attack on Coventry. It was helped by bright moonlight as well as by a special 'pathfinder' force. But its effectiveness was not equalled in the big attacks that followed on other cities—such as those on Birmingham, South-ampton, Bristol, Plymouth, and Liverpool. On December 29 much damage was caused in London, particularly the centre of the City, but attacks then eased off until the weather improved in March. A series of heavy attacks culminated in a very damaging raid against London on the night of May 10, the anniversary of the launching of the 1940 Blitzkrieg in the West. But in the sky over Britain the 'Blitz', as it was called, came to an end on May 16—after which the bulk of the Luftwaffe was sent eastward for the coming invasion of Russia.

The German air offensive from July until the end of October, 1940, had caused much more damage and disruption than was admitted, and the effects would have been even more serious had there been greater persistency in pressing, and repeating, attacks on the main industrial centres. But it had not succeeded in its object of destroying the R.A.F's fighter strength and the British people's morale.

In the course of the Battle of Britain, from July until the end of October, the Germans had lost 1,733 aircraft—not the 2,698 claimed by the British— while the R.A.F. lost 915 fighters—not the 3,058 claimed by the enemy.

CHAPTER 9

COUNTERSTROKE FROM EGYPT

When Hitler's attack on the West reached a point—with the breach of the improvised Somme–Aisne front—where the defeat of France became certain, Mussolini brought Italy into the war, on June 10, 1940, in the hope of gaining some of the spoils of victory. It appeared to be an almost completely safe decision from his point of view and fatal to Britain's position in the Mediterranean and Africa. This was the darkest hour in her history. For although a large proportion of her army in France had escaped by sea, it had been forced to leave most of its weapons and equipment behind, and in that unarmed state faced an imminent threat of invasion by the victorious Germans. There was nothing available to reinforce the small fraction of the British Army that guarded Egypt and the Sudan against the imminent threat of invasion from the Italian armies in Libya and Italian East Africa.

The situation was all the worse because Italy's entry into the war had made the sea-route through the Mediterranean too precarious to use, and reinforcements had to come by the roundabout Cape route—down the west coast of the African continent and up the east coast into the Red Sea. A small instalment of 7,000 troops, which had been ready for despatch in May 1940, did not reach Egypt until the end of August.

Numerically, the Italian armies were overwhelmingly superior to the scanty British forces opposing them, under General Sir Archibald Wavell who, on Mr Hore-Belisha's proposal, had been appointed in July 1939 to the newly created post of Commander-in-Chief, Middle East, when the first steps were taken to strengthen the forces there. But even now there were barely 50,000 British troops facing a total of half a million Italian and Italian colonial troops.

On the southerly fronts, the Italian forces in Eritrea and Abyssinia mustered more than 200,000 men, and could have pushed westwards into the Sudan—which was defended by a mere 9,000 British and Sudanese troops—or southwards into Kenya, where the garrison was no larger. Rugged

*for continuation westward see page 280

Capture of Sidi Barrani

Sidi Barrani DEC.10

Maktila DEC.9

Buq-Buq

4th ARMD. BDE.

Tummar W.

Tummar E.

7th ARMD. BDE.

Nibeiwa DEC.9

To Mersa Matruh

7th RTR & 4th INDIAN DIV.

Rabia

Railway

'PICCADILLY'

DEC 7/8 O'CONNOR'S FORCE FROM MERSA MATRUH

| 0 | Miles | 20 |
| 0 | Kilometres | 30 |

Italian fortified camps

Copyright © Cassell & Co. Ltd 1970

The Leap to El Agheila

MEDITERRANEAN SEA

Derna

| 0 | Miles | 100 |
| 0 | Kilometres | 200 |

Benghazi FEB.7

Barce Akhdar

Jebel

Mechili

Tobruk JAN.22

Bardia JAN.6,1941 Fort Capuzzo

Msus

Sidi Barrani

7th ARMD. DIV.

Beda Fomm FEB.5

C Y R E N A I C A

Antelat

Agedabia

L I B Y A

EGYPT

El Agheila FEB.9

Copyright © Cassell & Co. Ltd 1970

The Western Desert*

| 0 | Miles | 50 | 100 | 150 |
| 0 | Kilometres | 100 | | 200 |

M E D I T E R R A N E A N   S E A

Sidi Azeiz
Bardia
Capuzzo
Sollum
Buq-Buq
Sidi Barrani
Mersa Matruh
Alexandria
Nile Delta
Halfaya Pass
Sidi Omar
Bir Sheferzen
Habata
Fuka
El Daba
El Alamein
Libyan Plateau
Fort Maddalena
Qattara Depression
CAIRO
Nile

E G Y P T

Copyright © Cassell & Co. Ltd 1970

The Battle of Beda Fomm

| 0 | Miles | 10 | 20 |
| 0 | Kilometres | | 30 |

To Benghazi 20 miles

Ghemines

Solluch

SUPPORT GROUP

Sceleidima

RETREATING ITALIAN COLUMNS

7th HUSSARS

3rd HUSSARS

(4th ARMD. BDE.)
FEB 5/6

FEB. 6/7
7th ARMD. DIV.
FROM MECHILI

FEB. 5/6
ITALIAN TANKS
ENGAGED BY
7th ARMD. DIV.

1st RTR.
(7th ARMD. BDE.)
FEB. 6

Beda Fomm

2nd RTR.
(4th ARMD. BDE.)
FEB. 5/6

The Pimple

FEB. 6/7

GULF OF
SIRTE

Antelat
FEB. 6/7
HQ. 7th ARMD. DIV.

PM. FEB. 5
'COMBEFORCE' ESTABLISH
BLOCKING POSITIONS

To El Agheila, 100 miles

Copyright © Cassell & Co. Ltd 1970

country and distance, together with Italian difficulties in holding down the recently conquered Ethiopians and their own inefficiency, formed the main protection of the Sudan during this perilous period. Except for two small frontier encroachments, at Kassala and Gallabat, no offensive move developed on the Italians' part.

On the North African front a still larger force in Cyrenaica under Marshal Graziani faced the 36,000 British, New Zealand, and Indian troops who guarded Egypt. The Western Desert, inside the Egyptian frontier, separated the two sides on this front. The foremost British position was at Mersa Matruh, 120 miles inside the frontier and some 200 miles west of the Nile Delta.

Instead of remaining passive, however, Wavell used part of his one incomplete armoured division as an offensive covering force right forward in the desert. It was very offensive, keeping up a continual series of raids over the frontier to harass the Italian posts. Thus at the outset of the campaign General Creagh's 7th Armoured Division—the soon-to-be famous 'Desert Rats'—gained a moral ascendency over the enemy. Wavell paid special tribute to the 11th Hussars (the armoured-car regiment) under Lieutenant-Colonel J. F. B. Combe, saying that it 'was continuously in the front line, and usually behind that of the enemy, during the whole period'.

On June 14 a mobile column under Brigadier J. A. C. Caunter made a surprise stroke against Fort Capuzzo, and captured this important frontier stronghold, though the British did not try to hold it permanently, as their strategy was to keep mobile—'masters of the desert'—while inducing the Italians to concentrate and provide targets. The published list of Italian casualties for the three months until mid-September amounted to 3,500, while the British were only just over 150—despite being often bombed and machine-gunned from the air, where the relatively numerous Italian aircraft met little interference at that time.

It was not until September 13 that the Italians, after massing more than six divisions, began a cautious move forward into the Western Desert. After advancing fifty miles, less than half way to the British position at Mersa Matruh, they sat down at Sidi Barrani, and there established themselves in a chain of fortified camps—which were too widely separated to support one another. Week after week then passed without any attempt to move on. Meanwhile further reinforcements reached Wavell, including three armoured regiments rushed out from England in three fast merchant ships, on Churchill's bold initiative.

Wavell now decided that, as the Italians did not come on, he would sally forth and strike at them. That stroke was to have an astonishing effect, leading to the destruction of the whole Italian army and the near-collapse of the Italians' hold on North Africa.

But such a dramatic result was unforeseen. The stroke was planned, not as a sustained offensive, but rather as a large-scale raid. Wavell thought of it as a sharp punch to stun the invaders temporarily while he diverted part of his strength down to the Sudan, to push back the other Italian army there. Thus, unfortunately, no adequate preparations were made to follow-up the overwhelming victory that was actually gained.

Much was due to a radical change which was made in the attack plan following a rehearsal that raised doubts about its practicability. An indirect approach to take the enemy's camps from the rear was substituted for a frontal assault that would probably have failed—the more probably because it would have had a minefield in its path. The change of method was suggested by a staff officer, Brigadier Dorman-Smith, who had been sent by Wavell to attend the rehearsal. But its advantages were immediately grasped by the commander of the Western Desert force, General O'Connor, and the run of victory that followed was mainly due to his executive handling—for the higher commanders, Wavell and Lieutenant-General H. M. Wilson, were too far distant to exert positive influence on a fast-moving battle. They did have an important, and unfortunate, negative influence—as will be related.

Dick O'Connor's force consisted of 30,000 men, against an opposing force of 80,000—but it had 275 tanks against 120. The fifty heavily armoured 'Matilda' tanks of the 7th Royal Tank Regiment, impervious to most of the enemy's anti-tank weapons, played a particularly decisive role in this and subsequent battles.

On the night of December 7, the force moved out from the Matruh position on its seventy-mile approach through the desert. Next night it passed through a gap in the enemy's chain of camps, and early on the 9th the infantry of the 4th Indian Division (General Beresford-Peirse) stormed Nibeiwa camp from the rear, with the 7th Royal Tanks as its spearhead. The garrison was taken by surprise, and 4,000 prisoners captured, while the attackers' casualties were small—among the tankmen only seven.

The Matildas then led the way northward against the camp called 'Tummar West', which was stormed in the early afternoon, while 'Tummar East' also fell before this day of triumph ended. Meanwhile the 7th Armoured Division* had driven on westward and reached the coast-road, thus getting astride the enemy's line of retreat.

* Commanded in this battle by Brigadier J. A. C. Caunter, as General Creagh was temporarily sick.

On the next day the 4th Indian Division moved north against the cluster of Italian camps close around Sidi Barrani. The enemy were now on the alert, while violent sandstorms were also a hindrance to the advance. But, after an initial check, a converging assault from both flanks—with two additional tank regiments sent back by the 7th Armoured Division—was launched in the afternoon, and the greater part of the Sidi Barrani position was overrun before the day ended.

On the third day the reserve brigade of the 7th Armoured Division was brought up for a further enveloping bound to the westward, and arrived on the coast beyond Buq-Buq to intercept a large column of retreating Italians. The capture here of a further 14,000 Italians and eighty-eight guns brought the total bag to nearly 40,000 prisoners, and 400 guns.

The remnants of the invading Italian army, after recrossing their own frontier, took refuge in the coast-fortress of Bardia. There they were speedily isolated by the encircling sweep of the 7th Armoured Division. Unfortunately, there was no backing-up infantry division at hand to take advantage of their demoralisation, for the British higher commanders had planned to take away the 4th Indian Division as soon as Sidi Barrani was captured and to bring it back to Egypt for despatch to the Sudan. Their remoteness from the battlefield made it hard for them to realise what a decisive victory O'Connor had won, or what an immense opportunity it offered, and they persisted in the order for the recall of the 4th Indian Division.

Thus on December 11, the third day of battle, the routed Italians were running westwards in panic while half the victor's force was marching eastwards—back to back! It was a strange spectacle, and entailed a fateful delay. For three weeks elapsed before the 6th Australian Division arrived from Palestine to aid in continuing the British advance.

On January 3, 1941, the assault on Bardia was at last launched, with twenty-two Matildas of the 7th Royal Tank Regiment leading the way as 'tin-openers'. The defence quickly collapsed, and by the third day the whole garrison had surrendered—45,000 prisoners, with 462 guns and 129 tanks. The Australian divisional commander (Major-General I. G. Mackay) said that each Matilda tank was worth a whole infantry battalion to him.

Immediately after the capture of Bardia, the 7th Armoured Division drove westward to isolate Tobruk until the Australians could come up to mount an assault on the coastal fortress. Tobruk was attacked on January 21 and fell next day—yielding a bag of 30,000 prisoners, 236 guns and eight-seven tanks. Only sixteen Matildas were left for use in this assault, but once again they made the decisive penetration. That night some of the men of the

R.T.R. listened in to a news broadcast, and heard the commentator say: 'We suspect that the assault was led by a famous cavalry regiment.' One tankman was so incensed that he gave the box a hearty kick, exclaiming: 'You have to be colonial, black, or cavalry, to get any credit in this —— war.' It was a justifiable reaction. For never in the history of warfare has a single fighting unit played such a decisive part in the issue of a series of battles as the 7th R.T.R. did at Sidi Barrani, Bardia, and Tobruk in turn.

The rapid progress of the British advance into Cyrenaica was the more remarkable since it was made under a fresh handicap. Reinforcements, transport, and aircraft that should have been sent to O'Connor were held back in Egypt, and a number of units were even taken away from him. For Mr Churchill's imagination was now chasing a different hare. Following the scent of his old venture in the First World War, and stimulated by the way that the Greeks were standing up to the Italians, he pictured the possibility of creating a powerful combination of the Balkan countries against Germany. It was an attractive picture, but unrealistic, for the primitive Balkan armies had no power to withstand Germany's air and tank forces, while Britain could send them very little help.

Early in January Churchill decided to press the Greeks to accept a contingent of British tank and artillery units, to be landed at Salonika, and ordered Wavell to make immediate preparations for despatching such a force—although it meant weakening O'Connor's small strength.

But General Metaxas, who was then head of the Greek Government, declined the proposal, saying that the force offered would be likely to provoke the German invasion without being nearly strong enough to counter it. Moreover the Commander-in-Chief, General Papagos, expressed the view that the British would be wiser to complete their conquest of Africa before attempting anything fresh, and splitting the effort.

This polite rebuff from the Greek Government coincided with O'Connor's capture of Tobruk, so the British Government now decided to allow him to push on another step and capture the port of Benghazi. That would complete the conquest of Cyrenaica, the eastern half of Italian North Africa. But the British Prime Minister continued to cherish his Balkan project, and Wavell was told not to give O'Connor any reinforcements that might subtract from the building up of a force for that theatre.

On receiving permission to push on, O'Connor once again achieved much more than could be expected from his meagre resources. (His mobile arm, the 7th Armoured Division, had shrunk to only fifty cruiser tanks, with ninety-five light tanks—which had very thin armour and no effective armour-piercing gun.) Finding the enemy in a strong position at Derna on the coast-road, he planned to lever them out of it by a flanking move as soon as further supplies and cruiser tanks reached him. These were expected in time for him to resume the advance on February 12.

But on the 3rd, air reconnaissance showed that the enemy was preparing to abandon the Benghazi corner, and to retreat to the Agheila bottleneck, where they could block the route from Cyrenaica into Tripolitania. Large columns were seen to be already on the way.

O'Connor immediately planned a bold stroke to intercept the enemy's withdrawal, employing only the depleted 7th Armoured Division under General Creagh, and despatching it across the desert interior with the aim of reaching the coast-road well beyond Benghazi. It had about 150 miles to go, from its position at Mechili—the first long stretch being across extremely rough country. It moved off with only two days' rations and a bare sufficiency of petrol—on one of the most daring ventures and breathless races in military history.

Caunter's 4th Armoured Brigade started at 8.30 a.m. on the 4th, preceded by the 11th Hussars' armoured-cars. (The other armoured brigade, the 7th, had been reduced to one unit only, the 1st Royal Tanks.) At midday an air report brought the disconcerting news that the retreating enemy were already south of Benghazi. In an attempt to hasten the interception, Creagh ordered Caunter to organise an entirely wheeled force of motor infantry and artillery, and send it ahead with the 11th Hussars under Colonel Combe. Caunter's objections to this were borne out by the confusion and delay caused in pulling out these units from the rear of the column, and in organising special transport and signals for them. Moreover, on the terribly rough ground that was met in the afternoon, the tanks almost overtook the wheeled force. Caunter pushed on until after midnight, by moonlight, before pausing to allow his tank crews a few hours' rest.

In the morning (of the 5th), with easier ground, 'Combeforce' made faster progress. By the afternoon it had established a blocking position south of Beda Fomm across the enemy's two routes of retreat. That evening it trapped a very surprised column of Italian artillery and civilian evacuees.

Meanwhile Caunter's tanks, closely following up, had arrived at about 5 p.m. on the enemy's line of retreat past Beda Fomm. They broke up two columns of artillery and transport before dark. That action fittingly capped an advance in which they had actually covered 170 miles in thirty-three hours—a record in armoured mobility that has never been equalled. The roadlessness and ruggedness of the country made the feat all the more astonishing.

Next morning, the 6th, the enemy's main columns began to appear on the scene, escorted by tanks. There were over 100 new Italian cruiser tanks in all, whereas Caunter had only twenty-nine cruiser tanks. Fortunately, the Italian tanks came along in packets, instead of in a concentrated body, and kept near the road, whereas the British tanks skilfully manoeuvred to gain fire-positions where their hulls were concealed and protected by folds in the ground. A series of these tank battles went on all day, the brunt being borne by the nineteen cruiser tanks of the 2nd R.T.R., which were reduced to seven by the afternoon—when the 1st R.T.R. of the other brigade arrived, with ten more cruisers. The 3rd and 7th Hussars, using their light tanks boldly, did much to distract and harass the enemy.

When night fell on the battlefield, sixty of the Italian tanks had been crippled, and a further forty were found abandoned in the morning, while only three of the British tanks had actually been knocked out. The Italian infantry and other troops surrendered in crowds when their protecting tanks were destroyed and they were left exposed.

Combe's force, acting as a back-stop, caught such fractions as managed to evade the 4th Armoured Brigade. The Italians' last effort to break out was made against this rear position soon after daylight, and headed by sixteen tanks, but was checked by the 2nd Battalion, Rifle Brigade.

Altogether 20,000 prisoners were taken in this battle of Beda Fomm, as well as 216 guns and 120 tanks. The total British strength, in both Caunter's and Combe's forces, was only 3,000 men. When Bardia and its garrison fell on January 4, Anthony Eden, who had just returned to the Foreign Office as Secretary of State after seven months at the War Office, had coined a new version of Churchill's famous phrase, saying 'never has so much been surrendered by so many to so few'. That was even more true of the crowning victory at Beda Fomm.*

The radiance of victory, however, was soon dimmed. The complete extinction of Graziani's army had left the British with a clear passage through the Agheila bottleneck to Tripoli. But just as O'Connor and his troops were hoping to race on there—and throw the enemy out of his last foothold in North Africa—they were finally stopped by order of the British Cabinet.

On February 12 Churchill sent Wavell a long telegram which, after expressing delight that Benghazi had been captured 'three weeks ahead of

---

* Much of the credit was due to a man who took no part in the campaign—Major-General P. C. S. Hobart, who had been appointed to command the armoured division in Egypt when it was originally formed in 1938, and had developed its high pitch of manœuvring ability. But his ideas of how an armoured force should be handled, and what it could achieve when operating in strategical independence of orthodox forces, had been contrary to the views of more conservative superiors. His 'heresy', coupled with an uncompromising attitude, had led to his removal from command in the autumn of 1939—six months before the German panzer forces, applying the same ideas, proved their practicability.

expectation', directed him to halt the advance, leave only a minimum force to hold Cyrenaica, and prepare to send the largest possible force to Greece. Almost the whole of O'Connor's air force was removed immediately, leaving only one squadron of fighters.

What had produced this somersault? General Metaxas had died suddenly, on January 29, and the new Greek Prime Minister was a man of less formidable character. Churchill saw an opportunity of reviving his cherished Balkan project, and was prompt to seize it. He again pressed his offer on the Greek Government—and this time they were persuaded. On March 7, with Wavell's agreement and the approval of the Chiefs of Staff and the three Commanders-in-Chief, Middle East, the first contingent of a British force of 50,000 troops landed in Greece.

On April 6 the Germans invaded Greece, and the British were quickly driven to a second 'Dunkirk'. They narrowly escaped complete disaster, being evacuated by sea with great difficulty, leaving all their tanks, most of their other equipment, and 12,000 men behind in German hands.

O'Connor and his staff were confident that they could have captured Tripoli. Such an advance required the use of Benghazi as a base-port and some of the transport there had been reserved for the gamble in Greece. But all this had been worked out. General de Guingand, who later became Montgomery's Chief of Staff, has revealed that the Joint Planning Staff in the Middle East were convinced that Tripoli could be captured and the Italians swept out of Africa before the spring.

General Warlimont, a leading member of Hitler's staff, has revealed that the German Supreme Command took the same view:

> We could not understand at the time why the British did not exploit the difficulties of the Italians in Cyrenaica by pushing on to Tripoli. There was nothing to check them.* The few Italian troops who remained there were panic-stricken, and expected the British tanks to appear at any moment.

On February 6, the very day that Graziani's army was being finally wiped out at Beda Fomm, a young German general, Erwin Rommel—who had brilliantly led the 7th Panzer Division in the French campaign—was summoned to see Hitler and told to take command of a small German mechanised force that was to be sent to the Italians' rescue. It would consist of two small-scale divisions, the 5th Light and the 15th Panzer. But the transportation of the first could not be completed until mid-April, and that of the second not until the end of May. It was a slow programme—and the British had an open path.

On the 12th Rommel flew to Tripoli. Two days later a German transport

*Liddell Hart: *The Other Side of the Hill*, p. 250n.

arrived, carrying a reconnaissance battalion and an anti-tank battalion, as a first instalment. Rommel rushed them up to the front, and backed up this handful with dummy tanks that he quickly got built, in the hope of creating an air of strength. These dummies were mounted on Volkswagens, the 'people's motor-car' that was cheaply mass-produced in Germany. It was not until March 11 that the tank regiment of the 5th Light Division arrived in Tripoli.

Finding the British did not come on, Rommel thought he would try an offensive move with what he had. His first aim was merely to occupy the Agheila bottleneck. This succeeded so easily, on March 31, that he decided to push on. It was evident to him that the British much overestimated his strength—perhaps deceived by his dummy tanks. Moreover the Germans had the balance of strength in the air, which helped to conceal from the British command their weakness on the ground, and led also to some of the misleading reports rendered by the R.A.F. during the subsequent battles.

Rommel was lucky, too, in his timing. The 7th Armoured Division had been sent back to Egypt at the end of February to rest and refit. Its place was taken by part of the newly arrived and inexperienced 2nd Armoured Division—the other part had gone to Greece. The 6th Australian Division had been sent to Greece, and the 9th which replaced it was short of both equipment and training. O'Connor too had been given a rest, and had been relieved by Neame, an untried commander. Moreover Wavell, as he later admitted, did not credit reports of an impending German attack. The figures justified his view, and he can hardly be blamed for not making allowance for a Rommel.

Disregarding higher orders to wait until the end of May, Rommel resumed his advance on April 2, with fifty tanks, followed up more slowly by two new Italian divisions. By mobility and ruse he sought to magnify his slight strength. Following the shock of Rommel's initial assault, his shadow loomed so large that his two slim fingers, nearly a hundred miles apart, became magnified into encircling horns.

The effect of this audacious thrust was magical. The British forces hastily fell back in confusion, and on April 3 evacuated Benghazi. In this emergency O'Connor was sent up to advise Neame, but in the retreat their unescorted car ran into the back of a German spearhead group, on the night of the 6th, and both were taken prisoner. Meanwhile the one British armoured brigade had lost almost all its tanks in the long and hasty retreat, while the next day the commander of the 2nd Armoured Division, with a newly arrived motor brigade and other units, was surrounded at Mechili and led to surrender—the strength of the encircling force being magnified by the dust-clouds that

Rommel's men raised, with lines of trucks, to disguise their weakness in tanks. The Italians were still lagging behind.

By April 11 the British were swept out of Cyrenaica and over the Egyptian frontier, except for a small force shut up in Tobruk. This was in its way as astonishing a feat as the earlier conquest of Cyrenaica, and had been even quicker.

The British had now to begin all over again their efforts to clear North Africa, and under much heavier handicaps than before—above all, the presence of Rommel. The price to be paid for forfeiting the golden opportunity of February 1941 was heavy.

CHAPTER 10

THE CONQUEST OF ITALIAN EAST AFRICA

When Fascist Italy entered the war in June 1940 on Mussolini's instigation, her forces in Italian East Africa—which since 1936 had included conquered Ethiopia—immensely outnumbered the British, as they did in North Africa. According to the Italian records the forces in that area amounted to some 91,000 white troops and close on 200,000 native troops—although the latter seems to have been largely on paper, and might more reasonably be estimated as about half the claimed number. In the early months of 1940, preceding Italy's entry into the war, the British strength was only some 9,000 British and native troops in the Sudan, and 8,500 British East African troops in Kenya.

In this vast theatre of war, a double theatre, the Italians were almost as slow to take the initiative as they were in North Africa. A prime reason was their awareness that they were unlikely to get further supplies of motor fuel and munitions through the British blockade. But that was hardly a good reason since it made it more important to exploit their great superiority of strength before the British forces in Africa could be adequately reinforced.

Early in July the Italians moved hesitantly forward from Eritrea, in the north-west, and occupied the town of Kassala, a dozen miles inside the Sudanese frontier, employing a force of two brigades, four cavalry regiments, and two dozen tanks—some 6,500 men—against an outpost held by a company, of about 300 men, of the Sudan Defence Force. Major-General William Platt, commanding in the Sudan, had then only three British infantry battalions for the whole of that large area, posted respectively at Khartoum, Atbara, and Port Sudan. Wisely, he did not throw them into the fight until he could see how the Italian invasion developed. Instead of pushing on, it stopped—after occupying a few other frontier posts such as Gallabat, just over the north-west frontier of Ethiopia, and Moyale, on the northern frontier of Kenya.

It was not until early in August that the Italians started a more serious offensive move, and that was launched against the easiest possible target—

Port Sudan
100 miles

RED SEA

YEMEN

ERITREA

Atbara

Keren
Agordat
Barentu

Massawa APR.8
Asmara APR.1

Keru
Kassala

Assab

Atbara

FRENCH
SOMALILAND

Nile

Amba Alagi

GEN. PLATT
4th INDIAN DIV.
5th INDIAN DIV.
SUDAN DEFENCE
FORCE

AOSTA SURRENDERS
MAY 19

Khartoum

Blue Nile

Gondar
Debra
Tabor

Dessye

Dire Dawa

Gallabat
Metemma

Lake
Tanna

E   T   H   I

ITALIAN RESISTANCE
CEASES NOV. 27

Ha
Ma
Mie

ANGLO-

Addis Ababa
APR.6

EGYPTIAN

Gimbi

Jimma

Shashamanna

SUDAN

Ganale Dory

White Nile

Yaballo

Moy

Lake
Rudolf

**The Fall of the Italian
East African Empire**

0   Miles   100   200   300

0   Kilometres   200   400

K   E

ADEN
PROTECTORATE

GULF OF
ADEN

Aden

ibouti

Berbera MAR.16

Tug Argan
Pass

BRITISH
SOMALILAND

Hargeisa

Jijiga MAR.17

P I A

ITALIAN
SOMALILAND

Obbia

Webbe Shibeli

INDIAN

OCEAN

Mogadishu
FEB.25.

Juba

EN. CUNNINGHAM
th AFRICAN DIV.
th AFRICAN DIV.
t S.AFRICAN DIV.

Kismayu

A

N

British Somaliland, the strip of coastal territory on the African shore of the Gulf of Aden. Even that very limited move was defensive in motive. Indeed, Mussolini had ordered the Italians to stay on the defence. But the Duke of Aosta, who was Viceroy of Ethiopia, and supreme commander in that area, felt that the French Somaliland port of Djibouti offered an easy entry for the British into Ethiopia, and did not trust the armistice agreement with the French. So he decided to occupy the adjoining and larger area of British Somaliland.

The British garrison there, under Brigadier A. R. Chater, consisted of only four African and Indian battalions, with a British battalion, the 2nd Black Watch, on the way. The Italian invading force comprised twenty-six battalions provided with artillery and tanks. But the small Somaliland Camel Corps effectively delayed its advance, and Major-General A. R. Godwin-Austen arrived on the scene to take over just as the invaders reached the Tug Argan Pass on the approaches to Berbera, the seaport capital. Here the defenders put up such a tough defence that the attackers were kept at bay in a four-day battle, but in default of further reinforcements or defensive positions, the British force was evacuated by sea from Berbera—most of it being shipped to augment the British build-up now taking place in Kenya. It had inflicted over 2,000 casualties at a cost to itself of barely 250, and left an impression on the Italians that had a far-reaching strategic effect on their future action.

The British forces in Kenya, under Lieutenant-General Sir Alan Cunningham, who took over in November 1940, comprised the 12th African Division under Godwin-Austen (1st South African, 22nd East African, and 24th Gold Coast Brigades), shortly reinforced by the 11th African Division.

By the autumn the forces in Kenya had been raised to about 75,000 men—27,000 South Africans, 33,000 East Africans, 9,000 West Africans, and about 6,000 British. Three divisions had been formed—the 1st South African, and the 11th and 12th African. In the Sudan there was now a total of 28,000 troops, including the 5th Indian Division, while the 4th Indian was to move there after taking part in the initial stage of the brilliant counterstroke against the Italians in North Africa. A squadron of tanks had been sent there from the 4th Royal Tanks. There was also the Sudan Defence Force.

Mr Churchill felt that such large British forces demanded more activity than had been shown, and he repeatedly pressed for more aggressive action than had yet been taken, or contemplated. Wavell, who was Commander-in-Chief of the Middle East, proposed in agreement with Cunningham that an advance from Kenya into Italian Somaliland should begin in May or June after the spring rains. Wavell's doubts were increased by the tough resistance which Platt's first advance on the northern front had met in November, when launched against Gallabat by the 10th Indian Brigade under Brigadier W. J. Slim, a resolute leader who later became one of the most illustrious high commanders in the war. The initial attack on Gallabat succeeded, but the follow-up attack on the neighbouring post of Metemma suffered a check against an Italian colonial brigade of almost equal strength. That was largely due to the unexpected failure of a British battalion which had just been inserted in this Indian brigade, contrary to Slim's advice, for supposed stiffening. As later events showed, the Italian forces in this northern sector were much tougher than those elsewhere.

The only hopeful episodes of the winter were the activities of Brigadier D. A. Sandford, a retired officer who had been recalled to service on the outbreak of war, and subsequently sent into Ethiopia to raise revolt among the highland chiefs around Gondar, activities that were supported and extended during the winter by the still more unorthodox Captain Orde Wingate with a Sudanese battalion and his elusive 'Gideon Force'. The exiled Emperor Haile Selassie was brought back, by air, to Ethiopia on January 20, 1941—and barely three months later, on May 5, he re-entered his capital, Addis Ababa, in company with Wingate—far earlier than even Churchill had imagined possible.

For under continued pressure from Churchill, and from Smuts in South Africa, Wavell and Cunningham had been spurred to open the invasion of Italian Somaliland from Kenya in February 1941. The port of Kismayu was captured with unexpected ease, thus simplifying the supply problem, whereupon Cunningham's forces crossed the Juba River, and pushed on some 250 miles to Mogadishu, the capital and larger port, which they occupied barely a week later, on February 25. Here they captured an immense quantity of motor and air fuel, the speed of the advance having forestalled the planned demolitions, as at Kismayu. Good air support was another important factor in the rapid advance.

Cunningham's forces then turned inland, into Southern Ethiopia, and by March 17 the 11th African Division occupied Jijiga, close to the provincial capital of Harar, after a 400 mile advance. That brought them close to the frontier of former British Somaliland, where a small force from Aden had re-landed on the 16th. By March 29, after some tougher resistance, Harar was occupied, and Cunningham's forces then swung westward towards the Ethiopian capital, Addis Ababa, 300 miles distant in the west centre of Ethiopia. Cunningham's forces occupied it barely a week later, on April 6— a month before the Emperor Haile Selassie returned to his capital, escorted by Wingate. The remarkably ready surrender of the Italians was hastened by reports of the atrocities committed by Ethiopian irregulars among Italian women.

In the north, however, the opposition was much stiffer, as it had been from the outset. Here General Frusci, who was in command, had about 17,000 well-equipped Italian troops in the front in the area of Eritrea, with over three divisions farther back. General Platt's advance, starting in the third week of January, was carried out by the powerful 4th and 5th Indian Divisions. The Duke of Aosta had ordered the Italian forces in Eritrea to fall back before the British advance developed, and as a result the first serious stand was made at Keru, sixty miles east of Kassala and forty miles inside the Eritrean frontier.

Harder resistance was met by the two Indian-columns in mountainous positions at Barentu and Agordat, respectively forty-five and seventy miles east of Keru. Fortunately the 4th Indian, under General Beresford-Peirse, reached the more distant objective first, and that eased the 5th Indian's advance on Barentu.

Wavell then realised the possibility of extending his objective, to the conquest of Eritrea as a whole, and gave fresh orders to General Platt accordingly. But the capital, Asmara, was more than 100 miles beyond Agordat (and the port of Massawa further still), while almost midway between lay the mountainous position of Keren, one of the strongest defensive positions in East Africa, and the only gateway to Asmara and Massawa, the Italian naval base.

The first attempts to force a passage, starting early on February 3, were a failure, and suffered repeated repulses in the following days. The Italian commander on the spot, General Carnimeo, showed splendid fighting spirit and tactical skill. After more than a week of effort the attack was abandoned, and a long lull followed. Not until mid-March was the offensive resumed, when the 5th Indian Division was brought up and ready to join in. Once again the struggle was a prolonged one, and a series of Italian counter-attacks threw back the attackers, but at last on March 27 a squadron of heavily armoured 'infantry' tanks of the 4th R.T.R. broke through the block and pierced the Italian front—the same factor that in the hands of the 7th R.T.R. had been decisive in the successive North African battles from Sidi Barrani to Tobruk.

That finished the battle of Keren, after fifty-three days. General Frusci's forces fell back southward into Ethiopia, and on April 1 the British occupied Asmara. Then they pushed on eastward to Massawa, fifty miles beyond, and produced its surrender, after a fight, on April 8. That ended the Eritrean campaign.

Meanwhile the remaining Italian forces, under the Duke of Aosta, had withdrawn southward into Ethiopia, planning a final stand in a mountain position at Amba Alagi, some eighty miles south of Asmara. He had only 7,000 troops left, with forty guns, and barely three months' supplies. Moreover Italian morale was dwindling as a result of reports about the Ethiopian treatment of prisoners. So the Duke, though a gallant soldier, was more than willing to agree to surrender on 'honourable terms', which took place on May 19—and brought the total of Italian prisoners to 230,000. There still remained isolated Italian forces under General Gazzera in the south-west of Ethiopia and in the north-west under General Nasi near Gondar, but these were rounded up in the summer and autumn respectively. That was the end of Mussolini's short-lived African Empire.

PART IV

THE SPREAD

1941

The Overrunning of the Balkans

- Axis and Axis allied countries
- German attacks Apr. 6/28, 1941
- International frontiers Sept. 1941

0 Miles 300
0 Kilometres 200

APR 6 GREEK-ITALIAN FRONT.

MAY 20 GERMAN PARACHUTE TROOPS LAND

Copyright © Cassell & Co. Ltd 1970

CHAPTER 11

THE OVERRUNNING OF THE BALKANS AND CRETE

Some claim that the despatch of General Wilson's force to Greece, though it ended in a hurried evacuation, was justified because it produced six weeks' postponement of the invasion of Russia. This claim has been challenged, and the venture condemned as a political gamble, by a number of soldiers who were well acquainted with the Mediterranean situation—notably General de Guingand, later Montgomery's Chief of Staff, who was on the Joint Planning Staff in Cairo. They argue that a golden opportunity of exploiting the defeat of the Italians in Cyrenaica, and capturing Tripoli before German help arrived, was sacrificed in order to switch inadequate forces to Greece that had no real chance of saving her from a German invasion.

This latter view was confirmed by events. In three weeks, Greece was overrun and the British thrown out of the Balkans, while the reduced British force in Cyrenaica was also driven out by the German Afrika Korps, which had been enabled to land at Tripoli. These defeats meant a damaging loss of prestige and prospect for Britain, and only hastened the misery that was brought on the Greek people. Even if the Greek campaign was found to have retarded the invasion of Russia, that fact would not justify the British Government's decision, for such an object was not in their minds at the time. It is of historical interest, however, to discover whether the campaign actually had such an effect. The most definite piece of evidence in support of this lies in the fact that Hitler had originally ordered preparations for the attack on Russia to be completed by May 15, whereas at the end of March the tentative date was deferred about a month, and then fixed for June 22. Field-Marshal von Rundstedt said that the preparations of his Army Group had been hampered by the late arrival of the armoured divisions which had been employed in the Balkan campaign, and that this was the key-factor in the delay, in combination with the weather.

Field-Marshal von Kleist, who commanded the armoured forces under Rundstedt, was still more explicit. 'It is true', he said, 'that the forces employed in the Balkans were not large compared with our total strength, but the proportion of tanks employed there was high. The bulk of the tanks that came under me for the offensive against the Russian front in southern Poland had taken part in the Balkan offensive, and needed overhaul, while their crews needed a rest. A large number of them had driven as far south as the Peloponnese, and had to be brought back all that way.'*

The views of Field-Marshals von Rundstedt and von Kleist were naturally conditioned by the extent to which the offensive on their front was dependent on the return of these armoured divisions. Other generals attached less importance to the effect of the Balkan campaign. They emphasised that the main role in the offensive against Russia was allotted to Field-Marshal von Bock's Central Army Group in northern Poland, and that the chances of victory principally turned on its progress. A diminution of Rundstedt's forces, for the secondary role of his Army Group, might not have affected the decisive issue, as the Russian forces could not be easily switched. It might even have checked Hitler's inclination to switch his effort southward in the second stage of the invasion—an inclination that, as we shall see, had a fatally retarding effect on the prospects of reaching Moscow before the winter. The invasion, at a pinch, could have been launched without awaiting the reinforcement of Rundstedt's Army Group by the arrival of the divisions from the Balkans. But, in the event, that argument for delay was reinforced by doubts whether the ground was dry enough to attempt an earlier start. General Halder's view was that the weather conditions were not in fact suitable before the time when the invasion was actually launched.

The retrospective views of generals are not, however, a sure guide as to what might have been decided if there had been no Balkan complications. Once the tentative date had been postponed on that account the scales were weighted against any idea of striking before the extra divisions had returned from the quarter.

But it was not the Greek campaign that caused the postponement. Hitler had already reckoned with that commitment when the invasion of Greece was inserted in the 1941 programme, as a preliminary to the invasion of Russia. The decisive factor in the change of timing was the unexpected coup d'état in Yugo-Slavia that took place on March 27, when General Simovich and his confederates overthrew the Government which had just previously committed Yugo-Slavia to a pact with the Axis. Hitler was so

---

* Liddell Hart: *The Other Side of the Hill,* p. 251.

incensed by the upsetting news as to decide, that same day, to stage an overwhelming offensive against Yugo-Slavia. The additional forces, land and air, required for such a stroke involved a greater commitment than the Greek campaign alone would have done, and thus impelled Hitler to take his fuller and more fateful decision to put off the intended start of the attack on Russia.

It was the fear, not the fact, of a British landing that had prompted Hitler to move into Greece, and the outcome set his mind at rest. The landing did not even check the existing Government of Yugo-Slavia from making terms with Hitler. On the other hand, it may have encouraged Simovich in making his successful bid to overthrow the Government and defy Hitler—less successfully.

Still more illuminating was the summary of the operations in the Balkan campaign given by General von Greiffenberg, who was Chief of Staff of Field-Marshal List's 12th Army which conducted the Balkan campaign.

Greiffenberg's account emphasised, remembering the Allied lodgement at Salonika in 1915 which ultimately developed into a decisive strategic thrust in September 1918, that Hitler feared in 1941 that the British would again land in Salonika or on the southern coast of Thrace. This would place them in the rear of Army Group South when it advanced eastward into southern Russia. Hitler assumed that the British would try to advance into the Balkans as before—and recalled how at the end of World War I the Allied Balkan Army had materially contributed to the decision.

He therefore resolved, as a precautionary measure before beginning operations against Russia, to occupy the coast of Southern Thrace between Salonika and Dedeagach (Alexandropolis). The 12th Army (List) was earmarked for this operation, and included Kleist's Panzer Group. The army assembled in Rumania, crossed the Danube into Bulgaria, and from there was to pierce the Metaxas Line—advancing with its right wing on Salonika and its left wing on Dedeagach. Once the coast was reached, the Bulgarians were to take over the main protection of the coast, where only a few German troops were to remain. The mass of the 12th Army, especially Kleist's Panzer Group, was then to turn about and be sent northward via Rumania, to go into action on the southern sector of the Eastern Front. The original plan did not envisage the occupation of the main part of Greece.

When this plan was shown to King Boris of Bulgaria, he said that he did not trust Yugo-Slavia, which might threaten the right flank of the 12th Army. German representatives, however, assured King Boris that in view of the 1939 pact between Yugo-Slavia and Germany they anticipated no danger from that quarter. They had the impression that King Boris was not quite convinced.

He was proved right. When the 12th Army was about to begin operations from Bulgaria according to plan, the coup which led to the abdication of the Regent, Prince Paul, was suddenly launched in Belgrade, just before the movement of troops began.

It appeared that certain Belgrade circles disagreed with Prince Paul's pro-German policy and wanted to side with the Western powers. Whether the Western powers or the U.S.S.R. backed the coup beforehand, we as soldiers cannot gauge. But at any rate it was not staged by Hitler! On the contrary it came as a very unpleasant surprise, and nearly upset the whole plan of operations of the 12th Army in Bulgaria.*

For example, Kleist's panzer divisions had to proceed immediately from Bulgaria north-westward against Belgrade. Another improvisation was an operation by the 2nd Army (Weichs), with quickly gathered formations based on Carinthia and Styria, southward into Yugo-Slavia. The flare-up in the Balkans compelled a postponement of the Russian campaign, from May to June. To this extent, therefore, the Belgrade coup materially influenced the start of Hitler's attack on Russia.

But the weather also played an important part in 1941, and that was accidental. East of the Bug-San line in Poland, ground operations are very restricted until May, because most roads are muddy and the country generally is a morass. The many unregulated rivers cause widespread flooding. The farther one goes east the more pronounced do these disadvantages become, particularly in the boggy forest regions of the Rokitno (Pripet) and Beresina. Even in normal times movement is very restricted before mid-May, but 1941 was an exceptional year. The winter had lasted longer. As late as the beginning of June the Bug was over its banks for miles.

Similar conditions prevailed farther north. General von Manstein, who was then commanding a spearhead panzer corps in East Prussia, said that heavy rain fell there during late May and early June. It is evident that if the invasion had been launched earlier the prospect would have been poor, and as Halder said, it is very doubtful whether an earlier date would have been practicable, quite apart from the Balkan hindrance. The weather of 1940 had been all too favourable to the invasion of the West, but the weather of 1941 operated against the invasion of the East.

When the Germans invaded Greece in April 1941, following the landing of a small British army of reinforcement at Salonika, the Greek Army was mainly aligned to cover the passages through the mountains from Bulgaria, where the German forces had assembled. But the expected advance down the Struma Valley masked a less direct move. German mechanised columns

---

* Blumentritt in Liddell Hart: *The Other Side of the Hill*, p. 254.

swerved westward from the Struma up the Strumitza Valley parallel with the frontier, and over the mountain passes into the Yugo-Slav end of the Vardar Valley. Thereby they pierced the joint between the Greek and Yugo-Slav armies, and exploited the penetration by a rapid thrust down the Vardar to Salonika. This cut off a large part of the Greek Army, anchored in Thrace.

The Germans followed up this stroke, not by a direct advance southward from Salonika past Mount Olympus, where the British army had taken up its position, but by another swerving thrust down through the Monastir Gap, farther west. The exploitation of this advance towards the west coast of Greece cut off the Greek divisions in Albania, turned the flank of the British and, by its threatened swerve back onto the line of retreat of the surviving Allied forces, produced the speedy collapse of all resistance in Greece. The bulk of the British and Allied forces were evacuated by sea to Crete.

The capture of Crete by an invasion delivered purely by air was one of the most astonishing and audacious feats of the war. It was, also, the most striking airborne operation of the war. It was performed at Britain's expense—and should remain a warning not to discount the risk of similar surprise strokes 'out of the blue' in the future.

At eight o'clock on the morning of May 20, 1941, some 3,000 German parachute troops dropped out of the sky upon Crete. The island was held by 28,600 British, Australian, and New Zealand troops, along with two Greek divisions amounting in numbers to almost as many.

The attack had been expected, as a follow-up to the German conquest of the Balkans, and good information about the preparations had been provided by British agents in Greece. But the airborne threat was not regarded as seriously as it should have been. Churchill has revealed that General Freyberg, V.C., who had been appointed to command in Crete on his suggestion, reported on May 5: 'Cannot understand nervousness; am not in the least anxious about airborne attack.'* He showed more concern about seaborne invasion—a danger which was, in the event, dispelled by the Royal Navy.

Churchill felt anxious about the threat, 'especially from the air'. He urged that 'at least another dozen "I" [Infantry] tanks' should be sent to reinforce the mere half dozen that were there.† An even more fundamental weakness was the complete lack of air support—to combat the German dive-bombers and intercept the airborne troops. Even the provision of anti-aircraft guns was scanty.

* Churchill: *The Second World War*, vol. III, 246.
† ibid, p. 249.

By the first evening, the number of Germans on the island had been more than doubled, and was progressively reinforced—by parachute drop, by glider, and from the second evening onwards by troop-carriers. These began landing on the captured Maleme airfield while it was still swept by the defenders' artillery and mortar-fire. The final total of German troops brought by air was about 22,000. Many were killed and injured by crashes on landing, but those that survived were the toughest of fighters, whereas their numerically superior opponents were not so highly trained and some were still suffering from the shock of being driven out of Greece. More important were their deficiencies in equipment, and especially the lack of short-range wireless equipment. Nevertheless, many of these troops fought hard, and their stiff resistance had important effects that only became known later.

Optimism continued to prevail for a time in British high quarters. In the light of reports received, Churchill told the House of Commons on the second day that 'the greater part' of the airborne invaders had been wiped out. Middle East Headquarters went on for two more days talking about the Germans being 'mopped up'.

But on the seventh day, the 26th, the British commander in Crete reported: 'In my opinion the limit of endurance has been reached by the troops under my command . . . our position here is hopeless.' Coming from such a stout-hearted soldier as Freyberg, this verdict was not questioned. Evacuation began on the night of the 28th, and ended on the night of the 31st—the Royal Navy suffering heavy losses from the enemy's dominant air force in its persistent efforts to bring away as many troops as possible. A total of 16,500 were rescued, including about 2,000 Greeks, but the rest were left dead or prisoner in German hands. The Navy had well over 2,000 dead. Three cruisers and six destroyers were sunk. Thirteen other ships were badly damaged, including two battleships and the only aircraft-carrier then in the Mediterranean Fleet.

The Germans had some 4,000 men killed, and about half as many wounded. Thus their permanent loss was less than a third of what the British had suffered, apart from the Greeks and local Cretan levies. But as the loss fell mostly on the picked troops of Germany's one existing parachute division, it had an unforeseen effect on Hitler that turned out to Britain's benefit.

At the moment, however, the collapse in Crete looked disastrous. It hit the British peoples all the harder because it followed hard on the heels of two other disasters. For in April the British forces had been swept out of Cyrenaica in ten days, by Rommel, and out of Greece within three weeks from the start of the German invasion. Wavell's winter success in capturing Cyrenaica from the Italians came to appear no more than a delusory break in the clouds. With this fresh run of defeats at German hands, and the spring renewal of the air 'Blitz' on England, the prospect was darker even than in 1940.

But Hitler did not follow up his third Mediterranean victory in any of the ways expected on the British side—a pounce upon Cyprus, Syria, Suez, or Malta. A month later he launched the invasion of Russia, and from that time on neglected the opportunities that lay open for driving the British out of the Mediterranean and the Middle East. If his forfeit was mainly due to his absorption in the Russian venture, it was also due to his reaction after the victory in Crete. The cost depressed him more than the conquest exhilarated him. It was such a contrast to the cheapness of his previous successes and far larger captures.

In Yugo-Slavia and Greece his new armoured forces had been as irresistible as in the plains of Poland and France, despite the mountain obstacles they met. They had swept through both countries like a whirlwind and knocked over the opposing armies like ninepins.

Field-Marshal List's army captured 90,000 Yugo-Slavs, 270,000 Greeks, and 13,000 British—at a cost to itself of barely 5,000 men killed and wounded, as later records showed. At the time British newspapers estimated the German loss as over a quarter of a million, and even a British official statement put them as 'probably 75,000'.

The blemish on Hitler's Cretan victory was not only the higher loss but the fact that it temporarily weakened the one new kind of land-fighting force he had which could reach out and seize places over the sea without risking interception by the British Navy—which still dominated the sea-scape, despite its heavy losses. In effect, Hitler had sprained his wrist in Crete.

After the war General Student, the Commander-in-Chief of the German Airborne Forces, revealed, surprisingly, that Hitler was a reluctant convert to the scheme of attacking Crete:

> He wanted to break off the Balkan campaign after reaching the south of Greece. When I heard this, I flew to see Göring and proposed the plan of capturing Crete by airborne forces alone. Göring—who was always easy to enthuse—was quick to see the possibilities of the idea, and sent me on to Hitler. I saw him on April 21. When I first explained the project Hitler said: 'It sounds all right, but I don't think it's practicable.' But I managed to convince him in the end.
>
> In the operation we used our one Parachute Division, our one Glider Regiment and the 5th Mountain Division, which had no previous experience of being transported by air.*

The air support was provided by the dive-bombers and fighters of

* This and the extracts on pages 138 and 139, from Student in Liddell Hart: *The Other Side of the Hill*, pp. 238–43.

Richtofen's 8th Air Corps, which had been a decisive instrument in forcing the gate into Belgium and France successively in 1940.

No troops came by sea. Such a reinforcement had been intended originally, but the only sea transport available was a number of Greek caiques. It was then arranged that a convoy of these small vessels was to carry the heavier arms for the expedition—anti-aircraft and anti-tank guns, the artillery and some tanks—together with two battalions of the 5th Mountain Division... they were told that the British Fleet was still at Alexandria—whereas it was actually on the way to Crete. The convoy sailed for Crete, ran into the fleet, and was scattered. The Luftwaffe avenged this setback by 'pulling a lot of hair' out of the British Navy's scalp. But our operations on land, in Crete, were much handicapped by the absence of the heavier weapons on which we had reckoned....

At no point on May 20 did we succeed complêtely in occupying an airfield. The greatest degree of progress was achieved on Maleme airfield, where the valuable Assault Regiment fought against picked New Zealand troops. The night of May 20–21 was critical for the German Command. I had to make a momentous decision. I decided to use the mass of the parachute-reserves, still at my disposal, for the final capture of Maleme airfield. If the enemy had made an organised counterattack during this night or the morning of May 21, he would probably have succeeded in routing the much battered and exhausted remnants of the Assault Regiment—especially as these were badly handicapped by shortage of ammunition.

But the New Zealanders made only isolated counterattacks. I heard later that the British Command expected, besides the airborne venture, the arrival of the main German forces by sea on the coast between Maleme and Canea, and consequently maintained their forces in occupation of the coast. At this decisive period the British Command did not take the risk of sending these forces to Maleme. On the 21st the German reserves succeeded in capturing the airfield and village of Maleme. In the evening the 1st Mountain Battalion could be landed, as the first air-transported troops— and so the battle for Crete was won by Germany.

But the price of victory was much heavier than had been reckoned by the advocates of the plan—partly because the British forces on the island were three times as large as had been assumed, but also from other causes.

Much of the loss was due to bad landings—there were very few suitable spots in Crete, and the prevailing wind blew from the interior towards the sea. For fear of dropping the troops in the sea, the pilots tended to drop them too far inland—some of them actually in the British lines. The weapon-containers often fell wide of the troops, which was another handicap that contributed to our excessive casualties. The few British tanks that were there shook us badly at the start—it was lucky there were not more than two dozen. The infantry, mostly New Zealanders, put up a stiff fight, though taken by surprise.

The Führer was very upset by the heavy losses suffered by the parachute units, and came to the conclusion that their surprise value had passed. After that he often said to me: 'The day of parachute troops is over.' ...

When I got Hitler to accept the Crete plan, I also proposed that we should follow it up by capturing Cyprus from the air, and then a further jump from Cyprus to capture the Suez Canal. Hitler did not seem averse to the idea, but would not commit himself definitely to the project—his mind was so occupied with the coming invasion of Russia. After the shock of the heavy losses in Crete, he refused to attempt another big airborne effort. I pressed the idea on him repeatedly, but without avail.

So the British, Australian, and New Zealand losses in Crete were not without compensating profit. Student's project of capturing the Suez Canal may have been beyond attainment, unless Rommel's panzer forces in Africa had also been strongly reinforced, but the capture of Malta would have been an easier task. Hitler was persuaded to undertake it a year later, but then changed his mind and cancelled it. Student said: 'He felt that if the British Fleet appeared on the scene, all the Italian ships would bolt for their home ports and leave the German airborne forces stranded.'

'Barbarossa': Hitler's Invasion Plan

first phase
second phase

Miles
Kilometres
0   500   400

CHAPTER 12

HITLER TURNS AGAINST RUSSIA

The whole outlook of the war was revolutionised when Hitler invaded Russia on June 22, 1941—a day before the anniversary of Napoleon's invasion of 1812. That step proved as fatal to Hitler as it had to his forerunner, though the end did not come so quickly.

Napoleon was forced to retreat from Russia before the end of the year, and the Russians entered *his* capital in April of the second year following his invasion. Hitler was not driven out of Russia until three years had passed, and the Russians did not enter *his* capital until April of the fourth year. He had penetrated twice as far into Russia as Napoleon had done, though failing to repeat Napoleon's illusory success in entering Moscow. His deeper penetration was due to superior means of mobility. But this was not adequate for the fulfilment of his purpose. Space spelt first his frustration, and then his defeat.

History repeated itself also in the auxiliary effects of the aggressor's suicidal step. It brought Britain reprieve from a situation that appeared hopeless in the eyes of most people outside her own insular boundaries. It was obvious to them how desperate was the position of a small island on the edge of a hostile continent, which enveloped it more closely than in Napoleonic times. The value of the sea-moat was diminished by the development of airpower. The industrialisation of the island had made it dependent on imports, and thus multiplied the menace of submarine power. By refusing to consider any peace offer the British Government had committed the country to a course that under such conditions was bound, logically, to lead through growing exhaustion to eventual collapse—even if Hitler abstained from attempting its quick conquest by invasion. The course of no compromise was equivalent to slow suicide.

The United States might pump in 'air' to keep Britain afloat, but that would merely suffice to prolong the process, not to avert the end. Moreover the measure of this respite was offset by Churchill's midsummer decision to pursue the bombing of Germany with all Britain's puny strength. Such bombing attacks could amount to no more than pin-pricks, but they inherently tended to hinder Hitler's inclination to turn his attention elsewhere.

But the British people took little account of the hard facts of their situation. They were instinctively stubborn and strategically ignorant. Churchill's inspiring speeches helped to correct the depression of Dunkirk, and supplied the tonic the islanders wanted. They were exhilarated by his challenging note, and did not pause to ask whether it was strategically warranted.

Deeper than the influence of Churchill was the effect of Hitler. His conquest of France and near approach to their shores aroused them as no earlier evidence of his tyranny and aggressiveness had done. They reacted once again in their long-bred way—intent to keep their teeth in Hitler's skin at any cost. Never was their collective characterisation as a bulldog so clearly demonstrated, and justified, in all its sublime stupidity.

Once again a conqueror of the West was confounded by a people who 'did not see that they were beaten'. Hitler understood them better than Napoleon, as *Mein Kampf* shows, and he had thus taken unusual pains to avoid wounding their pride. But he had reckoned on their practical sense, and was baffled that they could not see the hopelessness of the outlook nor recognise that the conditions framed in his peace offer were extraordinarily easy considering the circumstances. In that state of confusion he hesitated as to what he should do next, and then turned in the same direction as Napoleon —to the conquest of Russia as the preliminary to a final settlement with Britain.

It was not a sudden turn of his mind, but made by degrees. It was also complex in causation—more complex than Napoleon's turn—and cannot be explained simply by any single factor or reason.

The heavy losses of the Luftwaffe over southern England were less decisive strategically, though more decisive tactically, than the check to the French fleet off Cape Finisterre in 1805. For Göring's defeat had no such instantaneous effect on Hitler's mind as Villeneuve's retreat had produced on Napoleon's. For the time being, Hitler persevered with his efforts to bend the British people's will, and merely changed the form of his pressure—from an attempted destruction of the defending air force to night bombing of the industrial cities. The intermittent relaxation of pressure was due, apart from weather, to a wavering of his mind. He seems to have been reluctant to proceed to extremes against Britain if he could possibly persuade her to accept peace, and he clung to the hope while pursuing the aim clumsily.

Meanwhile his mind was moving with increasing momentum in another direction, under the influence of his economic needs and fears, multiplied by his prejudices. Although his pact with Stalin had paved the way for his victory in the West, his conquests there had been largely the product of circumstances, whereas he had always contemplated the overthrow of Soviet Russia. For him that idea was more than a matter of expediency in pursuit of ambition; anti-Bolshevism was his most profound emotional conviction.

This eastward impulse was strongly influenced by Britain's resistance, but its revival had begun before Britain's rejection of his peace offer.

Early in June 1940, while Hitler was still engaged in the French campaign, Stalin had seized the opportunity to occupy Lithuania, Estonia, and Latvia. Hitler had agreed that the Baltic States should be within the Soviet Union's sphere of influence, not to their actual occupation, and he felt that he had been tricked by his partner, although most of his advisers realistically considered the Russian move into the Baltic States to be a natural precaution, inspired by fear of what Hitler might attempt after his victory in the West. Hitler's deep distrust of Russia had been shown in the way he worried throughout the campaign in the West at having left only ten divisions in the East, facing a hundred Russian divisions.

Then on June 26, again without notice to her partner, Russia addressed an ultimatum to Rumania, demanding the immediate restoration of Bessarabia, and the surrender of northern Bukovina in addition—as a 'small compensation' for the way that Russia had been 'robbed' of the former province in 1918. The Rumanian Government was allowed only 24 hours for its answer, and when it yielded to the threat the Russian troops swarmed in at once, by air as well as overland.

That was worse than a 'slap in the face' for Hitler, since it placed the Russians ominously close to the Rumanian oilfields on which he counted for his own supply, now that he was cut off from oversea sources. In the following weeks he became increasingly nervous about that risk, and anxious about its bearing on the air offensive against England. He became correspondingly suspicious of Stalin's intentions. On July 29 he spoke to Jodl about the possibility of having to fight Russia if she tried to seize the Rumanian oilfields. A few weeks later, as a countermove, he began the transfer of two armoured and ten infantry divisions to Poland. A directive of September 6 to the Counter-Intelligence Service, said: 'The Eastern territory will be manned more strongly in the weeks to come. These regroupings must not create the impression in Russia that we are preparing for an offensive in the East.' The strength of the German forces was to be camouflaged by frequent changes of area:

> On the other hand, Russia will realise that strong and highly-trained German troops are stationed in the Government-General, in the Eastern provinces, and in the Protectorate. She should draw the conclusion that we are ready to protect our interests, particularly in the Balkans, with strong forces against Russian seizure.

This directive had a predominantly defensive note. It showed concern to provide a deterrent to Russian aggression rather than foreshadowing German aggression. But because of the distance that separated his front from the oilfields he had to safeguard, he could not count on being able to give them direct protection, and was prompted to consider an offensive diversion on the Polish front. The idea of such a diversion soon developed into that of a major invasion—to forestall the particular risk by excising the whole danger.

In mid-September reports came that the Russian propaganda service had switched to a line of anti-German talk within the Red Army. This showed the Russians' suspicious reaction to the first increase of the German forces in the East, and their promptness to prepare their troops for a Russo-German conflict. But to Hitler's mind it was evidence of their offensive designs. He began to feel that he could not afford to wait—until he had completed and consolidated his victory in the West—before dealing with Russia. His fears, ambitions, and prejudices reacted on one another, giving impetus to the fresh turn of his thought. In that state of mind his suspicions were easily quickened. Puzzled by the way that the British did not seem to realise their hopeless situation, he looked to Russia for the explanation. Over and over again as the months went on he said, to Jodl and others, that Britain must be hoping for Russian intervention, or she would have given in. Already there must be some secret agreement. The despatch of Sir Stafford Cripps to Moscow, and his conversations with Stalin, were confirmation of it. Germany must strike soon, or she would be strangled. Hitler could not see that the Russians, likewise, might have fears of his aggression.

The plan for an offensive against Russia had already been sketched out when General Paulus (later to become famous as commander of the army that was trapped by the Russians at Stalingrad) became Deputy Chief of the General Staff at the beginning of September. He was instructed 'to examine its possibilities'. The objectives defined were, first, the destruction of the Russian armies in western Russia; and then an advance into Russia deep enough to secure Germany against the risk of air attack from the east, carried as far as a line from Archangel to the Volga.

By the beginning of November the plan was completed in detail, and then tested in a couple of war games. Hitler had now become less anxious about a Russian offensive—yet more inclined to take the offensive against Russia. The preparation and contemplation of vast strategic plans always intoxicated him. The doubts which his generals expressed, when he disclosed the trend of his mind, merely served to make it more definite. Had he not proved right on each issue where they had doubted his capacity to succeed? He must prove them wrong again, and more strikingly—their doubts showed that for all their subservience, they still had an underlying distrust of him as an amateur. Moreover, his admirals and his generals were apprehensive about an oversea move against England—and he could not remain passive. He had set on foot plans for a move through Spain against Gibraltar, to close the western end of the Mediterranean, but that was too small an operation to satisfy his gigantic ambition.

A fresh development at the end of October had an influence on his decision—and a greater one ultimately on its outcome. This was Mussolini's invasion of Greece, launched without reference to Hitler, who was incensed by his junior partner's disregard for his guidance, by the way it upset his own programme, and by the possibility that the Italians might establish themselves in his intended sphere. Although the last risk soon waned with the Italian reverses, Mussolini's independent initiative led Hitler to expedite his own Balkan moves. It formed a fresh reason for deferring the completion of his western programme, and accentuated the easterly turn of his mind. As he had to outstrip his associates in a race for control of the Balkans, he would settle with Russia next, and leave the British problem until later. It was not a clearcut decision even yet, but it was the thought uppermost in his mind.

On November 10 Molotov arrived in Berlin to discuss a wide range of questions, including the German suggestion that Russia should definitely join the Axis. At the end of the conversations an agreed communiqué was issued, saying: 'The exchange of ideas took place in an atmosphere of mutual trust, and led to a mutual understanding on all important questions interesting Germany and the Soviet Union.' Privately, too, the German participants were fairly well satisfied with the results, which were summed up thus on the 16th.

> For the time being there will be no fixed treaty. Russia appears willing to join the Three Power Pact after several further questions have been clarified. ... Molotov is notified of contemplated German action in the Balkans in support of Italy and raises no objection. He suggests the creation of conditions suitable for Russian influence in Bulgaria, similar to German influence in Rumania, but this suggestion is not entered into by the Germans. Germany, however, expresses her disinterestedness in Turkey's domination of the Dardanelles and sympathy with Russian desires for bases there. ...

But 'mutual trust' was entirely lacking, and the diplomatic phrase never had a more hollow ring. On the 12th Hitler's War Directive No. 18 had said:

> Political discussions have been initiated with the aim of clarifying Russia's attitude for the time being. Irrespective of the results of these discussions, all preparations for the East which have already been verbally ordered will be continued.

While the diplomats were talking the military plans were progressing. Hitler himself did not find the result of the conversations as satisfactory as others did, regarded Russia's further questions about the Three Power Pact as pure evasion, and was dominated by his growing desire to take the offensive. Raeder, who saw him on the 14th, noted that 'the Leader is still inclined to instigate the conflict with Russia'. After Molotov left, Hitler saw a number of his executives and made it plain to them that he was going to invade Russia. Their attempts to dissuade him from the venture were in vain. When they argued that it meant war on two fronts—a situation which had proved fatal to Germany in the First World War—he retorted that it was impossible to rely on Russia remaining quiet until Britain's resistance was broken. To overcome Britain required an expansion of the air force and navy, which meant reducing the army, but no such reduction was feasible while Russia remained a menace. The situation had been changed by 'Russia's unreliability, as evident in the Balkan States'. So 'Operation Sealion' would have to be postponed.

On December 5 Hitler received Halder's report on the eastern plan, and on the 18th issued 'Directive No. 21—Case Barbarossa.' It opened with the decisive statement: 'The German armed forces must be prepared to crush Soviet Russia in a quick campaign before the end of the war against England.'

> For this purpose the Army will have to employ all available units, with the reservation that the occupied countries will have to be safeguarded against surprise attacks. The concentration of the main effort of the Navy remains unequivocally against England!
>
> If the occasion arises, I shall order the concentration of troops for action against Soviet Russia eight weeks before the intended beginning of operations. Preparations requiring more time are—if this has not already been done—to begin immediately, and are to be completed by May 15, 1941. [This was considered the earliest possible date for suitable weather conditions.] Great caution has to be exercised so that the intention to attack will not be recognised. . . .
>
> The mass of the Russian Army in Western Russia is to be destroyed in daring operations by driving four deep wedges with tanks, and the retreat of the enemy's battle-ready forces into the wide spaces of Russia is to be prevented.

The directive went on to say that if these results did not suffice to cripple

Russia, her last industrial area in the Urals could be eliminated by the Luftwaffe. The Red Fleet would be paralysed by the capture of the Baltic bases. Rumania would help by pinning down the Russian forces in the south and by providing auxiliary service in the rear—Hitler had sounded the new Rumanian dictator, General Antonescu, in November about participating in an attack on Russia.

The phrase 'if occasion arises' has an indefinite sound, but there seems little doubt that Hitler's intention was fixed. The qualification may be explained by a later passage in the directive: 'All orders which shall be issued by the High Commanders in accordance with this instruction have to be clothed in such terms that they may be taken as measures of precaution in case Russia should change her present attitude towards ourselves.' The plan was to be cloaked by an elaborate deception programme, and it came naturally to Hitler to take the lead in this respect.

Moreover, deception had to be practised on his own people as well as on the enemy. So many of those to whom he broached the project were troubled about the risks of invading Russia, especially as it meant a two-front war, that he thought it wise to wear the appearance of reserving a final decision. This would give them time to become acclimatised to the change of wind, while giving him time to produce more persuasive evidence of Russia's hostile intentions. His generals, in particular, expressed such doubts that he was anxious about the effect of their half-heartedness. Although he could command obedience under the oath they had given him, that would not suffice to produce in their minds the determination required for success. As he had to make use of them as professional instruments it was necessary to convince them.

On January 10 a fresh treaty was signed with Russia that embodied the results of the November conversations with Molotov on frontier and economic questions. The surface was thus made to look smoother. But Hitler's private view was expressed in his comment that Stalin was an 'ice-cold blackmailer'. At the same time disquieting reports came from Rumania and Bulgaria about Russian activity there.

On the 19th Hitler was visited by Mussolini, and at this meeting spoke of his difficulties with Russia. He did not reveal his own offensive plans, but significantly mentioned that he had received a strong protest from Russia about the concentration of German troops in Rumania. An important sidelight on his own thought was contained in his remark: 'Formerly Russia would have been no danger at all, for she cannot imperil us in the least; but now in the age of airpower, the Rumanian oilfields can be turned into an expanse of smoking debris, by air attack from Russia and the Mediterranean,

GERMAN ARMY GROUPS IN THE EAST*
Showing Changes of Designation and Commanders
June 1941 – May 1945

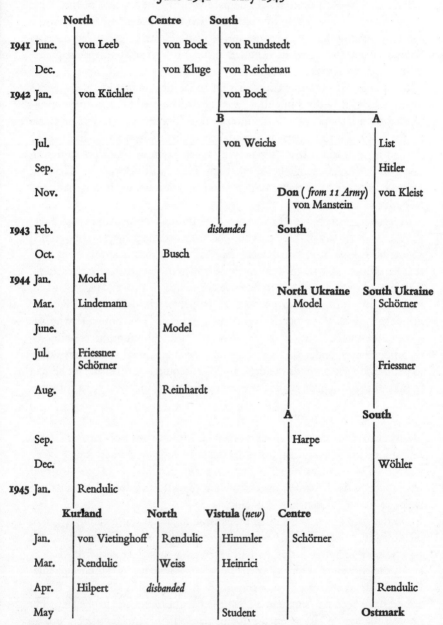

	North	Centre	South	
1941 June.	von Leeb	von Bock	von Rundstedt	
Dec.		von Kluge	von Reichenau	
1942 Jan.	von Küchler		von Bock	
			B	**A**
Jul.			von Weichs	List
Sep.				Hitler
Nov.			**Don** (*from 11 Army*) von Manstein	von Kleist
1943 Feb.			*disbanded*	**South**
Oct.		Busch		
1944 Jan.	Model			
			North Ukraine	**South Ukraine**
Mar.	Lindemann		Model	Schörner
June.		Model		
Jul.	Friessner Schörner			Friessner
Aug.		Reinhardt		
			A	**South**
Sep.			Harpe	
Dec.				Wöhler
1945 Jan.	Rendulic			
	Kurland	**North**	**Vistula** (*new*)	**Centre**
Jan.	von Vietinghoff	Rendulic	Himmler	Schörner
Mar.	Rendulic	Weiss	Heinrici	
Apr.	Hilpert	*disbanded*		Rendulic
May			Student	**Ostmark**

* Reproduced by kind permission of Lieutenant-Colonel Albert Seaton from Appendix B of his book *The Russo-German War, 1941–1945* (London: Arthur Barker, 1970).

and the life of the Axis depends on these oilfields.' That was also his argument to his own generals who suggested that, even if the Russians were intending an invasion, the risk could be adequately met by increasing the defensive strength of the German forces behind the frontier, instead of launching an offensive into Russia.

On February 3 Hitler approved the final text of the 'Barbarossa' plan, following a conference of his military chiefs at Berchtesgaden, in which the points of the plan were unfolded. Keitel gave an estimate of the enemy's strength in western Russia as approximately 100 infantry divisions, twenty-five cavalry divisions, and the equivalent of thirty mechanised divisions. This was close to the mark, for when the invasion was launched the Russians had available in the west 88 infantry divisions, seven cavalry divisions, and fifty-four tank and motorised divisions. Keitel then said that the German strength would be not quite so large, 'but far superior in quality'. Actually the invading armies comprised 116 infantry divisions (of which fourteen were motorised), a cavalry division, and nineteen armoured divisions—besides nine lines-of-communication divisions. The enumeration of strength was not calculated to allay the disquiet of the generals, for it showed they were embarking on a great offensive without any odds in their favour, and with marked adverse odds in the decisive element—the armoured forces. It was clear that the planners were gambling heavily on the superiority of quality.

Keitel continued: 'Russian operational intentions are unknown. There are no strong forces at the frontier. Any retreat could only be of small extent, since the Baltic States and the Ukraine are vital to the Russians for supply reasons.' That seemed reasonable at the time, but proved an over-optimistic assumption.

The invading forces were to be divided into three army groups, and their operational tasks were outlined. The northern one (under Leeb) was to attack from East Prussia through the Baltic states towards Leningrad. The central one (under Bock) was to strike from the Warsaw area towards Minsk and Smolensk, along the Moscow highway. The southern one (under Rundstedt) was to attack south of the Pripet Marshes, extending down to Rumania, with the Dnieper and Kiev as its objectives. The main weight was to be concentrated in the central group, to give it a superiority of strength. It was reckoned that there would be bare equality in the north, and an inferiority of strength in the southern sector.

In his survey, Keitel remarked that Hungary's attitude was still doubtful, and emphasised that arrangements with those countries that might co-operate with Germany could be made only at the eleventh hour, for reasons of secrecy. Rumania, however, had to be an exception to this rule, because her co-operation was 'vital'. (Hitler had just previously seen Antonescu again, and asked him to permit German troops to pass through Rumania to support the Italians in Greece, but Antonescu had hesitated, arguing that such a step might precipitate a Russian invasion of Rumania. At a third meeting Hitler promised him not only the return of Bessarabia and northern Bukovina, but the possession of a stretch of southern Russia 'up to the Dnieper' as a recompense for Rumanian aid in the attack.)

Keitel added that the Gibraltar operation was no longer possible as the bulk of the German artillery had been sent east. While 'Operation Sealion' had also been shelved, 'everything possible should be done to maintain the impression among our own troops that the invasion of Britain is being further prepared'. To spread the idea certain areas on the Channel coast and in Norway were to be suddenly closed, while as a double bluff the eastward concentration was to be represented as a deception exercise for the landing in England.

The military plan was coupled with a large-scale economic 'Plan Oldenburg' for the exploitation of the conquered Soviet territory. An Economic Staff was created, entirely separate from the General Staff. A report of May 2, on its examination of the problem, opened with the statements: 'The war can only be continued if all armed forces are fed by Russia in the third year of the war. There is no doubt that many millions of people will starve to death in Russia if we take out of the country the things necessary for us.' It is not clear whether this was simply a cold-blooded scientific statement or intended as a warning against excessive aims and demands. The report went on to say: 'The seizure and transfer of oil seeds and oil cakes are of prime importance; grain is only secondary.' An earlier report by General Thomas, Chief of the War Economy Department of the OKW (Armed Forces General Staff), had pointed out that the conquest of all European Russia might relieve Germany's food problem, if the transport problem could be solved, but would not meet other important parts of her economic problem—the supply of 'india rubber, tungsten, copper, platinum, tin, asbestos, and manila hemp would remain unsolved until communication with the Far East can be assured'. Such warnings had no effect in restraining Hitler. But another conclusion, that 'the Caucasian fuel supply is indispensable for the exploitation of the occupied territories', was to have a very important effect in spurring him to extend his advance to the point of losing his balance.

The 'Barbarossa' plan suffered even worse from a preliminary upset that had far-reaching delayed effect. This was due to the psychological effect, on

Hitler, of the double diplomatic rebuff he received from Greece and Yugo-Slavia, with British backing.

Before striking at Russia Hitler wanted to have his right shoulder free—from British interference. He had hoped to secure control of the Balkans without serious fighting—by practising armed diplomacy. He felt that after his victories in the West it ought to succeed more easily than ever. Russia had smoothed his way into Rumania by her push into Bessarabia; Rumania had fallen into his arms on the recoil. The next step also proved easy. On March 1 the Bulgarian Government swallowed his bribe and committed itself to a pact whereby the German forces were allowed to move through its territory and take up positions on the Greek frontier. The Soviet Government broadcast its disapproval of this departure from neutrality, but its abstention from anything more forcible made Hitler more sure that Russia was not ready for war.

The Greek Government was less responsive to Hitler's diplomatic approaches, as was natural after the way Greece had been invaded by his Axis partner. Nor did the Greek Government wilt at his threats. The spirit of the Greek people had been aroused and was heightened by their success in repelling Mussolini's invasion. In February arrangements had been made for their reinforcement by British troops, and these began to land a few days after the Germans' entry into Bulgaria.

The challenge provoked Hitler to put under way his attack on Greece—which was launched a month later. This was a needless diversion from his main path. For the force that Britain could furnish was not large enough to be capable of doing more than cause a slight irritation to his right shoulder, and the Greeks were fully occupied in dealing with the Italians.

The adverse effect on his Russian plan was intensified by the events in Yugo-Slavia. Here his approach had a favourable start. Under German pressure the Yugo-Slav Government agreed to link itself to the Axis on a compromise basis of being released from military obligations, but with the secret condition that the Belgrade-Nish rail line towards the Greek frontier was to be available for German troops. The Yugo-Slav representatives signed the Pact on March 25. Two days later a military coup d'état was carried out in Belgrade by General Simovich, the Chief of the Yugo-Slav Air Force, and a group of young officers. They seized control of the radio station and the telephone centre, turned out the Government, established a new one under Simovich's leadership, and then defied the German demands. British agents had helped to foster the plot, and when the news of its success reached London Churchill announced in a speech: 'I have great news for you and the whole country. Early this morning Yugo-Slavia found its soul.' He went on to declare that the new Government would receive 'all possible aid and succour' from Britain.

The coup revolutionised the Balkan situation. Hitler could not tolerate such an affront, and Churchill's glee infuriated him. He at once decided to invade Yugo-Slavia as well as Greece. The necessary moves were made so swiftly that he was able to launch the blow ten days later, on April 6.

The direct results of this Balkan defiance were pitiful. Yugo-Slavia was overrun within a week, and her capital devastated by the opening air attack. Greece was overrun in just over three weeks, and the British force hustled back into its ships, after a long retreat with little fighting. It had been out-manoeuvred at each stage. The outcome reflected on Churchill's judgement, and on that of those who supported him by declaring the feasibility of a successful military intervention—in view not merely of Britain's loss of credit but of the vast burden of misery that was cast on the people of Yugo-Slavia and Greece. The sense of being let down had lasting effects. Moreover, it is one of the ironies of history that the ultimate issue of Churchill's initiative was the resurrection of Yugo-Slavia in the form of a state hostile to all he represented.

But the indirect results of the episode were vital, and they reflected on Hitler's judgement. Operating with such a small margin of force—even when reckoned as quantity × quality—he could not afford to conduct a campaign in Yugo-Slavia and Greece at the same time as his invasion of Russia. A particular handicap was his numerical disadvantage in tanks compared with the Russians. A quick conquest of the Balkans depended on employing panzer divisions, and he would need every one of them that could be collected before he could venture to launch the offensive in Russia. So on April 1 'Barbarossa' was postponed—from the middle of May to the second half of June.

It remains an amazing military achievement that Hitler was able to conquer two countries so quickly that he could keep the new date of entry into Russia. Indeed, his generals considered that if the British had succeeded in holding Greece 'Barbarossa' could not have been carried out. In the event, the delay was only five weeks. But it was a factor in forfeiting his chance of victory over Russia, which can be coupled with the Yugo-Slav coup d'état, a fortuitous delay in August—from indecision of mind—and with the early coming of winter that year.

By May 1 the British had re-embarked from the southern beaches of Greece, save for those who were cut off and captured. That same day Hitler fixed the date of 'Barbarossa'. His directive summarised the respective strengths and then added:

Estimate of the course of operations—Presumably violent battles on the frontiers, lasting up to four weeks. In the course of the further development weaker resistance is expected. A Russian will fight on an appointed spot to his last breath.

On June 6 Keitel issued the detailed timetable for the venture. Besides enumerating the forces to be employed in the invasion, it showed that forty-six infantry divisions had been left in the West facing Britain, though no more than one was motorised, and only one armoured brigade had been left there. Operations 'Attila' (the seizure of French North Africa) and 'Isabella' (the counter to a possible British move in Portugal) could 'still be executed at ten days' notice, but not simultaneously'. 'Luftflotte 2 has been withdrawn from action and transferred to the East, while Luftflotte 3 has taken over sole command in the conduct of air warfare against Britain.'

These orders intimated that negotiations with the Finnish General Staff, to secure their co-operation in the attack, had begun on May 25. The Rumanians, already secured, were to be informed of the final arrangements on June 15. On the 16th the Hungarians were to be given a hint to guard their frontier more strongly. On the following day all schools in eastern Germany were to be closed. German merchant ships were to leave Russia without attracting notice, and outward sailings were to cease. As from the 18th 'the intention to attack need no longer be camouflaged'. It would then be too late for the Russians to carry out any large-scale reinforcement measures. The latest possible time for the cancellation of the offensive was given as 1300 hours on the 21st, and the codeword in that contingency would be 'Altona'—for starting the attack it would be 'Dortmund'. The hour fixed for crossing the frontier was 0330 on the 22nd.

Despite German precautions, the British Intelligence Service obtained remarkably good information of Hitler's intentions long in advance, and conveyed it to the Russians. It even accurately predicted the exact date of the invasion—a week before it was finally fixed. But its repeated warnings were received with an attitude of disbelief, and of continued trust in the Soviet-German Pact, which the British found as baffling as it was exasperating. They felt that the Russian disbelief was genuine—that feeling was reflected in Churchill's broadcast when the news of Hitler's attack came—and when the Red Army suffered initial disasters they ascribed these partly to the results of it being taken by surprise.

A study of the Russian press and broadcasts would hardly have supported that impression. From April onwards they contained significant indications of precautionary measures, while showing an awareness of German troop movements. At the same time there were much more prominent references to Germany's strict observance of the Pact, combined with denunciations of British and American attempts to sow discord between Russia and Germany, especially by spreading rumours of German preparations to strike at Russia. A broadcast of this nature on June 13, in Stalin's distinctive style, remarked that 'the despatch of German troops into the east and north-east areas of Germany must be assumed to be due to motives which have no connection with Russia'—a remark that might well encourage Hitler to assume that his deception programme had here succeeded in making the desired impression. Double bluff can be met by redoubling. The same broadcast answered foreign reports of the call-up of Russian reservists by explaining that this was merely for training prior to the usual summer manoeuvres. On the 20th Moscow wireless gave a glowing account of the military exercises that were in progress, near the Pripet Marshes—which may have been calculated to fortify confidence at home. It also announced that the civil air raid defences of Moscow were to be tested 'under realistic conditions' on Sunday, the 22nd. Even so, foreign reports of a coming German invasion were once again described as 'delirious fabrications by forces hostile to Russia'.

The Germans were informed of the British efforts to warn the Russians. Indeed, on April 24 their naval attaché in Moscow reported: 'The British Ambassador predicts June 22 as the day of the outbreak of war.' But this did not lead Hitler to vary the date. He may have reckoned on the Russians' discounting any report from British quarters, or have felt that the actual day did not matter.

It is difficult to gauge how far Hitler believed that the Russians were unprepared for his blow. For he often veiled his thoughts from his own circle. Reports from his observers in Moscow had been telling him since the spring that the Soviet Government was apprehensively passive and anxious to appease him; that there was no danger of Russia attacking Germany as long as Stalin lived. As late as June 7 the German Ambassador there reported: 'All observations show that Stalin and Molotov, who alone are responsible for Russian foreign policy, are doing everything to avoid a conflict with Germany.' Confirmation of this seemed to come not only from the way the Russians were keeping their deliveries under the trade agreement, but by their sops to Hitler of withdrawing diplomatic recognition of Yugo-Slavia, Belgium, and Norway.

On the other hand, Hitler often declared that Nazi diplomats in Moscow were the worst-informed in the world. He also furnished his generals with reports of an opposite nature—that the Russians were preparing an offensive, which it was urgent to forestall. Here he may have been deliberately deceiving them, rather than believing the reports himself, for he was having continued difficulty with his generals, who were still putting up arguments for abstaining from the invasion. Or a belated realisation that the Russians were not so unready as he had hoped may have led him, on the rebound, to assume that their intentions were similar to his own. After crossing the frontier the generals found little sign of Russian offensive preparations near the front, and thus saw that Hitler had misled them.

CHAPTER 13

THE INVASION OF RUSSIA

The issue in Russia depended less on strategy and tactics than on space, logistics, and mechanics. Although some of the operational decisions were of great importance they did not count so much as mechanical deficiency in conjunction with excess of space, and their effect has to be measured in relation to these basic factors. The space factor can be easily grasped by looking at the map of Russia, but the mechanical factor requires more explanation. A preliminary analysis of it is essential to the understanding of events.

As in Hitler's previous invasions everything turned on the mechanised forces, though they formed only a small fraction of the total forces. The nineteen panzer divisions available amounted to barely one tenth of the total number of divisions, German and satellite. The vast residue included only fourteen that were motorised and thus able to keep up with the armoured spearheads.

Altogether the German Army possessed twenty-one panzer divisions in 1941 compared with ten in 1940. But that apparent doubling of its armoured strength was an illusion. It had been achieved mainly by dilution. In the Western campaign the core of each division was a tank brigade of two regiments—each comprising 160 fighting tanks. Before the invasion of Russia a tank regiment was removed from each division, and on each 'rib' a fresh division was formed.

Some of the best qualified tank experts argued against the decision, pointing out that its real effect was to multiply the number of staffs and of unarmoured auxiliary troops in the so-called armoured forces while leaving the scale of armoured troops unchanged, and thus diminishing the punch that each division could deliver. Of its 17,000 men, only some 2,600 would now be 'tank men'. But Hitler was obdurate. Seeing the vastness of Russia's spaces he wanted to feel that he had a larger number of divisions that could strike deep, and he reckoned that the technical inferiority of the Russian forces would compensate the dilution of his own. He could also stress the fact that owing to the increasing output of the later Mark III and Mark IV types, two-thirds of the armoured strength of each division would now consist of medium tanks—with larger guns and doubled thickness of armour—whereas in the Western campaign two-thirds had been light tanks. The power of its punch would thus be increased even though the scale was halved. That was a good argument up to a point, and for the moment.

The reduction in the scale of tanks, however, emphasised the fundamental flaw in the German 'armoured division'—that the bulk of its elements were unarmoured and lacked cross-country mobility. The greatest development which the tank had produced in warfare—more important even than its revival of the use of armour—was its ability to move off the road, to be free from dependence on the smooth and hard surface of a prepared track. Whereas the wheeled motor-vehicle merely accelerated the pace of marching, and reproduced the effect of the railway in a rather more flexible form, the tank had revolutionised mobility. By laying its own track as it moved it dispensed with the need to follow a fixed route along a prefabricated track, and thus superseded one-dimensional by two-dimensional movement.

The significance of that potentiality had been realised by the original British exponents of mechanised warfare. In the pattern of armoured force they had proposed at the end of World War I all the vehicles, including those which carried supplies, were to be of the tracked cross-country type. Their vision had not been fulfilled even in the German Army, which had done more than any other to make use of it.

In the reorganised panzer division of 1941 there were less than 300 tracked vehicles in all, while there were nearly 3,000 wheeled vehicles, mostly of a road-bound type. The superabundance of such vehicles had not mattered in the Western campaign, when a badly disposed defence suffered a far-reaching collapse and the attacker could profit by a network of well-paved roads in exploiting his opportunity. But in the East, where proper roads were scarce, it proved a decisive brake in the long run. The Germans here paid the penalty for being, in practice, twenty years behind the theory which they had adopted as their key to success.

That they succeeded as far as they did was due to their opponents being still more backward in equipment. For although the Russians possessed a large numerical superiority in tanks, their total quantity of motor vehicles was so limited that even their armoured forces did not have a full scale of motor transport. That proved a vital handicap in manœuvring to meet the German panzer drives.

The Germans' armoured strength in this offensive totalled 3,550 tanks, which was only eight hundred more than in the invasion of the West. (The Russians, however, claimed in August that they had destroyed 8,000.)

The total Red Army tank strength, according to Stalin's despatch to Roosevelt of 30 July 1941, amounted to 24,000, of which more than half were in Western Russia.

Early on Sunday morning, June 22, the German flood poured across the frontier, in three great parallel surges between the Baltic Sea and the Carpathian Mountains.

On the left, the Northern Army Group under Leeb crossed the East Prussian frontier into Russian-occupied Lithuania. On the left centre, east of Warsaw, the Central Army Group under Bock started a massive advance against both flanks of the bulge that the Russian front formed in northern Poland. On the right centre there was a sixty-mile stretch of calm, where the German flood was divided by the western end of the Pripet marshland area. On the right, the Southern Army Group under Rundstedt surged forward on the north side of the Lwow bulge formed by the Russian front in Galicia, near the Carpathians.

The gap between Bock's right and Rundstedt's left was deliberately left to gain concentration of force and the clearest possible run. The speed of the German advance was thereby increased in the first stage. But since this Pripet sector was left untouched, the Russians were granted a sheltered area where their reserves could assemble under cover, and from which, at a later stage, they could develop a series of flank counterattacks southward which put a brake on Rundstedt's advance on Kiev. This would have mattered less if Bock's advance north of the Pripet Marshes had succeeded in its aim of trapping the Russian armies around Minsk.

The German offensive had its centre of gravity on the left centre. Here Bock was entrusted with the leading role for which he had been originally cast in the invasion of the West, only to see it transferred from his army group to Rundstedt's. For his decisive mission he was given the larger part of the armoured forces, two panzer groups under Guderian and Hoth, while the other army groups had one apiece. Bock also had the 4th and 9th Armies, each of three infantry corps.

The panzer groups (later redesignated panzer armies) each comprised four to five panzer divisions, and three motorised divisions.

While all the German leaders agreed that the issue would turn on the use of these panzer groups, a conflict of opinion arose as to the best way of using them. This 'battle of theories' was of far-reaching importance. Some senior commanders wanted to destroy the Russian armies in a decisive battle of the classic encirclement pattern, to be brought off as soon as possible after crossing the frontier. In framing such a plan they adhered to the orthodox theory of strategy that had been formulated by Clausewitz, established by Moltke, and developed by Schlieffen. They favoured it all the more strongly because of their anxiety over the risk of pushing far into Russia before the main Russian armies were beaten. To ensure the success of the plan they insisted that the panzer groups must co-operate with the infantry corps in the battle by wheeling inwards from either flank, as pincers, and closing round the rear of the enemy forces to complete the ring.

The tank experts, headed by Guderian, had a different idea. They wanted the panzer groups to drive as deep as they could as fast as they could—following the course that had proved so decisive in France. Guderian argued that his group and Hoth's should lose no time in exploiting their cut-through in the direction of Moscow, and at the least reach the Dnieper before wheeling in. The sooner they gained that line the more likely that the Russians' resistance would be dislocated as that of the French had been, and the more chance that the Dnieper might serve the same anvil purpose that the English Channel had fulfilled in 1940. In Guderian's view, the encirclement of the Russian forces in the space between the two panzer thrusts should be left to the infantry corps, helped by relatively small detachments which the panzer groups might switch inward as they raced onward.

The 'battle of theories' was decided in favour of orthodoxy—by the decision of Hitler. For all his boldness he was not bold enough to stake his fortunes on the card to which he owed his previous coups. His compromise with conservatism turned out more adversely than in 1940. Although the tank experts themselves were given a higher place than in 1940, they were refused the chance of fulfilling it in the way they considered best. Hitler's decision was influenced not only by his doubts of their way but by his vivid imagination—his mind was filled by a vision of rounding up the bulk of the Red Army in one gigantic ring.

That vision became a will-o'-the-wisp, luring him deeper and deeper into Russia. For the first two attempts did not succeed. The third brought a bigger bag of prisoners, but carried him beyond the Dnieper. At the fourth attempt over half a million Russians were trapped, but winter weather intervened to check the Germans' exploitation of the yawning gap in the front. Each of the staged battles had consumed time in the process of opening and closing the pincers, with the result that the strategical object was missed in trying to complete the tactical design.

Whether Guderian's method would have proved more successful remains an open question. But it was supported even at the time by some of the ablest members of the German General Staff who did not belong to the tank school of thought, and in retrospect their judgement was still more definitely in its favour. While recognising the difficulties of reinforcement and supply to such a deep-thrusting advance they felt that these could have been overcome by making full use of the available air transport and by stripping the panzer forces of impedimenta—pushing forward their fighting elements, and concentrating on the maintenance of these, while leaving the accessory motorised columns to follow on. But that idea of moving light in Sherman style was too contrary to the convention of European warfare to gain general acceptance at this stage.

The 'battle of theories' having been settled in favour of orthodox strategy, the plan was designed to produce a vast encirclement that should net, and ensure the annihilation of, the main Russian forces before the Dnieper was reached. To increase the chances, the plan for Bock's front embraced a short-range encircling manœuvre by the infantry corps of the 4th and 9th Armies and a longer-range manœuvre outside it by the panzer groups, which were to drive deeper than the former before wheeling inwards. That telescopic pattern went some way, though not far enough, to meet the views of Guderian, Bock and Hoth.

The axis of the advance was along the great motor-road to Minsk, and Moscow. This ran through the sector of the 4th Army, under Kluge, to which Guderian's panzer group was attached. The entry was barred by the fortress of Brest-Litovsk, which itself was covered by the River Bug. Thus the initial problem was to secure a bridgehead over the river and clear away the fortress obstacle, so that the subsequent advance could gain momentum from the use of the motor-road.

In weighing the problem, the question arose whether the panzer divisions should wait until the infantry divisions had made a gap, or whether they should co-operate in the breakthrough, alongside the infantry divisions. The second course was adopted, to help in saving time. While infantry divisions were used to capture the fortress, they were flanked by a couple of panzer divisions on either side. After forcing the passage of the Bug, these swept round Brest-Litovsk and converged on the stretch of the motor-road beyond it. As another aid to celerity all the forces engaged in the breakthrough were temporarily placed under Guderian's executive control. And when the breakthrough was achieved the panzer group sped forward independently—like a shell from a gun.

Through the wideness of the front and their by-passing tactics, as well as the suddenness of the attack, Bock's armies made a deep penetration at many points. On the second day the armoured forces on his right wing reached Kobryn, forty miles beyond Brest-Litovsk, while his left wing captured the fortress and rail-centre of Grodno. The Russian salient in northern Poland—the Bialystok salient—was visibly changing its shape and being pinched into a wasp-waist. The pinch became more severe in the following days as the wings converged on Baranovichi threatening to cut off all the Russian forces in the forward zone. The progress of the manœuvre was helped by the ineffectiveness of the Russians' numerically strong tank forces.

But the Germans' progress was retarded by the extremely tough resistance of the Russians. The Germans usually out-manœuvred their opponents but they could not outfight them. Surrounded forces were sometimes compelled to surrender, but this often came only at the end of prolonged resistance—and their stubbornly slow reaction to a strategically hopeless situation and the delay put a serious brake on the attacker's plans. It counted all the more in a country where communications were sparse.

The effect was first seen in the opening attack at Brest-Litovsk. Here, the garrison of the old citadel held out for a week in spite of intense bombardment from massed artillery and from the air, exacting a heavy price from the assaulting troops before it was at last overwhelmed. That initial experience, repeated at other points, opened the Germans' eyes to what was in store for them, while the stiff opposition that was met at many road-centres put a brake on their by-passing movements by blocking the routes needed by their road-bound supply columns.

The dawning sense of frustration was deepened by the character of the country that their invasion traversed. The impression it made was aptly expressed by one of the German generals:

> The spaces seemed endless, the horizons nebulous. We were depressed by the monotony of the landscape, and the immensity of the stretches of forest, marsh and plain. Good roads were so few, and bad tracks so numerous, while rain quickly turned the sand or loam into a morass. The villages looked wretched and melancholy, with their straw-thatched wooden houses. Nature was hard, and in her midst were human beings just as hard and insensitive—indifferent to weather, hunger, and thirst, and almost as indifferent to life and losses, pestilence, and famine. The Russian civilian was tough, and the Russian soldier still tougher. He seemed to have an illimitable capacity for obedience and endurance.

The first attempted encirclement reached a climax around Slonim, a hundred miles beyond the original front, where the inner pincers almost closed round the two Russian armies that had been assembled in the Bialystok salient. But the Germans were not quick enough in completing the encirclement, and about half of the enveloped forces managed to escape, though in small and unco-ordinated groups. The preponderance of unmechanised troops in the German 4th and 9th Armies was a handicap on the fulfilment of the design.

The main armoured forces on the wings drove more than a hundred miles deeper, crossed the 1939 Russian frontier, and then wheeled inwards beyond Minsk—which was captured on June 30, the ninth day. That night one of Guderian's wide-flung spearheads reached the historic Beresina river near Bobruisk—ninety miles south-east of Minsk, and less than forty miles from the Dnieper. But the effort to close the ring failed, and with the failure of their grand encirclement Hitler's dream of a quickly decisive victory faded. Sudden rain—for which the French had prayed in vain the previous summer—came to the rescue of the hard-pressed Russians. It turned the sandy soil into mud.

That was far worse a handicap in Russia than it would have been in France, since it not only cramped tactical manœuvring across country but held up strategic road movements. For the one good tarred road in the whole area was the new highway that ran past Minsk direct to Moscow, and that was only of partial service to Hitler's plan—which contemplated, not a race for Moscow, but a widecast encircling manœuvre that had to use the soft-surfaced roads on either flank. Following the rainstorms of early July, these 'quicksands' sucked down the invader's mobility, and multiplied the effect of the stubborn resistance offered by many isolated pockets of Russian troops within the area that the Germans had overrun. Although over 300,000 prisoners were taken in the double battle of encirclement around Bialystok and Minsk, roughly the same number was able to slip out before the net was drawn tight. Their extrication was of importance in providing a means of stiffening the next defensive line—which ran in front and behind the Dnieper.

The nature of the country also became an increasing brake in this crucial stage. South-east of Minsk lies a vast stretch of forest and swamp, while the Beresina is not a clear-cut river-line but a bunch of streams winding through a black peat marsh. The Germans found that only on two roads—the main highway through Orsha, and the one to Mogilev—were the bridges built to carry heavy loads. On the other roads they were rickety wooden structures. Although the Germans had moved fast, they found that the Russians had blown up the bridges that mattered most. The invaders also began to come upon minefields for the first time, and suffered the more delay from these because of the way that the advance was confined to the roads. The Beresina was almost as effective in checking Hitler's advance as in wrecking Napoleon's retreat.

All these factors multiplied the impediment to the intended process of closing the trap round the Russians in the area west of the Dnieper.

The frustration of the grand encirclement now drew the German Command into that advance beyond the Dnieper which they had hoped to avoid. They were already over 300 miles deep into Russia. The pincers opened out again to execute the design of a fresh encirclement, aimed to close in behind the Russians on the line of the Dnieper, beyond Smolensk. But the first two days of July had passed in the process of trying to close the Minsk trap and in bringing up the infantry corps of the 4th and 9th Armies—some of which marched twenty miles a day for two and a half weeks in coming up to help in breaking through the Stalin line.

This assault proved easier than the German Command had anticipated, as the retreating Russians had not time to reorganise for a proper stand nor to improve the defences, which were far from complete. The Dnieper itself was the biggest obstacle, but Guderian's armoured divisions overcame this by swift surprise attacks at a number of points away from the main crossings. By the 12th the Germans had breached the Stalin line over a wide front between Rogachev and Vitebsk, and were racing for Smolensk. The ease of the breakthrough suggested that there would have been more gain than risk in allowing an armoured force to push ahead in the first place, as Guderian had wished.

The difficulties of the country, as increased by the bursts of rain, were a greater check than the disorganised opposition. In these circumstances a heavy forfeit was paid for the time lost in the pause. For each heavy shower temporarily reduced the invaders' mobility to stagnation. From the air, it was a strange spectacle—stationary 'panzer' blobs strung out across the landscape for a distance of a hundred miles and more.

The tanks might have continued to advance, but these and the other tracked vehicles formed only a small part of each so-called armoured division. Their supplies and their massive infantry element were carried in wheeled vehicles of a large and heavy type, which could not move off the road, nor move on it if the surface turned into mud. When the sun came out again, the sandy roads dried quickly—and the procession then moved on. But the cumulative delay was a serious handicap on the strategic plan.

This was not outwardly apparent because of the relatively rapid advance by Guderian's panzer group along the main highway to Smolensk—which was entered on the 16th. The stretch of over a hundred miles between the Dnieper and the Desna was covered within a week. But Hoth's panzer group on the northern wing was delayed by the swamps as well as the rainstorms, on its course. Its slow progress naturally affected the fulfilment of Hitler's encirclement plan, and gave the Russians more time to rally their forces around Smolensk. Stiffer resistance on both flanks was met in the final stage of the effort. Indeed, the resistance was almost too stubborn, for the pincers came within ten miles of closing, and the Germans reckoned that half a million Russians were caught in the trap. Although a large part were extricated, a further 300,000 nevertheless went into captivity by 5 August,

That incomplete victory left the Germans with an unsolved problem. It meant that their path to Moscow, a further 200 miles ahead, was still blocked by considerable forces—which were being continuously increased by newly mobilised reinforcements. At the same time the Germans' capacity to mount a fresh effort was cramped by the difficulty of bringing up reinforcements on their side over the bad roads.

That spelt an inevitable delay, but nothing like the length of the delay that now occurred. For October came before the advance on Moscow was resumed. The best two months of the summer were allowed to pass while Bock's armies were halted on the Desna. The causes are to be found in Hitler's uncertainty of mind, coupled with the progress of Rundstedt's armies south of the Pripet marshes.

On that southern front the Germans had enjoyed no initial superiority of force. Indeed, they had started with odds against them that on paper looked formidable. The Russians' South-western Army Group under Marshal Budenny comprised thirty tank and motorised divisions, five cavalry divisions, and forty-five infantry divisions in southern Poland and the Ukraine; of these, six tank and motorised divisions, three cavalry divisions, and thirteen infantry divisions were in Bessarabia, facing the Rumanians. In armour it had nearly twice the strength of Marshal Timoshenko's Western Army Group which had faced the main German drive. Altogether, Budenny had about 5,000 tanks, of various types, whereas Kleist's panzer group—which formed Rundstedt's armoured punch—consisted of only 600 tanks. Moreover, a large proportion of the latter had been engaged in the Greek campaign, and been allowed little time for overhaul before they were launched into this greater venture.

Rundstedt had to depend for an advantage on surprise, speed, space—and the opposing commanders. Budenny, the famous old cavalry hero of the Civil War, was most aptly described by one of his own officers as 'a man with an immense moustache, but a very small brain'. Some of the best Russian commanders had been eliminated in the pre-war purges, and those who had survived as politically safe were often militarily unsafe. It was only after these too solid seniors had been weeded out under the test of war that the pick of a younger generation came to the top.

Rundstedt's main effort was concentrated on his left wing, along the Bug. That plan made the most of his limited strength, while profiting by the fact that his starting line lay well behind the flank of the Lwow salient formed by the Russian zone in Galicia. The attack was thus delivered from a natural wedge, which had only to be driven in a little further before it began to threaten the communications of all the Russian forces near the Carpathians. After Reichenau's 6th Army had forced the crossings of the Bug, Kleist's armoured forces were launched in a drive through the breach towards Luck and Brody.

Surprise helped not only to facilitate his initial breakthrough, but to nullify the potentially dangerous countermove which the Russians might otherwise have made. Knowing that they had twenty-five divisions facing Hungary's Carpathian frontier, Rundstedt had anticipated that these might swing round and strike at his right flank as he advanced towards Luck. Instead, they retreated. (That reaction, coupled with the lack of preparedness found in the Russians' forward zone, led Rundstedt and other German commanders to doubt whether there had been any justification for Hitler's argument that the Russians were about to take the offensive.)

Even with this flying start, Rundstedt's forces were not able to make such rapid progress as Bock's in the left centre. Guderian urged the importance of keeping the Russians on the run, and allowing them no time to rally. He was convinced that he could reach Moscow if no time was wasted, and that such a thrust at the nerve-centre of Stalin's power might paralyse Russia's resistance. Hoth shared his views and Bock endorsed them. But Hitler reverted to his own original idea in a directive of July 19 for the next stage of operations. The panzer forces were to be taken away from Bock, in the centre, and sent to the wings—Guderian's panzer group was to wheel southward to help in overcoming the Russian armies facing Rundstedt in the Ukraine, while Hoth's panzer group was to turn northward to aid Leeb's attack on Leningrad.

Once again Brauchitsch temporised, instead of at once pressing for a different plan. He argued that before any further operations were started, the panzer forces must have a rest to overhaul their machines and get up replacements. Hitler agreed the necessity for such a pause. Meanwhile the high-level discussion about the course to be followed went on, and it continued even after the panzer forces could have resumed their drive.

After several weeks had slipped away in such discussions, the Chief of the General Staff, Halder, spurred Brauchitsch to put forward proposals for a speedy advance on Moscow. Hitler retorted with a new and more definite directive on August 21, which began:

> I am not in agreement with the proposals submitted by the Army, on August 18, for the prosecution of the war in the East. Of primary importance before

the outbreak of winter is not the capture of Moscow, but rather the occupation of the Crimea, of the industrial and coal-mining area of the Donetz
basin, the cutting of the Russian supply routes from the Caucasian oilfields. . . .

Accordingly, he gave orders that to clear the way to these southern
objectives, part of Bock's army group (including Guderian's panzer forces)
was to turn south and help to overcome the Russian armies around Kiev that
were opposing Rundstedt.

When these orders were received, Halder tried to get Brauchitsch to
tender their joint resignation. But Brauchitsch said it would be a useless
gesture, as Hitler would simply reject their resignation. As for arguments,
Hitler brushed these aside with the remark, which he often repeated: 'My
generals know nothing about the economic aspects of war.' All that he would
concede was that after the Russian armies in the Kiev area had been wiped
out, Bock should be allowed to resume his advance on Moscow, and
Guderian's panzer forces be returned to him for the purpose.

The Kiev encirclement was in itself a great success, and raised rosy expectations. Guderian thrust downward across the Russians' rear while Kleist's
panzer group thrust upward. The two pincers met 150 miles east of Kiev,
closing a trap in which over 600,000 Russians were caught, according to the
German claim. But it was late in September before the battle ended as poor
roads and rainy weather had slowed down the pace of the encircling manœuvre. The brightness of victory was darkened by the shadow of winter, carry
ing its historic menace to an invader of Russia. The two wasted months of
the summer proved fatal to the prospects of reaching Moscow.

The renewed advance began on September 30. Its prospects looked bright
when Bock's armies brought off a great encirclement round Vyasma, where
a further 600,000 Russians were captured. That left the Germans momentarily with an almost clear path to Moscow. But the Vyasma battle had not
been completed until the end of October, the German troops were tired, the
country became a morass as the weather got worse, and fresh Russian forces
appeared in front of Moscow.

Most of the German generals wanted to break off the offensive and take up
a suitable winter-line. They remembered what had happened to Napoleon's
army. Many of them began to re-read Caulaincourt's grim account of 1812.
But on the higher levels a different view prevailed. This time it was not entirely
due to Hitler, who was becoming impressed, and depressed, both by the
increasing difficulties and by the wintry conditions. On November 9 he
sombrely remarked: 'The recognition that neither force is capable of annihi-
lating the other will lead to a compromise peace.' But Bock urged that the

German offensive must be continued. Brauchitsch and Halder agreed with him—Halder telling a conference of the higher staff on November 12 that there was good reason to believe that Russian resistance was on the verge of collapse.

Brauchitsch and Halder, as well as Bock, were naturally the more reluctant to call a halt because of their earlier struggle in getting Hitler to accept their arguments for capturing Moscow rather than pursuing objectives in the south. So the push for Moscow was resumed on November 15, when there was a momentary improvement in the weather. But after two weeks' struggle in mud and snow, it was brought to a halt twenty miles short of Moscow.

Even Bock came to doubt the value of trying to push on, although he had just previously been declaring: 'The last battalion will decide the issue.' But Brauchitsch, from far in the rear, continued to insist that the offensive must be continued at all costs. He was a sick man, and desperately worried by Hitler's anger about the poor results achieved.

On December 2 a further effort was launched, and some detachments penetrated into the suburbs of Moscow, but the advance as a whole was held up in the forests covering the capital.

This was the signal for a Russian counteroffensive of large scale, prepared and directed by Zhukov. It tumbled back the exhausted Germans, lapped round their flanks, and produced a critical situation. From generals downwards, the invaders were filled with ghastly thoughts of Napoleon's retreat from Moscow. In that emergency Hitler forbade any retreat beyond the shortest possible local withdrawals, and in this situation he was right. His decision exposed his troops to awful sufferings in their advanced positions facing Moscow—for they had neither the clothing nor equipment for a Russian winter campaign—but if they had once started a general retreat it might easily have degenerated into a panic-stricken rout.

Hitler had lost his chance of capturing Moscow by his August decision to halt the advance in that direction, and turn aside to clear a path into southern Russia. The forfeit of Moscow was not compensated by what his armies attained in the south. After the great round-up at Kiev, Rundstedt overran the Crimea and the Donetz basin, but without Guderian's tanks was frustrated in his drive for the Caucasian oilfields. His troops succeeded in reaching Rostov on the Don, but in an exhausted state, and were soon pushed out by the Russians. He then wanted to fall back to a good defensive line on the Mius River, but Hitler forbade such a withdrawal. Rundstedt replied that he could not comply with such an order, and asked to be relieved of his command. Hitler promptly replaced him, but immediately after this the front was broken and Hitler was forced to accept the necessity of a retreat. That was in the first week of December—simultaneously with the repulse at Moscow.

That same week Brauchitsch asked to be relieved on grounds of sickness, the next week Bock did likewise, and a little later Leeb resigned when Hitler rejected his proposal for a withdrawal on the northern front near Leningrad. So all the four top commanders departed.

Hitler appointed no successor to Brauchitsch, but took the opportunity to make himself the direct Commander-in-Chief of the Army. By Christmas he had got rid of Guderian, the principal agent of his earlier victories, who had withdrawn his exhausted troops without Hitler's permission.

A fundamental factor in the failure of the invasion was the invaders' miscalculation of the reserves that Stalin could bring up from the depths of Russia. In that respect the General Staff and its Intelligence Service were as much deceived as Hitler. The fatal error is epitomized in one pregnant sentence of Halder's diary in mid-August: 'We underestimated Russia: we reckoned with 200 divisions, but now we have already identified 360.'

That largely cancelled out the wonderful success of the start. Instead of having a path swept clean of defenders, the Germans had now to deal with fresh armies that had arrived on the scene. The massive Soviet mobilization system succeeded in getting under way well out of the reach of the German armies, and from the winter of 1941 onwards the Germans were always to be outnumbered on the Russian front. Thanks to their own superior technique and training, they eventually succeeded in destroying these armies in successive great battles of encirclement—but then became bogged in the autumn mud. By the time that the winter frost had hardened the ground, they again found fresh armies blocking the route, and they themselves were too exhausted to struggle on to their goal.

Next to their miscalculation of Russia's resources, the most fatal factor had been the way that Hitler and his top generals had wasted the month of August in arguing as to what should be their next move—there was an amazing state of mental haziness on the topmost level of the German Command.

Lower down, Guderian in particular had a clear idea of what he wanted to do—to drive for Moscow as fast as he could, leaving the infantry armies to mop up the disorganised bodies that he had cut through. In 1940 he had won the Battle of France in that way. It would have meant running big risks, but might have captured Moscow before the Russian second-line armies were ready to cover it. Far greater risks developed, and fatally, from the course that was followed.

As it was, Russia owed her survival more to her continued primitiveness than to all the technical development achieved since the Soviet revolution. That reflection applies not only to the toughness of her people and soldiers—their capacity to endure hardships and carry on under shortages that would have been paralysing to Western peoples and Western armies. A greater asset still was the primitiveness of the Russian roads. Most of them were no better than sandy tracks. The way that they dissolved into bottomless mud, when it rained, did more to check the German invasion than all the Red Army's heroic sacrifices. If the Soviet régime had given Russia a road system comparable to that of Western countries, she would have been overrun almost as quickly as France.

But this conclusion has a converse. Hitler lost his chance of victory because the mobility of his army was based on wheels instead of on tracks. On Russia's mud-roads its wheeled transport was bogged when the tanks could move on. If the panzer forces had been provided with *tracked* transport they could have reached Russia's vital centres by the autumn in spite of the mud.

CHAPTER 14

ROMMEL'S ENTRY INTO AFRICA

In 1941 the course of the war in Africa went through a series of startling changes that upset expectation on either side in turn but had no conclusive issue. It was a war of swift movement—but see-saw movement, repeatedly tilting up and down. The year had begun with the British throwing the Italians out of Cyrenaica, but then a German force arrived on the scene under the leadership of General Erwin Rommel, and barely two months later the British were thrown out of Cyrenaica except for a foothold which they retained at the small port of Tobruk. Rommel in turn was repulsed in two successive attacks on Tobruk, but then the British suffered reverses in two successive attempts to relieve the besieged garrison. After five months' pause to build up strength, they made a bigger effort in November that produced a see-saw battle of a month's duration, with repeated changes of fortune before the exhausted remains of the opposing army was forced to withdraw once again to the western border of Cyrenaica. But even then Rommel delivered a frontier riposte in the last week of the year, which proved a foreshadowing of another dramatic reversal of the British advance.*

Rommel's opening thrust at the end of March 1941, and its far-reaching exploitation, created all the greater shock because the possibility of an early advance by the enemy had been discounted on the British side. In an appreciation of the situation that Wavell sent to the Chiefs of Staff in London on March 2, after a warning report that German troops had begun to arrive in Tripoli, he emphasised that they would need to build up their strength to two divisions or more before attempting a serious attack, and concluded that the difficulties 'make it unlikely that such an attack could develop before the end of the summer'. In contrast, Churchill's messages showed apprehension that the Germans would not wait to complete an orthodox build-up,

* For maps, see pp. 110–11.

and a strong sense of the need for offensive counteraction, although over-optimistic about the capacity of the actual British forces. On March 26 he telegraphed to Wavell:

> We are naturally concerned at rapid German advance to Agheila. It is their habit to push on wherever they are not resisted. I presume you are only waiting for the tortoise to stick his head out far enough before chopping it off. It seems extremely important to give them an early taste of our quality.*

But quality was lacking, both technically and tactically. Although the depleted 2nd Armoured Division that was posted in the forward area still had three armoured units to Rommel's two, and a numerically favourable balance of gun-armed tanks, a large proportion of these were captured Italian M.13s that had been taken over by British crews to compensate the shortage of British cruiser tanks, while almost all were in badly worn condition. The prospects of such a scratch force were diminished by Wavell's instructions that 'if attacked' it was to fall back and 'fight a delaying action'. For by abandoning the bottleneck position east of Agheila at Rommel's initial onset, on March 31, it opened the way for him to enter a desert expanse where he could exploit a wide choice of alternative routes and alternative objectives to its own confusion, while being itself in no fit state for such strenuous manœuvring. In the days that followed, Rommel allowed it no respite. Most of its tanks were lost, not in fighting, but through breaking down or running out of fuel in a prolonged and disjointed series of withdrawals.

In less than a week the British had fallen back more than 200 miles from their position on the western border of Cyrenaica. In less than a fortnight they were 400 miles back, on the eastern border of Cyrenaica—and western frontier of Egypt—except for a force invested at Tobruk. The decision to hold on to this small port, and the retention of that position as a 'thorn in the enemy's side', had a far-reaching influence on the course of the African campaign during the next twelve months.

The swiftly spreading collapse had naturally tended to shake the confidence of commanders and troops on the British side, while leading them to magnify the strength of the attackers. At a distance it was easier to keep account of the enemy's limited strength and strategic handicaps. Churchill in London, duly weighing them, telegraphed to Wavell on April 7:

> You should surely be able to hold Tobruk, with its permanent Italian defences, at least until or unless the enemy brings up strong artillery forces. It seems difficult to believe that he can do this for some weeks. He would

---

* Churchill: *The Second World War*, vol. III, p. 178.

run great risks in masking Tobruk and advancing upon Egypt, observing that we can reinforce from the sea and would menace his communications. Tobruk therefore seems to be a place to be held to the death without thought of retirement. I should be glad to hear of your intentions.*

Wavell had already decided to hold Tobruk if possible, but when he flew there from Cairo on the 8th he reported that the situation had greatly deteriorated, and sounded so dubious about the prospects of defending the place that Churchill, in conclave with the Chiefs of Staff, drafted a still more emphatic message saying that 'it seems unthinkable that the fortress of Tobruk should be abandoned'. Before the message was despatched, however, word came from Wavell that he had made up his mind to hold on there for a time, and assemble a mobile force on the frontier to divert the enemy and ease the pressure, while striving 'to build up old plan of defence in Mersa Matruh area'—200 miles farther back. In the event there was no further withdrawal, thanks to the stubborn defence of Tobruk, though nearly eight months passed before it was relieved.

The main part of the garrison was provided by the 9th Australian Division under General Morshead, which had got back safely from the Benghazi area. In addition the 18th Infantry Brigade (of the 7th Australian Division) had arrived by sea, and was followed by detachments of the 1st and 7th Royal Tank Regiment with which a small armoured force of fifty odd tanks was built up.

Rommel's attack opened on Good Friday, April 11, with probing thrusts. The main attack was launched early on Easter Monday, against the middle stretch of the southern face of the thirty-mile perimeter, some nine miles from the port. It broke through the thin defences, and the leading panzer battalion drove on two miles northward, but was there checked by the defender's artillery, and then squeezed out of the narrow pocket it had made, losing sixteen tanks out of the thirty-eight engaged—a total that revealed the slenderness of Rommel's strength. The Italians attempted an attack on the 16th, but their effort quickly collapsed, and nearly a thousand surrendered when counterattacked by an Australian battalion.

The Italian Supreme Command in Rome, already uneasy about Rommel's deep advance, now begged the German Supreme Command to restrain his adventurous initiative and reported intention of thrusting into Egypt. Halder, the Chief of the German General Staff, was equally anxious to curb any action overseas that might require reinforcement at the expense of the German forces in the main theatre that were now preparing to invade Russia. He also had an instinctive dislike of Hitler's inclination to back

* Churchill: *The Second World War*, vol. III, p. 183.

dynamic leaders, such as Rommel, who did not conform to General Staff pattern. So Halder's deputy, General Paulus, was sent on a visit to Africa 'to head off this soldier gone stark mad', as Halder bitingly wrote in his diary. Paulus came, saw, and checked—but after administering an admonition, he sanctioned a fresh assault on Tobruk.

The assault was launched on April 30, by which time some advance elements of the 15th Panzer Division—though not its tank regiment—had arrived from Europe to reinforce the 5th Light Division. This time the blow was aimed at the south-western corner of the defences, and delivered under cover of darkness. By daylight on May 1 the German infantry had made a breach more than a mile wide, and the leading wave of tanks then started an exploiting drive towards Tobruk, ten miles away. But after advancing a mile they ran unsuspectingly on a minefield that had been newly laid, as a trap, and seventeen tanks out of forty were disabled—though all except five got back safely, after their tracks had been repaired under fire. The second wave of tanks and infantry wheeled south-eastward along the back of the perimeter to roll up the defences. But after a lateral advance of nearly three miles they were finally checked by the combination of fire from artillery deployed behind the minefield, a counterattack by twenty British tanks, and the continued resistance of several Australian posts which they had failed to subdue. As for the Italian supporting troops, they were slow in backing up and quick in backing out.

Next day only thirty-five German tanks out of the initial 70-odd remained fit for action, and the attack was suspended. On the night of the 3rd, Morshead launched a counterattack with his reserve infantry brigade, but this in turn failed, and the situation became one of mutual frustration. The south-western corner of the perimeter remained in Rommel's grip, but it was evident that his strength was not adequate for the capture of Tobruk, and Paulus, before returning home, imposed a veto on any attempt to renew the attack. So a state of siege developed, which lasted until late in the year—after the failure of two early efforts by Wavell to drive Rommel back and bring relief to the garrison.

The first of these, in mid-May, had a tentativeness that was expressed in its codename, 'Operation Brevity', but greater weight was given and much greater hopes attached to its mid-June successor, 'Operation Battleaxe'. The outcome was poor compensation for the heavy risks that had been taken, on Churchill's initiative, to ensure its success—the risk of providing a large reinforcement of tanks for Egypt at a time when the forces defending England were still ill-equipped, and when Hitler had not yet turned away to attack Russia; also, the further risk of despatching this reinforcement by the Mediterranean route, 'running the gauntlet' of the enemy's air forces.

Churchill's bold readiness to run such double risks, in the endeavour to gain success in Africa and preserve the British position in Egypt, was in striking contrast to the attitude of Hitler and Halder, who were agreed in trying to curtail the German commitment in the Mediterranean theatre. In October, when General von Thoma had been sent on an exploratory visit to Cyrenaica, he had reported that a force of four panzer divisions would be needed, and should suffice, to ensure success in the invasion of Egypt, but Mussolini had been as unwilling to accept such a scale of German help as Hitler was to provide it. Rommel's small force of two divisions had only been despatched there after the Italian defeat, in an effort to preserve Tripoli. Even when he had shown how far he could go with such a small panzer force, Hitler and Halder remained unwilling to provide the relatively small reinforcement that would in all probability have decided the issue. By that refusal they forfeited the chance of conquering Egypt and ousting the British from the Mediterranean area at a time when the British were still weak— while they were led to make a much greater commitment, and sacrifice, in the long run.

But in Britain, despite her still scanty resources, a convoy with large armoured reinforcements had already been assembled in April for despatch to Egypt. It was about to sail when a telegram came from Wavell, on April 20, emphasising the gravity of the situation and the urgency of his need for more armour. Churchill immediately proposed*, and got the Chiefs of Staff to agree, that the five fast ships carrying the tanks should turn east at Gibraltar and take the short cut through the Mediterranean—which would save nearly six weeks in time of arrival. He also insisted that the scale of the reinforcement should be increased and a hundred of the latest cruiser tanks included, although the Chief of the Imperial General Staff, General Dill, opposed such a subtraction from the slender strength available at home to meet a possible spring invasion.

This 'Operation Tiger' was the first attempt to pass a convoy through the Mediterranean since the Luftwaffe had made its appearance there in January. Helped by misty weather, the convoy was successfully taken through without suffering damage from the air, though one of the ships, with fifty-seven

* In a personal minute that day for the Chiefs of Staff, he pungently wrote: 'The fate of the war in the Middle East, the loss of the Suez Canal, the frustration or confusion of the enormous forces we have built up in Egypt, the closing of all prospects of American co-operation through the Red Sea—all may turn on a few hundred armoured vehicles. They must if possible be carried there at all costs.' (The Second World War, vol. III, p. 218.)

tanks, was sunk by a mine in passing through the Sicilian Narrows. The other four ships reached Alexandria safely on May 12, with 238 tanks (135 Matildas, eighty-two cruiser, and twenty-one lights)—which was four times as many as those which Wavell had been able to scrape together for the defence of Egypt.

Without waiting for this large reinforcement, however, Wavell had decided to take advantage of Rommel's rebuff at Tobruk, and reported acute shortage of supplies, by trying an offensive stroke with the scratch force assembled near the frontier, under Brigadier Gott. This was 'Operation Brevity'. Wavell's initial aim was to recapture the frontier positions near the coast—which he knew were lightly held—and scupper their garrisons before the enemy reinforced them. He hoped to do more than that, as he told Churchill in a telegram on May 13: 'If successful will consider immediate combined action by Gott's force and Tobruk garrison to drive enemy west of Tobruk.'

Two tank units were brought up to provide the punch for Gott's force— the 2nd R.T.R., equipped with twenty-nine old-type cruisers which had been reconditioned, and the 4th R.T.R. with twenty-six Matildas, heavily armoured, relatively slow, and officially classified as 'infantry tanks'. The 2nd R.T.R. with a support group of motorised infantry and artillery was to move round the desert flank of the fortified positions to Sidi Azeiz, and block the enemy's route of reinforcement and retreat. The 4th R.T.R. was to lead the motorised 22nd Guards Brigade in the direct assault.

After a thirty-mile approach march by night, the Italian-held post at the top of the Halfaya Pass was stormed by surprise early on May 15 and several hundred prisoners taken, though seven Matildas were knocked out by the defenders' artillery as they closed in. Two other posts, Bir Waid and Musaid, were quickly taken, but surprise had passed before Fort Capuzzo was reached, and when a German battle-group intervened by flank action the attack became disjointed. Although the fort was eventually captured, it was later evacuated. Meanwhile the flanking move to Sidi Azeiz had been broken off under threat of a counterattack. On the other hand, the enemy commander on the frontier had been so impressed by the apparent strength of the attack that he was led to start withdrawing.

Thus by nightfall both sides were in process of falling back. But while the German-Italian withdrawal was promptly countermanded by Rommel, who was rushing a panzer battalion to the scene from Tobruk, Gott had decided on a retirement to Halfaya, and the troops were already on the move, before a stand fast order reached him from the distant higher command. When daylight came the Germans found the battlefield empty—

much to their relief, as the reinforcing panzer battalion had run out of petrol, and was immobilised until a refill arrived late that day.

The British withdrawal did not stop at Halfaya, but left a small garrison there. The Germans were quick to take advantage of its exposed position, and recaptured the Pass on the 27th by a sudden converging stroke from several directions. Its recapture was a valuable gain to them, as it seriously hampered the next and heavier British offensive, 'Battleaxe'. Moreover, during the interval Rommel laid traps for the British tanks at Halfaya as well as at other forward posts by digging in batteries of 88-mm. guns, converted most effectively from an anti-aircraft to an anti-tank role.

That emergency step proved of great importance for the issue of the coming battle. At this time nearly two-thirds of the German anti-tank guns were still the old 37-mm., developed five years before the war, and much inferior to the British 2-pounder tank and anti-tank gun. They could do little against the British cruiser tanks and were helpless against the Matildas. Even the new 50-mm. anti-tank gun, of which Rommel now had fifty odd, could only pierce the Matilda's thick armour at very close range. But the wheeled 88-mm. was capable of penetrating the Matilda's frontal armour (77 mm. thick) at a range of 2,000 yards. Rommel had only twelve of these guns, but one battery (of four) was posted at Halfaya and another at Hafid Ridge—two points which the British aimed to capture at the outset of their attack.

That was fortunate for Rommel, for in many respects he stood at a serious disadvantage when the attack was launched, particularly in the number of tanks—the prime arm in these desert battles. No further reinforcements had arrived from Germany, and he had barely a hundred gun-armed tanks available when the battle opened, more than half of which were with the force investing Tobruk, eighty miles back. On the other side, the arrival of the 'Tiger' convoy enabled the British to deploy some 200 gun-armed tanks—which gave them a 4 to 1 advantage in the opening stage. Much depended on whether they could exploit this advantage to smash the enemy forces in the frontier area before Rommel could bring up the rest of his tanks (5th Panzer Regiment) from distant Tobruk.

Unfortunately for the British, the chances were diminished by an 'infantry-minded' planning of the offensive. This trend was fostered by the mixture of tank types and, in the event, led to a dissipation of the numerical advantage.

The arrival of the 'Tiger' convoy had enabled Wavell to reconstitute two armoured brigades for the new offensive, but so few tanks were left after the abortive 'Brevity' attack in mid-May that the total was only enough to equip two of the three regiments in each brigade.* Moreover the number of new cruiser tanks that had arrived sufficed only to equip one regiment, and of the earlier cruisers only enough remained for a second regiment. The two regiments of the other brigade were equipped with Matildas, 'infantry tanks'—which strongly influenced the Command decision to use this brigade at the outset to assist the infantry in a direct assault on the enemy's fortified position, instead of concentrating all available tank strength to crush the enemy's panzer forces in the forward area. The consequences of that decision proved fatally frustrating to the development of the offensive.

The aims of 'Operation Battleaxe' were ambitious—as set by Churchill, they were to gain a 'decisive' victory in North Africa and 'destroy' Rommel's forces. Wavell expressed a cautious doubt about the possibility of such complete success, but said that he hoped the attack would 'succeed in driving the enemy back west of Tobruk'. That was the object defined in the operation instructions he gave to General Beresford-Peirse who, as commander of the Western Desert Force, was to conduct the offensive.

The plan of attack comprised three stages, opening with an assault on the fortified area Halfaya-Sollum-Capuzzo by the 4th Indian Division, aided by the 4th Armoured Brigade (which was equipped with Matilda tanks), while the rest of the 7th Armoured Division covered the desert flank. In the second stage, the 7th Armoured Division was to make an exploiting drive for Tobruk, with both its armoured brigades. In the third stage, this division together with the Tobruk garrison was to push on westwards. It was a plan that contained the seeds of its own frustration. For by detaching half the armour to help the infantry in the first stage, it more than halved the chances of defeating the enemy's panzer regiment in the forward area before this could be reinforced by the other panzer regiment from Tobruk, and thus greatly diminished the chances of achieving the second and third stages of the British plan.

To reach the enemy's frontier positions the attacking force had to make a thirty-mile approach march, which started in the afternoon of June 14. The

* Churchill urged that a further hundred tanks—the number required to equip a third regiment for each brigade—should be sent out by the Mediterranean route, but the Admiralty were reluctant to run the risk again. Churchill bitterly remarks in his memoirs: 'I should not have been deterred from seeking and obtaining a Cabinet decision upon the issue but for the fact that General Wavell himself did not press the point, and indeed took the other side. This cut the ground from under my feet.' (*The Second World War*, vol. III, p. 223.) So the convoy went round the Cape and did not reach Suez until mid-July.

final bound, of eight miles, was made by moonlight in the early hours of the 15th, and the battle opened with the right wing's attack on the enemy's outlying position at the Halfaya Pass. But the defenders were better prepared than in May, while the chance of surprise was forfeited by the planning decision that the tanks should not deliver the assault until the artillery had sufficient light for shooting. That decision proved the worse because the one battery allotted to support the Halfaya assault became stuck in the sand. It was broad daylight when the squadron of Matildas leading this attack started on the last lap of the advance, and the first news that came back was from its commander's voice on the radio: 'They are tearing my tanks to bits.' That was his last message. Of the thirteen Matildas, only one survived the 'tank trap' of four 88s that Rommel had placed at what the British troops aptly called 'Hellfire Pass'.

Meanwhile the centre column had been pushing on across the desert plateau towards Fort Capuzzo, spearheaded by a whole regiment of Matildas. There were no 88s in the path, and the garrison's resistance crumbled in face of this massed menace. The fort was captured, and two counterattacks repulsed later in the day.

But the brigade of cruiser tanks leading the left column, which was intended to turn the enemy's flank, had run into Rommel's tank trap on the Hafid Ridge, and there been checked. Renewing the attack in the late afternoon, it only pushed deeper into the trap, with heavier loss. By that time the bulk of the forward panzer regiment had come on the scene, and it developed a counter flank threat which caused the remaining British tanks to fall back slowly to the frontier wire.

By nightfall on the first day, the British had lost more than half their tanks, mainly in the two anti-tank traps, whereas Rommel's tank strength was almost intact, and with the arrival of his other panzer regiment from Tobruk the balance shifted in his favour.

On the second day Rommel seized the initiative by using the whole of his 5th Light Division from Tobruk to envelop the British left flank in the desert in conjunction with a strong counterattack at Capuzzo by the 15th Panzer Division. This counterattack at Capuzzo was repulsed—the British here enjoying the advantage of the defensive in well-chosen and concealed positions. But the combined effect of the frontal and flank threats disjointed the British plan for a renewed offensive effort that day, and by nightfall the Germans' enveloping move had made ominous progress.

Pressing this advantage, Rommel switched the whole of his mobile forces to the desert flank in the early hours of the third day, with the aim of making a scythe-like sweep to the Halfaya Pass and cutting the British lines of retreat. When the menace became manifest in mid-morning, the British higher commanders issued orders, after hasty consultation, for a precipitate retreat of their disjointed forces. The advanced portion at Capuzzo had a very narrow escape, but the stubborn resistance of the remaining British tanks there gained time for the extrication of the lorry-borne infantry, and by the fourth morning the British forces were back on the line—thirty miles back—from which they had started.

The human losses in the three days' 'Battleaxe' battle were slight—less than a thousand killed, wounded and missing on the British side, and about the same on the other side. But the British lost ninety-one tanks and the Germans only 12. Being left in possession of the battlefield they were able to recover and repair most of their damaged tanks, whereas the British in their hasty retreat had to abandon many which were merely disabled by mechanical troubles, and could have been repaired if time had been allowed. The disproportionate tank losses emphasised the failure of this offensive to fulfil the high hopes, and far-reaching aims, with which it had been launched.

Tobruk, 'Brevity' and 'Battleaxe' marked a fresh turn in the tactical trend of the war. Hitherto, it had been an almost complete reversal of the ascendancy of the defensive that had prevailed during World War I and the previous half-century. Since September 1939 the offensive had been so repeatedly and sweepingly successful in every theatre, when carried out by fast-moving armoured forces, that both public and military opinion had come to regard the defensive as inherently weak, and to believe that any attack was bound to prevail. But 'Battleaxe' showed, as Tobruk and 'Brevity' had foreshadowed, how effective defence could be—even in such open country as the North African desert—if conducted with skill and based on an understanding of the properties of modern instruments. From this time onwards, as the war continued and experience grew, it became increasingly evident that defence, in a more mobile form, had regained the advantage it held in World War I, and could only be overcome by a great superiority of strength or a very high degree of skill—in upsetting the opponent's balance.

Unfortunately for the prospects of the next British attempt to crush Rommel and clear North Africa, the lessons of 'Battleaxe' were either missed or misunderstood. The most important point missed by the British higher headquarters in their conclusions was the part that the 88s had played in the defence. They discounted reports that this heavy anti-aircraft gun was being used as an anti-tank gun. When they came belatedly to realise that fact in the autumn, after further heavy tank losses from its fire, they remained obstinately sure that such a bulky weapon could only be used from a dug-in position. Thus they failed to foresee and evolve tactics to counter the next advance in Rommel's defensive tactics—that of using the 88s in a mobile role.

Another important development missed, by the British fighting troops as well as by their higher commanders, was the enemy's increasingly bold use of his normal anti-tank guns in close combination with his tanks—not only in defence but also in attack. In the coming battles that combination became a dominant factor, exerting an even greater influence on the issue than the 88s. Indeed, the principal cause of the disproportionately heavy loss of tanks on the British side appears, in analysis, to have been the way that the German 50-mm. anti-tank guns, comparatively small and handy, were pushed out ahead of their own tanks to concealed positions in hollows. That was not realised by the British tank crews, who could not know whether an armour-piercing shot that penetrated their armour had been fired by a tank or anti-tank gun—and naturally tended to ascribe it to the most visible opponent. That mistaken deduction led, in the aftermath, to a mistaken belief that their own tanks and tank-guns were inferior to the enemy's—and thereby to a spreading loss of confidence.

Besides the points that were missed in reviewing the course of the summer campaign, there was also an important one which was misunderstood, with serious effect on the British plan for the next offensive. Wavell in his Despatch, drafted nearly three months after 'Battleaxe', reached the conclusion that the prime 'cause of our failure was undoubtedly the difficulty of combining the action of cruiser and "I" [Infantry] tanks. . . .' But in fact the combination had not been tried, nor its possibility tested. The two regiments of Matildas had been detached from the armoured division and placed under the commander of the infantry division at the outset, and he had clung on to them throughout the battle, instead of releasing them after the first phase as intended in the plan. With intelligent combination the 'I' tanks could have played a valuable part in the armoured battle, operating as a strong offensive pivot of manœuvre for the cruiser tanks. There was only a slight difference of speed between the Matildas and the A.10 cruisers, which had effectively co-operated with the faster cruisers in the first Libyan campaign and in 'Battleaxe' itself. The Germans, both at this time and later, proved capable of combining tank types with as large a difference of speed as that between the faster British cruisers and the Matildas.

Unfortunately, the untested assumption that the combination was too difficult led to a complete division between the cruiser and 'I' tank brigades in the next British offensive—which became a battle waged, on the British side, in two separate compartments.

CHAPTER 15

'CRUSADER'

The frustration of the mid-summer effort of 1941 to gain a decisive victory in Africa, and sweep the enemy out of that continent, made Churchill more intent than ever to achieve that aim. He was determined to renew the effort as soon as possible, with stronger forces. To this end, he poured reinforcements into Egypt and brushed aside his military advisers' reminders about the longstanding decision that the defence of the Far East, and particularly of Singapore, was the second priority after the defence of Britain itself, and before the Middle East. The Chief of the Imperial General Staff, Sir John Dill, tried to remind Churchill of the carefully weighed decision, as between the two regions and risks, but was too gentle a personality and too deferential by habit to maintain it in face of Churchill's force of personality, argument, and position.

Yet the danger in the Far East had now become acute, while the British forces there remained pitifully weak. Although Japan had stayed out of the war hitherto, the steps which Roosevelt and Churchill took in July to cut off her economic resources were bound to make her strike back in the only way possible for her—by force of arms. Her hesitancy allowed America and Britain more than four months' grace for developing their defence in the Pacific, but they failed to profit by it—and in Britain's case that neglect was largely due to the way that Churchill's interest and efforts had become focused on North Africa. Thus Rommel indirectly produced the fall of Singapore—and as much by the personal impression he made on a personality-minded Prime Minister as by his potential threat to the Nile Valley and the Suez Canal.*

For the renewed offensive in Africa, codenamed 'Operation Crusader', the British forces were much increased and also re-equipped. The four tank units were increased to fourteen, so that four complete armoured brigades (each of three units) were provided for the striking force, while the Tobruk garrison

---

* For maps, see pp. 110–11.

was given one brigade (of two tank units and an additional squadron), sent in by sea, for use in the breakout to meet the striking force. (For the main part the brigades were equipped with the new Crusader cruiser tanks or with the new American Stuart tanks, the fastest of any in the field, but there were four units of 'I' tanks, Matildas or Valentines.) Three more motorised infantry divisions were brought up, making a total of four, besides a fresh division in Tobruk—where the British 70th relieved the 9th Australian that had borne the brunt of the siege.

By contrast, Rommel received very few reinforcements from Germany, and no additional tank units to augment his original four. The 5th Light Division was rechristened the 21st Panzer Division, but was not given an increased scale of tanks, and all that he could manage in the way of enlarging his force was to improvise an unmotorised infantry division (at first called the Afrika Division, and later the 90th Light) out of some extra artillery and infantry battalions. The Italian force of three divisions (one armoured) was augmented by three more small infantry divisions—but their value was much diminished by their obsolete equipment and lack of motor transport, so that they could only be used in a static role, and were an awkward handicap on Rommel's strategic freedom of manœuvre.

In the air, also, the British now had a big advantage. Their strength was built up to a total of nearly 700 aircraft immediately available for the support of the offensive, against a total of 120 German aircraft and 200 Italian.

In armour, the British superiority was even greater. When the offensive was launched the British had more than 710 gun-armed tanks (of which some 200 were 'I' tanks), while the enemy had only 174 German gun-armed tanks and 146 Italian—which were of obsolete type, and little value. Thus the British had a superiority well exceeding 2 to 1 over the enemy as a whole, and more than 4 to 1 over the Germans—whose two panzer divisions, with their two tank units apiece, were regarded by the British Commander-in-Chief as 'the backbone of the enemy's army'. Moreover, Rommel had no tanks in reserve, other than a few under repair, whereas the British had some 500 in reserve or in shipment on the way—so that they were much more capable of maintaining a prolonged fight. In the outcome, that reserve eventually turned the scales of the battle.*

Rommel's chief asset, in countering the heavy odds against him in tanks, was that by the autumn two-thirds of his ordinary anti-tank guns were of

* The figures of the comparative tank strengths and resources are those tabulated in the British Official History, pp. 30-1. The figures given for the British operational strength—a total of 713 (including 201 'I' tanks) were arrived at by deduction from a number of differing records, differently compiled. On another calculation from the records, the total comes to 756 (including 225 'I' tanks).

the new long-barrelled 50-mm. type—which was about 70 per cent superior in penetration to his old 37-mm. gun, and 25 per cent superior to the British 2-pounder gun. Thus his defence was no longer so dependent on his handful of 88s as it had been in the summer.

Besides despatching large reinforcements to Egypt, and most of Britain's newly manufactured equipment, Churchill also provided the striking force there with a new set of commanders. Four days after the failure of 'Battleaxe', Wavell was removed from command and replaced by Sir Claude Auchinleck, the Commander-in-Chief in India, while the force commander and the armoured division commander were replaced soon afterwards. Churchill had become increasingly impatient with Wavell's cautiousness, and the disappointing result of 'Battleaxe' clinched his decision to appoint a new commander-in-chief. But he found, to his renewed irritation, that Auchinleck was firm in resisting his pressure for an early renewal of the offensive and insisted on waiting until fully prepared and strong enough to ensure a good chance of decisive success. So the next offensive, 'Operation Crusader', was not launched until mid-November, five months after 'Battleaxe'. Meanwhile the greatly enlarged force was renamed Eighth Army, and command given to Lieutenant-General Sir Alan Cunningham—who had conducted the clearance of Italian Somaliland and the subsequent advance from the south into Ethiopia which led to the ejection of the Italians. The new army was divided into the 13th Corps under Lieutenant-General A. R. Godwin-Austen, and the 30th (armoured) Corps under Lieutenant-General C. W. M. Norrie. But with the exception of Norrie, a cavalryman, none of the new commanders had experience in handling tanks and in operating against armoured forces, and he was brought in as a substitute when the expert tankman originally chosen to command the armoured corps was killed in an air crash shortly before the offensive opened.

The 13th Corps included the New Zealand and 4th Indian Divisions, with a brigade of infantry tanks. The 30th Corps included the 7th Armoured Division with two armoured brigades (the 7th and 22nd), the 4th Armoured Brigade Group, the 22nd Guards (Motor) Brigade, and the 1st South African Division. The 2nd South African Division was in reserve.

The basis of the offensive plan was that the 13th Corps would pin down the enemy troops who were holding the frontier positions, while the 30th Corps swept round the flank of these fortified positions 'to seek out and destroy' Rommel's armoured force—and then link up with the Tobruk garrison, seventy miles beyond the frontier, which was to break out to meet the 30th Corps. Thus the two corps, and their respective armour, would be operating in widely separate areas—rather than with combined effect. The most formidable part of the British armour, the brigade of Matildas and Valentines, would make no contribution to the armoured battle but merely be employed in small packets with the infantry. And when the advance developed this separated distribution soon spread into dispersion, with consequent weakness everywhere.

Thereby the British forfeited the opening advantage gained by their strategic outflanking move, which had taken the enemy by surprise and temporarily confused him. The British attack became disjointed—and to a large extent had disjointed itself. As Rommel caustically said: 'What difference does it make if you have two tanks to my one, when you spread them out and let me smash them in detail? You presented me with three brigades in succession.'

The source of the trouble lay in the hoary maxim, long inculcated in every official military manual and at Staff College, that 'the destruction of the enemy's main armed forces on the battlefield' is the prime objective, and the only sound one for a military commander. Between the wars that maxim came to be applied even more fervently by infantry-minded commanders when considering how they should use the tanks placed at their disposal, and they were apt to say: 'Kill off the enemy's tanks, and then we can get on with the battle.' The persistence of that habit of thought was all too manifest in the instructions given to the Eighth Army, and its armoured corps: 'Your immediate objective is the destruction of the enemy's armoured forces.' But an armoured force is not in itself suited to be an immediate objective. For it is a fluid force, not easily fixed—as infantry formations can be. The aim of destroying it is more likely to be attained indirectly, by drawing it to cover or retrieve some point of key importance. In trying to 'kill' Rommel's elusive panzer forces in a too direct way, the British armour not only became stretched and scattered but let itself be drawn all too easily into his gun-lined tank traps.

The British 30th Corps crossed the frontier early on November 18 and then began a right wheel towards Tobruk ninety miles distant. The advance was covered by an 'air umbrella', but this protection against discovery and interference was not immediately needed, as a heavy storm in the night had swamped the enemy's airfields and his aircraft were grounded. Nor, for the same reason, did it matter that the advance was slowed down by the bad going. Rommel had no inkling of the 'storm of steel' that was about to burst upon him. His mind was focused on the preparation for his own intended assault on Tobruk, and his striking force had moved thither in readiness to deliver it, although he had placed a strong covering force in the desert to the south as a check on interference.

By nightfall on the 18th the British armoured columns were astride the Trigh el Abd, and next morning pushed on northward—their thirty-mile frontage becoming stretched to fifty miles in the course of driving back Rommel's screen. The ill-effects of that overstretch were not long in developing.

In the centre, the two leading regiments of the 7th Armoured Brigade reached and captured the enemy airfield on top of the escarpment at Sidi Rezegh—only twelve miles from the Tobruk perimeter. But the rest of the brigade and the division's Support Group did not come up until next morning, the 20th, and by then Rommel had rushed up part of the Afrika Division, with a large number of anti-tank guns, to hold the top edge of the escarpment and block the path. No reinforcements arrived to build up the British force there. For the two other armoured brigades had run into trouble, one far to the west and the other far to the east, while the 1st South African Division had also been diverted westward.

What had happened on the western flank was that the 22nd Armoured Brigade had run into Italian tanks, and in driving them back had been led to attack the Italians' fortified position near Bir el Gubi. The 22nd was a brigade composed of yeomanry regiments which had not long been mounted in tanks and also came fresh to the desert war. In a too gallant assault—carried out in the immortal spirit of the 'Charge of the Light Brigade' at Balaclava— they were heavily hammered by the Italians' dug-in guns, and lost more than forty of their 160 tanks. Under the impression that the attack was going well, the corps commander diverted the South Africans thither to occupy Bir el Gubi.

On the eastern flank the 4th Armoured Brigade Group, which had become strung out over a twenty-five-mile stretch in chasing a German reconnaissance unit, had been suddenly taken aback by the appearance of a strong German armoured force near its rear—and its rearmost unit was badly mauled before one of the other two units returned to help in checking the enemy. This blow was the sequel to Rommel's first countermove and was delivered by a strong battle-group (including the two tank units of the 21st Panzer Division) which had been sent southward to explore the situation.

It was lucky for the British armour on this flank that it did not have to meet a concentrated blow by the whole Afrika Korps next morning. That respite was due to a misleading report received by its commander, Cruewell, which led him to imagine that the most dangerous British advance was coming along the northerly route, the Trigh Capuzzo. So he moved both his panzer divisions thither, towards Capuzzo—and found the area empty. Blinded by lack of air reconnaissance, the Germans were still groping in the 'fog of war'. Worse still, the 21st Panzer Division ran out of fuel on this eastward excursion, and was temporarily stranded. Only the 15th Panzer Division was able to return that day, and in the afternoon it struck the still isolated 4th Armoured Brigade at Gabr Saleh—so that this brigade for the second day in succession bore the brunt of the German counterblow, and suffered another mauling. Although the British higher commanders had good information about the enemy's movements they were slow to take advantage of the respite, and opportunity, provided by the Afrika Korps' temporary departure from the scene. No immediate step was taken to concentrate the three widely scattered armoured brigades. But towards midday, when the danger to the 4th Armoured Brigade became manifest, the 22nd was sent eastward to reinforce it, instead of moving up to join the 7th at Sidi Rezegh as previously intended. But the 22nd had a long way to go, on this switch from one flank to the other, and did not arrive until nightfall. It was thus too late to help in the fight.

Yet all this time the New Zealand Division and the 'I' tank brigade of the 13th Corps had been lying only seven miles away, at Bir Gibni—panting to advance and eager to help. But it was not called on to take a hand in the armoured battle, and its offers to help were declined. It is an extraordinary revelation of how far the 'two-compartment' idea was carried in conducting this battle.

When morning came, on November 21, the British armoured brigades at Gabr Saleh found that the enemy had vanished from their front. This time it was not for a blow in the air—for Rommel had by now gained a clear picture of the British lay-out, and had ordered Cruewell to strike a concentrated blow, with both panzer divisions, against the British advanced force at Sidi Rezegh.

Norrie had just told this force to drive on towards Tobruk, and ordered the Tobruk garrison to start its breakout attack. But before the drive got going it was thrown out of gear. At 8 a.m. two German armoured columns were seen approaching from south and east. Two of the three British armoured units at Sidi Rezegh were hurriedly diverted to meet them. Thus only one (the 6th Royal Tanks) was left to lead the drive for Tobruk, and was soon shattered by the enemy's well-posted guns, which were able to concentrate on this single unit. It was another 'Charge of the Light Brigade' —a too light brigade in this case. Meanwhile the other two armoured units were assailed by the full weight of the Afrika Korps. One of them, the 7th Hussars, was overrun and almost wiped out by the 21st Panzer Division.

The other, the 2nd Royal Tank Regiment, attacked the 15th Panzer Division so boldly and with such effect, thanks to its superior skill in firing on the move, that the enemy turned away. But the Germans attacked afresh in the afternoon, and cleverly employed their new tactics of pushing forward anti-tank guns unobtrusively ahead of their tanks and round the opponent's flanks. In this way they took such heavy toll that the rapidly dwindling remnant of the 7th Armoured Brigade was only saved from annihilation by the long-awaited and belated arrival of the 22nd Armoured Brigade from Gabr Saleh—the 4th did not come up until next day. As for the breakout attack from Tobruk, this drove four miles deep into the German–Italian investing position, but was then suspended in view of the setback which the 30th Corps had suffered—and the breakout force was thus left in an awkwardly deep and narrow salient.

When dawn broke on the fifth day the Afrika Korps had again disappeared —but this time only to replenish its fuel and ammunition. Even that short lull was not to Rommel's liking, and about midday he arrived at the headquarters of the 21st Panzer Division, which had stayed near the battlefield, and launched it on an indirect approach and attack. Driving westward through the valley north of Sidi Rezegh, the panzer regiment wheeled round and struck at the western flank of the British position there. Sweeping up the slope, it overran the airfield and overwhelmed part of the Support Group before the two remaining British armoured brigades were able to intervene. Their belated counterattacks were not coordinated, and ended in a state of confusion as darkness fell. But that was not the end of a bad day. For the 15th Panzer Division, returning to the battle area at dusk after its 'day off', hit the rear of the 4th Armoured Brigade and surrounded the leaguer in which its headquarters and reserve, the 8th Hussars, were lying. Taken by surprise, most of the personnel, tanks, and wireless links were captured. The brigade commander had been directing the counterattack at Sidi Rezegh, and thus escaped capture—but when dawn came on the 23rd he found himself left with a mutilated and scattered brigade while short of the means to direct and reassemble its fragments. That plight paralysed his action on what proved a still more critical day.

It was a compensation, though not immediately, that the headquarters of the Afrika Korps suffered a similar fate early on the 23rd. This came about because Cunningham had at last given the order for the 13th Corps to start advancing—although only in a limited way. The New Zealanders took Capuzzo on the 22nd, and one brigade (the 6th) was then told to push on towards Sidi Rezegh. Soon after dawn on the 23rd it bumped into and overran the Afrika Korps H.Q. Cruewell only escaped capture because he had just gone off to conduct the next phase of the battle. But his loss of operational staff and wireless links became a serious handicap in the days that followed—more of a handicap than was realised by the British, who were concerned with their own troubles and growing afflictions.

November 23 was a Sunday—in England the 'Sunday next before Advent' and in Germany 'Totensonntag', the 'Sunday of the Dead'. In the light of what happened in the desert that day it was grimly apt that the battle was subsequently given that name by the Germans.

During the night the British force at Sidi Rezegh had withdrawn a short step southward, to await reinforcement by the 1st South African Division, which was now being brought up. But the junction was never achieved. For a concentrated thrust by the two panzer divisions, emerging from the early morning mist, took the British and South Africans by surprise and split them apart, as well as sweeping through their transport leaguers and producing a stampede. The disaster would have been greater if the panzer divisions had not been called off at this moment by a signal from Cruewell, who had not got a clear picture of the situation, and wanted to link up with the Italian Ariete Division before attempting a decisive blow. But the Italians were cautiously slow in advancing, and it was not until the afternoon that Cruewell launched his attack, from the south, against the major portion of Norrie's advanced forces, the now isolated 5th South African Brigade and 22nd Armoured Brigade—some of the smaller fragments had managed to slip out of the trap in the interval. By the time he struck, a good defence had been organised. His concentrated attack eventually succeeded in bursting into the position and overwhelming the defenders—of whom some 3,000 were captured or killed. But the Afrika Korps lost over seventy of its remaining 160 tanks.

The tank losses suffered in this one direct attack on a defensive position largely offset the material profit gained by skilful manœuvre during the previous days. Indeed the crippling cost of this tactical success was strategically more damaging to the Germans than anything else in the course of 'Operation Crusader'. While the 30th Corps had suffered much heavier losses—and had only some seventy tanks left fit for action out of the 500 with which it had started—the British had a large reserve from which to restore their tank strength, whereas Rommel had no such reserve.

On November 24 the battle took another dramatic turn. For Rommel now sought to exploit his success by a deep thrust to, and over, the frontier—into the rear area of the Eighth Army—with all his mobile forces. Rather than lose time while they were assembling, he set off with the 21st Panzer Division as soon as it was ready to move, and himself took the lead—telling the 15th to follow, and being promised that the Italian Mobile Corps (Ariete armoured and Trieste motor divisions) would back up the panzer divisions, to close the ring round the British forces.

His initial intention, as indicated by his overnight report to Berlin and Rome, was to take advantage of the splintered state of the British forces and relieve the German–Italian frontier garrisons. But during the night his aim expanded, according to the evidence of his principal staff officers, and their statements are borne out by the headquarters war diary, which recorded that: 'The Commander-in-Chief decided to pursue the enemy with his armoured divisions, to restore the situation on the Sollum front, and at the same time advance against rearward communications of the British in the area of Sidi Omar. . . . This would mean that they would soon be compelled to give up the struggle.'

Rommel was striking at the mind of the opposing commander, as well as against the rear of the opposing forces and their supplies. At that moment such a stroke had greater promise than Rommel knew. For on the previous day, following the disastrous outcome of the armoured battle, Cunningham had thought of retreating over the frontier, and had only been stopped by the arrival of Auchinleck—who flew up from Cairo and insisted on a continuance of the struggle. Rommel's dash for the frontier, however, then caused a stampede among those who were in its path, and naturally produced still greater alarm at Eighth Army Headquarters.

By four o'clock in the afternoon, Rommel reached the frontier at Bir Sheferzen—having covered sixty miles in five hours' drive through the desert. On arrival, he immediately sent a battle-group through the frontier wire on a north-eastward drive to the Halfaya Pass, to dominate the Eighth Army's coastward route of retreat and supply, while extending the threat to its rear. After leading the battle-group some distance on its way, Rommel turned back, but was stranded in the desert by engine trouble. Luckily for him, Cruewell happened to pass the spot in his own command vehicle, and picked him up. But darkness was falling, and they could not find a gap in the frontier wire. Thus the two commanders, together with their chiefs of staff, spent the night amid the British and Indian troops in that area—dependent for their safety only on the natural instinct of ordinary soldiers to 'let sleeping generals lie'. For Cruewell's command vehicle was one that had been captured from the British. That also helped them to slip away at dawn unchallenged and get back safely to the headquarters of the 21st Panzer Division.

But on returning there, after twelve hours' 'detention', Rommel found that the 15th Panzer Division had not yet arrived on the frontier, while the

Ariete Division had come to a halt at an early stage of its follow-up advance
—on sighting the 1st South African Brigade in position across its path. The
transport columns bringing up fuel supplies had also failed to arrive. These
delays not only hindered but diminished the development of Rommel's
counterstroke. He could not carry out his plan of sending a battle-group
eastward to Habata, the British railhead, to block both the descents of the
escarpment and the main inland route to Egypt along its crest. He also had to
drop his idea of sending another battle-group southward to the Jarabub
Oasis, along the track past Fort Maddalena, where the Eighth Army's
advanced headquarters lay—a move which would have multiplied the confusion and alarm there. Even in the frontier zone, the day slipped away
without any more fruitful action than an abortive and costly attack on Sidi
Omar by the already weak tank regiment of the 21st Panzer Division. When
the stronger 15th Panzer Division belatedly appeared on the scene, its northward sweep along the near side of the frontier merely achieved the destruction of a field workshop where sixteen British tanks were under repair.

Such a slight development of the menace that had loomed so large the
day before allowed the British a chance to recover their breath and their
balance. Moreover, early on the third day, November 26, Cunningham was
replaced as Commander of the Eighth Army by Auchinleck's Deputy Chief
of the General Staff, Neil Ritchie—appointed in this emergency as a way of
ensuring that the battle should be continued whatever the risks. It was very
fortunate for the British that the enemy's drive had missed the two big
supply dumps south of the Trigh el Abd on which they were largely dependent for the possibility of continuing the battle and resuming their
advance. The panzer divisions' south-eastward drive from Sidi Rezegh
passed well north of the dumps, but the Italians' line of advance, if they had
pushed on, would have come closer to the dumps.

But although Rommel's thrust had lost momentum, the British situation
remained very precarious on the morning of the 26th. The 30th Corps was
so disrupted that it did nothing during the day to relieve the enemy's threat
to the rearward parts of the 13th Corps—and these, besides being widely
separated, were also isolated by wireless breakdowns. The Germans, however, were also suffering from intercommunication trouble, due to loss of
wireless links, and it was far more detrimental in their case. For their prospects depended on quick and co-ordinated action to develop the threat to the
British rear, whereas the best thing that the British troops there could do
was to stand firm in their frontier positions while the advanced part of the
13th Corps continued to push on westward and link up with the Tobruk
force in a double threat to Rommel's rear. This threat had now begun to

produce a succession of signals from Panzer Group H.Q., back at El Adem, calling for the return of the panzer divisions to relieve the pressure.

These disturbing calls from the rear combined with wireless breakdowns and fuel shortages in the forward area to upset the continuation of Rommel's counterstroke. He had ordered Cruewell that morning, the 26th, 'to clear the Sollum front quickly'—by a simultaneous attack with the 15th Panzer Division on one side and the 21st on the other. But he was dismayed to find that the 15th had moved back to Bardia early in the morning to replenish its fuel and ammunition, and then, just as it was returning to the battlefield, he found that the 21st had withdrawn from Halfaya, on a misinterpreted order, and was likewise on its way back to replenish at Bardia. So no action developed that day, and in the evening Rommel reluctantly decided to let the 21st Panzer Division continue its return journey to Tobruk. Next day he ordered the 15th to follow suit—after an early morning attack in which it succeeded in overwhelming the headquarters and support elements of the rearmost New Zealand brigade. That was the fade-out finish of a counter-stroke that had opened so promisingly.

Retrospective comment on it has naturally been influenced by the knowledge that the thrust failed. Tactically minded critics have taken the view that Rommel should, instead, have concentrated on a more local exploitation of his success at Sidi Rezegh: finishing off what remained of 30th Corps, or crushing the New Zealand Division in its advanced position, or capturing Tobruk—thus clearing his flank and line of supply. But none of these tactical courses offered as great a chance of decisive strategic results against the British, while they carried more risk to him of losing time and being decisively weakened in a fruitless assault. The balance of numbers was so heavily against Rommel from the outset that he was bound to be beaten in a prolonged battle of attrition. If he tried to follow up and wipe out the remaining tanks of the 30th Corps, they could always evade battle—being faster than his own. The other courses meant attacking infantry and artillery in defensive positions. Since he could not afford to fight a battle of attrition, it would have been folly to pursue any of these tactical courses if any better prospect was open. Such a prospect was provided, inherently, by the course he chose— a deep strategic thrust with all his mobile forces. The chances were increased by the fact that he had at last induced Mussolini to put the Italian Mobile Corps under his command.

Rommel's stroke has often been criticised, after the event, as rash. But the history of war shows that a stroke of this kind has many times been successful —especially through its moral effect on the opposing troops and, even more, on their commanders. It was supported, too, by Rommel's own experience.

Twice previously, in April and June, he had produced a British retreat—in the first case a collapse—by a similar strategic thrust that was made in lesser strength and did not reach such a threatening position. Two months later—in January 1942—he produced another collapse by a fourth deep thrust—although it did not go so far as the November one towards cutting the British line of retreat. Moreover, when he launched his November thrust the opposing forces were more scattered and splintered than in any of the three cases when his strategic ripostes were successful.

The causes of his failure on this occasion have already emerged in the account of those crucial days—the delay of the 15th Panzer Division and the inertia of the Italian Mobile Corps in backing up the Rommel-led drive of the 21st Panzer Division; the consequent loss of momentum and spread in the exploiting 'shock-wave'; the fumbling and futile action on the frontier: due in part to lack of accurate information, wireless breakdowns, and misinterpreted orders; the creation by the British of a threat to their opponent's rear; Auchinleck's determination to continue the battle, and press this counter-threat, instead of retreating; the replacement of the Eighth Army's commander at a critical moment. His successor, being appointed in such circumstances, was bound to continue the battle whatever the risks—and this turned out a fortunate decision, although it might have proved fatal. (Two months later, the successor's reaction to a lesser threat was similar to his predecessor's in November.)

There is another factor which deserves attention, and emphasis, in any military analysis of the episode, and its lessons. The decision to continue the battle would have been of no avail, and merely led to worse disaster, if the stampede which Rommel produced had become more widespread. But most of the 'fragments' of the 30th Corps which were not in his path stayed in or near their previous positions, even though isolated, and so did those of the 13th Corps. The very fact of being so split up, and in the 30th Corps so stunned by the battering suffered in the previous days, helped to check the usual tendency of such scattered bodies to fall back towards their base. In this case, the enemy had so clearly outstripped them in his eastward drive that it must have seemed safer to 'stay put', on the edge of the whirlpool, even though the continued arrival of supplies was uncertain.

When Rommel's strategic counterthrust failed to achieve its purpose, the first question was whether he could recover from the miscarriage, and the next question was whether he could possibly regain the upper hand. Astonishingly, in view of his weakness, he succeeded in his answer to both questions. Yet he was unable to profit by his regained advantage, and had to retreat in the end, through the accumulating effects of attrition. That eventual issue tends to show that he was right in trying his deep, and seemingly rash, strategic counterthrust of November 24—as the one move that offered a good chance of tilting the scales decisively in his favour.

When the Afrika Korps turned back westward, with its sixty remaining tanks (of which a third were light tanks), its chances of retrieving the situation at Tobruk by direct action looked dim, while its own situation appeared very precarious. For the New Zealand Division's westward advance, supported by nearly ninety Valentine and Matilda tanks, broke through Rommel's investing curtain on the night of the 26th and linked up with the British force at Tobruk—which comprised more than seventy tanks (including twenty lights). Meanwhile a fresh delivery from the base had brought the tank strength of the 7th Armoured Division up to nearly 130, so that in all the British now had a superiority of 5 to 1 in tanks (and 7 to 1 in gun-armed tanks). If they had been used in a fully concentrated way the Afrika Korps would have had a poor prospect of survival, and the 7th Armoured Division alone should have been able to crush it.

The Afrika Korps was in jeopardy during the first stage of its withdrawal, and all the more because the 21st Panzer Division was delayed by a blocking position on its route, and could give no aid to the 15th Panzer Division when this was intercepted and assailed on the afternoon of November 27 by the two armoured brigades of the 7th Armoured Division—with three times as many tanks as it had. One brigade (the 22nd) barred its path, while the other (the 4th) attacked the marching column from the flank, and caused havoc among the transport. Although the Germans managed to check the attack after some critical hours, their own westward march along the Trigh Capuzzo track was brought to a halt. But as dusk approached the British tanks withdrew southward into the desert to lie up for the night in a protective leaguer, in accordance with their usual practice. That allowed the Germans to push on westward under cover of darkness. On the next day the British armoured brigades renewed their attack, but were kept at bay by the enemy's anti-tank screen—and when night came the Germans were again able to push on unopposed.

Thus by the morning of the 29th the Afrika Korps linked up again with the rest of Rommel's forces, and relieved the pressure on them. Next day Rommel concentrated against the isolated 6th New Zealand Brigade on the Sidi Rezegh ridge, while using the Ariete Division to cover his flank, and his operation, against interference from the British armour lying to the south. His tanks, having got round to the far side of the position, struck from the west while his infantry attacked from the south. By evening the 6th New Zealand Brigade had been driven off the ridge, but a remnant got away and rejoined the main part of the division in the valley below, near Belhamed. The British armour, although brought up to strength again by a fresh delivery of tanks and concentrated under the 4th Armoured Brigade, made no vigorous effort to break through Rommel's 'curtain' and come to the rescue. The commanders had been lured so often into traps, and suffered so much from the enemy's skilful combination of tanks with anti-tank guns, that they had now become excessively cautious.

Early on December 1 Rommel's forces closed in around the New Zealanders at Belhamed, cutting the 'corridor' between them and the Tobruk force. About 4.30 a.m. the 4th Armoured Brigade was ordered to drive north 'with all speed' at first light and 'at all costs' engage the enemy tanks. It moved off about 7 a.m., reached the Sidi Rezegh airfield at 9 a.m. and, after descending the escarpment, made contact with the New Zealanders. A counterattack was then planned against the enemy tanks—estimated as 'about forty'. But by this time part of the New Zealanders had been overrun, and a general withdrawal was ordered. What was left of the New Zealand Division retreated eastward to Zaafran (and then during the night to the frontier), while the 4th Armoured Brigade made a southward withdrawal of twenty-five miles to Bir Berraneb.

The outcome of this third round of the battle was an astonishing achievement on the part of an enemy force that had been outnumbered 7 to 1 in fighting tanks at the start of the round, and when it ended was still outnumbered 4 to 1 by the total of those on the British side.

Auchinleck now flew up to Eighth Army headquarters again. Correctly gauging the underlying weakness of Rommel's forces, he was determined to continue the battle, having fresh forces, and reserves of tanks, which he could bring up for the purpose. The 4th Indian Division was relieved on the frontier by the 2nd South African, and sent forward to join the 7th Armoured Division in an outflanking move to cut Rommel's line of supply and retreat.

When Rommel received news of this new and strong threat, he decided to pull back westward, and concentrate his remaining tanks in a stroke to dislocate the British outflanking move. So on the night of December 4 the Afrika Korps slipped away to the west, abandoning the investment of Tobruk.

That morning the leading brigade of the 4th Indian Division had launched an attack on the Italian position at Bir el Gubi (twenty miles south of Sidi Rezegh), but the assault broke down under the defenders' fire. The assault was renewed next morning, but again repelled. During these operations the

British armour had covered the northern flank of the attack against interference from Rommel, but unfortunately it moved back to leaguer in the afternoon of the 5th, with the intention of trying out a new system of leaguering. At 5.30 p.m. Rommel's panzer forces suddenly appeared on the scene, at Bir el Gubi, and overran part of the unshielded Indian brigade—the rest managed to escape as darkness fell.

Following this setback, the commander of the 30th Corps, Norrie, decided to postpone his intended flank advance to Acroma—a postponement that forfeited the chance of cutting Rommel's line of retreat. The 4th Armoured Brigade was ordered to seek and destroy the enemy's armour before a renewed advance was attempted. But the aim was not achieved, and examination of the records reveals little evidence of effort to fulfil it, although a fresh delivery of forty tanks had brought the brigade's total up to 136—almost three times the remaining strength of the Afrika Korps. The brigade spent the next two days in position near Bir el Gubi, with occasional short moves hopefully but vainly intended to draw the enemy into a direct assault on the gun positions of the 4th Indian Division.

On December 7, Rommel decided to withdraw to the Gazala line, having been notified that no reinforcements were likely to arrive before the end of the year; that night the Afrika Korps began to disengage. The British were slow to realise what was happening, and it was not until December 9 that their armour started on a drive for 'Knightsbridge', the road-junction south of Acroma. It was checked by an enemy rearguard eight miles short of Knightsbridge—and showed more concern to protect itself than to trap the enemy. By the 11th Rommel's forces had got back safely to Gazala, where a defensive position had earlier been prepared, as a reserve line.

On December 13, Godwin-Austen's 13th Corps, which had now taken over charge of the pursuit, launched its attack on the Gazala line. The frontal attack was checked, but the Italian Mobile Corps covering Rommel's inland flank gave way rapidly under pressure, and the British left wing reached Sidi Breghisc, fifteen miles behind the Gazala line. But a panzer counterattack then brought the envelopment to a halt.

On the 14th, before renewing the assault, Godwin-Austen sent the 4th Armoured Brigade on a wider flank circuit—to Halegh Eleba, a multiple track junction midway between Gazala and Mechili. This move to get astride Rommel's rear started at 2.30 p.m., and the brigade lay up for the night after trekking twenty miles due south. Starting again at 7 a.m., with sixty miles to cover in its circuit, it was delayed by bad going and did not reach Halegh Eleba until 3 p.m., four hours late by timetable—and too late to aid the main attack by drawing off Rommel's panzer reserve as planned.

Moreover, it then sat tight and did nothing to make itself felt, so that the enemy did not become aware of its presence until next morning.

Meanwhile the main attack on the 15th had been a failure. An assault near the coast had gained a foothold in the Gazala position, but an enveloping attack was upset by a panzer counterstroke at midday, which nipped off an advanced part of the attacking force.

The British higher command still hoped that the strong armoured brigade it had placed in the enemy's rear would have decisive results by the next day. But on the morning of the 16th the brigade moved twenty miles south in order to refuel in complete security, and when it returned in the afternoon at a point nearer the front, it was checked by an anti-tank screen—and retired southward again to leaguer for the night. It recorded an interchange of fire, at long range, but no casualties. The impression left on the analyst is that the predominant desire was to see the enemy go—and he went, along the open path that was left for his passage.

For even the small losses incurred in the successful panzer counterstroke on the 15th had left the Afrika Korps with barely thirty tanks, whereas the British now had nearly 200 on the scene. Weighing the situation, Rommel saw that it was impossible to hold on for long to the Gazala line, and decided to take a long step back, and get well out of reach, while awaiting reinforcements. He would go back to the Mersa Brega bottleneck on the Tripolitanian frontier, a position ideal for defence. It had also been the springboard for his first offensive, and would serve that purpose again. So on the night of December 16 he began his withdrawal—the Afrika Korps and the Italian Mobile Corps travelling by the desert route while the Italian infantry divisions marched back along the coast-road.

The pursuit was slow to get moving. The 4th Armoured Brigade did not start until 1 p.m. next day, and two hours later halted for the night twelve miles short of its earlier position at Halegh Eleba, while administrative preparations were made for a further advance. On the 18th it advanced along a desert route to a point south of Mechili, but on swinging northwards just missed catching the tail of the enemy's retreating columns.

Meanwhile the 4th Indian Division, mounted in motor transport and accompanied by infantry tanks, pressed on nearer the coast, through the rugged hill-country of the Jebel Akhdar. Derna was taken on the morning of the 19th—but the bulk of the enemy's foot-marching columns had already passed safely through the bottleneck. An attempt to intercept them farther west was hampered by the difficult country and shortage of petrol, and only a few fragments were caught. A large proportion of the pursuing forces were now grounded for lack of petrol.

Motorised infantry were employed to lead the chase across the desert chord of the great Benghazi bend. Reaching Antelat on December 22 they found the enemy's panzer force (with thirty tanks) posted near Beda Fomm—to cover the coastwise retreat of the Italian foot-marching forces—and were kept at bay until the 26th, when Rommel's rearguard fell back another thirty miles to Agedabia. Meanwhile the re-equipped 22nd Armoured Brigade had come up to reinforce the pursuit force. Following up the enemy rearguard, the Guards Brigade launched a frontal assault on Agedabia—which failed—while the 22nd Armoured Brigade made a turning move thirty miles deeper in the desert, through El Haseiat. This suffered an unexpected reverse. For on the 27th its own flank was suddenly assailed by a German panzer force, and then surrounded in further fighting three days later. Although some thirty of the British tanks managed to escape, sixty-five were lost. In making this riposte Rommel had been helped by the arrival of two fresh tank companies (thirty tanks) which had been landed at Benghazi on the 19th, just before the port was evacuated—the first reinforcement which had reached him since the opening of 'Crusader'.

The British reverse at El Haseiat was a disappointing and frustrating end to the long pursuit—a cold douche to the exhilaration of ultimate success in the battle around Tobruk. But substantial profits were gained through Rommel's enforced retreat, which left the German–Italian garrisons on the frontier isolated and without hope. Bardia surrendered on January 2, and the two remaining frontier posts on the 17th. This brought the number of prisoners captured in the frontier positions to 20,000, including those taken earlier at Sidi Omar, and the total Axis casualties to 33,000—compared with just under 18,000 on the British side. But nearly two-thirds of the Axis loss were Italians, and of the 13,000 Germans a considerable part were administrative personnel, whereas the bulk of the British loss in the six weeks' battle was in the fighting troops, and included many highly trained desert veterans, who were difficult to replace.

The disadvantage of having to rely on inexperienced troops, particularly in the desert, would be shown once again in the next battle. This came in the third week of January—when Rommel, supposedly crippled, delivered another of his unexpected strokes: with startlingly similar result to his opening stroke in 1941.

CHAPTER 16

UPSURGE IN THE FAR EAST

From 1931 onward the Japanese were aggressively engaged in expanding their footholds on the Asiatic mainland at the expense of the Chinese, who were weakened by internal conflict, and to the detriment of American and British interests in that sphere. In that year they had invaded Manchuria and converted it into a Japanese satellite state. In 1932 they penetrated China itself, and from 1937 on pursued a consistent effort to establish their control of that vast area, but became enmeshed in the toils of guerrilla warfare, and eventually sought a solution of the problem in further expansionist moves, southward, aimed to shut off the Chinese from outside supplies.

Following Hitler's conquest of France and the Low Countries in 1940, the Japanese took advantage of France's helplessness by getting her to agree, under threat, to their 'protective' occupation of French Indo-China.

In reply President Roosevelt demanded, on July 24, 1941, the withdrawal of Japanese troops from Indo-China—and to enforce his demand he issued orders on the 26th freezing all Japanese assets in the United States and placing an embargo on oil supply. Mr Churchill took simultaneous action, and two days later the refugee Dutch Government in London was induced to follow suit—which meant, as Churchill had remarked, that 'Japan was deprived at a stroke of her vital oil supplies'.

In earlier discussions, as far back as 1931, it had always been recognised that such a paralysing stroke would force Japan to fight, as the only alternative to collapse or the abandonment of her policy. It is remarkable that she deferred striking for more than four months, while trying to negotiate a lifting of the oil embargo. The United States Government refused to lift it unless Japan withdrew not only from Indo-China but also from China. No Government, least of all the Japanese, could be expected to swallow such humiliating conditions, and such 'loss of face'. So there was every reason to expect war in the Pacific at any moment, from the last week of July onwards. In these circumstances the Americans and British were lucky to be allowed

The Pacific: December 8,1941

Japanese occupied territory December 1941

four months' grace before the Japanese struck. But little advantage was taken of this interval for defensive preparation.

On the morning of December 7, 1941, a Japanese naval force with six aircraft-carriers delivered a shattering air attack on Pearl Harbor, the American naval base in the Hawaiian Islands. The stroke was made ahead of the declaration of war, following the precedent of the attack on Port Arthur in 1904, Japan's opening stroke in her war against Russia.

Until early in 1941 Japan's plan in case of war against the United States was to use her main fleet in the southern Pacific in conjunction with an attack on the Philippine Islands, to meet an American advance across the ocean to the relief of their garrison there. That was the move that the Americans were expecting the Japanese to make, and their expectations had been reinforced by the recent Japanese occupation of Indo-China.

Admiral Yamamoto, however, had in the meantime conceived a new plan—of a surprise attack on Pearl Harbor. The striking force made a very roundabout approach via the Kurile Islands and came down from the north upon the Hawaiian Islands undetected, then launched its attack before sunrise, with 360 aircraft, from a position nearly 300 miles from Pearl Harbor. Four of the eight American battleships were sunk, one was beached, and the others badly damaged. In little over an hour the Japanese had gained control of the Pacific.

By this stroke the way was cleared for an uninterrupted seaborne invasion of American, British and Dutch territories in that ocean. While the main Japanese striking force had been steaming towards the Hawaiian Islands, other naval forces had been escorting troopship convoys into the Southwest Pacific. Almost simultaneously with the air attack on Pearl Harbor, landings began in the Malay Peninsula as well as in the Philippines.

The former were aimed at the great British naval base at Singapore, but there was no attempt to attack it from the sea—the kind of attack which the defence had been primarily designed to meet. The approach was very indirect. While a landing was made at Kota Bharu on the north-east coast of the Malay Peninsula, to seize airfields and distract attention, the main forces were disembarked on the Siamese neck of the peninsula, some 500 miles north of Singapore. From these landing-places in the extreme north-east the Japanese forces poured down the *west* coast of the peninsula, successively outflanking the lines on which the British forces attempted to check them.

The Japanese profited not only by their unexpected choice of such a difficult route but by the opportunities for unexpected infiltration which the thick vegetation often provided. After almost continuous retreat for six weeks the British forces were forced to withdraw from the mainland into the island of Singapore, at the end of January. On the night of February 8, the Japanese launched their attack across the mile-wide straits, got ashore at numerous points, and developed fresh infiltrations along a broad front. On February 15, the defending forces surrendered, and with them was lost the key to the South-west Pacific.

In a smaller, separate operation, the Japanese had launched an attack on the British base at Hong Kong, starting on December 8, and forced the surrender of the colony, with its garrison, by Christmas Day.

On the main Philippine island of Luzon, the initial landings north of Manila had been quickly followed by a landing in the rear of the capital. Under this dislocating leverage, and the converging threat, the American forces abandoned most of the island and fell back into the small Bataan Peninsula, before the end of December. There, by contrast, they were only open to frontal assault on a narrowly contracted front, and succeeded in holding out until April before they were overwhelmed.

Long before that, and even before the fall of Singapore, the Japanese tide of conquest was spreading through the Malay Archipelago. On January 11, Japanese forces landed in Borneo and Celebes, and stronger ones followed on the 24th. Five weeks later, on March 1, the Japanese launched an attack on Java, the core of the Dutch East Indies, after the island had been isolated by flanking moves. Within barely a week, the whole of Java had fallen into their hands like a ripe plum.

But the apparently imminent threat to Australia did not develop. The main Japanese effort was now directed in the opposite direction, westward, towards the conquest of Burma. The direct but wide-fronted advance from Thailand upon Rangoon was an indirect approach to their major object on the Asiatic mainland as a whole, the paralysis of China's power of resistance. For Rangoon was the port of entry for Anglo-American supplies of equipment to China, by way of the Burma Road.

At the same time, this move was shrewdly designed to complete the conquest of the western gateway to the Pacific, and there establish a firm barrier across the main routes by which any overland Anglo-American offensive might subsequently be attempted. On March 8, Rangoon fell, and within a further two months the British forces were driven out of Burma, over the mountains, back into India.

The Japanese had thus secured a covering position so naturally strong that any attempt at reconquest would be badly handicapped and bound to be a very slow process.

A long time passed before the Allies built up forces sufficient to attempt the recovery of Japan's conquests—beginning at the south-eastern end. Here they benefited from the preservation of Australia, which provided them with a large-scale base close to the chain of Japanese outposts.

Japan was the only country in an advanced industrial state outside Europe and North America—due to the rapid process of modernisation which had begun under the Emperor Meiji from 1868 onward. Yet at heart Japanese society remained 'feudal', where the warrior was exalted, not the manufacturer or merchant. The Emperor was divine, and the ruling class all-powerful. Moreover the influence of the military was immense. Fervently patriotic, and often bitterly anti-foreign, they hoped to establish their country's domination over the whole of eastern Asia, particularly China. From the 1930s onward they had, by threats and assassinations, virtually assumed control of Japanese policy.

Japan's approach to political and strategic problems was much influenced by the fact that she had never suffered defeat since her modernisation began. Her people's belief in her invincibility became widespread after the war with Russia of 1904-5, when both on land and sea her forces had demonstrated their superiority—and shown that the dominance of Europeans over the rest of the world's peoples could be breached.

In August 1914 Japan, as Britain's ally since 1902, had taken Tsingtao and Shantung, the German concessions in China, together with the Marshall, Caroline, and Mariana groups of islands in the Pacific, all of which were German colonies. The gains were confirmed by the Treaty of Versailles in 1919, at the end of the First World War—thus leaving Japan the predominant power on the west side of the Pacific. Despite this, her people were dissatisfied with her war gains, and left with the feeling that she was a 'have-not' power, like Italy. So the Japanese came to feel that they had something in common with Italy and with Germany.

The sense of frustration probably developed from the failure of Japan's attempt to control China, in 1915, when her '21 Demands' had to be withdrawn under American protest. Significantly, China was always the main goal for the Japanese Army from the Sino-Japanese War of 1895 onward. Although at the end of the First World War the Imperial Defence Policy named the United States as the prime potential enemy, in accord with the naval view, the Army was always more apprehensive about Soviet Russia, whose large land forces in the Far East were regarded as a much greater threat to Japan's continental designs.

Then came a series of humiliations for Japan in the years 1921-4. First, the British politely declined to renew the alliance with Japan. That break was to some extent prompted by various signs of Japanese expansionist plans in the Pacific, but the definite decision was made under strong American pressure. The Japanese took it as an insult, and a sign that the white peoples were lining up against them. Their indignation was increased by successive American legislative steps to restrict Japanese immigration, culminating in the Act of 1924 that excluded Asiatics as immigrants. The double 'loss of face' was bitterly resented.

Meanwhile the British had announced plans for building a Far East naval base at Singapore, adequate for a battle-fleet. That was obviously intended as a check upon Japan, and interpreted by the Japanese as a challenge.

All this reacted to the detriment of the Japanese political leaders, who came under increasing attack for having accepted a 3–5–5 basis in relation to the American and British battlefleets under the Washington naval limitation treaty of 1921. Other grievances were that they had agreed to return Shantung Province to China, and later had signed the Nine-Power Treaty of 1922 guaranteeing the integrity of China.

Actually, and ironically, the Treaty of Washington assisted Japan's subsequent expansionist moves by weakening checks upon her in the Pacific— the projected American and British naval bases there being either delayed or weakly fortified. She herself found it easier to evade the specifications of gun-power and tonnage during the thirteen-year period before she openly repudiated the treaty.

The more liberal political leaders of Japan also suffered from the world economic crisis that developed in 1929, as she was particularly hard hit by it, with a resulting growth of discontent that the militarists were able to exploit in pressing their argument that expansion was the solution for Japan's economic problem.

In September 1931 the 'Mukden incident' gave the local Japanese Army leaders a pretext, and opportunity, to expand into Manchuria, and turn it into their puppet state of Manchukuo. Their troops guarding the South Manchurian railway, under treaty right, attacked and disarmed the Chinese garrisons in Mukden and neighbouring towns on the excuse of self-defence against a threatened attack. The facts were obscure, and obscured, thus helping the Japanese to overrun the whole of Manchuria within the next few months. Although the occupation was not recognised by the League of Nations, or the United States, protests and widespread criticism gave the Japanese an incentive to withdraw from the League in 1933. Three years later they joined with Nazi Germany and Fascist Italy in the Anti-Comintern Pact.

In July 1937, an alleged clash at the Marco Polo Bridge, another highly suspicious 'incident', led to the Japanese Kwantung Army invading North China proper. The invasion continued and extended during the next two years, but the Japanese became increasingly bogged down in the struggle against the Chinese nationalist forces under Chiang Kai-Shek, while in their attack at Shanghai in the summer of 1937 they suffered a repulse. This, however, turned out to their advantage in the long run, as it spurred them to correct tactical faults and tendencies to overconfidence dating back to the Russo-Japanese War—although not before they had suffered a further lesson, at the hands of the Soviet Army, in a clash over the disputed frontier of West Manchuria. Here, in the Nomonhan region, a Japanese force of some 15,000 men was encircled, and over 11,000 were lost, when the Russians brought up five mechanised brigades with three infantry divisions, in August 1939.

In that same month the unexpected news of the Nazi–Soviet Pact caused a revulsion, and the return of moderate Japanese Governments. But that reaction only continued until Hitler's conquest of Western Europe in 1940, and in July 1940 a pro-Axis Government under Prince Konoye was put into power by the Army. Japanese expansion in China was then accelerated, while at the end of September Japan signed the 'Tripartite Pact' with Germany and Italy, by which these three undertook to oppose any fresh country that joined the Allies—a pact aimed primarily against intervention by America.

In April 1941 the Japanese further re-insured themselves by a neutrality pact with Soviet Russia. That promised to release Japanese forces for southerly expansionist operations—although even then suspicion of Russia and her designs led the Japanese to allot only eleven divisions for such operations, while thirteen were kept in Manchuria, and twenty-two in China.

On July 24 the Japanese, with the reluctant compliance of the Vichy Government, took over French Indo-China. Two days later President Roosevelt 'froze' all Japanese assets, an action that was quickly followed by the British and Dutch Governments. Thus trade with Japan was brought to a stop, particularly in oil.

Japan imported 88 per cent of her peacetime oil consumption. At the time of the embargo she held stocks sufficient for three years of normal use, or half that period at full war consumption. Moreover, a Japanese War Office survey had shown that stocks would be exhausted before the three years that were reckoned as necessary to finish the war in China, so a victory there seemed all the more important. The only available resource left lay in the oilfields of the Dutch East Indies, and it was reckoned that although the Dutch were likely to destroy their installations there before capture these could be repaired and brought into use before home stocks were too badly depleted. Oil from Java and Sumatra would save the situation, and enable China's conquest to be completed.

Conquest of the region, including Malaya, would also bring possession of four-fifths of the world's rubber output, and two-thirds of its tin output. That would not only be a very valuable gain for Japan, but hit her opponents worse than the loss of the oil.

These were the main factors that Japan's leaders had to consider when faced with the trade embargo. Unless America could be induced to lift it, they were faced with a choice between abandoning their ambitions—in which case an Army coup at home might follow—or seizing the oil and fighting the white powers. It was a stark alternative. If they continued the campaign in China, but withdrew from Indo-China and stopped southward expansion, they might obtain some mitigation of the embargo, but Japan herself would be becoming weaker—and less able to withstand any further demands by the United States.

Natural hesitation to make an all-or-nothing choice may explain the puzzle why the Japanese were so tardy in striking, and deferred a decision for four months. There was also the natural instinct of military chiefs to desire ample time for completing preparations, and prolonged arguments over the strategy to be adopted. One school of thought even optimistically hoped, and argued, that America might continue to stand aside if Japan confined herself to seizing Dutch and British territory.

On August 6 Japan besought the United States to lift the embargo. That same month came the American decision to hold the whole of the Philippine Islands in the event of war, and the Japanese request for the cessation of the flow of American reinforcements thither. It met a firm reply, warning the Japanese against further aggression.

After two more months of internal argument, Prince Konoye's Government was replaced by one under General Hideki Tojo—an event that was probably decisive. Even so, there was further prolonged discussion, and the decision for war was not taken until November 25. One precipitating factor was a report showing oil stocks as having shrunk by a quarter of their total between April and September.

Even then, the Commander-in-Chief of the Japanese Combined Fleet, Admiral Yamamoto, was given orders the same day that the attack on Pearl Harbor was to be cancelled if by any chance the continued negotiations in Washington were successful.

The naval strengths in the Pacific in December 1941 are summarised in the following table:*

	CAPITAL SHIPS	AIRCRAFT CARRIERS	HEAVY CRUISERS	LIGHT CRUISERS	DESTROYERS	SUBMARINES
BRITISH EMPIRE	2	—	1	7	13	—
U.S.A.	9	3	13	11	80	56
NETHERLANDS	—	—	—	3	7	13
FREE FRENCH	—	—	—	1	—	—
ALLIES TOTAL	11	3	14	22	100	69
JAPAN	10	10	18	18	113	63

The main point to note is that while the two sides were closely balanced in most respects, the Japanese had a great advantage in aircraft-carriers, the crucial arm. Moreover, what such a table cannot show are qualitative differences. The Japanese force was compact and well-trained, especially in night-fighting; it did not suffer command or language difficulties as on the Allied side. There were 6,000 miles of ocean between the two main bases of the Allies, Pearl Harbor and Singapore. Materially, the Japanese Navy was much better. It had many newer ships, while most of them were somewhat better-armed and faster. Of the capital ships, only H.M.S. *Prince of Wales* was a match in these respects for the better Japanese battleships.

In Army strength, the Japanese employed only eleven divisions, out of their overall total of fifty-one, for their operations in the South-west Pacific. That was under a quarter of a million fighting troops, and with administrative troops probably a total of about 400,000. Allied numbers are more uncertain. In deciding to attack, the Japanese estimated the British as having 11,000 in Hong Kong, 88,000 in Malaya, and 35,000 in Burma—a total of 134,000; the Americans as having 31,000 of their men in the Philippines, with about 110,000 Philippine troops; the Dutch as having 25,000 regulars and 40,000 militia. Superficially, to launch a far-reaching offensive with such small odds might seem a daring gamble. In reality, it was a well-

* Figures from Roskill: *The War at Sea*, vol. I, p. 560.

calculated gamble, as sea and air control would usually give the Japanese local superiority of numbers, while this would be multiplied by experience and superior quality of training—particularly in amphibious landings, jungle warfare, and night attacks.

In air strength the Japanese employed only 700 out of their total of 1,500 first-line Army aircraft, but these were reinforced by 480 Naval aircraft, of the 11th Air Fleet, based on Formosa—as well as 360 allocated for the Pearl Harbor stroke. Originally, the fleet carriers were allotted, and needed, to provide air cover for the southern operations. But in November, barely four weeks before the war, the range of the Zero fighters—which outclassed the Allied fighters available—was increased, so that they could fly the 450 miles from Formosa to the Philippines, and back. Thus the carriers were freed for the Pearl Harbor stroke.

Opposed to these powerful Japanese air forces were 307 American operational aircraft in the Philippines, including thirty-five long-range B.17 bombers, but otherwise inferior in quality; 158 first-line British aircraft in Malaya, mostly of obsolete types; and 144 Dutch in their territories. In Burma, the British then had only thirty-seven fighters. The Japanese superiority in quantity was multiplied by superiority in quality—particularly that of the Zero fighters.

The Japanese also owed much to their development of amphibious warfare, for such an oceanic area of islands and gulfs. Their one serious weakness was the relatively small size of their merchant marine—little more than 6 million tons of shipping—but that did not become a decisive handicap until later in the war.

In sum, the Japanese started the war with a great all-round advantage, especially in quality. In the opening stage, their only real danger lay in the possibility of a prompt intervention by the American Pacific Fleet—but that danger they forestalled by their Pearl Harbor stroke.

Intelligence is a further factor, of which sufficient account is rarely taken in setting out the balance of strength. In general, the Japanese were good in this way, owing to long and careful study of the areas beforehand—but the Allies enjoyed one immense advantage in that the Americans had broken the Japanese diplomatic code in the summer of 1940 (an achievement due to Colonel William F. Friedman). From then on, all Japanese Foreign Office or Command secret messages could be read by the Americans, and during the pre-war negotiations they knew the latest Tokyo proposals before they were presented. Only the exact date, and operational points of attack, were not passed to the Japanese ambassador.

Although the Americans were taken by surprise at Pearl Harbor, their knowledge of the Japanese codes was inherently a great basic advantage, and became such as they learnt to use it better.

Japanese strategy was geared to the dual aim, defensive and offensive, of securing the required oil supplies that would enable her to overcome a China that would in the same sweeping process be shut off from the supplies needed to maintain resistance. In taking the risk of challenging America, a power whose potential was vastly greater than their own, the Japanese leaders drew encouragement from the turn of events in Europe, where the Axis now dominated almost the whole Continent, and Soviet Russia was so hard pressed by Hitler's onslaught that she could hardly intervene in the Far East. If the Japanese fulfilled their dream of establishing a concentric defensive ring from the Aleutian Islands in the north round to Burma in the south, they hoped that the United States, after vain efforts to break through the ring, would eventually come to accept Japan's conquests and the establishment of what she called 'The Greater East Asia Co-Prosperity Sphere'.

The plan had a basic likeness to Hitler's concept of establishing offensively a defensive barrier from Archangel to Astrakhan, to shut out and keep out the Asiatic border.

Originally, the Japanese plan had been to seize the Philippines, then await the American recovery-move—which was expected to come through the mandated island territories—while concentrating her own forces to repel it. (Under the three-stage war-plan, the Japanese reckoned to complete the capture of the Philippines in fifty days, that of Malaysia in 100 days, and all the Dutch East Indies after 150 days.) But in August 1939, Admiral Yamamoto, an ardent believer in the value of aircraft-carriers, was appointed to command the Japanese Combined Fleet. He shrewdly saw the necessity of an immediate, and surprise, stroke to paralyse the United States Pacific Fleet—which he termed 'a dagger pointed at the throat of Japan'—and delay its countermoves. The Japanese Naval Staff rather dubiously and reluctantly accepted his argument.

The opening attack-problem was complicated by the timetable—and the zone differences (Sunday, December 7 in Hawaii would be Monday, December 8 in Malaya). But it was arranged that all the main operations would begin between 1715 hours and 1900 hours Greenwich Mean Time, and all assaults would take place in the early morning by local time.

On the American side, it had long been considered politically deplorable to abandon the Philippines, but the military argument that it was impossible to defend these islands, 5,000 miles from Pearl Harbor in Hawaii, had prevailed, so that the plan was only to maintain a foothold—on the fortified

Bataan peninsula in Luzon, near the capital Manila. In August 1941, however, the plan was changed and the decision taken to hold all the Philippines.

One factor in the change was the pressure of General Douglas MacArthur, who had been military adviser to the Philippine Government since 1935, and then at the end of July 1941 had been recalled to active duty in the United States Army and appointed Commanding General in the Far East; President Roosevelt's high opinion of MacArthur's judgement had earlier been shown by the way he had himself in 1934 extended MacArthur's four-year tenure as Chief of Staff of the United States Army by a year. Another factor was that President Roosevelt had come to feel that since Germany had become entangled in Russia he could venture to take a firmer line with Japan—as he had done in imposing the oil embargo. The third factor was the optimism aroused by the advent of the long-range B.17 bombers—which, it was hoped, would effectively hit not only Formosa but Japan herself. She, however, struck before any large number of B.17s reinforced the air force in the Philippines. Moreover, what was not seriously considered by the American Chiefs of Staff was a Japanese stroke at Pearl Harbor.

CHAPTER 17

JAPAN'S TIDE OF CONQUEST

The execution of the plan of attack on Pearl Harbor owed as much to Admiral Yamamoto's impulsion as had its adoption. For many months a stream of information, particularly about American ship movements, flowed in from the trained naval Intelligence officers who had been posted to the Japanese consulate in Honolulu. In the Japanese fleet itself the crews of ships and aircraft were intensively trained for the operation, and to carry it out in all kinds of weather; at least fifty practice flights were made by the bomber crews.

As already mentioned, the plan was much helped by the recently increased range of the Zero fighter type, which freed the carrier fleet from having to aid the South-west Pacific operations. It profited also from the evidence of the British naval attack on Taranto in November 1940, where the British Fleet Air Arm had succeeded, with only twenty-one torpedo-bombers, in sinking three Italian battleships lying in a strongly fortified harbour. Even then it had not been considered possible to launch aerial torpedoes in water where the depth was less than 75 feet—which was about the average at Taranto—and Pearl Harbor had thus been regarded as immune from that kind of attack, as the depth there was only 30–45 feet. But by 1941 the British, applying their experience at Taranto, had become able to launch aerial torpedoes in barely 40 feet depth of water, by fitting wooden fins that prevented them from 'porpoising' and hitting the shallow sea-bottom.

Learning these details from their embassies in Rome and London, the Japanese were stimulated to press on with similar experiments. Moreover, to make their planned attack more effective, their high-level bombers were equipped with 15-inch and 16-inch armour-piercing shells fitted with fins so that they would fall like bombs. Dropped vertically, no deck-armour could withstand them.

The United States Pacific Fleet could have countered the 'Taranto' danger by fitting its larger ships with anti-torpedo nets—and that possibility worried the Japanese—but Admiral Husband E. Kimmel, its Commander-in-Chief, had taken the view, like the Navy Department, that the cumbersome nets then available would be too much of a hindrance to quick movement of ships and to boat traffic. As the event showed, that decision virtually doomed the fleet at Pearl Harbor.

A combination of factors determined the date of the attack. The Japanese knew that Admiral Kimmel always brought his fleet back into Pearl Harbor during the weekend, and that the ships would not be fully manned then, thus increasing the effect of a surprise attack. So a Sunday was the natural choice. After mid-December the weather was likely to be unfavourable for amphibious landings in Malaya and the Philippines, as the monsoon would be at its peak, and unfavourable also for the refuelling at sea of the force to attack Pearl Harbor. On December 8 (Tokyo time), a Sunday at Hawaii, there would be no moonlight, and the consequent cloak of darkness would aid the surprise approach to Hawaii of the carrier force. The tides there would also be favourable for landings, an idea which was originally considered, although eventually rejected for lack of troopships and because the approach of such an invasion force was likely to be detected.

In choosing the approach route of the naval striking force, three alternatives were considered. One was a southerly route via the Marshall Islands, and another was a central route via the Midway Islands. These were the shorter, but they were discarded in favour of a northerly approach from the Kurile Islands—which would mean refuelling—because this avoided the shipping routes and also carried less risk of being spotted by the American reconnaissance aircraft patrols.

The Japanese also benefited from the use of what has been called the 'unequal leg' attack. Approaching in darkness, the carriers launched their planes at first light when at the nearest point to the target, then turned away from the target but not on a directly reversed route, and were rejoined by their aircraft at a point farther from the target than when they had been launched. Thus the Japanese aircraft flew one short, and one long, leg— whereas pursuing American aircraft would have to fly two long legs, one out and one back. That disadvantage had not been considered by the American defence planners.

The targets, in order of importance, were: the American carriers (it was hoped by the Japanese that as many as six, and at least three, would be at Pearl Harbor); the battleships; the oil tanks and other port installations; the aircraft on the main bases at Wheeler, Hickam, and Bellows Field. The force used for this stroke by the Japanese was six carriers, carrying a total of 423 aircraft, of which 360 were employed in the attack—104 high-level bombers,

Attack on Pearl Harbor Dec 7, 1941

1st ATTACK
2nd ATTACK
45 FIGHTERS
34 FIGHTERS
54 HIGH-LEVEL BOMBERS
55 DIVE BOMBERS
40 TORPEDO BOMBERS
40 DIVE BOMBERS
50 HIGH-LEVEL BOMBERS
WHEELER FIELD
O A H U
Pearl Harbor
HICKHAM FIELD
Honolulu

0 Miles 15

Invasion of Hong Kong Dec 8/26, 1941

JAPANESE OCCUPIED CHINA

(NEW TERRITORIES)

GINDRINKERS LINE

Kowloon

Lantao   Victoria

Hong Kong

0 Miles 10

Invasion of the Philippine Islands Dec 10/June 9* 1941

*Resistance on Mindanao (S. Philippines) ended on this day

0 Miles 300
0 Kilometres 200

JAP. 14th ARMY (Homma) from Formosa

Batan Is.

Camiguin DEC. 10

Aparri DEC. 10

Vigan DEC. 10

L U Z O N

Ilagan

P A C I F I C   O C E A N

Lingayen Gulf

Lingayen DEC. 22

PHILIPPINE ISLANDS

Cabanatuan

DEC. 24 FROM RYUKYU IS.

JAN. 6 / APR. 9 US FORCES IN PENINSULA

Ipo

Bataan Peninsula

Corregidor

Manila JAN. 2

Lamon Bay

DEC. 12 FROM PALAU

MAY 6 LAST US RESISTANCE IN N. PHILIPPINES ENDS

Nasugbu

Batangas

Legaspi

Mindoro

Copyright © Cassell & Co. Ltd 1970

Invasion of Burma
December 1941/May 1942

| 0 | Miles | 300 |
| 0 | Kilometres | 400 |

Invasion of Malaya & Singapore
Dec 8,1941/Feb 15,1942

| 0 | Miles | 100 |
| 0 | Km. | 100 | 200 |

CHINA

BURMA ROAD to Chungking

INDIA

Chindwin

Kohima

MANIPUR

Tamu

Myitkyina

Lashio

Ava Mandalay

BURMA

Yenangyaung

Irrawaddy

Salween

Prome

Sittang

Pegu

Biling

Rangoon
MAR.8

JAN.20 JAPANESE LAUNCH MAIN ATTACK

Moulmein

JAP. 15th ARMY (Iida)

THAILAND

Tavoy

Bangkok

Tenasserim
mid-DEC.

Chumphon

Kra Isthmus

Nakhon

Singora

GULF OF SIAM

Nakhon

JAP. 25th ARMY (Yamashita) from Hainan

THAILAND

Kra Isthmus

Singora

Patani

Jitra

KEDAH

Penang

Kota Bharu

Ipoh

MALAYA

Kampar

Slim

Kuala Trengganu

Kuantan
JAN 6

SELANGOR

Kuala Lumpur
JAN.11

Tampin JAN.13

Malacca

Gemas

Endau
JAN.21

JOHORE

Johore Bahru

Singapore

FEB 15
BRITISH & EMPIRE FORCES END RESISTANCE

SUMATRA

Copyright © Cassell & Co. Ltd 1970

135 dive-bombers, and forty torpedo-bombers, with eighty-one fighters. The escorting force consisted of two battleships, three cruisers, nine destroyers, and three submarines, with eight accompanying tankers; it was under Admiral Nagumo. There was also planned to be a simultaneous attack by midget submarines, to take advantage of the expected chaos.

On November 19 the submarine force left Kure naval base in Japan, with five midget submarines in tow. The main task force assembled on the 22nd at Tankan Bay in the Kurile Islands, and left on the 26th. On December 2 it received word that the attack orders were confirmed, so ships were darkened; even then there was the proviso that the mission would be abandoned if the fleet was spotted before December 6—or if a last-minute settlement was reached in Washington. On the 4th the final refuelling took place, and speed was increased from 13 to 25 knots.

Continuous reports were reaching it, via Japan, from the Honolulu consulate, so there was disappointment when on the 6th, the eve of the stroke, no carriers were reported in Pearl Harbor. (Actually one was on the Californian coast, another was taking bombers to Midway, and another had just delivered fighters to Wake, while three were in the Atlantic.) However, eight battleships were reported to be in Pearl Harbor, and without torpedo nets, so Admiral Nagumo decided to go ahead. The aircraft were launched between 0600 and 0715 hours (Hawaii time) next morning, about 275 miles due north of Pearl Harbor.

There were two late warnings that might have made a difference to the outcome, but did not. The first was that the approach of the Japanese submarine force was detected, several times from 0355 hours onward; one of the submarines was sunk at 0651 by U.S. destroyers and another at 0700 by naval aircraft. Then the most northerly of the six American radar stations on the island detected a large force of aircraft, evidently over a hundred, approaching soon after 0700. But this was interpreted by the information centre as being a number of B.17s that was expected from California—although it comprised only twelve planes and these were coming from the east, not the north.

The attack started at 0755 and went on until 0825; then a second wave, of dive-bombers and high-level bombers, struck at 0840. But the use of the torpedo-bombers in the first wave had been the decisive factor.

Of the eight American battleships, the *Arizona, Oklahoma, West Virginia* and *California* were sunk, and the *Maryland, Nevada, Pennsylvania,* and *Tennessee* were severely damaged.* Sunk, too, were three destroyers and four smaller vessels, while three light cruisers and a seaplane tender were

* The *Nevada* was beached; the *California* was later refloated.

badly damaged. Of American aircraft, 188 were destroyed, and sixty-three damaged. The Japanese loss was only twenty-nine planes destroyed and seventy damaged—apart from the five midget submarines which were lost in an attack that was a complete failure. Of human casualties, the Americans had 3,435 killed or wounded; while the Japanese figure is more uncertain, the killed were under a hundred.

The returning Japanese aircraft landed on the carriers between 1030 and 1330 hours. On December 23 the main task force itself arrived back in Japan.

The coup brought three great advantages to Japan. The United States Pacific Fleet was virtually put out of action. The operations in the Southwest Pacific were made secure against naval interference, while the Pearl Harbor task force could be employed to support those operations. The Japanese now had more time to extend and build up their defensive ring.

The main drawbacks were that the stroke had missed the U.S. carriers—its prime target, and key one for the future. It had also missed the oil tanks and other important installations, whose destruction would have made the American recovery much slower, as Pearl Harbor was the only full fleet base. Coming as a surprise, apparently before any declaration of war, it aroused such indignation in America as to unite public opinion behind President Roosevelt, and in violent anger against Japan.

Ironically, the Japanese had intended to keep within the bounds of legality while profiting from the value of surprise—in other words, going as close to the border as they could without violating it. Their reply to the American demands of November 26 was timed so that it should be sent to the Japanese Ambassador in Washington in the late evening of Saturday, December 6, and was to be delivered to the United States Government at 1300 hours on the Sunday—which would be 0730 in the morning by Hawaii time. That would give the United States scant chance—about half an hour—of notifying its commanders in Hawaii and elsewhere that war had come, but could be claimed as legally correct by international law. Owing, however, to the length of the Japanese Note (5,000 words) and delays in decoding it at the Japanese Embassy, it was not ready for delivery by the Ambassador until 1420 hours Washington time—which was about 35 minutes *after* the start of the Pearl Harbor attack.

The violence of the American denunciation of Pearl Harbor as barbarous behaviour, and the way it came as a surprise, were astonishing in the light of history. For the Japanese attack had a close parallel with their attack on the Russian fleet at Port Arthur, and had been foreshadowed by it.

In August 1903, negotiations had begun between Japan and Russia for a settlement of their differences in the Far East. But after $5\frac{1}{2}$ months, the

Japanese Government came to the conclusion that the Russian attitude offered it no satisfactory arrangement, and on February 4, 1904, decided to use force. On the 6th, negotiations were broken off—but without any declaration of war. The Japanese fleet, under Admiral Togo, sailed secretly for Port Arthur, the Russian naval base. On the night of the 8th, Togo launched his torpedo-boats against the Russian squadron anchored at Port Arthur. Taking it by surprise, he disabled two of its best battleships, and a cruiser—with the result that Japanese naval supremacy was henceforth established in the Far East. It was only on the 10th that the Japanese declaration of war was issued and the Russian at the same time.

The attitude of the British, who had made an *entente* with Japan two years before, was in ironical contrast to the way they echoed the American denunciation of Japan's behaviour thirty-seven years later. A comment in *The Times* in February 1904 was:

> The Japanese navy, thanks to the masculine decision of the Mikado and his advisers, has taken the initiative, and has opened the war by an act of daring. ... Owing to its position in the outer roadstead, the Russian squadron was open to, and invited, attack. The invitation has been accepted with a promptness and a punctuality that do high honour to the navy of our gallant allies. ... The moral effect of this exploit promises to be enormous, and may influence and colour the whole conduct of the war.... By these acts of vigour, the Japanese navy have profited by the initiative conferred on them by statesmanship, and have established a moral mastery of the situation.

The article on 'Japan' in the 1911 edition of the *Encyclopaedia Britannica* also praises the action of Japan in choosing war, and for taking up arms 'against a military dictatorship and a policy of selfish restrictions'.

On October 21, 1904—the 99th anniversary of Trafalgar—Admiral Sir John Fisher became First Sea Lord in Britain. He promptly began to urge on King Edward VII, and in other influential quarters, a suggestion that the rising danger presented by the growth of the German fleet should be forestalled by 'Copenhagening' it—that a sudden attack should be launched upon it without any declaration of war. He even went so far as to put out propaganda for such a coup. His constant advocacy of such a course naturally came to the ears of the German Government, and as naturally, was taken more seriously than in English political quarters.

It is not clear whether Admiral Fisher's proposals had been mooted prior to the success of the Japanese coup at Port Arthur. In any case, the coup by which Nelson crippled the Danish fleet at Copenhagen without any declaration of war was a famous part of England's naval history, familiar to every sailor. Togo, as a young naval officer, had spent seven years in England studying his profession. Thus the influence of Nelson's Copenhagen coup on Admiral Togo's initiative in 1904 may well have been as great as Admiral Togo's influence on Fisher's scheme.

For Americans, the Pearl Harbor coup of 1941 came as such a surprise, despite the lesson of history, that the shock produced not only widespread criticism of their authorities, headed by President Roosevelt, but a deep suspicion that factors more sinister than blindness and confusion were responsible for the disaster. Such a suspicion became rife, particularly among Roosevelt's critics and political opponents, and has long persisted.

But while it is clear that President Roosevelt had long been hoping and seeking for a way of bringing America's weight into the war against Hitler, the evidence of complacency and miscalculation in army and navy headquarters suffices to outweigh the arguments of American 'revisionist' historians that Roosevelt planned or contrived the Pearl Harbor disaster for that purpose, and the slender evidence on which such arguments have been based.

THE FALL OF HONG KONG

The early loss of this British outpost in the Far East was the clearest of all examples how strategy, and common sense, can be sacrificed vainly for the sake of fanciful prestige.* Even the Japanese never committed such folly 'for face' as did the British in this case. It was palpably the weak point in Britain's position, and inherently far more difficult to hold than Singapore. This island port, adjoining the coast of China, was barely 400 miles from the Japanese air bases on Formosa whereas it was 1,600 miles from the British naval base at Singapore.

In a review of the situation early in 1937 the British Chiefs of Staff put Japan second to Germany as a possible enemy, and rated Singapore along with Britain herself as the keystones on which the survival of the British Commonwealth would depend, therefore emphasising that no consideration for the security of British interests in the Mediterranean should be allowed to interfere with the despatch of a fleet to Singapore. In discussing Hong Kong, they agreed that the period before relief could not be less than ninety days, and went on to say that even if a reinforced garrison could hold the colony the

---

* In March 1935, General Dill, who had become Director of Military Operations and Intelligence, asked me to go to the War Office for a talk with him about current and prospective defence problems. The discussion focused on the Far East, and particularly on the question of trying to hold Hong Kong in the event of war with Japan. According to a note of the discussion made that evening: 'I suggested, and he appeared to agree, that it would be better to risk its loss by holding it too lightly than to strengthen it so much as to make it, morally, a "Verdun" or "Port Arthur" with great danger to our prestige if lost.'

port itself could be neutralised by Japanese air forces operating from Formosa. But, in a more hopeful and less realistic way than the facts of the situation warranted, they rejected the logical conclusion on the ground that evacuation of the garrison would entail a loss of prestige, and of necessary encouragement to China in resisting the Japanese. Their own conclusion was that 'Hong Kong should be regarded as an important though not vital outpost to be defended for as long as possible.'* That conclusion foredoomed the garrison.

Two years later, early in 1939, a new review of the situation produced the same general conclusion, but showed a very significant change in putting the security of the Mediterranean before the Far East in order of priority. That inherently made a defence of Hong Kong more hopeless still, and all the more so because a Japanese expeditionary force was now ensconced on the Chinese mainland north and south of Hong Kong, thus isolating this British possession and exposing it to land attack.

In August 1940, following the fall of France, the situation was reviewed afresh by the new team of Chiefs of Staff—in which Dill represented the Army, as he was now C.I.G.S. This time they faced the fact that Hong Kong was indefensible, and recommended the withdrawal of the garrison—then four battalions. Their view was accepted by the War Cabinet, now led by Mr Churchill. But nothing was done to implement the conclusion. Moreover, a year later they veered round again, and advised Churchill to accept the Canadian Government's offer of two battalions to reinforce the garrison—an offer, and reversal of policy, that was prompted by the optimistic view of Major-General A. E. Grasett, himself a Canadian, who had recently been commanding in Hong Kong, and on his way back to England had told the Chief of the Canadian General Staff that such an addition would make the place strong enough to withstand attack for a long period. In advising acceptance of the offer, the Chiefs of Staff in Britain expressed the view that even at the worst it would enable the garrison to maintain a 'more worthy' defence of the island—another 'prestige' argument. On October 27, 1941, the two Canadian battalions sailed for Hong Kong, thus enlarging the vain sacrifice by nearly 50 per cent.

The Japanese attack from the mainland opened early on December 8, being delivered by a well-armed force more than a division strong (twelve battalions), with ample air cover and artillery support. By next day the British had fallen back to the so-called Gindrinkers Line in the Kowloon peninsula, and early on the 10th a key redoubt here had been seized by a Japanese detachment. This coup precipitated an early abandonment of the

* *Official History: The War Against Japan*, vol. I, p. 17.

Gindrinkers Line and withdrawal to Hong Kong island, while the Japanese were still moving up for their planned attack on the Line.

Initial attempts to cross the straits were repelled, but served to stretch out the defending force. Then on the night of the 18th/19th the main Japanese force landed in the north-east corner, and its concentrated thrust soon drove through to Deep Water Bay in the south, splitting the defending force. One part of it surrendered on the evening of Christmas Day, and the other part followed suit next morning. Despite its reinforcement, Hong Kong had held out for barely eighteen days—a fifth of the time expected. The Japanese casualties were under 3,000, while they had captured the whole of the reinforced garrison, nearly 12,000 men. The loss of the island came in the centenary year of its occupation, and the 99th anniversary of its formal cession, by China, to Britain.

THE FALL OF THE PHILIPPINES

At 0230 hours on December 8 news of the Japanese attack on Pearl Harbor reached, and alerted, the United States Command in the Philippines. Meanwhile, morning fog on Formosa delayed the planned Japanese air-strike against the islands. But that handicap turned out to the advantage of the Japanese. For on the American side there was a confusion—which has been a continuing cause of controversy—as to whether the B.17s were to bomb Formosa in immediate reply. As a result of this they were ordered to fly around the great island of Luzon to avoid being caught on the ground. At 1130 hours they landed to prepare for their strike—just as the delayed Japanese aircraft arrived overhead. Owing to the defective American warning system, most of the American aircraft were knocked out on that first day, especially the B.17 bombers and the modern P.40E fighters. The balance of air strength thus swung to the Japanese, who dominated the air from then on with their 190 Army and 300 land-based Naval planes operating from Formosa. On the 17th, the ten remaining B.17s were withdrawn to Australia, and from Admiral Hart's pretentiously named Asiatic Fleet its handful of surface ships were also sent away, leaving only his twenty-nine submarines in the area.

As to land forces, despite the new decision—on MacArthur's insistence—that the whole of the Philippines should be held, he had contrarily if shrewdly kept most of the 31,000 regulars (Americans and Filipino Scouts) near Manila, so that the far-stretching coastlines were covered only by low-grade Philippine troops, nominally about 110,000 in total. That decision, however wise strategically, meant that the Japanese would meet little difficulty in getting ashore wherever they chose to land.

The attack was entrusted to the Japanese 14th Army under General Homma. He employed 57,000 men in the landings and initial operations. Relatively, the number was not large, thus making surprise and air superiority the more essential. It was also necessary for the Japanese to capture some outlying islands and weakly-defended coastal regions so that airfields could be quickly built for their short-range Army aircraft.

On the opening day, they seized the main island of the Batan group, 120 miles north of Luzon, and on the 10th made another bound to Camiguin Island, just north of Luzon. That same day two other detachments landed on the north coast itself, at Aparri and Vigan, while on the 12th a fourth one coming from the Palau Islands landed unopposed at Legaspi in the far southeast of Luzon. These paved the way for the main landings, which took place in the Lingayen Gulf, only 120 miles north of Manila, beginning on December 22. Eighty-five transports carried General Homma's 43,000 troops. On the 24th another force of 7,000, coming from the Ryukyu Islands, landed in Lamon Bay on the east coast, opposite Manila. None of these forces met any serious opposition, as the raw and poorly equipped Philippine Army crumbled quickly, especially when tanks advanced on them, and the Americans moved to their aid too late. The Japanese casualties hitherto had been less than 2,000.

MacArthur, realising that he could not fulfil his hope and plan of crushing the invaders before they were properly established ashore, had already on the 23rd reverted to the original plan of withdrawing to the Bataan Peninsula, with all that remained of his forces. His decision was precipitated by reports that overestimated, by almost double, the strength of the Japanese— and discounted most of his own Philippine troops. On the 26th Manila itself was declared an open city. Despite the initial state of confusion, MacArthur's troops managed to carry out a step by step withdrawal, under pressure, and were established in the Bataan Peninsula by January 6—helped by the fact that the Japanese strength was actually about half their own.

But once back in this peninsula—which was about twenty-five miles long and twenty miles wide—the Americans suffered from having to feed over 100,000 mouths, including civilians, instead of the 43,000 reckoned in the original plan. Moreover the peninsula was extremely malarious, so that very soon barely a quarter of the American forces were fit enough to fight.

The opening Japanese attacks on the peninsular position were repulsed, and so were the amphibious flanking attacks they attempted. On February 8, after a month's effort, they suspended their attacks as their forces had become so weak—10,000 being sick with malaria, while their 48th Division had been sent off to help the attack on the Dutch East Indies. By the beginning of March only 3,000 troops were manning the Japanese lines, but the Americans, unaware of this situation, made no attempt to take the offensive. Moreover their own effectives were now down to a fifth of their numbers, and their morale suffered from MacArthur's departure for Australia on March 10. It was also evident that no effort was being made to come to their relief—a decision made early in January by the authorities in Washington.

By the end of March the Japanese were reinforced with over 22,000 fresh troops, as well as by more aircraft, and many more guns. Their attacks were resumed from April 3 onward, and the Americans were pushed backward down the peninsula, until on April 9 the remaining commander there, General King, surrendered unconditionally to avoid 'mass slaughter'.

The fight now shifted to the fortified island of Corregidor, which had a garrison of nearly 15,000 men (including those on three smaller islands adjoining it). But only two miles separated it from the Bataan peninsula, which enabled the Japanese to maintain a heavy artillery bombardment over the straits as well as continuous air attacks. This pounding went on week after week, gradually pulverising the defences and putting most of the American guns out of action, while also hitting the island's water supply. The bombardment rose to an intensity of 16,000 shells on May 4. Just before midnight on the 5th, 2,000 Japanese troops crossed the straits, and landed. They met fierce resistance and lost more than half their strength before they got ashore, but the landing of tanks turned the scale and caused the defenders to crumble—although only three tanks actually went into action. Next morning, May 6, General Wainwright, who had been commanding Corregidor since leaving the peninsula, sent out a broadcast message of surrender—to avoid vain loss.

General Homma at first refused to accept such a local surrender while American and Filipino detachments in the southern islands continued to maintain a guerrilla-type struggle, as were others in the more remote parts of Luzon. Wainwright then agreed to order a general surrender, for fear that the now disarmed garrison of Corregidor would be massacred. But some of these detachments still refused to comply—in loyalty to MacArthur's urgings, from Australia, and it was not until June 9 that their resistance ceased.

The Americans had lost some 30,000 troops in the campaign, and their Filipino allies some 110,000. While a large proportion of the latter had melted away by desertion, the total of both who surrendered on the Bataan peninsula was about 80,000, and a further 15,000 on Corregidor. The

Japanese casualties, though more difficult to determine, seem to have been only about 12,000, apart from the sick.

Nevertheless, despite the initial collapse, the defenders of the Philippines eventually held out much longer than anywhere else—four months on Bataan, and six months in all—although they had no effective support or supply from outside the Philippines.

THE FALL OF MALAYA—AND SINGAPORE

In the Japanese plan, the task of conquering Malaya and Singapore was allotted to General Yamashita's 25th Army, comprising three divisions with supporting troops—a combat strength of about 70,000, and a total strength of about 110,000. Moreover the sea-transports available only sufficed to carry a quarter of the force direct across the Gulf of Siam—17,000 combat troops, and 26,000 in all. This advanced fraction was to seize the northern airfields. The bulk of Yamashita's army was to move overland, from Indo-China through Thailand and down the Kra Isthmus to reinforce the sea-borne force as soon as possible, then pursuing the advance down the west coast of the Malay Peninsula.

Outwardly, it was a remarkably small expedition for such a far-reaching aim—and indeed less in numbers than the British total of 88,000 under General Percival defending Malaya (composed of 19,000 British troops, 15,000 Australian, 37,000 Indian, and 17,000 Malays). But these were a mixed lot, poorly equipped and trained in comparison with Yamashita's three divisions—the Imperial Guards, the 5th, and the 18th—were among the best in the whole Japanese Army. They were supported by 211 tanks—whereas the British in Malaya had none—and 560 aircraft—nearly four times as many as the British aircraft in Malaya, while much superior in quality. Moreover, the Japanese reckoned that the monsoon, prevailing from November to March, would hinder British moves to counter their advance, as during this bad weather only the better roads would be passable. They also reckoned that the mountainous backbone of Malaya, up to 7,000 feet high and covered with dense jungle, would split the defence, and aid their intended switch from the east coast to the west.

The basic irony of the British dispositions was that the ground forces were widely dispersed to guard airfields that contained no adequate air force, and that these airfields had been built to cover a naval base that contained no fleet. The Japanese were to be the main beneficiaries from both airfields and naval base.

The chief Japanese landings were made at Singora and Patani on the

Thai neck of the Malay Peninsula, with four subsidiary landings farther north on the coast of Thailand. The third in importance of the landings was made at Kota Bharu, just inside the frontier of Malaya. This force was intended, after seizing the British airfield there, to carry out a diversionary move down the east coast while the main advance was being made down the west coast. These landings were made in the early hours of December 8, local time—the landing at Kota Bharu, by a force of 5,500 Japanese, was actually over an hour before the stroke at Pearl Harbor. The airfield there was abandoned to the Japanese after a short fight, while those in Thai territory were taken still more easily. The intended British forestalling advance, 'Operation Matador', started too late because of reluctance to cross the frontier before Thailand's neutrality had been violated by the Japanese. British air reconnaissance had discovered a Japanese fleet in the Gulf of Siam on December 6, but bad weather obscured its further moves, and aims. The preparatory moves for the 'Matador' offensive merely upset British dispositions for defence. By the morning of December 10 the Japanese 5th Division had already swung across to the west coast and penetrated the frontier of Malaya, advancing by two roads into Kedah.

That day a decisive disaster befell the British at sea.

After the decision in July to cut off Japan's oil supplies, Winston Churchill had belatedly 'realised the formidable effects of the embargoes' and a month later, on August 25, proposed the despatch of what he called a 'deterrent' naval force to the East. The Admiralty were planning to assemble there the *Nelson*, the *Rodney*, and four older battleships, together with a battlecruiser and two to three aircraft-carriers. Churchill preferred to employ 'the smallest number of the best ships', and proposed to send one of the new *King George V* type battleships, with a battlecruiser and an aircraft-carrier, telling the Admiralty, on August 29:

> I cannot feel that Japan will face the combination now forming against her of the United States, Great Britain, and Russia. . . . Nothing would increase her hesitation more than the appearance of the force I mentioned, and above all a *K.G.V.* This might indeed be a decisive deterrent.*

Accordingly the *Prince of Wales* and the battlecruiser *Repulse* sailed for Singapore—but without any aircraft-carrier. The one that had been earmarked ran ashore in Jamaica and had to be docked for repairs. There was another actually in the Indian Ocean, and within reach of Singapore, but no orders were given for her to move there. Thus the two big ships had to depend for air cover upon shore-based fighters, and these were scanty—even apart from the early loss of the northern airfields.

---

* Churchill: *The Second World War*, vol. III, p. 774.

The *Prince of Wales* and *Repulse* reached Singapore on December 2, and next day Admiral Sir Tom Phillips arrived to take command of the 'Far Eastern Fleet'. On the 6th, as already mentioned, a large Japanese convoy of transports was reported to be sailing from Indo-China in the direction of Malaya. By midday on the 8th Phillips heard that they were disembarking their troops at Singora and Kota Bahru, covered by at least one battleship of the *Kongo* class, five cruisers, and twenty destroyers. In the late afternoon Phillips gallantly sailed north with what was called Force Z—his two big ships and an escort of four destroyers—to strike at the transports, although no shore-based air cover could be provided so far north now that the airfields there were lost.

In the evening of the 9th the weather cleared, and with it Phillips's cloak of obscurity. His Force Z was spotted from the air, so he turned south and headed for Singapore. But that night a signal came from there reporting, mistakenly, that a Japanese landing had been made at Kuantan, a midway point. Reckoning that surprise might be possible, and the risk justified, he altered course for Kuantan.

The Japanese were well prepared for any interception move by Force Z, whose arrival at Singapore had been broadcast to the world. Their élite 22nd Air Flotilla, with the best pilots of the Naval Air Arm, was based on the airfields near Saigon, in the south of Indo-China. Moreover, a patrol line of twelve submarines covered the approaches from Singapore to Kota Bharu and Singora. Already, in the early afternoon of the 9th, Force Z's northward move had been sighted and reported by the most easterly submarine of this screen. When the report came, the 22nd Air Flotilla, which had been preparing for a raid on Singapore, hurriedly exchanged its bombs for torpedoes and set off for a night attack on Force Z, but failed to find it because of Phillips's southward turn. However the air flotilla set off again just before dawn, and this time Force Z was found, near Kuantan. The Japanese employed thirty-four high-level bombers and fifty-one torpedo-bombers, the former opening the attack soon after 1100 hours and the latter following, in successive waves. Both kinds of bombing proved remarkably accurate—despite the fact that it was against ships manœuvring at high speed, not static and taken by surprise as at Pearl Harbor. Moreover the *Prince of Wales* with 175 anti-aircraft guns could pump out 60,000 shells a minute. Both ships were sunk, the *Repulse* by 1230 and the *Prince of Wales* by 1320. The escorting destroyers managed to save over 2,000 men out of 2,800 in the two ships' crews, though Admiral Phillips himself was among those lost. The Japanese abstained from interference with the rescue work. They lost only three aircraft.

Before the war the heads of the Admiralty had scorned the idea that battleships could be sunk by air attack, and Churchill had tended to support their view. The delusion even persisted until the fatal days of December 1941. Moreover, as Churchill wrote: 'The efficiency of the Japanese in air warfare was at this time greatly under-estimated both by ourselves and by the Americans.'*

This stroke settled the fate of Malaya—and Singapore. The Japanese were able to continue their landings unchecked, and establish air bases ashore. The superiority of their air force over the meagre British air strength in Malaya was decisive in crumbling the resistance of the British troops and enabling their own troops to push down the Malay Peninsula and force the backdoor into Singapore. Its fall was the consequence of earlier oversight and mis-judgement—mainly in London.

From December 10 onwards, the British retreat down the west coast became almost continuous. Road blocks such as the large one at Jitra were either overcome by Japanese tanks and artillery or by flank threat from Japanese infantry infiltrating through the bordering jungle. The commander in northern Malaya, General Heath, hoped to make a stand on the Perak River, but this line was turned by the Japanese column thrusting obliquely down from Patani. A strong position behind, at Kampar, was turned by flank action from the sea that was carried out by troops using small craft captured in the advance.

On December 27, Lieutenant-General Sir Henry Pownall took over as C.-in-C. Far East from Air Chief Marshal Sir Robert Brooke-Popham.

The British fell back at the beginning of January to the Slim River, covering Selangor Province, and the approaches to the southern airfields near Kuala Lumpur. But on the night of the 7th/8th a company of Japanese tanks broke through the ill-organised defence and raced on to seize the road-bridge—which was nearly twenty miles beyond the front line. The British troops north of the river were cut off, losing some 4,000 troops and their equipment—at a cost to the Japanese of only six tanks and a few infantry. The 11th Indian Division was shattered. The disaster entailed the early abandonment of central Malaya and jeopardised the chance of holding northern Johore long enough for adequate reinforcements to reach Singapore by sea from the Middle East.

On the very day of the disaster General Wavell arrived in Singapore on his way to Java to take up the new, emergency post of Supreme Com-mander, A.B.D.A. (American, British, Dutch, Australian) Command. Pownall then became Chief of Staff A.B.D.A., Far East Headquarters being

* Churchill: *The Second World War*, vol. III, p. 551.

abolished. Wavell decided that the defence was now to be based on Johore, the best troops and the reinforcements being kept there. That meant a quicker withdrawal, instead of the gradual one planned by General Percival. Kuala Lumpur was abandoned on January 11, and the bottleneck position at Tampin on the 13th (instead of the 24th). It also, by giving the Japanese access to the better road system in Johore, enabled them to employ two divisions simultaneously, instead of in turn—which nullified a tough defence of Gemas by the Australians. Thus the withdrawal through Johore became even quicker than intended.

Meanwhile, a corresponding withdrawal of the British force on the east coast had led to the abandonment of Kuantan and its airfield on January 6; of Endau on the 21st, following a seaborne threat; and by the 30th both 'Eastforce' and 'Westforce' were back at the extreme southern end of the Malay Peninsula. The rearguards crossed the straits next night, into Singapore Island. The Japanese Army Air Force, less effective than the Naval air arm, had done little to harry the retreat, and only proved effective against airfields.

Thus the Japanese had conquered Malaya in fifty-four days. Their total casualties were only about 4,600—whereas the British had lost about 25,000 (mainly prisoners), and a large quantity of equipment.

It was on the night of Sunday, February 8, 1942, that the two leading divisions of the Japanese invading force, which had swept down the 500-mile length of the Malay Peninsula, crossed the narrow channel which separates Singapore Island from the mainland. The crossing was made on an eight-mile stretch of the thirty-mile straits, which here were less than a mile in width. This sector was held by three battalions of the 22nd Australian Brigade.

Armoured landing craft carried the first waves of attackers, but the rest followed in any sort of boats that could be collected, and a number of the Japanese even swam across—with their rifles and ammunition. Some of the craft were sunk, but most of the assault troops landed safely, helped by failures on the defenders' side that have never been satisfactorily explained. The beach searchlights were not employed, means of communication failed or were not used, and the artillery was slow to put down its intended curtain of defensive fire.

By daylight 13,000 Japanese were ashore, and the Australians had fallen back to inland positions. Before midday the invaders' strength had risen to more than 20,000, and they had established a deep lodgement in the northwestern part of the island. Later a third Japanese division landed, making the total well over 30,000.

There were two more divisions close behind on the mainland, but General Yamashita did not consider that he could effectively deploy them in the island advance. He did, however, feed in a lot of fresh men as replacements during the days that followed.

Numerically, the defenders had more than sufficient strength in the island to repel the invasion, particularly as it came in the sector where it was most expected. General Percival, even now, had some 85,000 troops under his command—mainly British, Australian, and Indian, with some local Malay and Chinese units. But the majority were ill-trained to match the Japanese attacking force, composed of troops specially selected for the purpose, and had been repeatedly outmanœuvred in the dense jungle country or rubber plantations. The leadership in general was poor.

The air force had been outnumbered and outclassed from the outset of the campaign, and the little that remained was withdrawn in the final stage. Lack of protection against the enemy's fierce and incessant air attacks was the more demoralising to troops whose spirits were already depressed by the long retreat down the Malay Peninsula.

The effect of the home Government's failure to provide such essential air cover was not redressed by the appeals that Churchill and his military advisers now sent that 'the battle should be fought to the bitter end at all costs', and that commanders 'should die with their troops' for 'the honour of the British Empire', carry out a 'general scorched-earth scheme' and destroy everything that might be useful to an occupier with 'no thought of saving the troops or sparing the population'. All this showed an extra-ordinary ignorance of psychology on the part of the authorities at home. The morale of the men in the fighting line was not raised by the sight of black smoke clouds billowing up behind them, from burning oil tanks. Nor did it encourage them to know that they were doomed to death or captivity. A year later, even the tough German veterans in Africa collapsed quickly when, after Hitler's order to hold Tunis at all costs, their front was pierced and behind them lay the sea, with the enemy in command of it. To call on troops to fight with 'backs to the wall' of such a nature is rarely effective in stiffening their spine.

At Singapore the end came on Sunday, February 15—exactly a week after the Japanese landing. By that time the defenders had been driven back to the suburbs of Singapore city, which lies on the south coast of the island. Food stocks were running low and the water supply was liable to be cut off at any moment. That evening General Percival went out under a white flag to capitulate to the Japanese commander. For a brave man it was a bitter step, but surrender was inevitable, and he chose to go himself in the hope of obtaining better treatment for his troops and the population.

These two black Sundays at Singapore were fatal to the imperial sway of what had been proudly called for many years 'the Empire on which the sun never sets'.

The failure to repel the Japanese Army's attack, however, was not the primary cause. The surrender of Singapore was the sequel to naval defeat—two months before.

It was also the tail end of a long chain of errors and oversights. The development of the new base and its defences had been pitifully slow. Political reluctance to spend money was not the only brake. In the years following the decision to build this base a violent argument raged in Whitehall as to the best means of defending it. The argument was fiercest of all in the Chiefs of Staff Committee—supposedly as united as a trinity. Trenchard, the Chief of the Air Staff, urged the paramount importance of aircraft. Beatty, the First Sea Lord, advocated big guns—while scorning the idea that aircraft could be a grave threat to battleships. Both were famous men, and strong men.

The Government hesitated to decide between their views, and the controversy still continued long after they had retired. On balance, the 'Senior Service' prevailed. The big guns were provided, but not the aircraft. Unfortunately, when the attack eventually came it did not come from the way the guns were pointing, but from behind.

In the 1930s various soldiers who studied the problem began to suggest that the attack might come through the backdoor, by way of the Malay Peninsula. It seemed the more likely because the naval base had been built on the north side of Singapore, in the narrow channel between the island and the mainland. Among the soldiers who took that view was Percival, when Chief General Staff Officer in Malaya 1936–7. It was endorsed by the then G.O.C., General Dobbie, who in 1938 began the construction of a defence line in the south of the Malay Peninsula.

Mr Hore-Belisha, who had now become War Minister, was quick to appreciate the necessity for increasing the small garrison—for a main feature of the programme he adopted on taking office was priority for Imperial Defence over Continental action. The danger of war with Germany and Italy combined was becoming so acute that a strengthening of the Mediterranean forces necessarily had first call, but he induced the Government of India to send two brigades to Malaya, for trebling the garrison there. More was hardly possible from the limited pre-war resources.

When war came in September 1939, Britain's resources began to multiply.

But as the war was then confined to the West it was natural that the bulk of them were devoted to that quarter. Then came the catastrophes of May and June 1940 when France collapsed and Italy entered the war. In that appalling crisis, the first need was to build up the defence of Britain, and the second to provide for the defence of the Mediterranean area. Those two needs were difficult enough to meet simultaneously. Indeed, Churchill's boldest and greatest action was seen in the risks he took to strengthen the defence of Egypt before Britain itself was secure against invasion.

It would be unjust to find fault with the provision made for Malaya during this period. Taking due account of the circumstances it was remarkable that the garrison was reinforced by six brigades during the winter of 1940-1. Unfortunately, there was no similar increase of air strength—which was more vital.

Early in 1940 the new G.O.C., General Bond, had expressed the opinion that the defence of Singapore depended on the defence of Malaya as a whole. For that purpose he estimated that three divisions were the minimum required, while suggesting that the R.A.F. should take over the main responsibility for the defence. The authorities at home adopted these views in principle, but with an important modification. Whereas the commanders in Malaya considered that a force of over 500 modern aircraft was required, the Chiefs of Staff Committee judged that some 300 should suffice, and said that even this total could not be provided until the end of 1941. Moreover, by the time the Japanese invasion came—in December 1941—the actual first-line air strength in Malaya was only 158, and most of them were out-of-date machines.

During 1941 the bulk of the modern fighter aircraft available, beyond the needs of Britain's air defence, were sent to support the abortive offensive campaigns in the Mediterranean area. In the second half of the year some 600 were sent to Russia. But Malaya received scarcely any. No long-range bombers were sent there, yet hundreds were used nightly in bombing attacks on Germany that were palpably futile at that stage of the war. It is evident that the needs of Malaya's defence received inadequate attention.

The clue to the puzzle is provided by Churchill himself in his war memoirs. Early in May the Chief of the Imperial General Staff, Sir John Dill, submitted a paper to the Prime Minister in which he argued against continuing to build up the striking forces in North Africa at the risk of Britain herself or Singapore.

> The loss of Egypt would be a calamity which I do not regard as likely.... A successful invasion alone spells our final defeat. It is the United Kingdom therefore and not Egypt that is vital, and the defence of the United Kingdom

must take first place. Egypt is not even second in order of priority, for it has been an accepted principle in our strategy that in the last resort the security of Singapore comes before that of Egypt. Yet the defences of Singapore are still considerably below standard.

Risks must of course be taken in war, but they must be calculated risks. We must not fall into the error of whittling away the security of vital points.*

Churchill was upset by this paper, for it ran contrary to his idea of taking the offensive against Rommel, and to his dream of gaining a decisive victory in North Africa at an early date. 'Compliance with this would have meant a complete reversion to the defensive. . . . There would be nothing in hand for taking the initiative.' In a sharp reply he said:

I gather you would be prepared to face the loss of Egypt and the Nile Valley, together with the surrender or ruin of the Army of half a million we have concentrated there, rather than lose Singapore. I do not take that view, nor do I think that the alternative is likely to present itself . . . should Japan enter the war the United States will in all probability come in on our side; and in any case Japan would not be likely to besiege Singapore at the outset, as this would be an operation far more dangerous to her and less harmful to us than spreading her cruisers and battle-cruisers on the Eastern trade routes.†

It is apparent that Churchill, in his exasperation, distorted the C.I.G.S's argument. It was not a question of weakening the defence of Egypt, but merely of postponing the offensive on which Churchill had set his heart, and about which he had exaggerated expectations. In the event the June offensive in North Africa proved a fiasco, and the renewed offensive in November, with large additional reinforcements, failed to gain any decisive result. Churchill's reply to Field-Marshal Dill also makes it clear how gravely he miscalculated the risk to Singapore. It is astonishing that, in retrospect, he remarked:

Many Governments I have seen would have wilted before so grave a pronouncement by the highest professional authority, but I had no difficulty in convincing my political colleagues, and I was of course supported by the Chiefs of the Navy and the Air. My views therefore prevailed and the flow of reinforcements to the Middle East continued unabated.‡

In July President Roosevelt sent his personal adviser, Harry Hopkins, on a mission to London to convey his misgivings about the wisdom of this policy and a warning of the risks involved elsewhere—'by trying to do too much' in the Middle East. The American military and naval experts endorsed

* Churchill: *The Second World War*, vol. III, p, 375.
† *ibid.*, p. 376.
‡ *ibid.*, p. 377.

the warning, and expressed the view that Singapore should be given priority over Egypt.

None of these arguments altered Churchill's view. 'I would not tolerate abandoning the struggle for Egypt, and was resigned to pay whatever forfeits were exacted in Malaya.' But he did not really expect danger there. He frankly says: 'I confess that in my mind the whole Japanese menace lay in a sinister twilight, compared with our other needs.' It is clear that the responsibility for the failure to reinforce Malaya's inadequate defences rests principally with Churchill himself—and was due to his insistence on launching a premature offensive in North Africa.

The immediate strategic effects of the loss of Singapore were disastrous, for it was quickly followed by the conquest of Burma and the Dutch East Indies—a two-pronged sweep that brought the Japanese menacingly close to India on the one flank and Australia on the other. Nearly four years of struggle followed, at immense cost, before Singapore was recovered as a result of Japan's own eventual collapse from exhaustion, and atomic bomb-shock.

But the longer and wider effects of Singapore's initial fall were beyond repair. Singapore had been a symbol—the outstanding symbol of Western power in the Far East, because that power had been erected and long maintained on British seapower. So much emphasis had been given since World War I to the creation of a great naval base at Singapore that its symbolical importance had come to surpass even its strategical value. Its easy capture, in February 1942, was shattering to British, and European, prestige in Asia.

No belated re-entry could efface the impression. The white man had lost his ascendancy with the disproof of his magic. The realisation of his vulnerability fostered and encouraged the post-war spread of Asiatic revolt against European domination or intrusion.

THE FALL OF BURMA

Britain's loss of Burma was an early sequel to the fall of Malaya, and enabled the Japanese to complete their capture of the western gateways to China, and the Pacific—thus completing the great defensive barrier visualised in their strategic design. Although a sequel, the Burma campaign was an independent operation, and was entrusted to the 15th Army under Lieutenant-General S. Iida.

This 'army' comprised only two divisions, and even with supporting troops totalled only 35,000 men. Its task was to occupy Thailand, including most of the Kra Isthmus, and cover the rear of the 25th Army while this was driving south into Malaya from the landings in the Singora area of the isthmus. The 15th Army was then to set out on its independent task of invading Burma, with Rangoon, the capital, as its immediate goal.

Such a large venture with so small a force was justified by the scantiness, both in quantity and quality, of the forces guarding Burma. Initially, these amounted to little more than a division in numbers, mostly consisting of recently raised Burmese units, with a stiffening of only two British battalions and an Indian brigade—while a second Indian brigade was on its way, to provide a general reserve. When the crisis came, most of the available reinforcements were diverted to Malaya, too late to save Singapore, and not until the end of January did the semi-trained and incomplete 17th Indian Division begin to arrive in Burma as a forerunner of the more substantial reinforcements that were promised. The air situation was even worse, as only thirty-seven aircraft were at first available to meet 100 Japanese—which were doubled by another air brigade after the fall of Manila early in January.

The Japanese invasion of Burma had started as early as mid-December, when a detachment of the 15th Army moved in to Tenasserim, on the western or Burmese side of the Kra Isthmus, to seize the three key airfields there and thus block the way for British air reinforcements to Malaya. On December 23 and 25 heavy Japanese air attacks were delivered on Rangoon, causing the Indian labour force to stream away, blocking the roads and abandoning work on the defences. On January 20 the direct attack opened with an advance from Thailand on Moulmein, which was occupied on the 31st after a stiff but confused struggle—in which the defenders, with the wide Salween River estuary at their backs, had a narrow escape from disaster, and capture.

At the end of December, Wavell had sent his Chief of the General Staff in India, Lieutenant-General T. J. Hutton, to take over the command in Burma, and he in turn had placed the miscellaneous troops defending Moulmein, and the approaches to Rangoon, under Major-General J. G. Smyth, V.C., the commander of the newly arriving 17th Indian Division.

After the fall of Moulmein, the Japanese pressed on north-west, and gained crossings of the Salween near there and some twenty-five miles up-river in the first fortnight of February. Smyth had been urging an adequate strategic withdrawal to a position where he could concentrate, but was not permitted to withdraw until too late to organise such a defence on the Bilin River, itself narrow and fordable at many points. That position was soon turned. Then came a race to get the troops back to the mile-wide Sittang

River, thirty miles behind (and seventy from Rangoon). Owing to the delayed start, the Japanese were able to forestall the British, despite the handicap of having to pursue their outflanking moves by jungle tracks, and the vital Sittang Bridge was blown up in the early hours of February 23, leaving most of Smyth's troops still on the east bank. Barely 3,500 got back, by devious ways, and of these less than half still had their rifles. By March 4 the Japanese, exploiting their advantage, reached and surrounded Pegu, a road and rail junction where the remnants of Smyth's troops and a few reinforcements were assembling.

The next day, General Sir Harold Alexander arrived to take over the command in Burma from General Hutton. That emergency decision by Churchill was quite natural in the circumstances, and the more so in view of the way that the early collapse had been unforeseen in higher quarters. But it was unjust to 'Tom' Hutton who had not only expressed doubt of the possibility of holding Rangoon but shown wise foresight in sending supplies to the Mandalay area 400 miles north of Rangoon, while hastening the construction of a mountain road from the State of Manipur, in India, as an overland link with Mandalay and the Burma Road to Chungking. During this period, and earlier, views at home were much influenced by Wavell's opinion that Japanese skill was overrated—a myth that could be punctured by vigorous counteraction.

On arrival, Alexander at first insisted that Rangoon must be held and ordered an offensive to restore the situation. But when that was attempted, it gained little, despite vigorous action by the newly-arrived 7th Armoured Brigade and some infantry reinforcements. So Alexander soon came round to accept Hutton's view, and on the afternoon of March 6 ordered the evacuation of Rangoon, after demolitions carried out the next afternoon. Thus on the 8th the Japanese, to their own surprise, entered a deserted city. Even so, the forces there had luck in escaping, up the road northward through Prome, by finding a gap in the Japanese encirclement.

There was now a temporary pause, during which the Japanese were reinforced by two more divisions, the 18th and 56th, as well as two tank regiments, and their air force was doubled—to over 400 planes. The British received far fewer troop reinforcements. In the air their three depleted fighter squadrons and the two of the American Volunteer Group (lent by Generalissimo Chiang Kai-Shek), totalling only forty-four Hurricanes and Tomahawks at the start, had effectively beaten off Japanese air raids on Rangoon, while inflicting disproportionately heavy losses on the attackers. But with the abandonment of Rangoon most of the British were withdrawn to India—where an initial reinforcement of some 150 planes, bombers and fighters, was received from the Middle East by the end of March. The loss of Rangoon had disrupted the early warning system, so that the remaining British planes were unable—as in Malaya earlier—to put up any effective resistance to the Japanese.

Early in April the strengthened Japanese 15th Army moved north up the Irrawaddy, towards Mandalay, in fulfilment of its aim of cutting and closing the Burma Road to China. The British, now amounting to some 60,000, were holding an east–west line 150 miles south of Mandalay—with the aid of the Chinese forces on their eastern flank. But the Japanese boldly moved round their western flank, enveloping its defenders, and capturing the Yenangyaung oilfields in mid-April. General Joseph Stilwell, the American officer who was Chiang-Kai-Shek's right hand, devised a plan to let the Japanese push up the Sittang River and then trap them by a pincer-move, but his plan was forestalled and distracted by a wider Japanese move, round the eastern flank, towards Lashio on the Burma Road. A rapid reflux took place on that flank, and it soon became clear that neither Lashio nor the use of the supply route to China could be preserved.

So Alexander wisely decided not to make a stand at Mandalay—as the Japanese hoped he would—but to withdraw towards the Indian frontier. The long withdrawal, of more than 200 miles, began on April 26, covered by rearguards, and the Ava bridge over the Irrawaddy was blown up on the 30th—the day before the Japanese flanking advance reached Lashio.

The principal problem now was to reach the Indian frontier, and Assam, before the monsoon began in mid-May and flooded the intervening rivers as well as the roads. The Japanese raced up the Chindwin River to intercept the British retreat, but the British rearguards managed to get through, by a deviation, and reached Tamu a week before the monsoon began. They lost much of their equipment in the final scurry, including all their tanks, but most of the troops were saved. Even so, their casualties in the Burma campaign had amounted to three times those of the Japanese— 13,500 against 4,500. That the forces in Burma got away at all, in their thousand-mile retreat, was largely due to the repeated interventions, by counterattack, from the tanks of the 7th Armoured Brigade—and the cool-headed way in which the retreat was handled after the decision to abandon Rangoon.

CEYLON AND THE INDIAN OCEAN

While the Japanese army in Burma was moving on, in a seemingly irresistible way, from Rangoon to Mandalay, the British were also suffering alarm from the entry of the Japanese Navy into the Indian Ocean. For the great island of Ceylon, off the south-east corner of India, was considered vital by the British—as a potential springboard for the Japanese Navy from which it could threaten Britain's troop and supply route to the Middle East round the Cape of Good Hope, and South Africa, as well as her sea-routes to India and Australia. Rubber from Ceylon, too, had become very important to Britain since the loss of Malaya.

Wavell was told by the British Chiefs of Staff that the preservation of Ceylon was more essential than that of Calcutta. For that reason, no less than six brigades were employed to hold Ceylon at a time when the forces in Burma were palpably inadequate and those in India perilously weak. Moreover a fresh naval force was also built up there in March, under command of Admiral Sir James Somerville—which comprised five battleships (although four of these were old and obsolete), and three carriers, one of which (the *Hermes*) was both old and small.

At the same time the Japanese were preparing an offensive move from Celebes into the Indian Ocean with a more powerful force, comprising five fleet carriers—those used in the Pearl Harbor attack—and four battleships. Thus the prospects of preserving Ceylon looked poor when that news came. But the threat was not so serious, nor so substantial as it appeared. For the Japanese naval offensive was basically defensive in aim. They had not the troops available to carry out an invasion of Ceylon. Their aim was a raid—to disperse the British naval force that was being built up there, and to cover their own troop reinforcements that were on the way to Rangoon by sea.

Expecting attack on April 1, Somerville's force had been divided into two parts—the faster and more effective part, Force A, being on patrol until it was sent to refuel at Addu Attol, a new secret base in the Maldive Islands some 600 miles south-west of Ceylon. The Japanese stroke actually came on April 5, when over a hundred planes attacked the harbour at Colombo, inflicting much damage and repelling the air counterattacks. A further attack came in the afternoon, from fifty bombers, which sank two British cruisers. Somerville's two-part force, too late to intervene, then retreated—the older battleships to East Africa, and the faster part to Bombay. But after a successful stroke at Trincomalee on the 9th, the Japanese fleet withdrew, its commerce raiding detachment having meanwhile sunk twenty-three ships (112,000 tons) in the Bay of Bengal during this brief raid.

It was another humiliating defeat for British seapower, but fortunately went no further. Indeed, if the British had not provoked such a stroke by trying to build up a naval force in Ceylon of a palpably obsolescent kind, the Japanese would probably not have attacked—as it was beyond their designed limits.

Another sequel, imposing renewed strain on Britain's relations with the French as well as diversion of force, was the despatch of a combined army and naval force to seize the harbour of Diego Suarez in the north of French-owned Madagascar—to forestall any possibility of the Japanese occupying it. This rather expensive move in May was followed by a larger expedition in September to take over the whole of the island. As in the case of sinking the French fleet at Mers-el-Kebir, the military port of Oran in Algeria in 1940, fear proved in the long term a bad counsellor.

PART V

THE TURN

1942

Russia: December 1941 – April 1942

FINLAND
Helsinki
L. Ladoga
Gulf of Finland
Volkhov
Tallinn
Tikhvin
ESTONIA
L. Peipus
ARMY GROUP NORTH
Novgorod
L. Ilmen
Rybinsk
Staraya Russa
Volga
Riga
Pskov
Kholm
Kalinin
LATVIA
Ostashkov
Velikye Luki
Rzhev
Klin
Moscow
LITHUANIA
Kaunas
Vitebsk
Demidov
Vyazma
Ryazan
Smolensk
Kaluga
Tula
Minsk
Mogilev
Dnieper
Roslavl
ARMY GROUP CENTRE
Briansk
Tambov
BELO - RUSSIA
Gomel
Orel
Livny
Yelets
Pinsk
Pripet
Beresyna
Desna
Kursk
Voronezh
Rovno
Konotop
Don
Kiev
Zhitomir
Kharkov
ARMY GROUP SOUTH
Izyum
Dnieper
UKRAINE
Donetz
Kirovograd
Dnepropetrovsk
Zaporozhe
Taganrog
HUNGARY
MOLDAVIA
Kishinev
Mariupol
Rostov.
Dniester
Odessa
Sea of Azov
RUMANIA
CRIMEA
Kerch
Bucharest
Novorossiisk
Sevastopol
BLACK SEA
BULGARIA

Miles 100 200
Kilometres 200 300

—— Limit of German advance into Russia December 5, 1941
▨ Reoccupied by Russian forces December 5, 1941, to end April 1942

Copyright © Cassell & Co. Ltd 1970

CHAPTER 18

THE TIDE TURNS IN RUSSIA

In 1940 the Germans had opened their campaign on April 9 with the spring upon Norway and Denmark. In 1941 they had opened it on April 6, with their offensive in the Balkans. But in 1942 there was no such early opening. That fact showed the exhausting effects on the Germans of their frustrated attempt in 1941 to gain a quick victory over Russia, and the extent to which their offensive effort had been absorbed there. For while weather conditions were unfavourable to an early spring move on the Russian front, there was no such hindrance to a move against the eastern or western ends of Britain's precarious position in the Mediterranean. Yet no fresh threat was developed in this key area of British oversea communications.

In the Russian theatre, the Red Army's winter counteroffensive continued for over three months after its December launching, though with diminishing progress. By March it had advanced more than 150 miles in some sectors. But the Germans maintained their hold on the main bastions of their winter front—such towns as Schlüsselburg, Novgorod, Rzhev, Vyasma, Briansk, Orel, Kursk, Kharkov, and Taganrog—despite the fact that the Russians were many miles in rear of most of these places, through pushing into the spaces between them.

These bastion-towns were formidable obstacles from a tactical point of view; strategically, they tended to dominate the situation, because they were focal points in the sparse web of communications. While their German garrisons could not prevent infiltration into the wide spaces between them, these communication-blocks cramped and curtailed the exploitation of any penetration so long as they remained intact. Thus they fulfilled, on a larger scale, the braking function which the French forts of the Maginot Line had been designed to perform—and might have succeeded in performing if the chains of forts along the French frontier had not ended at a half-way point which allowed the Germans ample room to outflank it.

As the Red Army failed to undercut these bastions sufficiently to cause their collapse, the deep advances it made in the intervening spaces tended to turn out to its own disadvantage later. For the bulges it made were naturally less defensible than bastion-towns, and thus absorbed an excessive quantity of troops in holding them, while they could more easily be cut off by flanking strokes from the German-held bastions, used as offensive springboards.

By the spring of 1942 the battlefront in Russia had become so deeply indented as to appear almost like a reproduction of Norway's coastline, with its fiords penetrating far inland. The way that the Germans had been able to hold on to the 'peninsulas' was remarkable evidence of the power of modern defence when skilfully and tenaciously conducted, and provided with adequate weapons. It was a lesson that went even beyond the Russian defence of 1941 in refuting the superficial deductions drawn from the swift offensive successes earlier in the war against soft opposition—from cases where the attacker had a decisive superiority in weapon-power or encountered an ill-trained and badly bewildered defence. It repeated on a much larger scale the experiences of the St. Mihiel salient in the First World War, and proved the possibilities that were foreshadowed by the four-years-long maintenance of that theoretically untenable projection. The experience of the 1941 winter campaign also tended to confirm the longer-view evidence of history that the effect of co-incidence is primarily psychological, and that the danger is greatest in the early stages—diminishing if the sudden shock of its realisation, by the partially encircled troops, does not produce an immediate collapse.

In retrospect, it is clear that Hitler's veto on any extensive withdrawal worked out in such a way as to restore the confidence of the German troops, and probably saved them from a widespread collapse, while his insistence on the 'hedgehog' system of defence brought the Germans important advantages at the outset of the 1942 campaign.

Nevertheless, they paid a heavy price indirectly for that rigid defence. Its success encouraged the belief that it could be as successfully repeated in the more adverse conditions of the following winters. A more immediate handicap was the strain to which their air force was subjected in the prolonged effort to maintain supplies by air, under winter conditions, to the garrisons of these more or less isolated bastion-towns. Because of the bad weather the accident rate was high, while an excessive number of aircraft had to be used to make up supply shortages in the intervals of good weather—on occasions over 300 transport planes had to be used in the day to provision a single army corps. The effort of providing air transport on such a scale to a whole chain of exposed forward positions damaged the air transport organization of the Luftwaffe, and the withdrawal of experienced air units to other theatres limited the Luftwaffe's combat effectiveness on the Russian front.

The tremendous strain of that winter campaign, on an army that had not been prepared for it, had also a serious delayed effect in other ways. Before the winter ended many divisions were reduced to barely a third of their original strength. They were never fully built up again, and it was well into the summer before they even reached a level sufficient to attempt active operations. Moreover, the additional divisions that were raised at home during the winter created a total figure that was basically fictitious. In 1942 and subsequently, divisions which had been almost destroyed in heavy fighting were maintained in existence, as a camouflage, without the gaps in their ranks being filled up. These nominal divisions sometimes comprised only two or three battalions.

Hitler had been told by his generals that an additional 800,000 men must be provided if the offensive was to be resumed in 1942. Albert Speer, the Minister for Armament Production, said it was not possible to release such a number from the factories for service in the army.

The deficit was eventually met by a radical change in organisation. Infantry divisions were reorganised on a basis of seven battalions instead of nine. The battle-strength of the infantry company was fixed at a maximum of 80 men, compared with 180 as formerly. That reduction served a dual purpose, as it was found that with the loss of trained officers the younger officers who replaced them as company commanders were apt to lose control when handling companies of the old bulk, while it was also found that larger losses occurred in the larger-size companies without much difference of effect.

The combined reduction in the number of battalions and number of men gave unreality in subsequent years to the tendency of the Allied Intelligence staffs to continue reckoning the number of German divisions as if they were of similar size to their own. It would have been a better approximation to count two German divisions as equivalent to one British or American division. Even that ratio ceased to be a true guide by the late summer of 1944, when few divisions actually approached their reduced nominal strength.

The 1942 campaign also saw an increase of the German Army's tank strength that was superficial rather than real. Two new armoured divisions were formed during the winter—partly through the conversion of the horsed cavalry division that it had hitherto preserved, only to find it of negligible value. Some additions were made in the tank holdings of the motorised infantry divisions, but barely half of the twenty existing armoured divisions were brought up to strength in tanks.

Thus, in sum, the Germans' balance-sheet represented a precarious foundation for a continuance of the offensive. Even by the most strenuous efforts they could barely regain their former level of numbers, and then only by increased drafts upon their allies' forces, poorer in quality than their own. They could have no margin to meet the losses of another costly campaign. A still greater handicap was their inability to develop their two main offensive assets, their air force and their armoured force, to the scale needed for an assured superiority.*

The unfavourable aspects of the situation were realised by the German General Staff, but its heads had diminished power to influence Hitler's decision. Hitler's pressure was too strong for them to resist, and the pressure of events was too strong for Hitler. He was compelled to go on and on.

The question of resuming the offensive in 1942 was under discussion in November 1941—even before the final attempt to capture Moscow. Rundstedt claimed to have argued in those November discussions not only for a changeover to the defensive, but the advisability of a withdrawal to the original starting line in Poland. Leeb was said to have agreed. While the other leading generals did not advocate so complete a change of policy, most of them felt an increasing anxiety as to where the Russian campaign was leading them, and showed no keenness for a resumption of the offensive. The failure of the December attack on Moscow and the trials of the winter reinforced their doubts.

But the weight of military opposition was weakened by the changes in the higher commands which followed the miscarriage of the 1941 campaign. Rundstedt had asked, and been allowed, to resign at the end of November, when Hitler overruled his proposal to discontinue the southern drive to the Caucasus and fall back to a winter defence line on the Mius River. He at least was relatively fortunate in the time and manner of his departure. When the failure of the whole campaign was plain to the world, the departure of Brauchitsch on December 19 was publicly announced in terms which implied that he was the man to blame. That act served the dual purpose of furnishing Hitler with a scapegoat and opening the way for him to take over direct command of the Army. Bock, the too zealous supporter of Hitler's last bid for Moscow, had reported sick in mid-December with a stomach ailment brought on by worry and strain and his resignation was

---

* These drawbacks could be deduced even by distant onlookers in the West. In a commentary I wrote in March 1942, my conclusion was that 'it would be reasonable to anticipate this summer not only a repetition of last autumn's German frustration but a definite change in the tide'.

accepted on December 20. Leeb remained for the moment, and it was less easy to blame him for failure to take Leningrad, since his planned attack on that city had been cancelled by Hitler's own order just as it was about to start—from a fear of the losses that might be incurred in street-fighting. But when Leeb saw that nothing could persuade Hitler to withdraw from the Demyansk salient he asked to be relieved.

The disappearance of Brauchitsch and the three original army group commanders diminished the restraining influence of Halder, the Chief of the General Staff. That effect, and Hitler's advantage, were deepened by the natural tendency of the successors to swallow their doubts and become initially more amenable to the Führer's desires. Hitler well understood the effect of promotion in seducing men's judgement and producing compliance. Professional ambition rarely resists that form of temptation.

Rundstedt was replaced by Reichenau; Bock by Kluge; and Leeb, later, by Küchler. Bock's departure from command of the Central Army Group was due to a temporary illness, and when Reichenau died suddenly from a heart-attack in January, Bock was reinstated as his successor. He was dropped finally in July, however, when the forces in the south were reorganised during the summer offensive. In this reorganisation a special 'Army Group A' was created out of Army Group South for the drive to the Caucasus, and command of it was given to Field-Marshal List. The remainder of 'Army Group South' was then redesignated as 'Army Group B' firstly under Bock and then under Weichs.

The plan to launch another great offensive crystallised in the early months of 1942. Hitler's decision was influenced by pressure from his economic experts. They told him that Germany could not continue the war unless she obtained oil supplies from the Caucasus, as well as wheat and ores—a view that was proved mistaken by the fact that Germany failed to secure the Caucasus oil yet managed to continue the war for three more years. But Hitler was the more responsive to such economic arguments because they coincided with his instinctive urge—to do something positive and offensive. The idea of a withdrawal was repugnant to him, whatever the relief and potential advantage it might bring. Since he recoiled from that step-back he saw nothing else he could do than to push forward again.

That instinct made him insensitive to uncomfortable facts. For example, the German Intelligence Service had information that 600–700 tanks a month were being produced by the Russian factories in the Urals and elsewhere. But when Halder gave him the evidence he slammed the table and declared that any such rate of production was impossible. He would not believe what he did not want to believe.

Hitler's Plans: Spring 1942

Short term - Caucasian oilfields
Long term - Moscow

Front line April 1942
Oil fields

Miles 0 — 300
Kilometres 0 — 500

Moscow

Vyasma

ARMY GROUP CENTRE

Orel

Kursk

Kazan

Ural Mts

?

?

Kuybyshev

Voronezh

Saratov

ARMY GROUP B

Kharkov

ARMY GROUP SOUTH

Donetz

Don

Volga

Ural

ARMY GROUP A

Stalingrad

Taganrog

Rostov

Astrakhan

Sea of Azov

Kerch

Kuban Pen.

CRIMEA

Sevastopol

Maikop

Grozny

CAPSIAN SEA

CASPIAN SEA

BLACK SEA

CAUCASUS MTS.

Batumi

Tiflis

Baku

TURKEY

PERSIA

Copyright © Cassell & Co. Ltd 1970

He was led, however, to recognise the limitation of Germany's resources to the extent of admitting the necessity of limiting the scope of his new offensive. As defined early in the spring, it was to be pursued on both flanks, but not on the whole front.

The main effort was to be made on the southern flank near the Black Sea. It would take the form of a drive down the corridor between the Don and Donetz rivers. After reaching and crossing the lower reach of the Don, between its southerly bend and Black Sea mouth, the drive was to turn south towards the Caucasus oilfields, while also extending eastward to Stalingrad on the Volga.

In formulating that dual aim Hitler originally entertained the idea that the capture of Stalingrad might open the way for a northward wheel to get astride the rear of the Russian armies that were covering Moscow, while some of his entourage even talked of an advance to the Urals. But, after much argument, Halder convinced him that this was an impossibly ambitious project, and the objective actually set was to extend the advance beyond Stalingrad only so far as to provide tactical security for that strategic keypoint. Moreover, the purpose in capturing Stalingrad was now defined as a means of providing strategic flank-cover for the advance into the Caucasus. For Stalingrad lay on the Volga, commanding the land bridge between that river and the Don, and as a focus of communications formed a potential cork for this bottleneck.

Hitler's 1942 plan also comprised a secondary offensive to capture Leningrad during the summer. Apart from the prestige value, this northern move was considered important as a means of securing overland communication with Finland and relieving her isolated situation.

On the rest of the Eastern front, the German armies were to remain on the defensive, merely improving their fortified positions. In brief, the German offensive of 1942 was to be confined to the two wings. That limitation was the measure of the extent to which German reserves were running short. Moreover, the intended drive on the southern wing could only be carried out by drawing more heavily on Germany's allies to furnish most of the rearward cover for the flanks of the advance as it pushed deeper.

The idea of such a deep advance on one flank, without any simultaneous pressure on the enemy's centre, ran contrary to the canons of strategy with which the German generals had been indoctrinated from youth onwards. It looked all the worse to them since the flank advance would have to run the gauntlet between the main Russian armies and the Black Sea. They felt still more uneasy at the thought that the protection of their inland flank would have to depend largely on Rumanian, Hungarian, and Italian troops. Hitler answered their anxious questions with the decisive statement that Germany could only maintain herself in the war by securing the oil supplies of the Caucasus. As for the risk of relying on allied troops to protect their flank, he said that these would be used to hold the line of the Don, and of the Volga between Stalingrad and the Caucasus—where the river lines themselves would help. The capture of Stalingrad, and the holding of that keypoint, would be entrusted to German troops.

As a preliminary to the main offensive, on the mainland, the German forces in the Crimea launched a stroke on May 8 to capture the easterly part of it, the Kerch peninsula, where the Russians had managed to check them in the autumn. A well-prepared attack, covered by a concentration of dive-bombers, made a breach in the defences. Pouring through, the Germans wheeled northward and penned a large part of the defenders against the coast, where the dive-bombers soon produced their surrender. With their own path thus cleared, the Germans swept down the fifty-mile long penin-sula. After a momentary check at the 'Tartar Ditch'—an historic line of defence twelve miles from the peninsula tip—they captured Kerch itself by May 16, and thus cleared the Russians out of the Crimea, except for the long-isolated fortress of Sevastopol in the south-western corner.

This coup had been conceived as a means of creating a leverage in aid of the main objective—by a jump across the Kerch Straits onto the Kuban peninsula, which forms the western end of the Caucasus. The German forces were to be used to open the way. But the main offensive made such rapid progress, along the overland route into the Caucasus, that this leverage became unnecessary.

The most effective factor in clearing the path for the German advance was a Russian offensive, towards Kharkov, which began on May 12, striking at Paulus's 6th Army, which was itself poised to eliminate the Soviet Izyum salient. This was a premature effort, beyond the powers of the Russian Army at this stage in face of the Germans' defensive skill. Ambitious aims, and ex-cessive anticipations, were suggested by Marshal Timoshenko's opening 'Order of the Day' —which started: 'I hereby order the troops to begin the decisive offensive.' The prolongation of this Kharkov offensive played into the Germans' hands, absorbing too large a part of the Russians' reserves, and thus laying them open to a deadly riposte. The Russians penetrated the German defences in the Kharkov area and fanned out north-west and south-west. By Hitler's order the projected offensive against the Izyum salient by Paulus's 6th Army and Kleist's 1st Panzer Army was advanced one day and the Russian offensive was brought to an end by Bock's counteroffensive. Two complete Soviet armies and the elements of two others were cut to pieces, and by the end of May 241,000 Red Army men went into captivity. Few reserves were in hand to meet the Germans when they launched their own main stroke in June.

The German offensive was 'staggered' both in siting and timing. It was planned to take place on the whole German front in South Russia, which ran back obliquely from the coast near Taganrog and along the Donetz towards Kharkov and Kursk. It was a battle-front in echelon. The parts farthest back, on the left, were to move first. The more advanced parts, on the right, were to wait for the left wing to come up before trying to advance, but meanwhile helped to exert a flanking leverage that weakened the resistance facing the left.

On the right was the 17th Army, with the 11th Army in the Crimea. Next to the 17th Army, farther back, was the 1st Panzer Army. After July 9 these two armies comprised List's 'Army Group A', destined to invade the Caucasus. On its left was Bock's 'Army Group B', which included the 4th Panzer Army, the 6th Army, the 2nd Army and the 2nd Hungarian Army. The two panzer armies were to deliver the decisive thrusts, both delivered from the Germans' rear flank against the Russians' most advanced positions—the 1st striking from the Kharkov sector, and the 4th from the Kursk sector. The 'infantry' armies were to follow on and back them up.

As an immediate preliminary to the main offensive, a siege assault was launched against the fortress of Sevastopol on June 7. This was carried out by Manstein's 11th Army. Although the resistance was tough, the Germans eventually prevailed through superior weight and skill, though it was not until July 4 that the fortress, and with it the whole Crimea, was completely in German hands. The Russians were thus deprived of their chief naval base in the Black Sea. But their fleet was still 'in being', although in fact it was to remain passive.

Meanwhile the opening of this move in the Crimea had been followed by another important diversionary offensive closer to the points where the main operation was being mounted. For on June 10 the Germans exploited their Izyum wedge by forcing the passage of the Donetz, and gaining a foothold on the north bank of the river. After expanding this by degrees into a large bridgehead they delivered a powerful armoured stroke northward from it on the 22nd, and in two days reached the junction of Kupiansk some forty miles north of the river. That created an invaluable flanking leverage to assist the easterly thrust of their main offensive, which was launched on the 28th.

On the left wing of the main offensive there was stiff fighting for several days before the Russian reserves ran short and the 4th Panzer Army broke through in the sector between Kursk and Belgorod. After that the advance

German Advance to Stalingrad

German armoured attacks

German infantry attacks

Front line, May 28, 1942

Front line, July 22

Front line, Nov 18

0 — Miles — 200
0 — Kilometres — 300

Belgorod

Volchansk

MAY 26

Kharkov

Kupiansk

6th ARMY

Krasnograd

Izyum

MAY 12

Slavyansk

1st PANZER ARMY

Russian offensive May 12, 1942

German counteroffensive May 17/26

0 — Miles — 50
0 — Km. — 80

Donetz

2nd ARMY

Kursk

4th PANZER ARMY

ARMY GROUP B

Belgorod

6th ARMY

Kharkov

Voronezh

Rossosh

C O R R I D O R'

Novaya Kalitva

Chertkovo

Izyum

ARMY GROUP SOUTH

1st PANZER ARMY

Millerovo

Donetz

Don

Volga

6th ARMY

Kalach

Stalingrad

ARMY GROUP A

Kamensk

17th ARMY

ARMY GROUP B

Taganrog

Rostov

Proletarskaya

Kotelnikovo

4th PANZER ARMY

Astrakhan

Manych

K A L M U K S T E P P E

Sea of Azov

Kerch

CRIMEA

Kuban

Krasnodar

ARMY GROUP A

Stavropol

Budenovsk

C A S P I A N S E A

Dnieper

MAY 8 11th ARMY

Kuban Pen.

Novorossiisk

Tuapse

Maikop

Laba

Armavir

1st PANZER ARMY

Pyatigorsk

Mozdok

NEW RAILWAY

Terek

C a u c a s u s

Nalchik

Grozny

Alagir

Ordzhonikidze

To Baku 150 miles

B L A C K   S E A

ROSTOV-TIFLIS HIGHWAY

M o u n t a i n s

Batumi

Tiflis

TURKEY

swept rapidly across the hundred-mile stretch of plain to the Don near Voronezh. This appeared to foreshadow a direct move across the Upper Don and beyond Voronezh, cutting the lateral rail-link from Moscow to Stalingrad and the Caucasus. Actually, the Germans had no such intention. The orders were to halt on reaching the river and turn it into a defensive flank-cover for the south-easterly continuation of the drive. The 2nd Hungarian Army came up to relieve the 4th Panzer Army, which then wheeled south-eastward down the corridor between the Don and the Donetz, followed by the 6th Army—which had the mission of taking Stalingrad.

The whole of the operations on this left wing tended to cloak the menace that was developing on the right wing. For while attention was focused on the thrust from Kursk towards Voronezh, a more dangerous thrust was being delivered by Kleist's 1st Panzer Army from the Kharkov sector. This profited by the ill-organised position on which the Russian forces stood after the check to their own offensive, as well as by the Kupiansk wedge in the Russians' flank. After achieving a quick breakthrough, Kleist's armoured divisions drove eastward down the Don–Donetz corridor to Chertkovo, on the railway from Moscow to Rostov. Then they made a southerly turn, past Millerovo and Kamensk towards the Lower Don at and above Rostov.

The left wing gained a crossing, with little opposition, on July 22—after an advance of some 250 miles from the starting line. Next day the right wing, arriving on the edge of the Rostov defences, drove a wedge into them. Lying on the west bank of the Don, the city was exposed to such thrusts, and in the rapid flux of the retreat its defences had not been properly organised. The German flanking moves accentuated the confusion, and the city quickly fell into their hands. Its capture cut the pipeline from the Caucasus, leaving the Russian armies dependent for their oil supply on what could be brought in tankers up the Caspian Sea and up the new rail route they had hurriedly laid along the steppes west of it. Russia had also lost another huge slice of her bread supply.

The one important offset to this spectacular sweep was that, though large bodies of Russian troops were overrun, the total captured was not nearly so large as in 1941. The pace had not been quite fast enough. That was due, not so much to the resistance met, as to the earlier loss of so many of the best-trained German tank troops, and the tendency to adopt more cautious methods. The panzer 'groups' of 1941 had been reorganised as panzer 'armies', with an increased proportion of infantry and artillery; this increase of support tended to cause a decrease of speed.

Although large numbers of Russian troops were momentarily isolated by the German advance, many of them were able to filter back before they could be rounded up. The south-easterly direction of the German sweep made it natural for them to fall back in a north-easterly direction, thus helping the Russian Command to gather them in or near the Stalingrad area, where they became an inherent threat to the flank of the German advance into the Caucasus. That effect had a vital bearing on the next phase of the campaign, when the German armies forked on divergent courses—part for the Caucasus oilfields, and part for the Volga at Stalingrad.

After crossing the Lower Don, Kleist's 1st Panzer Army wheeled south-eastward into the valley of the Manych River—which is linked by a canal with the Caspian Sea. By blowing up the big dam here, and flooding the valley, the Russians momentarily upset the tanks' onrush. But after two days' delay the German forces succeeded in crossing the river and then continued their drive into the Caucasus, fanning out on a wide front. Encouraged by the lack of opposition and the openness of the country, Kleist's right column drove almost due southward through Armavir to the great oil centre of Maikop, 200 miles south-east of Rostov, which it reached on August 9. On the same day the van of his centre column swept into Pyatigorsk, 150 miles to the east of Maikop, in the foothills of the Caucasus Mountains. His left column took a still more easterly direction, towards Budenovsk. Mobile detachments had been sent racing ahead, and as a result the pace of this early August onrush beyond the Don was terrific.

But the pace slowed down almost as suddenly as it had developed. The prime causes were a shortage of fuel and an abundance of mountains. That dual brake was subsequently reinforced by the distant effect of the struggle for Stalingrad, which drained off a large part of the forces that might have been used to give a decisive impetus to the Caucasus advance.

It was difficult to keep up the flow of fuel supplies required for such a far-ranging sweep, and the difficulty was increased because it had to come by rail through the Rostov bottleneck, and the track had to be converted from the wide Russian to the central European gauge—the Germans could not venture to send supplies by sea while the Russian fleet remained in being. A limited amount was forwarded by air, but the total that came through by rail and air was insufficient to maintain the momentum of the advance.

The mountains were a natural barrier to the attainment of the German objective, but their effect was increased by the increasingly stubborn resistance that was met on reaching this area. Earlier, there had been little difficulty in swerving round the Russian forces which tried to oppose the advance, and the latter had tended to retreat before they were cut off, instead of fighting on stubbornly as in 1941. The change may have been due to a more elastic defensive strategy, though the German Command was convinced, from the interrogation of prisoners, that there was a growing tendency on the part of troops who were by-passed to look for a way of getting back to their homes, especially among those who came from Asiatic Russia. But when the Caucasus was reached the resistance became stiffer. The defending forces here were largely composed of locally recruited troops, who felt that they were protecting their own homes, and were familiar with the kind of mountainous country in which they were fighting. Those factors multiplied the strength of the defence, whereas the nature of the country cramped the attackers by canalising the flood-like advance of their armoured forces.

While the 1st Panzer Army had been carrying out its flanking sweep into the Caucasus, the 17th Army had been following up on foot through the bottleneck of Rostov, whence it turned south towards the Black Sea coast.

After the capture of the Maikop oilfields the Caucasus front was divided afresh, and further objectives allotted. The 1st Panzer Army was given responsibility for the main stretch between the River Laba and the Caspian Sea. Its first objective was to capture the mountain stretch of the great highway running from Rostov to Tiflis; its second objective was Baku, on the Caspian. The 17th Army was responsible for the narrower area from the Laba back to the Kerch Straits. Its first task was to advance southward from Maikop and Krasnodar, across the western end of the Caucasus range, to capture the Black Sea ports of Novorossiisk and Tuapse. Its second objective was to force a passage down the coastal road beyond Tuapse, and thus open the way to Batumi.

While the coastal road south from Tuapse was overhung by high mountains, the first task of the 17th Army looked relatively easy, since it had less than fifty miles to go before reaching the coast, and this western end of the mountain chain sloped away into foothills. But the task did not prove easy. The advance had to cross the Kuban River, which had wide marshy borders near its mouth, and the hills farther east were rugged enough to be difficult obstacles. It was nearly the middle of September before the 17th Army captured Novorossiisk. It never reached Tuapse.

The 1st Panzer Army, on the main line of advance, made better progress by comparison, but at a diminishing pace and with increasing pauses. Fuel shortage was the decisive handicap in the advance to the mountains. The panzer divisions were sometimes at a standstill for several days on end, awaiting fresh supplies. This handicap cost the Germans their best chance—of rushing the passes while surprise lasted, and before the defences were strengthened. When it came to a matter of fighting a way into the mountains the 1st Panzer Army was handicapped because most of the expert mountain troops had been allotted to the 17th Army for its attempt to reach Tuapse and open the coast road to Batumi.

The first serious check occurred on reaching the Terek River—which covered the approaches to the mountain road over to Tiflis, as well as the more exposed Grozny oilfields north of the mountains. The Terek has nothing like the awe-inspiring breadth of the Volga, but its swift current made it an awkward obstacle. Kleist then tried a manœuvre to the east, downstream, and succeeded in forcing a passage near Mozdok, in the first week of September. But his forces were held up again in the densely wooded hills beyond the Terek. Grozny lay only fifty miles beyond the Mozdok crossing, but all the German efforts failed to bring it within their grasp.

An important factor in this frustration was the way that the Russians switched a force of several hundred bombers to the airfields near Grozny. Their sudden appearance proved the more effective, as a brake on Kleist's advance, because most of his anti-aircraft units and much of his air force had been withdrawn from him to help the German forces at Stalingrad. Thus the Russian bombers were able to harass Kleist's army without hindrance, while they also increased its ordeal by setting alight large tracts of the forest through which it was struggling to advance.

The Russians provided a wider distraction by bringing cavalry divisions down the Caspian coast to harass his exposed eastern flank. Operating over the steppes against a widely stretched defensive screen, the Russian cavalry found unusually good scope for their particular qualities. In that vast plain they were able to penetrate his outposts wherever they chose, and cut off supplies. The Russians' growing concentration on this flank was helped by the railway they had built from Astrakhan southward. This was laid across the flat expanse of the steppes without any foundation, and neither cuttings nor embankments were required. The Germans soon found that they gained little by cutting it, since as soon as any section of it was destroyed a fresh set of rails was quickly laid. At the same time the enemy was equally intangible, and his flanking menace continuously increased. Although German mobile detachments penetrated as far as the Caspian shore, the sight of that sea was a 'mirage in the desert'.

Throughout September and October, Kleist went on trying to push south from Mozdok, by surprise attacks at different points. At each attempt he was blocked. Then he decided to switch his weight from his left centre to his right centre, for a pincer-stroke against Ordzhonikidze, the gateway to the Daryal Pass, which carries the mountain highway to Tiflis. This stroke was launched in the last week of October, and for it he was given such air support as could be spared. His right pincer captured Nalchik in a westerly flanking move, and then Alagir—the beginning of the alternative military road over the Mamison Pass. From Alagir it thrust on to Ordzhonikidze in conjunction with a converging thrust up the Terek valley. Rain and snow delayed the final stage, but Kleist's forces were almost within reach of their immediate goal when the Russians launched a well-timed and well-aimed counterattack. This produced the sudden collapse of a Rumanian mountain division, which had done well in the advance but was feeling the strain of the effort. As a result Kleist had to fall back and abandon his plan. The front was then stabilised, with the Germans still facing the mountain barrier which they had vainly tried to pierce.

This final repulse in the central Caucasus coincided with the opening of the great Russian counteroffensive at Stalingrad.

A final effort in the western Caucasus had also been planned, but this never matured. For it Hitler had, very belatedly, decided to play the airborne trump which he had so carefully preserved. The Parachute Division—still called the 7th Air Division as a camouflage—had been assembled in and near the Crimea for a swoop onto the coastal road from Tuapse to Batumi, in conjunction with a renewed push by the 17th Army. But then the Russian counteroffensive at Stalingrad took place, and was followed by a new Russian attack near Rzhev—where Zhukov's armies had nearly broken through in their August attempt to give indirect relief to Stalingrad. Hitler was so alarmed at the dual threat that he cancelled his last bid for Batumi, and ordered the parachute forces to be rushed north by rail to Smolensk, as a reinforcement to the central front.

All these failures and dangers were the fruit of frustration at Stalingrad, where a subsidiary purpose had developed by degrees into a principal effort that drew away the land and air reserves needed to fulfil the primary aim, and ultimately drained Germany's strength to no purpose.

It was ironical that in the first phase the Germans should have paid forfeit for fulfilling the canons of orthodox strategy, and subsequently paid forfeit for disregarding them. Out of the original convergence arose a fatal divergence of effort.

The direct advance on Stalingrad was carried out by the 6th Army, under Paulus. It pushed down the north side of the corridor between the Don and the Donetz. Helped by the great armoured drive that was proceeding on the south side, the 6th Army made good progress at first. But as the advance extended its strength dwindled, as more and more divisions had to be detached to cover the ever-extending northern flank along the Don. The shrinkage was increased by the wastage due to long and rapid marches in

great heat, as well as to battle-losses. That shrinkage in turn became a handicap in overcoming the successive stands made by the retreating Russians.
Harder fighting entailed heavier losses, and thus less power to deal with the
next stand.

The effect became pronounced when the 6th Army approached the great
eastern bend of the Don. On July 28 one of its mobile spearheads reached the
river near Kalach—350 miles from the starting line and barely forty miles
distant from the western bend of the Volga at Stalingrad. But this was a
flash in the pan, and the general advance was delayed by stubborn Russian
resistance in the Don bend. The narrowed front and the lower proportion of
mobile troops in the 6th Army, compared with the panzer armies, handicapped its manœuvring power. A fortnight passed before the Germans were
able to crush the Russian forces in the bend. Even then it was a further ten
days before they established bridgeheads across the river.

On August 23 the Germans were ready to begin the final stage of their
advance on Stalingrad. It took the form of a pincer-attack, by the 6th Army
from the north-west, and by the 4th Panzer Army from the south-west.
That same night German mobile units reached the banks of the Volga
thirty miles above Stalingrad and came close to the bend of the Volga fifteen
miles south of the city. But the pincers were kept well apart by the defenders.
In the next phase the Germans developed an attack from the west, thus completing the semi-circle of pressure, and the tenseness of the situation was
manifested in the tone of the call to the Russian troops to hold on at all costs
to the last man. They responded to the call with wonderful endurance, for
they were fighting under nerve-racking conditions that were also hard for
the problem of supply and reinforcement. The two-mile wide river behind
their backs was not wholly a disadvantage. With such troops, it helped to
stiffen resistance as well as complicating it.

Along the arc of Russian defence, attack followed attack in seemingly end-
less succession, with frequent changes of site and method, but with only
slight progress to compensate the attackers' cost. At times the defence was
pierced, but the thrust could never be driven deep enough to cause more than
a local withdrawal. More often, the attacks failed to penetrate. As check
followed check, the psychological importance of the place increased—as
with Verdun in 1916. In this case it was multiplied by the name that the
place bore. 'Stalingrad' was an inspiring symbol for the Russians, and a
hypnotic symbol for the Germans—especially for their Leader. It hypnotised
Hitler into a state in which he lost sight of strategy, and lost all regard for the
future. It became more fatal than Moscow—because its name meant more.

The unprofitableness, and risks, of the continued effort were apparent to any analyst of war experience who kept a clear head. Such repetitive attacks rarely pay unless the defending forces are isolated from reinforcement or their country's reserves are running short—whereas in this case it was the Germans who were less able to bear a prolonged process of attrition.

Despite Russia's immense losses, her reserves of manpower remained much greater than those of Germany. Her most serious shortage was in equipment; a shortage due to the 1941 losses which had partly accounted for her renewed defeats in 1942. Artillery was lacking, and was substituted to a large extent by mortars that were brought up on trucks. Tanks and all forms of motor-transport were other serious deficiencies. But towards the end of the summer an increasing flow of fresh equipment came from the new factories in the back areas, as well as from American and British supplies. At the same time the much extended call-up of men that had been applied after the outbreak of war was bearing fruit, and the volume of new divisions from Asia was rising.

The Stalingrad battle-area lay so far east that it was the more accessible to this inflow from the east. That helped the defence of the city, and while the scale of the direct reinforcement was cramped by its awkward situation, the mounting strength of the Russian armies on the northern flank had an in-direct effect which was equivalent to an important reinforcement. Their counter-pressure on that flank would have turned the scales long before it did, if it had not been handicapped by material deficiencies in the pre-dominant weapons of modern warfare. But the effect increased as the Germans, through becoming entangled in a localised attrition battle, used up their limited reserves of men and machines. In that kind of battle their expenditure was higher proportionately, being the attackers, and they could afford it less.

The dangers of the process were soon appreciated by the General Staff. On returning from his daily conference with Hitler, Halder would often throw out his hands in a gesture of exasperation and depression that told his assistants of one more vain effort to make Hitler see reason. His arguments against a continuance of the offensive became more urgent as winter came nearer, and the combined effect frayed Hitler's nerves, so that their relations became intolerable to both. In discussing plans Hitler continued his airy habit of waving his hand over the map in big sweeps, although the advances were now so slight that they were hardly discernible. As he became less able to sweep aside the Russians, he became more inclined to sweep obstructive counsellors out of his office. He had always felt that 'the old generals' were half-hearted about his schemes, and the more these failed to progress the more he felt that the General Staff was the brake.

So at the end of September Halder took his departure—following some of his assistants—and was succeeded by Kurt Zeitzler, a much younger man who at the time was Chief of Staff to Rundstedt in the West. In 1940 Zeitzler had been Chief of Staff of Kleist's panzer group, and it was largely due to his bold supply planning that the long-range armoured sweep from the Rhine to the English Channel had proved administratively possible. Apart from that important qualification, Hitler felt that he would have less difficulty in dealing with a younger soldier over the longer-range problem of advancing to the Caspian and the Volga—especially where the latter started with the spur of sudden promotion to the highest post. Zeitzler at first justified his confidence in this respect, for he did not worry Hitler with continual objections as Halder had done. But Zeitzler himself became worried within a short time, and as the prospect of gaining Stalingrad faded he began to argue with Hitler that the idea of maintaining the German front so far forward was impracticable. When events proved the truth of his warning Hitler did not like his advice any the better, and in 1943 took a distant attitude towards him, so that his advice became more and more ineffectual.

The same basic factors that governed the frustration of the Germans' attack on Stalingrad turned it into a faial reverse, by assisting the eventual Russian counteroffensive.

The more closely the Germans converged on the city, the more their own power of manœuvre became cramped, whereas the narrowing of the frontage helped the defender in moving his reserves more quickly to a threatened point on the diminished arc. At the same time, the Germans forfeited the advantage which they had formerly enjoyed from their power of distraction. During the opening drive of the summer campaign, as far as the Don, uncertainty as to their aim had helped to paralyse opposition, but now their aim had become obvious—and the Russian Command could commit its reserves with assurance. Thus the attacker's increasing concentration of force on Stalingrad became decreasingly effective as such—concentrated attack meeting concentrated defence.

At the same time, the Germans' concentration at Stalingrad increasingly drained reserves from their flank-cover, which itself was already strained by having to stretch so far—nearly 400 miles from Voronezh along the Don to the Stalingrad 'isthmus', and as far again from there to the Terek, across the Kalmuk Steppes. While these barren wastes restricted the weight of any

Russian counterstroke against the second stretch, that limitation did not apply to the Don sector, which, though covered by the river, was liable to become very vulnerable when the river froze or the Russians found unguarded spots for a crossing in strength. Moreover, they had succeeded in retaining a bridgehead over the Don near Serafimovich, 100 miles west of Stalingrad.

The danger to this long-stretched flank was foreshadowed by a number of small exploratory attacks that the Russians delivered from August onwards. These showed them how thinly held it was, and that it was mainly entrusted to Germany's allies—Hungarians from Voronezh southward; Italians around the point where it turned eastwards, near Novaya Kalitva; Rumanians near the final southward bend west of Stalingrad, as well as beyond Stalingrad. That long flank-front had only a slight German stiffening of odd regiments, or occasionally divisions, interspaced among the allied troops. Divisional sectors were up to forty miles long, and there were no properly fortified positions. The railheads were often a hundred miles or more behind the front, and the country was so bare that little timber was available for constructing defences.

An uncomfortable realisation of these handicaps led the German General Staff to tell Hitler as early as August that it would be impossible to hold the line of the Don, as a defensive flank, during the winter. Their warning was not appreciated. All defensive considerations were subordinated to the aim of capturing Stalingrad.

The cramping character of this too direct offensive became more marked after the middle of September, when the Germans penetrated into the straggling suburbs, and then into the factory area. To become entangled in street-fighting is always a handicap on the offensive, and it was specially detrimental to an army whose advantage lay mainly in a superior manœuvring power. At the same time the defence was able to make use of workers' units, who fought with the ferocity of men whose own homes are the immediate stake. In such circumstances, that local infusion was an important addition to the strength of the defending forces—the 62nd Army under General Chuikov and part of the 64th Army under General Shumilov—during the crucial weeks until the flow of reinforcements began to turn the tide. For the 62nd Army had been badly mauled in the fighting west of the Don, while few immediate resources could be found for it by General Eremenko, who was placed in charge of the sector as a whole.

The Germans' arrival in the built-up area also tended to split up their offensive into a string of localised attacks—which diminished its tidal force. The same limitation fostered a revival of the habit—to which infantry-minded commanders of the old school were prone—of employing tanks in driblets, instead of a flood. Many of the attacks were delivered with a mere twenty or thirty tanks, and although a few of the bigger efforts packed a punch of a hundred tanks, this figure meant only one tank to some 300 men engaged. With so small a proportion it was natural that the anti-tank weapons kept the upper hand. But while these paltry numbers conduced to poor tactics they revealed a growing material deficiency. This became equally marked in the declining scale of air support. The Germans were running short of the two weapons upon which they had mainly depended for their success. As a natural result the burden on the infantry became heavier, and the price of any advance higher.

On the surface, the defenders' position came to appear increasingly peril-ous, or even desperate, as the circle contracted and the enemy came closer to the heart of the city. The most critical moment was on October 14, but the German attack was stemmed by General Rodimtsev's 13th Guards Division. Even after this crisis was overcome the situation remained grave, because the defenders now had their backs so close to the Volga that they had little room left in which to practise shock-absorbing tactics. They could no longer afford to sell ground to gain time. But beneath the surface funda-mental factors were working in their favour.

The attackers' morale was being sapped by increasing losses, a growing sense of frustration, and the coming of winter, while their reserves were so fully absorbed as to leave the overstretched flanks without resiliency. They was thus becoming ripe for the counterstroke which the Russian Command were preparing, and for which it had now accumulated sufficient reserves to make it effective against such overstrained opponents.

The counterstroke was launched on November 19 and 20, and was well-timed. It started in the interval between the strong first frosts, which harden the ground for rapid movement, and the heavy snows, which clog manœuvre. It was to catch the Germans at the pitch of exhaustion, just as they were feeling most acutely the natural reaction from the failure of their offensive to bring them victory.

The counterstroke was shrewdly aimed strategically and psychologically—exploiting the indirect approach in a double sense. A pair of pincers, each composed of several prongs, was inserted in the flanks of the Stalingrad attack, so as to isolate the 6th Army and 4th Panzer Army from Army Group B. The pincers were driven in at places where the flank-cover was largely provided by Rumanian troops. The plan was devised by a brilliant trium-virate of the Russian General Staff, Generals Zhukov, Vasilevsky, and Voronov. The principal executants were General Vatutin, commander of the South-western front, General Rokossovsky, commanding the Don front, and General Eremenko, commanding the Stalingrad front.

Here it should be mentioned that the Eastern Front as a whole was divided by the Russians into twelve 'fronts' directly under General Headquarters in Moscow. Instead of organising them permanently in larger groups, it now became the Russian practice to send a senior general and staff from General Headquarters to co-ordinate the several 'fronts' concerned in any particular series of operations. The 'fronts' comprised an average of about four 'armies' apiece—which were smaller than in the West—and each of these usually controlled the divisions in it direct without the interposition of army corps headquarters. The armoured and motorised troops were organised in groups of brigades that were called 'corps', but were equivalent to large divisions; and these corps were controlled by the 'front' commander.

The corps system was re-introduced by the Russians in the summer of 1943, before the new system had a chance to be tested fully. For by cutting out links in the chain of command, and giving the higher commanders a larger number of 'sub-units' to handle, operations should be quickened and flexibility of manœuvre developed. Every additional link in the chain is a *drawback*—in the most literal sense. It tends to cause loss of time both in getting information back to the higher commander, and in getting his orders forward to the real executants. Moreover, it weakens his power of control, both by making his impression of the situation more remote, and by diminishing the force of his personal influence on the executants. Hence the fewer the intermediate headquarters, the more dynamic operations tend to become. On the other hand, an increase in the number of sub-units handled by one headquarters improves the power of manœuvre by providing more flexibility. A more flexible organisation can achieve greater striking effect because it has more capacity for adjustment to varying circumstances, and for concentration at the decisive point. If a man had only one or two fingers in addition to his thumb he would find it much more difficult to get a properly adjusted grip on any object, or opponent, than he can with four fingers and a thumb. His hand would have less flexibility and less capacity for concentrated pressure. That cramping limitation was seen in the armies of the Western Powers, where most formations and units were divided into only two or three manœuvrable parts.

North-west of Stalingrad, Russian spearheads thrust down the banks of the Don to Kalach and the railway running back to the Donetz Basin. Southeast of Stalingrad the prongs of the left pincers thrust westward to the railway

The Tide Turns in Russia

———	Front line November 18, 1942
◀━━	Russian attacks Nov. 19/Jan 13
▷━━	Manstein's counterattack, December 12/18

Miles 0 — 150
Kilometres 0 — 200

Livny
Kursk
Stary Oskol
Voronezh
VORONEZH FRONT
Belgorod
Kharkov
Novaya Kalitva
Don
SOUTH-WEST FRONT
Serafimovich
DON FRONT
TRAPPED 6th ARMY
NOVEMBER 19, 1942 RUSSIAN COUNTER-OFFENSIVE BEGINS.
VIII ITAL. ARMY
ARMY GROUP B
Chir
Millerovo
Kalach
Stalingrad
STALINGRAD FRONT
Donetz
ARMY GROUP SOUTH
Morozovsk
Gukovo
Stalino
ARMY GROUP DON
Volga
Kotelnikovo
Mius
Taganrog
Rostov
Mariupol
Proletarskaya
Astrakhan
Sea of Azov
Salsk
Manych
Elista
Tikhoretsk
ARMY GROUP A
Kerch
Kuban Pen.
Krasnodar
Armavir
Stavropol
Novorossiisk
Maikop
1st PANZER ARMY
END DEC. 1942 RUSSIAN OFFENSIVE BEGINS.
Tuapse
C A U C A S U S
Pyatigorsk
BLACK SEA
M T S.
Mozdok
Grozny
CAUCASUS FRONT
CASPIAN SEA

running south to Tikhoretsk and the Black Sea. After cutting this line they pressed on towards Kalach, and by the 23rd the encirclement was completed. It was welded more firmly in the days that followed, enclosing the 6th Army and a corps of the 4th Panzer Army. In those few days of swift movement the Russians had turned the tables strategically while keeping their defensive tactical advantage—that double score which the indirect approach often achieves. For the Germans were now forced to continue attacking—not to break in, but to break out. Their efforts in reverse were as unsuccessful as their earlier efforts to drive forward.

Meanwhile, another powerful Russian force had burst out of the Serafimovich bridgehead, and spread over the country west of the Don bend, in a multi-pronged drive south into the Don–Donetz corridor, to link up on the Chir with the left pincer thrusting on from Kalach. This outer-circle movement was of vital importance to the success of the whole plan, for it upset the enemy's base of operations and dropped an iron curtain across the more direct routes by which relieving forces might have come to the aid of Paulus.

Thus the German reply, in mid-December, was delivered from the southwest, beyond the Don, up the line from Kotelnikovo to Stalingrad. The troops for it came from a scratch force hastily assembled under Manstein's 11th Army Headquarters, which had to be withdrawn from Army Group Centre, Manstein's 11th Army being redesignated 'Army Group Don'. Its small size hardly justified such an impressive title, and for his attempt to relieve Stalingrad he had to depend on meagre reserves, including the 6th Panzer Division, which had been sent by rail from Brittany in France.

By skilful tactics Manstein made the most of his scanty armour, and succeeded in driving a deep wedge into the Russian covering position. But this hastily improvised advance was checked thirty miles short of the beleaguered Army, and then gradually forced back by Russian pressure on its own flank. With the frustration of this attempt any hope of relieving Paulus passed, for the German Command had no reserves for another attempt. Manstein, however, hung on to his own exposed position as long as he could, and longer than was safe, in order to cover the air lifeline by which a meagre flow of supplies was carried to the doomed army.

Meanwhile, on December 16, the Russians started a fresh outer-circle manœuvre far to the west. General Golikov, commanding the Voronezh front, launched his left wing across the Middle Don at a number of points on a sixty-mile stretch between Novaya Kalitva and Monastyrshchina—a stretch that was held by the 8th Italian Army. Crossing the hard-frozen Don at first light, tanks and infantry followed up a heavy bombardment which had already put many of the Italians to flight. Snowstorms helped to blind such little opposition as was met, but did not hold up the Russians, who rapidly pushed south towards Millerovo and the Donetz. At the same time Vatutin's forces struck south-westward from the Chir towards the Donetz. Within a week the converging drives had swept the enemy out of almost the whole of the Don–Donetz corridor. While the defence had been too thin and the rout too rapid for many prisoners to be secured in the first bound, larger numbers of the retreating enemy were overrun and rounded up in the next stage, so that by the end of the second week—which was also the end of the year— the bag reached a total of 60,000.

The sweep threatened the rear of all the German armies on the Lower Don and in the Caucasus. But deepening snow and the stubborn resistance of the German troops at Millerovo and several other communication-centres north of the Donetz averted the danger for the moment.

Nevertheless the menace was so palpable, and its extension so probable, that Hitler was at last brought to realise the inevitability of a disaster greater even than the Stalingrad encirclement if he persisted in his dream of conquering the Caucasus, and compelled the armies there to cling on while their flank was exposed for 600 miles back. So, in January, the order was sent that they were to retreat. The decision was taken just in time for them to escape being cut off. Their successful extrication prolonged the war, but it preceded the actual surrender of the Stalingrad armies in making clear to the world that the German tide was on the ebb.

The course of the Russian counteroffensive had been marked by the skill with which General Zhukov chose his thrust-points—as much on psychological as on topographical grounds. He hit the moral soft-spots in the enemy's dispositions. Moreover, he had shown his ability to develop an alternative kind of threat once his striking forces lost the immediate local tide, and the chance it carried of producing a general collapse. As a concentrated thrust has a diminishing effect in straining a defender's resisting power, he had renewed the initial effect by developing a widely distributed series of thrusts, aimed to extend the strain. That usually tends to be the more profitable, and less self-exhausting, form of strategy when a counteroffensive grows into an offensive and no longer enjoys its initial recoil-spring impetus.

Beneath all the other factors, material and moral, that governed the course of events lay the basic condition of the ratio between space and force. Space was so *wide* on the Eastern front that an attacker could always find room for outflanking manoeuvre if he did not concentrate upon too obvious an objective—such as Moscow in 1941, and Stalingrad in 1942. Thus the Germans had been able to gain their offensive successes without a superiority in numbers, so long as they kept a qualitative superiority. The fact that space was so *deep* on the Eastern front was, however, a saving factor for the Russians during the time they were unable to match the Germans in mechanised power and manœuvrability.

But the Germans had lost that technical and tactical advantage, while they had also used up much of their manpower. With that shrinkage of their forces the wide spaces of Russia had turned to their disadvantage, endangering their capacity to hold such an extended front. The question now became whether they could recover their balance by contracting their front, or whether they had expended so much of their strength as to leave them no chance.

CHAPTER 19

ROMMEL'S HIGH TIDE

The campaign of 1942 in Africa saw even more violent and far-reaching reversals of fortune than had taken place in 1941. It started with the rival armies facing one another on the Western border of Cyrenaica—exactly where they had stood nine months before. But when the new year was three weeks old Rommel launched one more of his strategic counterstrokes, which went more than 250 miles deep, and swept the British two-thirds of the way back to the Egyptian frontier before they rallied. There the front crystallised, on the Gazala line.

Near the end of May, Rommel struck again, forestalling a British offensive—just as his own had been forestalled in November. This time, after another whirling battle of breath-catching changes, the British were driven to retreat—so fast and so far that they did not rally until they reached the Alamein line, the final gateway into the Nile Delta. This time Rommel's exploiting thrust had gone more than 300 miles deep in a week. But its momentum, and his strength, were by then nearing exhaustion. His efforts to push on to Alexandria and Cairo were checked, and he was desperately close to defeat before the battle ended in mutual exhaustion.

At the end of August, after being reinforced, he made one more effort for victory. But the British had been more heavily reinforced and—under a new team of commanders, headed by General Sir Harold Alexander and General Sir Bernard Montgomery—his thrust was parried, and he was forced to yield most of his slight initial gains.

Then in late October the British resumed the offensive, in greater strength than ever before—and this time decisively. After a thirteen-day struggle, Rommel's resources were finished, and his tanks almost completely used up. His front then collapsed, and he was fortunate in escaping with the remnants of his army. They were too weak to make any further serious stand, and by the end of the year, eight weeks later, he had been driven back to Buerat in Tripolitania—a thousand miles back from Alamein. Even that was only a halt in a retreat that ended at Tunis, in the following May, with the complete extinction of the German and Italian forces in Africa.*

At the beginning of January 1942 the British regarded their repulse at Agedabia as no more than a momentary interruption of their advance on Tripoli. They were busy with plans and the build-up for this operation—which was too aptly named 'Acrobat'. Before the month ended they had done a string of somersaults, backwards.

On January 5 a convoy of six ships, which had succeeded in slipping through the British naval and air curtain, reached Tripoli with a fresh batch of tanks that brought Rommel's strength up to just over a hundred. With that aid, and in the light of a report about the weakness of the British advanced forces, he started to plan an immediate counterstroke—keeping his intention secret. He launched it on January 21. On the 23rd the Italian War Minister arrived at his headquarters to raise objections, but by then Rommel's spearhead had already driven a hundred miles eastward, and the British were moving eastward even faster.

The British advanced force, at the moment when Rommel struck, was formed mainly of a newly arrived armoured division, the 1st, whose armoured brigade (of 150 cruiser tanks) was composed of three converted cavalry regiments—with little experience of armoured operations, and no experience of desert operations. Their handicap was increased because Rommel's new batch of Panzer III tanks were better armoured (with plates of 50 mm. thickness) than the older ones, while the German anti-tank gunners had been practising a further development of their offensive tactics in combination with their own tanks. This development is described by Heinz Schmidt:

> With our twelve anti-tank guns we leap-frogged from one vantage-point to another, while our Panzers, stationary and hull-down, if possible, provided protective fire. Then we would establish ourselves to give them protective fire while they swept on again. The tactics worked well and, despite the liveliness of his fire, the enemy's tanks were not able to hold up our advance. He steadily sustained losses and had to give ground constantly. We could not help feeling that we were not then up against the tough and experienced opponents who had harried us so hard on the Trigh Capuzzo.†

Worse still, the three British armoured regiments were brought into action separately. They lost nearly half their tanks in the first engagements,

* For map, see pp. 110-11.
† Schmidt: *With Rommel in the Desert*. pp. 125-6.

when the Germans attacked them by surprise near Antelat. Rommel's advance was then temporarily halted by the intervention of the Italian War Minister, General Cavallero, who refused to allow the Italian Mobile Corps to follow up the Afrika Korps. But the British failed to profit from this pause, and the absence of any strong countermove on their part emboldened Rommel to thrust forward again on the 25th, to Msus, bursting through the line held by the Guards Brigade and the 1st Armoured Division, which fell back northward, away from his line of advance, with its remaining thirty tanks.

Rommel's deep and threatening thrust to Msus produced a hasty order that the 4th Indian Division at Benghazi was to evacuate this port, now crammed with supplies, and withdraw to the Derna–Mechili line. The withdrawal was countermanded that night, and the preparation of a counteroffensive ordered, following the arrival of Auchinleck, who had flown up from Cairo to see Ritchie at Eighth Army headquarters. But his intervention did not prove so fitting or effective as in November. For it resulted in the British becoming spread out and static in trying to cover the 140 miles stretch between Benghazi and Mechili, while Rommel, from his central position at Msus, was allowed time and freedom to develop his action, as well as a choice of alternative objectives.

This variability of threat on his part produced 'orders, counterorders, and disorders' in the British command during the days that followed. One sequel was that the corps commander, Godwin-Austen, asked to be relieved of his command because of the way that the army commander was issuing orders directly to the subordinate commanders. Worse results followed.

Since Rommel's strength was small, he decided to turn westward against Benghazi as his next move, to quench any threat to his rear from that direction, while making a show of driving eastward to Mechili. The feint hypnotised the British command so that they hurried reinforcements to Mechili, while the widely stretched 4th Indian Division was left unsupported. Rommel's rapid switch towards Benghazi came as a shock, and produced a hurried abandonment of the port, with all its accumulated stores. Exploiting the shock effect, he sent two small battle-groups to drive eastward. By their bold blend of thrust and threat they caused the British to abandon a series of possible defensive positions, and fall back to the Gazala line—although the bulk of the Afrika Korps, owing to shortage of supplies, had not yet advanced farther east than Msus. It was on February 4 that the British Eighth Army retreated into the shelter of the Gazala defences, but it was not until the beginning of April that Rommel, after overcoming the hesitation of the Italian higher command, was able to move up his forces close to the British position.

By this time the Gazala position was being developed, by constructing field works and laying extensive minefields, from a line into a Line—in the fortified sense of the term. But its preparation for defence was soon over-shadowed by the planning for a renewed British offensive, and while it became a suitable springboard for that purpose, it was less suitable for defence —being too linear, and lacking in depth. Except in the coastal sector, the fortified points were too far apart to give one another effective fire-support. They extended fifty miles southward from the coast, with increasing gaps. The left flank position at Bir Hacheim, held by the 1st Free French Brigade under General Koenig, was sixteen miles beyond that at Sidi Muftah. Another complication for the defence was the forward base and railhead established at Belhamed, with a view to the renewed offensive. It was an obvious target for an outflanking thrust by the enemy, and the need to cover the vast amount of supplies piled up there was a constant worry to the British commanders in the battle, cramping their freedom of manœuvre.

Policy and planning also suffered from a conflict of views on the British side about the practicability and desirability of an early offensive. From February onward, Mr Churchill urged early action, pointing out that the British had 635,000 men standing idle in the Middle East theatre while the Russians were fighting desperately and Malta, closer at hand, was being reduced to an extremity by Kesselring's sustained air attack. But Auchinleck, who had a shrewd sense of the technical and tactical defects of the British forces, wished to wait until Ritchie's strength was raised to a level sufficient to make sure of nullifying Rommel's superiority in quality. Finally Churchill, overruling his arguments, decided to send him definite orders to attack which he 'must obey or be relieved'. But Rommel struck first, on May 26—again forestalling the British, whose offensive was intended to start in mid-June.

Reinforcements had brought both sides up to a strength greater than at the start of the November battle, 'Operation Crusader', although the number of divisions remained the same—three German (of which two were armoured) and six Italian (one armoured) against six British (two armoured). Reckoned in terms of divisions, as both statesmen and generals commonly do, Rommel was attacking with nine against six—and such military arith-metic has been used to account for the British defeat.

But the realities in comparative strength were very different, and showed how misleading it can be to reckon in 'divisions'. Four of the five low-strength Italian infantry divisions were unmotorised, so that they could play no active part in a mobile battle of manœuvre, such as this Battle of Gazala became. The British Eighth Army had not only an abundance of motor transport, but also two independent motor brigade groups and two 'Army' tank brigades additional to its six divisions, while one of its two armoured divisions (the 1st) had two armoured brigades instead of one—as was now the normal pattern. In all, the Eighth Army had fourteen tank units on the scene, and three more on the way, to meet Rommel's seven—of which only the four German were equipped with effective tanks.

In numbers, the British had 850 tanks in the Eighth Army's armoured formations, and 420 more available to send up as reinforcements. Their opponents had 560 tanks altogether, but 230 of these were obsolete and unreliable Italian tanks, and fifty of the 330 German were light tanks. Only the 280 German gun-armed medium tanks would really count in a fight, and there was none available in reserve, apart from about thirty under repair and a new batch of some twenty just landed at Tripoli. Thus on a realistic reckoning the British had a numerical superiority of 3 to 1 for the opening clash of armour, and of more than 4 to 1 if it became a battle of attrition.

In artillery, the British had a numerical superiority of 3 to 2, but that advantage was partly offset because all their guns were distributed among the divisions, whereas Rommel made very effective use of a mobile reserve of fifty-six medium guns which he kept under his own control.

In the air, the two sides were more closely balanced than in any other battle. The British Desert Air Force had a first-line strength of approximately 600 aircraft (380 fighters, 160 bombers, and 60 reconnaissance) against a German-Italian total of 530 (350 fighters, 140 bombers, 40 reconnaissance). But the 120 German Me 109s were qualitatively superior to the British Hurricanes and Kittyhawks.

A greater question is the qualitative balance between the tanks of the two sides. After the Eighth Army's defeat, the British very naturally took the view that their tanks were inferior to the enemy's, and that view was expressed as a fact in Auchinleck's official Despatch. But it is not borne out by analysis of the technical and test data of their respective guns and armour. Most of the German medium tanks were armed with the short 50-mm. gun, which had a penetration slightly inferior to the 2-pounder gun, of higher muzzle-velocity, with which all the British-built tanks were armed. In armour, most of the German tanks in 1941 had been more thinly protected than the newer British cruisers (30 mm. maximum armour against 40 mm.), but were now better protected except on the turret, some of the recent arrivals having thicker hull plates (50 mm.), and the rest having additional strips fitted on the most exposed parts of the hull. All the German tanks, however, were more vulnerable than the Matildas (78 mm. of armour) and Valentines (65 mm. of armour).

A new German medium tank—the Panzer III(J) Special—came into action in this battle, armed with a long 50-mm. gun similar to their anti-tank gun. But only nineteen of these tanks had reached the front, while a further batch of the same number had been landed at Tripoli. This reinforcement was far outweighed by the arrival in Egypt of more than 400 of the new American Grant tanks. By the time that the battle opened the two British armoured divisions at Gazala had been equipped with nearly 170 of these Grants— which were armed with a 75-mm. gun that had a penetration even better than the long 50-mm. gun in the German Panzer III(J) Specials, and also better protection (57 mm. thickness of armour compared with 50 mm.). Thus there is no basic justification for the oft-repeated assertion that the tanks used by the British were inferior to the German. On the contrary, the British had a qualitative advantage as well as a very large superiority in numbers.*

In anti-tank guns, too, the British had now regained the qualitative advantage through the arrival of their 6-pounder (57-mm.), which was 30 per cent superior in penetration to the long 50-mm. anti-tank gun of the Germans. Sufficient of the new 6-pounders had arrived to equip both the motorised infantry brigades and the motor battalions of the armoured brigades. Although the German 88-mm. gun still remained the most formidable 'tank-killer', Rommel had only forty-eight of these guns, and their high mounting made them much more vulnerable than any of the standard anti-tank guns on either side.

Analysis of the technical factors provides no adequate explanation of the Eighth Army's defeat at Gazala. The evidence clearly shows that it was basically due to the Germans' superior tactics in general, and especially to their tactical combination of tanks with anti-tank guns.

The fortified Gazala Line was held by the 13th Corps, now commanded by Lieutenant-General 'Strafer' Gott, with two infantry divisions forward —the 1st South African on the right, and the 50th on the left. The 30th Corps, still under Norrie, and comprising most of the armour, was to cover the southern flank and was also to counter any panzer thrust in the centre— which, rather strangely, the British commanders regarded as Rommel's more likely course. This dual task led to the British armour being

* For a fuller examination of this matter, see Liddell Hart: *The Tanks*, vol. II, pp. 92–8, and 154–6.

ill-positioned, the 1st Armoured Division being kept near the Trigh Capuzzo, while the 7th Armoured Division (which had only one armoured brigade) was posted some ten miles southward and stretched widely out to cover and support the French brigade that was holding Bir Hacheim. Auchinleck had written to Ritchie suggesting a closer concentration, but unfortunately his suggestions were not carried out by the men on the spot.

On the moonlit night of May 26 Rommel moved swiftly round the British flank with his three German divisions and the two of the Italian mobile corps—while the four unmotorised Italian divisions 'made faces' at the Gazala Line. Although his outflanking move (with more than ten thousand vehicles) was spotted and reported before dark, and again at dawn as it swept round Bir Hacheim, the opposing commanders still thought that his main attack would come in the centre in accord with their expectation. The British armoured brigades were slow to move, and thus came into action piecemeal, while the two outlying motor brigades on the southern flank were disrupted while separated and unsupported. The headquarters of the 7th Armoured Division was overrun and the commander, Major-General F. W. Messervy, captured—although he later managed to escape. It was his second mishap within a few months, for he had been commanding the 1st Armoured Division when it was surprised and shattered by Rommel at Antelat in January.

But Rommel, despite his opening success, did not succeed in cutting through to the sea—and thus cutting off the divisions in the Gazala Line, as he had hoped. His panzer divisions had a shock on encountering, for the first time, the Grant tanks with their 75-mm. guns. They found themselves coming under destructive fire at ranges too long for them to hit back, and only succeeded in making headway when they brought up anti-tank guns, including three batteries of 88s, while their own tanks worked round the flanks of the British armour—whose units as well as brigades were separated, and thus the more susceptible to such flanking leverage. Even so, the panzer divisions had advanced only three miles north of the Trigh Capuzzo by nightfall, at heavy cost—and were still nearly twenty miles short of the sea coast. Rommel himself wrote in his diary: 'Our plan to overrun the British forces behind the Gazala Line had not succeeded. . . . The advent of the new American tank had torn great holes in our ranks . . . far more than a third of the German tanks had been lost in this one day.'*

Rommel's renewed effort to reach the sea on the second day brought little progress and more loss. By nightfall his bid for quick victory had already failed, although the British had done nothing to exploit his loss of balance—

* *The Rommel Papers*, pp. 207–8.

their best chance of producing his downfall. But his situation was the more perilous because of the long detour his supply columns had to make round Bir Hacheim, under constant risk of interception by the British armoured and air forces. He himself had a narrow escape from capture when he went forward in his car—and was the more lucky because on his return to his battle headquarters he found that 'during our absence the British had over-run my Staff'. The Afrika Korps had only 150 tanks left fit for action, and the Italians 90, while the British still had 420 in hand.

After another abortive day, he ordered his striking force to take up a defensive position. That was a precarious position. For it lay beyond the fortified Gazala Line, and left him separated from the rest of his forces by the British garrison and their far-stretching belt of minefields. To fight 'with one's back to the wall' is grim, but to fight with one's back to a mined barrier is worse.

During the days that followed, the British air force rained bombs on this position, which was aptly christened 'the Cauldron', while the Eighth Army attacked it on the ground. The newspapers were filled with tri-umphant reports that Rommel was now trapped, while in the British military headquarters there was a comfortable assurance that he could be dealt with at leisure, and was bound to surrender.

Yet by the night of June 13 the whole outlook had changed. On the 14th Ritchie abandoned the Gazala Line, and started a rapid retreat to the frontier which left the troops in Tobruk isolated. By the 21st Rommel had captured that fortress and 35,000 men in it, together with an immense amount of stores. It was the worst British disaster of the war except for the fall of Singapore. Next day the remainder of the Eighth Army abandoned its position on the frontier near Sollum, and beat a hasty retreat eastward through the desert with Rommel on its heels.

What had caused such a dramatic turnabout? Rarely has there been such a tangled battle, and the threads have never been properly unravelled. The 'mystery of the Cauldron' has continued to baffle those who have tried to write its story from the British side, and been made more puzzling by myths that sprang up.

Besides the myth that Rommel possessed superiority in tanks, another myth is that the scales were turned and the bulk of the British tanks lost in one fatal day, June 13. In reality that was only the culmination of a series of disastrous days. The basic clue to the 'mystery of the Cauldron' is to be found in Rommel's notes. On the evening of May 27:

> In spite of the precarious situation and the difficult problems I looked for-ward full of hope to what the battle might bring. For Ritchie had thrown

his armour into the battle piecemeal and had thus given us the chance of engaging them on each separate occasion with just enough of our own tanks. . . . They should never have allowed themselves to be duped into dividing their forces. . . .*

He then recorded that he took up what seemed his perilously exposed defensive position . . .

on the certain assumption. . .that the British would not dare to use any major part of their armoured formations to attack the Italians in the Gazala line [while strong German panzer forces stood in a position to threaten their rear]. . . . Thus I foresaw that the British mechanised brigades would continue to run their heads against our well-organised defensive front, and use up their strength in the process.†

Rommel's calculation worked out all too well. The British persisted in a series of piecemeal assaults on his position, at heavy cost. Such direct assaults proved the worst form of caution. While beating them off, he overwhelmed the isolated 'box' at Sidi Muftah held by the 150th Infantry Brigade, which lay behind his back, and cleared a passage through the minefield for his supplies.

Four days later, on June 5, Ritchie launched a larger-scale attack on Rommel's position. But this again was executed in a piecemeal way, while the defenders benefited from the long interval they had been allowed to organise and fortify their position. The complex attack plan suffered from a series of hitches and became a disjointed succession of too direct assaults, which were beaten off in turn. By the second evening the British tank strength had melted, through battle losses and breakdowns, from some 400 down to 170. Moreover, exploiting the attackers' state of confusion Rommel launched a sudden pincer-like riposte on the first evening that scattered one of the brigades of the 5th Indian Division, then closed round the back of another, which was wiped out next day, together with all the artillery supporting the division. The capture of four regiments of artillery, as well as 4,000 prisoners, was a very important 'bag'.

The British armoured brigades were kept at bay while this operation was proceeding. Their relieving efforts were spasmodic and unco-ordinated— the breakdown of control being all the worse since the commander of the 7th Armoured Division, Messervy, had been chased off the scene the previous evening when the headquarters of the 5th Indian Division was overrun by the German tanks, his second exit from the stage in this battle.

Meanwhile Rommel was also carrying out the amputation of another

* *The Rommel Papers*, p. 208.
† *ibid.*, p. 211.

important section of the Eighth Army's position. For on the evening of June 1, immediately after excising the Sidi Muftah 'box', he had sent off a German battle-group and the Trieste Division to attack the still more isolated 'box' at Bir Hacheim on the southern flank held by the 1st Free French Brigade. It proved so tough that Rommel was compelled to go down and take personal command of the assault forces, and he says: 'Nowhere in Africa was I given a stiffer fight.' It was only on the tenth day that he penetrated the defences—and most of the French got away under cover of night.

Rommel was now free to make a fresh and longer pounce. Although the British armoured brigades had been brought up by fresh reinforcements to a total of 330 tanks—more than double the remaining strength of the Afrika Korps—their confidence was badly shaken, and the Germans were smelling the scent of victory. On June 11 Rommel struck eastward, and the next day cornered two of the three British armoured brigades between his panzer divisions—forcing the British to fight in a cramped area where he could batter them with converging fire. They might have made more effort to get out of the trap if they had not been deprived of leadership through Messervy being again cut off from his troops—for the third time in three weeks—by the enemy's advance, when on his way to see the army commander. By mid-afternoon on the 12th the two armoured brigades were trapped, and remnants only escaped, while the third brigade, coming down to the rescue, suffered heavy losses from the well-posted Germans. On the 13th Rommel turned northward, and squeezed the British out of the 'Knightsbridge Box', while continuing to harry what remained of the British armour. By nightfall it had shrunk to barely a hundred tanks. Rommel now for the first time had a superiority in tank strength—and, being in possession of the battlefield, he could recover and repair many of his damaged tanks, unlike the British.

The two divisions holding the Gazala Line were now in imminent danger of being cut off and trapped, for on June 14 Rommel sent the Afrika Korps driving north past Acroma towards the coast-road. But it was delayed by the minefield there, which it did not get through until late in the afternoon, and the panzer-troops were by now so tired that they fell asleep where they halted at nightfall—heedless of Rommel's calls to press on and cut the coast-road. That was very fortunate for the South Africans, whose motor-convoys were pouring back along the road throughout the night. But part of their rearguard was cut off when the panzer forces raced on to the sea in the morning. The other division in the Gazala Line, the British 50th, only managed to escape by breaking out westward through the Italian front, followed by a long circuit south and then east to the frontier.

The 1st South African Division, after slipping out along the coast-road, also continued its retreat back to the frontier—over a hundred miles distant and seventy miles beyond Tobruk.

Such a long step back was contrary to Auchinleck's intention, and his instructions to Ritchie were that the Eighth Army should rally and stand on a line west of Tobruk. But Ritchie failed to tell his Commander-in-Chief that the Gazala Line divisions were going back to the frontier, and by the time Auchinleck became aware of this it was too late to stop them. Worse still, the British forces 'fell between two stools'.

For on June 14, as the British were falling back, Mr Churchill sent an emphatic message saying: 'Presume there is no question in any case of giving up Tobruk.' He repeated this admonition in telegrams on the 15th and 16th. That long-distance advice from London conduced to the crowning blunder. For the hasty step of leaving part of the Eighth Army in Tobruk, while the rest withdrew to the frontier, gave Rommel the chance to overwhelm the isolated force in Tobruk before its defence was properly organised.

Quickly turned eastward again by Rommel, after their thrust to the coast, the panzer forces swept round the Tobruk perimeter, capturing or isolating the 'boxes' that had been established in the Eighth Army's rear, and drove on to capture the airfields at Gambut, east of Tobruk. In this drive, they brushed aside the remnants of the British armoured brigades—which then retreated to the frontier. But Rommel did not pursue them, yet. For as soon as he had secured the Gambut airfields, he turned his forces back westward, and with astonishing quickness mounted an attack on Tobruk. Its reinforced garrison comprised the 2nd South African Division (which included the 11th Indian Brigade) under General Klopper, the Guards Brigade, and the 32nd Army Tank Brigade—with seventy tanks. But, after seeing Rommel's panzer forces drive on eastward, they did not expect an attack, and were not prepared to meet it. At 5.20 a.m. on June 20, a hurricane bombardment started against a sector in the south-east of the perimeter, by artillery and dive-bombers, followed by an infantry assault. By 8.30 a.m. the German tanks were pouring through a breach in the defences, and Rommel himself was on the spot to speed up the exploiting flow. By the afternoon the panzer forces had overcome the resistance of the confused defenders, and drove into Tobruk. By morning the garrison commander, General Klopper, came to the conclusion that continued resistance was hopeless, and retreat impossible, so he took the fateful decision to surrender. Although a few small parties managed to escape, 35,000 troops were taken prisoner.

The consequence of that disaster was the headlong retreat into Egypt of Ritchie's surviving force, with Rommel in hot chase. In maintaining this pursuit Rommel was greatly helped by the huge haul of stores he had made at Tobruk. According to Bayerlein, the Chief of Staff of the Afrika Korps, 80 per cent of Rommel's transport at this time were captured British vehicles. But while this great catch provided him with the transport, fuel, and food to maintain his mobility, it did not restore his fighting strength. When the Afrika Korps moved up to the frontier on June 23 it had only forty-four tanks left fit for action, and the Italians only fourteen. Nevertheless Rommel determined to follow again the maxim 'press hard on the heels of a rout'.

Field-Marshal Kesselring flew in from Sicily the day after Tobruk's fall to argue against a further advance in Africa—calling for the return of his air force units for an attack on Malta, as earlier agreed. The Italian Supreme Command in Africa were also averse to pushing on, and on the 22nd Bastico actually gave Rommel an order to halt—whereat Rommel replied that he would not 'accept the *advice*', and jocularly invited his official superior to dine with him in Cairo. He could afford to take liberties after such a victory, and all the more because a signal from Hitler's headquarters brought the news of his promotion to field-marshal in reward for the victory. At the same time, Rommel appealed direct to Mussolini and Hitler for permission to drive on. Hitler and his military advisers had become very dubious about the intended assault on Malta, feeling that the Italian Navy would fail to back them up in face of the British Navy, and that the German parachute troops dropped on Malta would be left stranded without supplies and reinforcements. A month earlier, on May 21, Hitler had decided that, if Rommel succeeded in capturing Tobruk, the attack on Malta, 'Operation Hercules', was to be dropped. Mussolini was also relieved by the possibility of a less formidable alternative to this labour of 'Hercules', and eager to embrace a more glorious prospect. So, early on the 24th, Rommel received a wireless message: 'Duce approves Panzerarmee intention to pursue the enemy into Egypt.' A few days later, Mussolini flew over to Derna, with a white charger following in another aircraft, ready for a triumphant entry into Cairo. Even Kesselring, according to Italian accounts, appears to have agreed that pursuit into Egypt was preferable to an assault on Malta.

The precipitate British retreat from the frontier, even before Rommel had arrived there, provided both a justification and confirmation of his boldness. It was a most striking demonstration of moral effect—and of Napoleon's oft-quoted dictum that 'in war the moral is to the material as three is to one'. For when Ritchie decided to abandon the frontier—'to gain time with distance' as he telegraphed to Auchinleck—he had three almost intact infantry divisions there, a fourth on the way up that was fresh, and three times as many tanks fit for action as the Afrika Korps.

But the shock of the news from Tobruk had caused Ritchie to abandon any attempt to hold the frontier—a decision which he took on the night of June 20, six hours before Klopper's decision to surrender.

Ritchie's intention was to make a stand at Mersa Matruh, and fight out the issue there with the divisions brought back from the frontier, reinforced by the 2nd New Zealand Division which was just arriving from Syria. But on the evening of June 25 Auchinleck took over direct command of the Eighth Army from Ritchie. After reviewing the problem with his principal staff officer, Eric Dorman-Smith, he cancelled the order to hold the fortified position at Matruh, and decided to fight a more mobile battle in the Alamein area. It was a hard decision, for not only did it mean many difficulties in getting away troops and stores, but it was bound to cause fresh alarm at home, particularly in Whitehall. In taking this decision, Auchinleck showed a cool head and strong nerve. Although a further withdrawal could not be justified by the balance of material strength, it was probably wise in view of the weaknesses of the Mersa Matruh position, which could be easily by-passed, and of the balance of morale. For although the troops pouring back from the frontier were not demoralised, their confidence was shaken and they were in a state of confusion. Major-General Sir Howard Kippenberger, the New Zealand commander and war historian, watched them arriving in the Matruh area, so 'thoroughly mixed up and disorganised' that he 'did not see a single formed fighting unit, infantry, armour, or artillery'.* Rommel allowed them no time to reorganise, and the speed of his pursuit nullified Ritchie's reason for abandoning the frontier 'to gain time with distance'.

On getting the 'release' from Rome, during the night of June 23/24, Rommel pushed on beyond the frontier and across the desert in the moonlight, and by the evening of the 24th he had covered more than a hundred miles—reaching the coast-road well east of Sidi Barrani, close on the heels of the British, although he only caught a small part of the rearguard. By the next evening his forces were close to the positions that the British had taken up at Matruh and to the south of it.

Because of the ease with which Matruh could be by-passed, the mobile forces of the 13th Corps (Gott's) had been posted in the desert to the south, supported by the New Zealand Division, while the Matruh defences were held by the 10th Corps (Holmes) with two infantry divisions. There was a gap of nearly ten miles between the two corps, covered by a minefield belt.

There was no pause to mount a carefully prepared attack. For lack of

* Kippenberger: *Infantry Brigadier*, p. 127.

strength, Rommel had to depend on speed and surprise. While the British armour had been brought up to a total of 160 tanks (of which nearly half were Grants), he had barely 60 German tanks (of which a quarter were light Panzer IIs) and a handful of Italian tanks. The total infantry strength of his three German divisions was a mere 2,500, and that of the six Italian divisions only some 6,000. It was sheer audacity to launch any attack with such a weak force—but audacity triumphed, with the aid of moral effect plus speed.

The three very diminished German divisions, leading the advance, started their attack on the afternoon of the 26th. Two of them had arrived opposite the gap already mentioned. The 90th Light was fortunate in arriving on the shallowest part of the mined belt, and by midnight was twelve miles beyond (it reached the coast-road, again, on the next evening and thus blocked the direct line of retreat from Matruh). The 21st Panzer took longer in getting through the doubled belt of mines that it met, but at daylight drove on twenty miles deep and then swung round on to the rear of the New Zealand Division at Minqar Qaim, scattering part of its transport before being checked. The 15th Panzer, farther south, ran into the British armour and was held in check most of the day. But the swift and deep thrust of the 21st Panzer, and its threat to the British line of retreat, had produced such an effect that in the afternoon Gott ordered a retreat—which soon developed into a very disorderly retreat. The New Zealand Division was left isolated, but succeeded in breaking through the enemy's thin ring after dark. The 10th Corps in Matruh received no word of the retreat of the 13th Corps until almost dawn on the next day—nine hours after its line of retreat had been blocked. Nearly two-thirds of the Matruh force managed to escape on the following night, however, by breaking out southward in small groups under cover of darkness. But 6,000 were taken prisoner—a number larger than Rommel's whole striking force—and a vast quantity of supplies and equipment was left behind, to Rommel's benefit.

Meanwhile his panzer spearheads were pushing on, so fast that they forestalled the British hope of making a temporary stand at Fuka. By their quick arrival on the coast-road there, in the evening of the 28th, they caught and overwhelmed the remnants of an Indian brigade which had been scattered in the opening attack, and next morning they trapped some of the columns that had escaped from Matruh. The 90th Light, which had been mopping up at Matruh, resumed its eastward drive along the coast-road that afternoon; by midnight it had travelled ninety miles, and overtaken the panzer spearheads. Next morning, June 30, Rommel wrote to his wife exultantly: 'Only 100 more miles to Alexandria!' By evening he was barely sixty miles distant from his goal, and the keys of Egypt seemed within his grasp.

PORTUGAL
SPAIN
Madrid
Lisbon
Barcelona
Algeciras
Gibraltar
Tangier
SPAN.
MOR.
Fez
Mehdia
Pt. Lyautey
Rabat
Fedala
Casablanca
Safi
Marrakesh
MOROCCO
(French)
Colomb-Béchar
Ain Sefra
Ghardaia
ALGERIA
(French)
Touggourt
Laghouat
Aflou
Maison Djelfa
Biskra
Blanch
Oran
Mersa Bou
Zédjar
Les Andalouses
La Sénia
Tafaraoui
Arzeu
Castiglione
Algiers
Bilda
Bougie
Djidjelli
Constantine
Tebessa
Bône
Souk
Ahras
Souk
el Arba
Beja
Bizerta
Tunis
Sousse
TUNISIA
Gafsa
Gabes
Sfax
Mareth
FRANCE
Marseilles
Toulon
Genoa
CORSICA
SARDINIA
ITALY
Rome
Naples
Taranto
SICILY
Pantelleria
(Ital.)
Malta
MEDITERRANEAN
SEA
GREECE
ALBANIA
YUGO-SLAVIA
Belgrade
LIBYA
Benghazi
El Agheila
Nofilia
Buerat
Homs
Tripoli
Tarhuna
Mareth

North–West Africa*

✠ Airports & airstrips

| 0 | Miles | 300 |
| 0 | Kilometres | 400 |

* for continuation eastward see pp. 110-11

Copyright © Cassell & Co Ltd 1970

CHAPTER 20

THE TIDE TURNS IN AFRICA

On June 30 the Germans moved up close to the Alamein line, a relatively short advance, while waiting for the Italians to arrive. This brief pause to gather strength turned out to the detriment of Rommel's chances. For that morning what remained of the British armoured brigades were still lying in the desert south of the coast route, unaware that they had been outstripped in their retreat by Rommel's armour. Only the thinness of the pursuing force saved them from being trapped and 'put in the bag' before they got back into the shelter of the Alamein line.

Rommel's momentary pause may have been caused by mistaken Intelligence reports about the strength of that defensive position. Actually, it comprised four 'boxes', which had been laid out in the thirty-five-mile stretch between the coast and the steep drop into the great Qattara Depression—which, because of the salt marsh and soft sand, limited an outflanking move. The largest and strongest 'box' lay on the coast at Alamein, and was occupied by the 1st South African Division The next, similar, to the south, was a newly-made one at Deir el Shein, occupied by the 18th Indian Brigade. The third, seven miles beyond, was the Bab el Qattara Box (called by the Germans Qaret el Abd) which was occupied by the 6th New Zealand Brigade. Then, after a fourteen mile gap, came the Naqb el Dweis Box held by a brigade of the 5th Indian Division. The intervals were covered by a chain of small mobile columns formed from these three divisions and remnants of the two that had garrisoned Mersa Matruh.

In making his plan of attack, for July 1, Rommel did not know of the existence of the new 'box' at Deir el Shein. Nor did he know that the British armour had been outstripped in its retreat by his advance, and was only just arriving back at Alamein. So he reckoned that it would probably be posted in the south to cover that flank. On this reckoning, he planned a pinning attack there, followed by a quick switch northward of the Afrika Korps for a breakthrough thrust in the stretch between Alamein and Bab el Qattara. But the Afrika Korps ran into the 'unknown' Deir el Shein Box,

To Sidi Abdel Rahman
7 miles

JULY 11
Tell el
Eisa

ITAL. XXI
CORPS

9th AUST.
DIV.

MEDITERRANEAN SEA

El Alamein

EL ALAMEIN
PERIMETER

ITAL. XX CORPS

ITAL. X CORPS

90th LT. DIV.

1st S. AFR.
DIV.

VIA BALBIA

To Alexandria
55 miles

15th PZ. DIV.

21st PZ DIV.

Miteiriya
Ridge

4th
ARMD. BDE.

XXX CORPS

Deir el Abyad

1800 HRS
JULY 1

Deir el Shein
18th IND. BDE.
El Mireir

Ruweisat Ridge

22nd ARMD. BDE.
1st ARMD. DIV.

Alam Halfa Ridge

JULY 2/4
ROMMEL'S ATTACKS ARE
TWICE REPULSED

JULY 3
'ARIETE' DIV.

6th NZ. BDE.

Bab el
Qattara

NZ. ARTILLERY

Alam Nayil
NZ. INF.

XIII CORPS

7th MOTOR BDE.

Deir el
Munassib

NZ. DIV.

Naqb el
Dweis

5th IND. BDE.

Qattara
Depression

7th ARMD. DIV.

Qaret el
Himeimat

BARREL TRACK

To Cairo
130 miles

First Alamein

8th Army Corps Headquarters

8th Army Divisional Headquarters

Miles 0 — 10
Kilometres 0 — 15

and was held up until the evening before it succeeded in capturing the 'box', with most of its defenders. But they had held out long enough to annul Rommel's hope of a quick breakthrough and its swift exploitation. The British armour arrived on the scene too late to save the 'box', but its belated appearance helped to check the Afrika Korps from continuing the advance. Rommel ordered it to push on by moonlight, but that intention was frustrated by the British aircraft which utilised the moonlight to bomb and disperse the German supply columns.

This day—Wednesday, July 1—was the most dangerous moment of the struggle in Africa. It was more truly the turning point than the repulse of Rommel's renewed attack at the end of August or the October battle that ended in Rommel's retreat—the battle which, because of its more obviously dramatic outcome, has come to monopolise the name of 'Alamein'. Actually, there was a series of 'Battles of Alamein', and the 'First Alamain' was the most crucial.

The news that Rommel had reached Alamein had led the British fleet to leave Alexandria, and withdraw through the Suez Canal into the Red Sea. Clouds of smoke rose from the chimneys of the military headquarters in Cairo as their files were hastily burned. In grim humour, soldiers called it 'Ash Wednesday'. Veterans of World War I remembered that it was the anniversary of the opening day of the Somme offensive in 1916, when the British Army lost 60,000 men—the worst day's loss in all its history. Seeing the black snowstorm of charred paper, the people of Cairo naturally took it as a sign that the British were fleeing from Egypt, and crowds besieged the railway station in a rush to get away. The world outside, on hearing the news, took it to mean that Britain had lost the war in the Middle East.

But by nightfall the situation at the front had become hopeful, and the defenders more confident—in contrast to the state of panic at the back of the front.

Rommel continued his attack on July 2, but the Afrika Korps had less than forty tanks left fit for action and the troops were dead-tired. Its renewed attack did not get going until the afternoon, and soon came to a halt on sighting two larger bodies of British tanks—one in its path and the other moving round its flank. Auchinleck had coolly gauged the situation, realised the weakness of Rommel's attacking forces, and planned what he hoped would prove a decisive counterstroke. His plan was not carried out as intended, and the hitches in execution frustrated his hopes, but it served to foil Rommel's aim.

Rommel made a further effort on July 3, but by then the Afrika Korps had only twenty-six tanks fit for action, and its eastward push that morning was checked by the British armour, although a renewed effort in the afternoon advanced nine miles before it was halted. A converging advance by the Ariete Division was also repelled, and during the action a New Zealand battalion, the 19th, captured almost the whole of the Ariete's artillery in a sudden counterattack on its flank—and 'the remainder took to their heels in panic'.* That collapse was a clear sign of overstrain.

Next day, July 4, Rommel ruefully wrote home: 'Things are, unfortunately, not going as we should like. The resistance is too great, and our strength is exhausted.' His thrusts had not only been parried but answered by upsetting ripostes. His troops were too tired as well as too few to be capable of making a fresh effort for the moment. He was forced to break off the attack and give them a breather, even though it meant giving Auchinleck time to bring up reinforcements.

Moreover Auchinleck had regained the initiative, and he came close to turning the tables decisively even before reinforcements arrived. His plan that day was broadly the same as on the previous day—to hold the Panzer-armee's attack in check with Norrie's 30th Corps, while Gott's 13th Corps in the south struck upward across the enemy's rear. But this time the bulk of the armour was kept in the north under the 30th Corps, although the 13th Corps included the recently reorganised 7th Armoured Division, now called a 'light armoured division' and composed of a motor brigade, armoured-cars, and Stuart tanks. It lacked punch, but had the mobility for a quick and wide drive round the enemy's rear while the strong New Zealand Division attacked his flank.

Unfortunately, a lack of wireless security allowed the German 'intercept' services to hear, and warn Rommel, of Auchinleck's design. The 21st Panzer Division was moved back to meet the enveloping attack, and that countermove may have increased the hesitation which the executive commanders showed in fulfilling Auchinleck's decisive intention. Similar hesitation was shown in the northern sector. When the 21st Panzer Division moved back, some of the 1st Armoured Division's Stuart tanks started to push forward, and this insignificant advance produced a very significant effect—a sudden panic among the scanty troops of the 15th Panzer Division (whose fighting strength now was only fifteen tanks and some 200 riflemen). Such a panic in such tough German troops revealed how badly overstrained they were. But nothing was done to seize the opportunity for a general attack—by the armoured division, and the corps—which might well have proved decisive.

* *The Rommel Papers*, p. 249.

That night Auchinleck, even more emphatically than before, ordered his forces to drive home their attack, saying in his orders: 'Our task remains to destroy the enemy as far east as possible and not to let him get away as a force in being . . . the enemy should be given no rest. . . . Eighth Army will attack and destroy the enemy in his present position.' But he did not succeed in passing his own vigorous spirit down the 'chain of command'. He had moved his tactical headquarters up close to 30th Corps H.Q., but that had been established nearly twenty miles behind the front, while it was equally far from 13th Corps H.Q. in the south. Panzerarmee H.Q. was only six miles behind the front, and Rommel himself was often up with the forward troops, applying a personal impulse on the spot. Rommel has been much criticised by more orthodox soldiers, German as well as British, for the frequency with which he was away from his headquarters and his fondness for taking direct control of the fight. But that direct control, although it caused some of his troubles, was a prime cause of his great successes. It revived in modern war the practice of, and influence exerted by, the Great Captains of the past.

On July 5 the 13th Corps did little, and the 30th Corps even less, to carry out Auchinleck's aim and orders. The brigades of the New Zealand Division, which were cast for the leading role in the attack on Rommel's rear, were not informed of their Commander-in-Chief's intentions, and the decisive action expected of them. Auchinleck may reasonably be criticised for leaving the bulk of the armour with the 30th Corps instead of sending it to reinforce the intended rear thrust by the 13th Corps, but there is little reason to think that it would have been more vigorously employed there than it was in the centre—where a vigorous thrust might easily have succeeded in view of the enemy's weakness. The 1st Armoured Division had now been brought up to a strength of ninety-nine tanks, while the 15th Panzer Division facing it had only fifteen left, and the whole Afrika Korps barely thirty.

The best excuse, and basically the truest explanation, was sheer tiredness—resulting from prolonged strain. That was the factor which in this first crucial phase finally settled the issue—as a stalemate settlement.

On balance, this was probably to the immediate advantage of the Germans and Italians, although to their ultimate disadvantage. The British situation was never so desperate as it outwardly appeared, whereas by July 5 Rommel's forces were nearer to complete collapse than they had ever been to complete victory.

During the short lull which followed, the remainder of the Italian infantry divisions came up, and these took over the now static front in the northern sector, thus setting free the Germans for the new thrust in the southern sector that Rommel was planning. But on July 8, when he was about to try this thrust, the fighting strength of his three German 'divisions' had risen to no more than fifty tanks and about 2,000 infantry, while that of the seven Italian 'divisions' (including the recently arrived Littorio armoured division) was only fifty-four tanks and about 4,000 infantry. The British were reinforced by the arrival of the 9th Australian Division, which had so vigorously defended Tobruk in 1941, and by two fresh regiments, which brought them up to a strength of more than 200 tanks. The Australian division was sent to join the 30th Corps, which was now given a new commander, Lieutenant-General W. H. Ramsden—previously commanding the 50th Division.

Rommel's intention to switch his effort southward fitted in well with Auchinleck's desires, and new plan—which was to use the Australians for an attack westwards along the coast-road. When the Germans moved south, the New Zealanders withdrew eastward, evacuating the Bab el Qattara Box, so that all the Germans gained by this thrust on July 9 was 'vacant possession' of this 'box'.

Early next morning, the Australians launched their attack near the coast, and speedily overran the Italian division holding that sector. Although they were checked, and some of the lost ground regained, by German troops who were rushed to the spot, this strong threat to Rommel's coast-road line of supply forced him to abandon his thrust in the south. Auchinleck promptly sought to exploit the effect by a thrust aimed at the now weakened centre of Rommel's line, on the Ruweisat Ridge. But, again, a well-conceived plan miscarried through mismanagement by the subordinate commanders, and lack of skilful combination between armour and infantry—to which the Germans owed so many of their successes.

The faulty tactical combination between the arms was made all the worse by the distrust that had long been growing among the infantry of the support they were likely to get from their own armour if, by pushing forward, they exposed themselves to counterattack from the panzer troops:

> At this time there was throughout the Eighth Army, not only in the New Zealand Division, a most intense distrust, almost hatred, of our armour. Everywhere one heard tales of the other arms being let down; it was regarded as axiomatic that the tanks would not be where they were wanted in time.*

Even so, the thrust and threat strained Rommel's meagre resources, while a counterattack he attempted in the north had little success. Although the British tanks were slow in meeting German tank counterstrokes against their

---

* Kippenberger: *Infantry Brigadier*, p. 180.

own infantry, they helped to frighten the Italian infantry into large surrenders. Writing home on July 17 Rommel said:

> Things are going downright badly for me at the moment, at any rate, in the military sense. The enemy is using his superiority, especially in infantry, to destroy the Italian formations one by one, and the German formations are much too weak to stand alone. It's enough to make one weep.*

Next day the 7th Armoured Division developed a threat to Rommel's southern flank, to extend the strain while Auchinleck prepared a new and heavier attack with further reinforcements which had now arrived. It was again aimed to achieve a breakthrough in the centre, but this time on the southern side of the Ruweisat Ridge, towards El Mireir. A fresh armoured brigade, the 23rd, which had just arrived (with 150 Valentines), was to be used in this attack—but one of its three regiments was sent to help the Australians in a subsidiary attack on the Miteiriya Ridge in the north.

The prospects looked all the better since the Eighth Army, with this additional brigade and fresh deliveries to the others, now had nearly 400 tanks on the scene. Rommel's tank strength was even lower than his opponents realised—the Afrika Korps had less than thirty left. But, by a combination of luck and judgement, they were posted just at the point where the main British thrust was looming—and, in the event, only a small proportion of the British tanks were actually brought into action there.

Auchinleck's plan this time was to burst through the enemy's centre by a wide-fronted night attack with infantry—the 5th Indian Division—advancing straight along the Ruweisat Ridge, and the valley south of it, after the resistance had been lowered by a northward sweeping flank attack of the New Zealand Division. Then, at daylight, the new 23rd Armoured Brigade was to drive through to the El Mireir end of the valley, and the 2nd Armoured Brigade would then pass to carry on the exploiting drive. It was a finely conceived plan, but required thorough working out of the detailed process by the executives, which it did not get. The successive steps were not adequately co-ordinated at a corps conference, and Gott's subordinates remained hazy about each other's part.

The attack was launched on the night of July 21, and the New Zealanders arrived on their objective. But then German tanks came up and counter-attacked them in the dark, causing confusion. At daylight they smashed the most advanced New Zealand brigade—while the 22nd Armoured Brigade, which was to have protected the flank of the New Zealand advance, had not appeared on the scene. For its commander, in contrast to the Germans, had declared that tanks could not move in the dark.

---

* The Rommel Papers, p. 257.

Meanwhile the 5th Indian Division's night attack had failed to reach its objectives. Worse still, it failed to clear a gap in the minefields for the follow-up advance of the 23rd Armoured Brigade. When its 40th and 46th Royal Tank Regiments were launched to the attack in the morning, they met the Indians falling back, but could get no clear information as to whether the mines in their path had been cleared. So they most gallantly drove on, and carried out what the New Zealanders, admiringly but too aptly, called 'a real Balaclava Charge'. They soon found that the minefield had not been gapped, and that they had charged into a triple trap—coming under intense fire from the German tanks and anti-tank guns when they ran onto the minefield and became stranded there. Only eleven tanks returned. The one redeeming aspect of this ill-fated attack was that these two fresh regiments of the R.T.R. had helped to restore the confidence of the infantry, and of the New Zealanders particularly, that they would not be left in the lurch by the excessive caution of their own armour. The other regiment of the brigade had shown a similar thrustfulness in the northern attack. But the price was heavy—altogether, 118 tanks were lost this day, compared with the Germans' loss of three. Even so, the British tank strength was still ten times as large as Rommel's. But the miscarriage of the initial attack had such a damping effect that little further effort was made to resume the attack and use the potentially overwhelming weight of the forces on the British side.

After four days' interval, for reorganisation and regrouping, one further attempt was made to break through Rommel's front—by a thrust in the north. It opened well with the Australians' capture of the Miteiriya Ridge by moonlight, and the 50th Division to the south of them also made a good start. But the commander of the 1st Armoured Division, which was to follow up and pass through, was not satisfied that a sufficiently wide gap had been cleared in the minefield. His delay spoilt the prospects of the attack as a whole. It was mid-morning before the leading tanks started to move through the minefield, and they were then pinned down by German tanks which had been rushed north. The infantry on the far side of the minefield were cut off, and then cut up by a counterattack. Meanwhile, the Australians had also been driven off the ridge, and a part of them similarly trapped.

Auchinleck now reluctantly decided to suspend the attack. Many of the troops were showing signs of exhaustion after the prolonged struggle, and an increasing tendency to surrender if isolated. It was also clear that the defence had the advantage on such a restricted front, and that the advantage would grow with the reinforcements that were now at last reaching Rommel —by the start of August his tank strength increased to more than five times what it had been on July 22.

While the battle ended in disappointment for the British, their situation was far better than when it opened. The final sentence of Rommel's account of the battle utters the final verdict: 'Although the British losses in this Alamein fighting had been higher than ours, yet the price to Auchinleck had not been excessive, for the one thing that had mattered to him was to halt our advance, and that, unfortunately, he had done.'*

Although the Eighth Army had suffered over 13,000 casualties during the July battle at Alamein, it had taken over 7,000 prisoners, including more than a thousand Germans. The price would have been lower, and the gains much greater, if the execution of the plans had been more vigorous and efficient. But, even as it was, the difference in the total loss on either side was not large, and Rommel was much less able to afford the loss. His frustration was almost certainly bound to prove fatal in view of the flood of British reinforcements that was now pouring into Egypt.

His own account makes it clear how perilously close to defeat he came by mid-July. Even clearer is his own confession at the time, in a letter to his wife on the 18th: 'Yesterday was a particularly hard and critical day. We pulled through again. But it can't go on like it for long, otherwise the front will crack. Militarily, this is the most difficult period I've ever been through. There's help in sight, of course, but whether we will live to see it is a question.'† Four days later, with reserves still fewer, his troops had to meet an even weightier blow, and were fortunate in surviving it.

Rommel's subsequent account of the battle pays a high tribute to the British Commander-in-Chief: 'General Auchinleck who had ... taken over command himself at El Alamein, was handling his forces with very considerable skill. ... He seemed to view the situation with decided coolness, for he was not allowing himself to be rushed into accepting a "second-class" solution by any moves we made. This was to be particularly evident in what followed.'‡

But each of the successive 'first-class' solutions which Auchinleck devised (with the aid of his fertile-minded chief staff officer, Dorman-Smith) went wrong in the third-class compartments of the executants' train. Its corridors also became blocked. One important cause of blockage was the presence of such a mixture of contingents from the different countries of the British Commonwealth, under such conditions of strain, and the way that the commanders were distracted by anxious questions and cautions from their respective Governments. While such anxiety was very natural after the un-

* *The Rommel Papers*, p. 260.
† ibid., p. 257.
‡ ibid., p. 248.

happy experience of recent months, it multiplied the usual friction of war.

It was also natural that the prevailing disappointment at the end of the battle in July should have renewed the impression of bad leadership left by the disaster in June, and developed an impulsive feeling that drastic changes were needed in the higher command. As usual, criticism was focused on the top of the ladder, rather than where the slips and bungles had occurred, lower down. There was better justification in the need to restore the confidence of the troops, which had been shaken afresh by the failure of Auchinleck's counteroffensive. In such conditions, a change of command is the easiest way to provide a tonic and may be essential as a stimulant—however unjust to the commander who is replaced.

Churchill decided to fly out to Egypt, to size up the situation, and arrived in Cairo on August 4—the fateful anniversary of Britain's entry into World War I. Although Auchinleck had 'stemmed the adverse tide', as Churchill recognised and said, it was not so apparent that the tide had actually turned, as can be seen in retrospect. Rommel still stood barely sixty miles from Alexandria and the Nile Delta—disturbingly close. Churchill was already thinking of making a change in the command, and his inclination turned into decision after finding that Auchinleck strongly resisted his pressure for an early renewal of the offensive, and insisted that it must be deferred until September in order to give the new reinforcements time to become acclimatised and have some training in desert conditions.

His decision was also influenced and fortified by discussion with Field-Marshal Smuts, the South African Prime Minister, who had flown to Egypt at his request. Churchill's first idea was to offer the command to the very able Chief of the Imperial General Staff, General Sir Alan Brooke—but Brooke, from motives of delicacy as well as of policy, did not wish to leave the War Office and take Auchinleck's place. So after further discussion, Churchill telegraphed to the other members of the War Cabinet in London that he proposed to appoint Alexander as Commander-in-Chief, and to give the command of the Eighth Army to Gott—a surprising choice in the light of this gallant soldier's fumbling performance as a corps commander in the recent battles. But Gott was killed in an air crash next day, on his way to Cairo. Montgomery was then, fortunately, brought out from England to fill the vacancy. Two fresh corps commanders were also flown out—Lieutenant-General Sir Oliver Leese to take over the 30th Corps and Lieutenant-General Brian Horrocks to fill the vacancy in the 13th.

But an ironical result of these changes was that the resumption of the British offensive was put off to a much later date than Auchinleck had proposed. For the impatient Prime Minister had to give way to Montgomery's firm determination to wait until preparations and training were completed. This entailed leaving the initiative to Rommel, and allowing him another chance to bid for victory in what was to be called the 'Battle of Alam Halfa' —but in effect only gave him 'enough rope to hang himself'.

During August only two fresh formations arrived to reinforce Rommel— a German parachute brigade and an Italian parachute division. Both came 'dismounted', for employment as infantry. But the losses in the divisions already engaged were made up to a considerable extent by drafts and fresh supplies of equipment—although much more arrived for the Italian divisions than for the German. By the eve of the attack, which Rommel was planning to deliver at the end of August, he had about 200 gun-armed tanks in the two panzer divisions, and 240 in the two Italian armoured divisions. While the Italian tanks were still of the old model, now more obsolete than ever, the German Panzer IIIs included seventy-four with the long 50-mm. gun, and twenty-seven of the Panzer IVs mounted the new long 75-mm. gun. That was an important qualitative gain.

But the British tank strength at the front had been brought up to a total of over 700 (of which some 160 were Grants). In the event, only some five hundred were used in the armoured battle—which this time was brief.

The fortified front was still held by the same four infantry divisions as in July, with strength rebuilt, and the 7th (Light) Armoured Division remained, while the 1st Armoured Division went back to refit and was replaced by the 10th (commanded by Major-General A. H. Gatehouse)—which comprised two armoured brigades, the 22nd and the newly arrived 8th, while the re-equipped 23rd was also put under its command after the battle started. A newly arrived infantry division was also brought to the front to hold the rearward position on the Alam Halfa Ridge.

No radical change was made in the defence that had been designed by Dorman-Smith and approved by Auchinleck while he was still in command. After the battle was won, it was widely reported that the plan was completely recast following the change of command. So it should be emphasised that Alexander, in his Despatch, stated the facts with an honesty shattering to such stories and claims. He said that when he took over the command from Auchinleck:

> The plan was to hold as strongly as possible the area between the sea and Ruweisat ridge and to threaten from the flank any enemy advance south of the ridge from a strongly defended prepared position on the Alam el Halfa ridge. General Montgomery, now in command of Eighth Army, accepted this plan in principle, to which I agreed, and hoped that if the enemy

Battle of Alam Halfa

German   Italian

→ ------→   Rommel's intended advance
→ - - - →   Rommel's actual advance
- - - - - - -   Eastern edge of Axis minefields

+ - + Main alignment of 8th Army's minefields

| 0 | Miles | 10 |
| 0 | Kilometres | 15 |

should give us enough time he would be able to improve our positions by strengthening the left or southern flank.*

The Alam Halfa position was reinforced before Rommel attacked, but its defence was not seriously tested—for the issue of the battle was decided by the well-judged positioning of the armour, and its very effective defensive action.

The northern and central sectors of the front were so strongly fortified that the southern stretch of fifteen miles, between the New Zealanders' 'box' on the Alam Nayil Ridge and the Qattara Depression, was the only part of the front where a quick penetration could possibly succeed. Thus in trying to achieve a breakthrough Rommel was bound to take that line of advance. That was obvious—and was what the defence plan evolved under Auchinleck had been designed to produce.

Surprise in aim-point was thus impossible, so Rommel had to depend on achieving surprise in time and speed. He hoped that if he broke through the southern sector quickly, and got astride the Eighth Army's communications, it would be thrown off balance and its defence disjointed. His plan was to capture the mined belt by a night attack, after which the Afrika Korps with part of the Italian Mobile Corps would drive on eastward for about thirty miles before daylight, and then wheel north-east to the coast towards the Eighth Army's supply area. This threat, he hoped, would lure the British armour into a chase, giving him the chance to trap and destroy it. Meanwhile the 90th Light Division and the rest of the Italian Mobile Corps were to form a protective corridor strong enough to resist counterattacks from the north until he had won the armoured battle, in the British rear. In his own account, he says that he 'placed particular reliance on the slow reaction of the British command, for experience had shown us that it always took them some time to reach decisions and put them into effect'.

But when the attack was launched, on the night of August 30, it was found that the mined belt was much deeper than expected. At daylight, Rommel's spearheads were only eight miles beyond it, and the bulk of the Afrika Korps was not able to start on its eastward drive until nearly 10 a.m. By that time its mass of vehicles was being heavily bombed by the British air force. The corps commander, General Walter Nehring, was wounded at an early stage, and during the rest of the battle, the Afrika Korps was commanded by its Chief of Staff, Lieutenant-General Fritz Bayerlein.

When it was clear that any surprise-effect had vanished, and that the rate of advance was badly behind time, Rommel thought of breaking off the attack. But after discussion with Bayerlein, and following his own natural inclination, he decided to continue it—although with modified aims and

* Alexander: *Despatch*, p. 841.

more limited objectives. As it was obvious that the British armour had been allowed time to take up its battle-positions, and could thus threaten the flank of a deeply extended drive, he felt bound to make 'an earlier turn north than we had intended'. He therefore ordered the Afrika Korps to make an immediate wheel, so that it headed for Point 132, the dominant feature of the Alam Halfa Ridge. This change of direction brought it towards the area where the 22nd Armoured Brigade was posted—and also towards an area of soft sand, cramping to manœuvre. The line of thrust originally planned had been well clear of this 'sticky' area.

The 8th Armoured Brigade's battle positions were some ten miles distant, to the south-east, from the 22nd—more directly placed to check a bypassing move, instead of trusting to the indirect check and threat of a flanking position. In accepting the risk of posting the brigades so far apart, Montgomery could rely on the fact that each of them was almost as strong in armour as the whole Afrika Korps, and should therefore be capable of holding out until the other brigade arrived to support it.

The 8th, however, did not reach its assigned position until 4.30 a.m.—it was fortunate that the enemy had been so much delayed, for under Rommel's original plan the Afrika Korps had been directed on that same area and intended to arrive there before dawn. A collision in the dark, or assault in the morning, before the 8th was firmly in position, might have produced an awkward situation, especially for troops who were in action for the first time.

As a result of Rommel having to wheel north earlier than he had intended, the attack fell directly on the 22nd Armoured Brigade, and on that alone—but not until late in the day. For continued air attacks, and the delayed arrival of fuel and ammunition convoys, had such a retarding effect on the advance that the Afrika Korps did not begin even the shortened northward wheel until the afternoon. On approaching Alam Halfa, and the battle positions of the 22nd Armoured Brigade, the panzer columns came under a storm of fire from the well-sited tanks and then from the supporting artillery of this all-arms brigade group—which was ably handled by its new and young commander, 'Pip' Roberts. Repeated advances and attempted local flank moves were checked—until nightfall closed down the fight, bringing well-earned respite to the defenders and spreading depression among the attackers.

The abortiveness of the attack was due, however, not only to these actual repulses. For fuel was so short in the Afrika Korps that in mid-afternoon Rommel had cancelled his orders for an all-out effort to capture Point 132.

Even when morning came on September 1, there was still such a shortage of fuel that Rommel was forced to give up the idea of carrying out any large operation that day. The most that he could attempt was a local and limited attack with one division, the 15th Panzer, to seize the Alam Halfa Ridge. The Afrika Korps was now in a very awkward predicament, and it suffered growing loss as the battering it had endured during the night from British bombers and the artillery of Horrocks's 13th Corps continued throughout the day. The diminished attacks of the German armour were successively checked, by a reinforced defence—for early that same morning Montgomery, now sure that the enemy was not driving on east towards his rear, had ordered the two other armoured brigades to concentrate alongside Roberts's.

By the afternoon Montgomery 'ordered planning to begin for a counter-stroke which would give us the initiative'. The idea was, by a wheeling attack southward from the New Zealanders' position, to cork the neck of the bottle into which the Germans had pushed. He also made arrangements to bring up the headquarters of the 10th Corps 'to command a pursuit force', that was 'to be prepared to push through to Daba with all reserves available'.

The Panzerarmee now had only one day's fuel issue left in hand—a quantity sufficient only for about sixty miles movement for its units. So, after a second night of almost continuous bombing, Rommel had decided to break off the offensive, and make a gradual withdrawal.

During the day, the Germans facing Alam Halfa were seen to be thinning out, and starting to move westward. But requests for permission to follow them up were refused—for it was Montgomery's policy to avoid the risk of his armour being lured into Rommel's traps, as had happened so often before. At the same time Montgomery gave orders that the southward attack by New Zealanders, reinforced by other troops, was to start on the next night but one, September 3/4.

But on September 3 Rommel's forces began a general withdrawal, and were only followed up by patrols. The 'bottling' attack was launched that night, against the enemy's rear flank, which was being guarded by the 90th Light and Trieste Divisions. The attack became badly mixed up, suffering heavy loss, and was broken off.

On the next two days, September 4 and 5, the Afrika Korps continued its gradual withdrawal, and no further effort was made to cut it off, while it was only followed up in a very cautious way, by small advanced parties. On the 6th the Germans halted on a line of high ground six miles east of their original front, and were obviously intending to make a strong stand there. Next day, Montgomery decided, with Alexander's approval, to break off the battle. So Rommel was left in possession of this limited gain of ground in the south. It was small consolation for his losses, and the decisive frustration of his original aims.

For the troops of the Eighth Army, the fact of seeing the enemy in retreat, even though only a few short steps back, far outweighed the disappointment of failing to cut him off. It was a clear sign that the tide had turned. Montgomery had already created a new spirit of confidence in the troops, and their confidence in him was confirmed.

The question remains, however, whether a great opportunity was missed of destroying the enemy's capacity for further resistance while the Afrika Korps was 'bottled'. That would have saved all the later trouble and heavy cost of assaulting him in his prepared positions. But so far as it went the Battle of Alam Halfa was a great success for the British. When it ended, Rommel had definitely lost the initiative—and, in view of the swelling stream of reinforcements to the British, the next battle was bound to be for Rommel a 'Battle Without Hope'—as he himself aptly called it.

In the clearer light of post-war knowledge of the respective forces and resources, it can be seen that Rommel's eventual defeat became probable from the moment his dash into Egypt was originally checked, in the July battle of First Alamein, and this accordingly may be considered the effective turning point. Nevertheless, he still looked a great menace when he launched his renewed and reinforced attack at the end of August, and as the strength of the two sides was nearer to an even balance than it was either before or later, he still had a possibility of victory—and might have achieved it if his opponents had faltered or fumbled as they had done on several previous occasions when their advantage had seemed more sure. But in the event the possibility vanished beyond possibility of recovery. The crucial significance of 'Alam Halfa' is symbolised in the fact that although it was fought out in the same area as the other battles of Alamein, it has been given a separate and distinctive name.

Tactically, too, this battle has a special interest. For it was not only won by the defending side, but decided by pure defence, without any counteroffensive—or even any serious attempt to develop a counteroffensive. It thus provides a contrast to most of the 'turning point' battles of the Second World War, and earlier wars. While Montgomery's decision to abstain from following up his defensive success in an offensive way forfeited the chance of trapping and destroying Rommel's forces—momentarily a very good chance —it did not impair the underlying decisiveness of the battle as a turning point in the campaign. From that time onwards, the British troops had an assurance of ultimate success which heightened their morale, while the opposing forces laboured under a sense of hopelessness, feeling that whatever their efforts and sacrifices they could achieve no more than a temporary postponement of the end.

There is also much to be learned from its tactical technique. The positioning of the British forces, and the choice of ground, had a great influence upon the issue. So did the flexibility of the dispositions. Most important of all was the well-gauged combination of airpower with the ground forces' plan. Its effectiveness was facilitated by the defensive pattern of the battle, with the ground forces holding the ring while the air forces constantly bombed the arena, now a trap, into which Rommel's troops had pushed. In the pattern of this battle, the air forces could operate the more freely and effectively because of being able to count on all troops within the ring as being 'enemy', and thus targets—in contrast to the way that air action is handicapped in a more fluid kind of battle.

Seven weeks passed before the British launched their offensive. An impatient Prime Minister chafed at the delay, but Montgomery was determined to wait until his preparations were complete and he could be reasonably sure of success, and Alexander supported him. So Churchill, whose political position was at this time very shaky after the series of British disasters since the start of the year, had to bow to their arguments for putting off the attack until late in October.

The exact date of D-day was determined by the phases of the moon, for the offensive was planned to start with a night assault—to hamper the enemy's defensive fire—while adequate moonlight was needed for the process of clearing gaps in his minefields. So the delivery of the assault was fixed for the night of October 23—full moon being on the 24th.

One key factor in Churchill's desire for an earlier attack was that the great project of a combined American and British landing in French North Africa, named 'Operation Torch', was now planned for launching early in November. A decisive victory over Rommel at Alamein would encourage the French to welcome the torch-bearers of liberation from Axis domination, and would also help to make General Franco more disinclined to welcome the entry of German forces into Spain and Spanish Morocco—a countermove that could upset and endanger the Allied landings.

But Alexander considered that if his attack, 'Operation Lightfoot', was launched a fortnight in advance of 'Torch', that interval 'would be long enough to destroy the greater part of the Axis army facing us, but on the other hand it would be too short for the enemy to start reinforcing Africa on any significant scale'. In any case, he felt, it was essential to make sure of success at his end of North Africa if there was a good result from the new landings at the other end. 'The decisive factor was that I was certain that to attack before I was ready would be to risk failure if not to court disaster.'

These arguments prevailed, and although the date he now proposed was nearly a month later than Churchill had earlier suggested to Auchinleck, the postponement to October 23 was accepted by him.

By that time, the British superiority in strength—both in numbers and quality—was greater than ever before. On the customary reckoning by 'divisions', the two sides had the appearance of being evenly matched—as each had twelve 'divisions', of which four were of armoured type. But in actual number of troops the balance was very different, the Eighth Army's fighting strength being 230,000, while Rommel had less than 80,000, of which only 27,000 were German. Moreover the Eighth Army had seven armoured brigades, and a total of twenty-three armoured regiments, compared with Rommel's total of four German and seven Italian tank battalions. More striking still is the comparison in actual tank strength. When the battle opened the Eighth Army had a total of 1,440 gun-armed tanks, of which 1,229 were ready for action—while in a prolonged battle it could draw on some of the further thousand that were now in the base depots and workshops in Egypt. Rommel had only 260 German tanks (of which twenty were under repair, and thirty were light Panzer IIs), and 280 Italian tanks (all of obsolete types). Only the 210 gun-armed German medium tanks could be counted upon in the armoured battle—so that, in terms of reality, the British started with a 6 to 1 superiority in numbers fit for action, backed by a much greater capacity to make good their losses.

In fighting power, for tank *versus* tank action, the British advantage was even greater, since the Grant tanks were now reinforced by the still newer, and superior, Sherman tanks that were arriving from America in large numbers. By the start of the battle the Eighth Army had more than 500 Shermans and Grants, with more on the way, while Rommel had only thirty—four more than at Alam Halfa—of the new Panzer IVs (with the high velocity 75-mm. gun) that could match these new American tanks. Moreover, Rommel had lost his earlier advantage in anti-tank guns. His strength in anti-tank '88s' had been brought up to eighty-six and although these had been supplemented by the arrival of sixty-eight captured Russian '76s', his standard German 50-mm. anti-tank guns could not penetrate the armour of the Shermans and Grants, or the Valentines, except at close range. That was all the worse handicap since the new American tanks were provided with high explosive shells that enabled them to knock out opposing anti-tank guns at long ranges.

In the air, the British also enjoyed a greater superiority than ever before. Sir Arthur Tedder, the Air Commander-in-Chief in the Middle East, now had ninety-six operational squadrons at his disposal—including thirteen

American, thirteen South African and one Rhodesian, five Australian, two Greek, one French and one Yugo-Slav. They amounted to more than 1,500 first-line aircraft. Of this total, 1,200 serviceable aircraft based in Egypt and Palestine were ready to aid the Eighth Army's attack, whereas the Germans and Italians together had only some 350 serviceable in Africa to support the Panzerarmee. This air superiority was of great value in harassing the Panzerarmee's movements and the immediate supply of its divisions, as well as in protecting the Eighth Army's flow of supplies from similar interruption. But much more important for the issue of the battle was the indirect and strategic action of the air force, together with the British Navy's submarines, in strangling the Panzerarmee's sea-arteries of supply. During September, nearly a third of the supplies shipped to it were sunk in crossing the Mediterranean, while many vessels were forced to turn back. In October, the interruption of supplies became still greater, and less than half of what was sent arrived in Africa. Artillery ammunition became so short that little was available for countering the British bombardment. The heaviest loss of all was the sinking of oil tankers, and none reached Africa during the weeks immediately preceding the British offensive—so that the Panzerarmee was left with only three issues of fuel in hand when the battle opened, instead of the thirty issues which were considered the minimum reserve required. That severe shortage cramped counter-manœuvre in every way. It compelled piecemeal distribution of the mobile forces, prevented their quick concentration at the points of attack, and increasingly immobilised them as the struggle continued.

The loss of food supplies was also an important factor in the spread of sickness among the troops. It was multiplied by the bad sanitary condition of the trenches, particularly those held by the Italians. Even in the July battle, the British had often been driven by the filth and smell to evacuate Italian trenches which they captured, and had thereby been caught in the open on several occasions by German armour before they could dig fresh trenches. But the disregard of sanitation eventually became a boomerang, spreading dysentery and infectious jaundice not only among the Italian troops but also among their German allies—and the victims included some of the key officers of the Panzerarmee.

The most important 'sick casualty' of all was Rommel himself. He had been laid up in August, before the Alam Halfa attack. He recovered sufficiently to exercise command during that battle but medical pressure subsequently prevailed, and in September he went back to Europe for treatment and rest. He was temporarily replaced by General Stumme, while the vacant command of the Afrika Korps was filled by General von Thoma—both of

Scale:
Miles: 0, 10, 20, 30
Kilometres: 0, 20, 30, 40, 50

El Daba

To Füka 30 mls.

Ghazal

**2130 HRS. OCTOBER 23
8th ARMY LAUNCHES ATTACK**

MEDITERRANEAN SEA

Sidi Abdel Rahman

OCT 28
90th LT. DIV.

15th PZ. DIV.
'LITTORIO'

OCT 28/29

10th ARMD.
DIV.

Tell el
Aqqaquir

Tell el Eisa

9th AUST. DIV.

51st (H) DIV.

1st ARMD. DIV.

NZ. DIV.

El Alamein

OCT
27

Kidney Ridge

10th
ARMD. DIV.

**NOVEMBER 4
1st, 7th & 10th ARMD
DIVS PASS THROUGH
BREACH**

1st S. AFR. DIV.

XXX CORPS

Miteiriya Ridge

X CORPS

RAHMAN TRACK

4th IND. DIV.

Ruweisat Ridge

21st PZ. DIV.

50th DIV.

'ARIETE' DIV.

XIII CORPS

OCT 25

44th DIV.

7th ARMD. DIV.

OCT 25

FR 1st FIGHTING BDE.

El Taqa Plateau

Qaret el
Himeimat

Qattara
Depression

Second Alamein

Axis armour   Axis minefields   8th Army attacks

Axis infantry   +—+ Western edge of 8th Army minefields   Main movement of Afrika Korps these commanders coming from the Russian front. Rommel's absence, and their inexperience of desert conditions, was an additional handicap in the planning and preparation of the measures to meet the impending British offensive. On the day after this opened, Stumme drove up to the front, ran into a heavy burst of fire, fell off his car, and died from a heart attack. That evening, Rommel's convalescence in Austria was cut short by a telephone call from Hitler to ask if he could return to Africa. He flew back there next day, October 25, arriving near Alamein in the evening—to take charge of a defence which had by then been deeply dented and had lost nearly half its effective tanks that day in fruitless counterattacks.

Originally, Montgomery's plan had been to deliver simultaneous right and left hand punches—by Oliver Leese's 30th Corps in the north and Brian Horrocks's 13th Corps in the South—and then push through the mass of his armour (concentrated under Herbert Lumsden in the 10th Corps) to get astride the enemy's supply routes. But early in October he came to the conclusion that it was too ambitious, 'because of shortcomings in the standard of training in the Army', and changed to a more limited plan. In this new plan, 'Operation Lightfoot', the thrust was concentrated in the north, near the coast, in the four mile stretch between the Tell el Eisa and Miteiriya ridges—while the 13th Corps was to make a secondary attack in the south, to distract the enemy, but not to press it unless the defence crumbled. This cautiously limited plan led to a protracted and costly struggle, which might have been avoided by the bolder original plan—taking account of the Eighth Army's immense superiority in strength. The battle became a process of attrition—of hard slogging rather than of manœuvre—and for a time the effort appeared to hover on the brink of failure. But the disparity of strength between the two sides was so large that even a very disparate ratio of attrition was bound to work in favour of Montgomery's purpose—pressed with the unflinching determination that was characteristic of him in all he undertook. Within the chosen limits of his planning, he also showed consummate ability in varying the direction of his thrusts and developing a tactical leverage to work the opponent off balance.

After fifteen minutes' hurricane bombardment by more than a thousand guns, the infantry assault was launched at ten o'clock on the night of Friday, October 23. It had a successful start—helped by the enemy's shortage of shells, which led Stumme to stop his artillery from bombarding the British assembly positions. But the depth and density of the minefields proved a greater obstacle, and took longer to clear, than had been reckoned, so that when daylight came the British armour was still in the lanes or held up just beyond them. It was only on the second morning, after further night attacks by the infantry, that four brigades of armour succeeded in deploying on the far side—six miles behind the original front—and they had suffered much loss in the process of pushing through such constricted passages. Meanwhile, the subsidiary attack of the 13th Corps in the south had met similar trouble, and was abandoned on the second day, the 25th.

But the wedge that had been driven into the defences in the north looked so menacing that the defending commanders threw in their tanks piecemeal during that day in efforts to prevent the expansion of the wedge. This action fulfilled Montgomery's calculation and enabled his armour, now established in good positions, to inflict heavy losses on these spasmodic counterattacks. By evening the 15th Panzer Division had only a quarter of its tank strength left fit for action—the 21st Panzer Division was still in the southern sector.

Next day, October 26, the British resumed the attack, but their attempt to push forward was checked, and their armour paid a heavy price for the abortive effort. The chance of developing the break-in to a breakthrough had faded, and the massive British armoured wedge was embedded in a strong ring of German anti-tank guns. Lumsden and his divisional commanders had already raised objections on the second night to the way that the armour was being used, to ram a passage through such narrow lanes, and the feeling that it was being misused became increasingly widespread among officers and men as losses multiplied in the still narrow-fronted pushes.

While maintaining an air of supreme confidence, Montgomery shrewdly realised that his initial thrust had failed, that the breach was blocked, that he must devise a fresh plan, and meanwhile give his main striking forces a rest. His readiness to vary his aim according to circumstances, on this and later occasions, was a better tonic to the troops and a greater tribute to his generalship than his habit of talking in retrospect as if everything had gone 'according to plan'. Ironically, that habit has tended to obscure and diminish the credit due to him for his adaptability and versatility.

The new plan was christened 'Operation Supercharge'—a good name to impress the executants that it was decisively different and carried a better promise of success. The 7th Armoured Division was brought north as a reinforcement. But Rommel also took the opportunity of regrouping his forces during the lull, and the 21st Panzer Division was already on its way north, followed by the Ariete. The secondary attack in the south by the British 13th Corps had not fulfilled its purpose of distracting the enemy's attention and making him keep part of his armour in the south. The switch northward, and the consequent closer concentration of both armies there, was tactically an advantage to Rommel. It left the British more dependent on sheer slogging power, and attrition. Fortunately for them, their numerical advantage was so large that attrition, even at a very adverse ratio, was bound to decide the issue in their favour if the 'killing' process was pursued with unflinching determination.

Montgomery's new offensive opened on the night of October 28—with a northward thrust towards the coast, from the big wedge that had been driven into the enemy's front. Montgomery's intention was to pinch off the enemy's coastal 'pocket', and then start an exploiting drive westward along the coast-road, towards Daba and Fuka. But the new thrust became hung up in the minefield, and its prospects waned with Rommel's quick countermove in switching the 90th Light Division to this flank. Even so, Rommel counted himself lucky when this attack came to a halt, for by now his resources were running low. The Afrika Korps had only ninety tanks left, while the Eighth Army still had more than eight hundred serviceable tanks on the spot—so that although it had paid a price of nearly four British tanks for one German, its ratio of superiority had risen, and was now 11 to 1.

Writing to his wife on the 29th, Rommel said: 'I haven't much hope left. At night I lie with my eyes wide open, unable to sleep, for the load that is on my shoulders. In the day I'm dead tired. What will happen if things go wrong here? That is the thought that torments me day and night. I can see no way out if that happens.'* It is very evident from this letter that the strain was wearing down not only the troops but also their commander, who was still a sick man. Early that morning he had thought of ordering a withdrawal to the Fuka position, sixty miles to the westward, but had been reluctant to take such a step back because it meant sacrificing a large part of his immobile infantry, and therefore deferred such a fateful decision in the hope that one more check would lead Montgomery to break off his offensive. In the sequel, the check to the coastward attack turned out to the British advantage. For if Rommel had slipped away at this moment, all the British planning would have been thrown out of gear.

As soon as Montgomery saw that his coastward thrust had miscarried, he decided to revert to his original line of thrust—hoping to profit by the north-ward shift of the enemy's scanty reserves. It was a well-judged decision, and another example of his own flexibility. But his forces were not as flexible, and the time consumed in regrouping prevented the fresh thrust being launched until November 2.

This further pause, following the repeated checks, deepened the depression and anxiety in London. Churchill was feeling bitter disappointment about the

* *The Rommel Papers*, p. 312.

slow progress of the offensive, and was with difficulty restrained from sending off an acid telegram to Alexander. The brunt fell on the C.I.G.S., General Sir Alan Brooke—who strove to reassure the Cabinet, but inwardly had growing doubts, and anxiously wondered whether 'I was wrong and Monty was beat'. Even Montgomery himself was no longer so confident as he outwardly appeared, and privately confessed his anxiety.

The start of the new attack, in the early hours of November 2, was again damping—and increased the feeling that the offensive might have to be broken off. For, once again, the minefields caused more delay, and the resistance proved tougher, than expected. When daylight came, the leading armoured brigade 'found itself on the muzzles of the powerful screen of anti-tank guns on the Rahman track, instead of beyond it as had been planned'.* In that cramped position it was counterattacked by what remained of Rommel's armour, and in the day's fighting lost three-quarters of its tank strength. The remainder gallantly held on, and thus enabled the follow-up brigades to push through the gap, but they in turn were held up just beyond the Rahman track. When nightfall put an end to the fight, the British had lost nearly two hundred more tanks in combat and mechanical casualties.

Gloomy as the situation looked after this further check—particularly when viewed from afar—the cloud was about to lift. For by the end of the day Rommel was at the end of his resources. It is amazing that the defence had held out so long. The hard core of it was the two panzer divisions of the Afrika Korps, but even at the start of the battle, their fighting strength had been only 9,000, and had withered in the fire to little more than 2,000. Worse still, the Afrika Korps was left with barely thirty tanks fit for action, whereas the British still had more than 600—so that their superiority over the Germans was now 20 to 1. As for the thin-skinned Italian tanks, they had been pulverised by the British fire, and many of the survivors had vanished from the battlefield in westward flight.

That night Rommel took the decision to fall back to the Fuka position in a two-step withdrawal. This was well in progress when, soon after midday on the 3rd, an overriding order came from Hitler—insisting that the Alamein position must be held at all costs. So Rommel, who had not previously suffered from Hitler's interference, nor learned the necessity of disobedience, stopped the withdrawal and recalled the columns that were already on the way back.

The turnabout was fatal to the chance of making an effective stand farther back, while the attempt to resume a stand at Alamein was futile. The

* Alexander: *Despatch*, p. 856.

westward withdrawal had been spotted and reported from the air early on the 3rd, and naturally stimulated Montgomery to continue and intensify his efforts. Although two attempts to get round the enemy's screen were checked during the day, a fresh infantry attack that night (by the 51st Highland and 4th Indian Divisions), made with a south-westerly slant, succeeded in piercing the joint between the Afrika Korps and the Italians. Soon after dawn on the 4th, the three armoured divisions passed through the breach and deployed—with orders to swing northward and bar the enemy's line of retreat along the coast-road. Their exploiting drive was reinforced by the motorised New Zealand Division, and a fourth armoured brigade, under its command.

There was now a magnificent opportunity of cutting off and destroying Rommel's entire army. The chance was all the greater because the commander of the Afrika Korps, Thoma, was captured in the confusion of the morning, and the order for retreat was not given until the afternoon—while Hitler's belated permission was not received until next day. But as soon as the retreat order was given by Rommel, the German troops moved very fast, packed into such motor transport as remained to them, while the British exploitation suffered from its old faults of caution, hesitation, slow motion, and narrow manoeuvre.

After passing through the gap and deploying, the three armoured divisions were directed northward to the coast-road at Ghazal, only ten miles behind the broken front. That narrow wheel gave the remnant of the Afrika Korps a chance to block them, by a quick and short side-step. After advancing a few miles they were checked by this thin screen, and kept in check until the afternoon, when the Panzerarmee began to withdraw as ordered. Then when darkness came the British cautiously halted for the night. That was the more unfortunate because they were well beyond, and behind, the bulk of what remained of the Panzerarmee.

Next day, November 5, the cutting-off moves were again too narrow and too slow. The 1st and 7th Armoured Divisions were at first directed on Daba, only ten miles beyond Ghazal, and the leading troops did not arrive at Daba until midday—to find that the retreating enemy had slipped past them. The 10th had been directed on Galal, fifteen miles further west, and there caught the enemy's tail, capturing some forty tanks—most of these being Italian tanks that had run out of fuel. No effort was made to chase the main retreating columns until the evening, and the British armour then halted for the night as usual, after a short advance of eleven miles—when six miles short of its new objective, the escarpment at Fuka.

The New Zealand Division and its attached armour had been told to go for Fuka when the breakthrough was achieved, but it was delayed in following the armoured divisions through the gap—partly owing to bad traffic control—and then lost more time in mopping up Italians in its path. So it was less than half way to Fuka when it halted at nightfall on the 4th. It arrived near its objective at midday on the 5th, but then halted in face of a suspected minefield—which was, in fact, a dummy that the British had laid to cover their own retreat to Alamein. Darkness was approaching before the New Zealanders pushed through it.

Meanwhile the 7th Armoured Division, after its too early wheel inwards at Daba, had been sent back into the desert to drive for Baqqush, fifteen miles beyond Fuka. But it was delayed in crossing the New Zealanders' tail, as well as by the suspected minefield—and then halted for the night.

Next morning these three pursuing divisions closed in around Fuka and Baqqush—but the retreating enemy had already slipped away westward. All they caught were a few hundred stragglers and a few tanks that had run out of fuel.

The main hope now of catching Rommel's columns depended on the 1st Armoured Division—which, after missing them at Daba, had been ordered to make a longer circuit through the desert and cut the coast-road west of Mersa Matruh. But its drive was twice halted by fuel shortage—the second time when only a few miles from the coast-road. That was all the more exasperating to its commander, because he and others had urged that at least one of the armoured divisions should be prepared for a long pursuit, to Sollum, by replacing some of the ammunition in the transport with extra fuel.

In the afternoon of November 6, rain started to fall in the coastal belt, and became very heavy during the night. That put a brake on all the pursuit moves, and ensured Rommel's get-away. After the event, it formed the main excuse for the failure to cut off his retreat. But, in analysis, it becomes clear that the best opportunities had already been forfeited before the rain intervened—by too narrow moves, by too much caution, by too little sense of the time-factor, by unwillingness to push on in the dark, and by concentrating too closely on the battle to keep in mind the essential requirements of its decisive exploitation. If the pursuit had driven deeper through the desert, to reach a more distant blocking point such as the steep escarpment at Sollum, it would have avoided the risk of interception either by resistance or weather—for while rain is a likely risk in the coastal belt it is rare in the desert interior.

During the night of the 7th Rommel withdrew from Mersa Matruh to Sidi Barrani, and there made another brief stand while his transport columns were filtering through the frontier bottleneck by the passes up the escarpment at Sollum and Halfaya, which were being heavily bombed by the British air force. For a time there was a huge traffic jam on the coast-road, a queue twenty-five miles long, but with well-organised traffic control most of it got through on the following night, despite the British bombing. So on the 9th, although about a thousand vehicles still had to pass through the bottleneck, Rommel ordered his rearguards to withdraw to the frontier.

Meanwhile Montgomery had organised a special pursuit force, consisting of the 7th Armoured and New Zealand Divisions, and grounded the other two armoured divisions as a safeguard against running out of fuel and giving Rommel a chance for one of his ripostes, against a stranded force. This longer pursuit started on the 8th, but the New Zealanders did not reach the frontier until the 11th, and although the two armoured brigades of the 7th Armoured Division, advancing through the desert south of the coast-road crossed it the afternoon before, they just missed catching the enemy's tail when it passed through Capuzzo on the 11th.

While Rommel had slipped out of Montgomery's clutches, successfully evading each successive attempt to cut off his retreat, he was too weak to re-establish a new defence line on the frontier, or farther back in Cyrenaica. His fighting strength at the moment was about 5,000 Germans and 2,500 Italians, with eleven German and ten Italian tanks, thirty-five German anti-tank guns, sixty-five German field-guns, and a few Italian guns. For although some 15,000 German fighting troops had got away, safely, two-thirds of them had lost all their fighting equipment, and a still larger proportion of the Italians who had escaped had left theirs behind. The Eighth Army, besides killing several thousand, had captured some 10,000 Germans and over 20,000 Italians—including administrative personnel—together with some 450 tanks and over 1,000 guns. That was a very big compensation for its own 13,500 casualties, as well as for the disappointment of seeing Rommel slip away 'to fight again another day'.

After a short pause to bring up supplies, the British advance was resumed. But it was a follow-up rather than a pursuit, and Rommel's past counter-strokes had left so deep an impression that the advance proceeded cautiously along the coastal circuit instead of driving across the desert chord of the Benghazi arc. The leading armour did not reach Mersa Brega until November 26, more than two weeks after crossing the eastern frontier of Cyrenaica —and long after Rommel had regained the shelter of that bottleneck position. The only serious trouble and danger to his forces during the retreat through Cyrenaica had come from shortage of fuel. At Mersa Brega he was reinforced by a fresh Italian armoured division, the Centauro, and elements of three Italian infantry divisions—although these, being unmotorised, were more of a complication than an asset.

There was now a further fortnight's pause while the British brought up reinforcements and supplies for an assault on the Mersa Brega position. Montgomery again prepared a plan 'to annihilate the enemy in his defences'—by pinning Rommel with a strong frontal assault, while sending another strong force on a wide outflanking manœuvre to block his line of retreat. The frontal assault was to be launched on December 14, preceded by large-scale raids on the night of the 11th/12th to distract attention from the outflanking manœuvre, which then started on its desert circuit. But Rommel slipped away during the night of the 12th—thus stultifying the British plan. He went back in a rapid bound to a position near Buerat, 250 miles west of Mersa Brega—and double that distance beyond the Eighth Army's new advanced base at Benghazi.

Rommel was still holding the Buerat position when the year ended, for this time there was a month's pause, for a move-up and build-up, before Montgomery was ready to resume his drive. But it was nonetheless clear that the tide of war in Africa had definitely turned. For there was little chance that Rommel's army could be brought up again to a strength capable of matching the Eighth Army's build-up capacity, while his rear areas, and possible rearward positions, were now imperilled by the Anglo-American First Army's advance eastward from Algeria into Tunisia.

Yet Hitler's illusions soon revived, while Mussolini desperately clung to his because he could not bear to see Italy's African empire crumbling away. Indeed, their illusions had become uppermost again even while it was still uncertain whether Rommel would succeed in evading his pursuers and extricating the remnants of his battered army. On reaching Mersa Brega safely he had received orders to hold that line 'at all costs', and prevent the British from penetrating into Tripolitania. As a reinforcement to that dreamland demand he was also put under Marshal Bastico's command again, as he had been before the advance into Egypt. When he saw Bastico on November 22 he had told him bluntly that the order 'resist to the end' on that desert frontier spelt the certain destruction of the remaining troops—'we either lose the position four days earlier and save the army, or lose both position and army four days later'.

Then Cavallero and Kesselring came to see Rommel on the 24th and he told them that, as barely 5,000 of his German troops had weapons, to hold the Mersa Brega position he would need the speedy delivery, before Montgomery attacked, of fifty Panzer IV tanks armed with the new long-barrelled 75-mm. guns, and fifty anti-tank guns of the same kind, besides an adequate supply of fuel and ammunition. It was a modest estimate of his need, but it was all too evident that there was no likelihood of its being met, as most of the available equipment and reinforcements was being diverted to Tunisia. Yet they still pressed the order to stand at Mersa Brega.

So, in the hope of getting Hitler to face the realities of the situation, Rommel flew to the Führer's headquarters near Rastenburg, in the East Prussian forests. He had a chilly reception, and when he suggested that the wisest course would be to evacuate North Africa, Hitler 'flew into a fury', and would not listen to any further argument. This explosion did more than anything before to shake Rommel's faith in his Führer. As he wrote in his journal: 'I began to realise that Adolf Hitler simply did not want to see the situation as it was, and that he reacted emotionally against what his intelligence must have told him was right.' Hitler insisted that 'it was a political necessity to continue to hold a major bridgehead in Africa and there would, therefore, be no withdrawal from the Mersa el Brega line'.*

But when Rommel went to Rome on the way back he found Mussolini more open to reason, while more aware of the difficulties of shipping sufficient supplies to Tripoli and getting them forward to Mersa Brega. So he had managed to obtain Mussolini's permission to prepare an intermediate position at Buerat, to move the non-motorised Italian infantry back there in good time and to withdraw the rest of his slender force if and when the British attacked. Rommel had been prompt to act on this permission and slip away in the darkness immediately the British showed signs of launching their attack. Moreover, he had made up his own mind that he was not going to stop at Buerat or in front of Tripoli, and provide Montgomery with a chance of trapping him. His plan, already formed, was to withdraw right back to the Tunisian frontier and the Gabes bottleneck, where he could not easily be outflanked and could deliver an effective counterstroke with the reinforcements that would be more closely at hand there.

* *The Rommel Papers*, p. 366.

CHAPTER 21

'TORCH'—THE NEW TIDE FROM
THE ATLANTIC

The Allied landings in French North Africa took place on November 8, 1942.* This entry into north-west Africa came a fortnight after the launching of the British offensive on Rommel's position at Alamein, in the extreme north-east of Africa, and four days after the collapse of that position.

At the 'Arcadia Conference' in Washington at Christmas 1941—the first Allied conference following the Japanese stroke at Pearl Harbor which brought the United States into the war—Mr Churchill put forward the 'North-west Africa Project' as a step towards 'closing and tightening the ring around Germany'. He told the Americans that there was already a plan, 'Gymnast', for a landing in Algeria if the Eighth Army gained a sufficiently decisive success in Cyrenaica for it to push westward to the Tunisian border. He went on to propose that 'at the same time United States forces, assuming French agreement, should proceed to land on the Moroccan coast by invitation'. President Roosevelt favoured the project, being quick to see its political advantages in grand strategy, but his Service advisers were dubious about its practicability while anxious lest it should interfere with the prospects of an early and more direct attack against Hitler's hold on Europe. The most they were willing to agree was that study of the operation, now re-christened 'Super-Gymnast', should continue.

During the next few months discussion concentrated on the project of a cross-Channel attack, to be launched in August or September, to meet Stalin's demand for the opening of a 'Second Front'. The Cotentin (Cherbourg) peninsula came to be the most favoured site, as urged by General Marshall, the Chief of Staff of the United States Army, and by Major-General Eisenhower, whom he had chosen and sent to London as Commander of the American forces in the European theatre. The British emphasised the drawbacks of a premature landing in Europe with inadequate strength, pointing out the risks of such a bridgehead being bottled up, or overwhelmed, without

* For map, see p. 280.

bringing appreciable relief to the Russians. But President Roosevelt swung his weight in support of the project, and committed himself, when Molotov visited Washington at the end of May, to an assurance that he 'hoped' and 'expected' to create 'a Second Front in Europe in 1942'.

A reversion to the project of a landing in north-west Africa was spurred on by the unexpected British collapse in north-east Africa which occurred in June, following Rommel's forestalling attack on the Gazala Line.

The battle of Gazala had already taken a bad turn when Churchill flew to Washington on June 17, with his Chiefs of Staff, for a fresh conference. On arrival Churchill went on by air to Hyde Park, Roosevelt's family home on the Hudson, for a private talk. Here he re-emphasised the drawbacks and dangers of a premature landing in France, while suggesting the revival of 'Gymnast' as a better alternative. The British and American Chiefs of Staff, meeting in Washington on June 21, had disagreed over the Cherbourg project but found themselves in complete agreement that the North Africa project was unsound.

Their combined negative conclusion about this project was soon reversed by the pressure of events, combined with Roosevelt's pressing desire for some positive action in 1942 that would fulfil, even if not so directly as intended, his promise to the Russians. On June 21, news came that the fortress of Tobruk had fallen to Rommel's assault and that the remains of the British Eighth Army were in retreat to Egypt.

During the weeks that followed, the British situation worsened, and the argument for direct or indirect American intervention in Africa was correspondingly strengthened. By the end of June, Rommel reached and started to attack the Alamein Line, following on the heels of the British retreat. On July 8 Churchill cabled to Roosevelt that 'Sledgehammer', the plan for a landing in France that year, must be discarded, and went on to urge, once again, the case for 'Gymnast'. He followed it up with a message through Field-Marshal Sir John Dill, who was now head of the British Joint Staff Mission in Washington: 'Gymnast affords the sole means by which the U.S. can strike at Hitler in 1942,' and that otherwise both the Western allies would have to remain 'motionless in 1942'.

The American Chiefs of Staff reacted to this contention with renewed objections to 'Gymnast'—Marshall's condemnation of it as 'expensive and ineffectual' was supported by Admiral King's declaration that it was 'impossible to fulfil naval commitments in other theatres and at the same time to provide the shipping and escorts which would be essential should that operation be undertaken'. They also agreed in viewing the British refusal to attempt a landing in France in 1942 as clear evidence that the British did not really want to risk it even in 1943. So Marshall, readily supported by King, proposed a radical change of strategy—that unless the British accepted the American plan for an early cross-Channel attack 'we should turn to the Pacific and strike decisively against Japan; in other words assume a defensive attitude against Germany, except for air operations; and use all available means in the Pacific'.

But the President objected to the idea of delivering such an ultimatum to his British allies, expressed his disapproval of the proposed strategic switch, and told his Chiefs of Staff that unless they could persuade the British to undertake a cross-Channel operation in 1942 they must either launch one into French North Africa or send a strong reinforcement to the Middle East. He emphasised that it was politically imperative to take some striking action before the year ended.

Faced with the President's decision, the Chiefs of Staff might have been expected to choose the course of temporarily reinforcing the British in the Middle East, rather than embarking on the 'Gymnast' plan which they had so strongly and persistently opposed. Moreover, after reviewing the two courses, Marshall's planning staff reached the conclusion that the former was the lesser of two evils. But contrary to expectation, he and King swung round in favour of 'Gymnast'. This became their preferred alternative when they flew to London in mid-July along with Harry Hopkins, as the President's representatives, and found that the British Chiefs of Staff were firmly opposed to Eisenhower's plan for an early landing near Cherbourg.

In choosing north-west Africa as the alternative, rather than a reinforcement to the Middle East, Marshall's prime reason, according to Harry Hopkins, was 'the difficulty of mixing our troops with the British in Egypt'. While a mixture would also occur in the case of a combined operation in north-west Africa, it was obvious that American reinforcements to the Middle East would have come under a British Commander-in-Chief.

The adoption of 'Super-Gymnast' was formulated at two further meetings of the Combined Chiefs of Staff, American and British, in London on July 24 and 25—and promptly endorsed by Roosevelt. Moreover, he emphasised in his cable that the landing should be planned to take place 'not later than October 30'—a directive that Hopkins had suggested, in a personal message, as a means 'to avoid procrastination and delays'. On Churchill's initiative the operation was rechristened 'Torch', as a more inspiring name. It was also agreed that the supreme command should be given to an American—an ointment to the sore feelings of the American Service chiefs that Churchill was very ready to provide—and on the 26th Eisenhower was told, by Marshall, that he was to have the post.

While the decision for 'Torch' was now definite, it had been made before the questions of time and site were settled, or even fully examined. Thus fresh conflicts of view arose over both these problems.

On the question of time the British Chiefs of Staff, spurred by Churchill, proposed October 7 as the target date. But the American Chiefs of Staff recommended November 7, as being 'the earliest reasonable date for landing of the forces based on availability of combat loaders'.

On the question of site, the respective views were even wider apart. The British urged that the landings should be made on the north coast of Africa, inside the Mediterranean, so that a quick advance to Tunisia would be possible. But the American Chiefs of Staff stuck to the limited objective of the 'Gymnast' plan, as modified in June, when it was envisaged as a purely American operation, and were anxious to confine the landings to the Casablanca area on the west coast—the Atlantic coast—of Morocco. They feared not only the dangers of French opposition but of hostile Spanish reaction and a German counterstroke to block the gateway into the Mediterranean by seizing Gibraltar. The British on this issue were dismayed by such a cautious approach to the strategic problem. They argued that it would allow the Germans time to seize Tunisia, stiffen or replace French opposition in Algeria and Morocco, and thus frustrate the aim of the Allied operation.*

Eisenhower and his staff were inclined to agree with the British view. His first outline plan, formulated on August 9, was devised as a compromise. It proposed simultaneous landings inside and outside the Mediterranean, but not farther eastward than Algiers—because of the risk of enemy air attacks from Sicily and Sardinia—except for a minor one at Bône to seize the airfield there (Bône is 270 miles east of Algiers but 130 miles short of Bizerta). This compromise did not satisfy the British planners, as it did not seem likely to fulfil the principal condition of success, which they defined as being: 'We must have occupied the key points of Tunisia within 26 days of passing Gibraltar and preferably within 14 days.' In their view, a major landing at Bône, or even farther east, was essential to achieve a quick enough advance to Tunisia.

These arguments impressed the President, who directed Marshall and King

* I was asked for my views on the question of the North-west Africa Project on June 28, immediately after the Washington Conference when its revival was mooted. On being told that the main landing was then intended to be at Casablanca, on the Atlantic coast, I pointed out that this site was 1,100 miles distant from Bizerta and Tunis, the strategic keys, and that the best chance of early success lay in capturing them as quickly as possible, which meant that the landings should be made as near them as possible. I also emphasised the importance of landing on the north coast, in Algeria, 'on the backs of the French' as a means to diminish the opposition that was likely to develop in face of a frontal attack at, and slow advance from, Casablanca.

to restudy the project. They had also impressed Eisenhower, who reported to Washington that the American members of his staff were now convinced of the soundness of the British reasoning, and that he was now drawing up a new plan that would eliminate the Casablanca landings, and advance the date of the others.

His staff produced (on August 21) a second outline plan which largely followed the British idea. Discarding the Casablanca landing, it provided for an American landing at Oran (250 miles east of Gibraltar) as well as for British landings at Algiers and Bône. But Eisenhower's own endorsement of it was tepid, and emphasised that such an expedition, wholly inside the Mediterranean, would be badly exposed on its flank. That conclusion tuned in with Marshall's opinion.

The second outline plan was as unpalatable to the American Chiefs of Staff as the first had been to the British. Marshall told the President that 'a single line of communication through the Straits is far too hazardous' and he was against any landing being made inside the Mediterranean farther east than Oran (600 miles short of Bizerta).

Churchill received the news of this cautious turn after returning from his visit with General Brooke to Egypt and Moscow—where Stalin had taunted them about the failure of the Western Powers to open a 'Second Front', with such scornful questions as 'Are you going to let us do all the work while you look on? Are you never going to start fighting? You will find it is not too bad when once you start!' That had, naturally, stung Churchill, but he had managed to arouse Stalin's interest in the potentialities of 'Torch', and had vividly depicted how it could indirectly relieve the pressure on Russia. So he was shocked to find that the Americans were proposing to whittle down the plan.

On August 27 he sent off a long cable to Roosevelt protesting that the changes which the American Chiefs of Staff suggested might be 'fatal to the whole plan', and that 'the whole pith of the operation will be lost if we do not take Algiers as well as Oran on the first day'. He emphasised the bad impression that a narrowing of the aim would have on Stalin.

Roosevelt's reply, on the 30th, insisted that 'under any circumstances one of our landings must be on the Atlantic'. So he proposed that the Americans should carry out the Casablanca and Oran landings, leaving the British to make the eastward ones. Moreover, mindful of British military action against Vichy French forces in North Africa, Syria and elswhere, he raised a fresh issue:

> I feel very strongly that the initial attacks must be made by an exclusively American ground force. . . . I would even go so far as to say I am reasonably

sure a simultaneous landing by British and Americans would result in full
resistance by all French in Africa, whereas an initial American landing without British ground forces offers a real chance that there would be no French
resistance, or only a token resistance. . . . It is our belief that German air or
parachute troops cannot get to Algiers or Tunis in any large force for at least
two weeks after the initial attack.*

The British were appalled at the idea of a week's pause before making
eastward landings, more important and urgent for the strategic goal than
the westerly ones, and were far from happy about the Americans' optimistic
estimate that the Germans could not intervene effectively in less than two
weeks.

Churchill was very willing to profit from the persuasive influence of the
American Ambassador to the Vichy Government, Admiral Leahy, towards
easing the way politically and psychologically. While he was 'anxious to
preserve the American character of the expedition', and therefore willing to
keep the British forces 'as much in the background as was physically
possible', he did not believe it possible to conceal the fact that the larger part
of the shipping, the air support, and the naval forces would be British—and
these elements would become visible first, before the ground forces. He
touched on these points in a tactful reply to Roosevelt on September 1, and
emphasised that if 'the political bloodless victory, for which I agree with
you there is a good chance, should go amiss, a military disaster of very great
consequences would ensue'. He continued:

> Finally, in spite of the difficulties it seems to us vital that Algiers should be
> occupied simultaneously with Casablanca and Oran. Here is the most friendly
> and hopeful spot where the political reaction would be most decisive
> throughout North Africa. To give up Algiers for the sake of the doubtfully
> practicable landing at Casablanca seems to us a very serious decision. If it led
> to the Germans forestalling us not only in Tunis but in Algeria, the results on
> balance would be lamentable throughout the Mediterranean.†

This good argument for maintaining the landing at Algiers as part of the
plan did not mention the importance of landings farther east, and nearer
Bizerta—an omission, and concession, which was of fateful consequence to
the chances of early strategic success.

Replying to Churchill's cable, on September 3, Roosevelt agreed that a
landing at Algiers should be included in the plan, while suggesting that
American troops should land first 'followed within an hour by British
troops'. Churchill immediately accepted this solution, provided that there
was such a reduction in the force earmarked for Casablanca as to make

* Churchill: *The Second World War*, vol. IV, p. 477.
† *ibid.*, pp. 479-80.

the Algiers landing effective. To this Roosevelt agreed, in a modified form, suggesting a reduction of 'one regimental combat team' at Casablanca, and another at Oran, to provide '10,000 men for use at Algiers'. Churchill cabled back on September 5: 'We agree to the military lay-out you propose. We have plenty of troops highly trained for landing. If convenient they can wear your uniform. They will be proud to do so. Shipping will be all right.' That same day, Roosevelt replied in a one word cable 'Hurrah!'

Thus the matter was finally settled in this exchange of cables between Roosevelt and Churchill. Three days later Eisenhower specified November 8 as the date of the landings, while declining Churchill's offer to put the British Commandos in American uniform, as he was anxious to preserve an all-American look to the initial landings. Churchill reconciled himself to the delay, and to the modification of the plan. Indeed, in a subsequent cable to Roosevelt on September 15, he submissively said: 'In the whole of "Torch", military and political, I consider myself your lieutenant, asking only to put my view-point plainly before you.'*

Roosevelt's 'Hurrah!' cable on September 5 settled what was aptly called 'the transatlantic essay competition'—although Marshall continued to express doubts, while his immediate political chief, Henry Stimson, the Secretary for War (i.e. for the Army) made a bitter complaint to the President about the decision to land in North Africa. But the President's decision enabled detailed planning to be pushed on in a hurried effort to remedy the effects of procrastination. The plan, however, carried the two-edged effects of a compromise. By diminishing the chances of a quickly decisive success in North Africa it made more certain the prolonged diversion of Allied effort in the Mediterranean—as American official historians have recognised and emphasised.†

In the final plan, the Atlantic coast landing to capture Casablanca was to be made by the all-American force under Major-General George S. Patton, with 24,500 troops, carried by the Western Naval Task Force under Rear-Admiral H. Kent Hewitt. It sailed direct from America—the main part from Hampton Roads in Virginia—and consisted of 102 ships, of which twenty-nine were transports.

The capture of Oran was entrusted to the Centre Task Force, which comprised 18,500 American troops under Major-General Lloyd R. Fredendall, but was escorted by a British naval force under Commodore Thomas Troubridge. It sailed from the Clyde, as it was composed of American

* Churchill: *The Second World War*, vol. IV, p. 488.
† See, in particular, the very able and penetrating analysis in *Strategic Planning for Coalition Warfare* 1941–1942, by Maurice Matloff and Edwin M. Snell.

troops who had been brought over to Scotland and Northern Ireland early in August.

For the operation against Algiers, the Eastern Naval Task Force was also entirely British, commanded by Rear-Admiral Sir Harold Burroughs, but the Assault Force consisted of 9,000 British and 9,000 American troops, and its commander, Major-General Charles Ryder, was American. Moreover, American troops were incorporated in the 2,000-strong British Commando units. This curiously mixed composition was inspired by the hope that putting Americans in the front of the shop-window would lead the French to assume that the assault force was all-American. On November 9, the day after the landings, overall command of all the Allied troops in Algeria was taken over by the commander of the newly created British First Army, Lieutenant-General Kenneth Anderson.

The assault forces for both Oran and Algiers sailed together from Britain in two large convoys, a slow one starting on October 22 and a fast one four days later. This timing was arranged so that they could pass through the Straits of Gibraltar simultaneously during the night of November 5, and from there they were covered by part of the British Mediterranean Fleet under Admiral Sir Andrew Cunningham. Its presence sufficed to deter the Italian fleet from interfering, even after the landings—so that, as Cunningham regretfully remarked, his powerful force had 'to be kept cruising idly'. But he had plenty of work on his hands, as he was Allied Naval Commander, under Eisenhower, and thus responsible for the whole of the maritime side of 'Torch'. Including storeships that had come in advance convoys early in October, over 250 merchantment sailed from Britain, of which some forty were transports (including three American), while the British naval force employed in the operation, as escort and cover, amounted to 160 warships of various types.

The diplomatic prelude to the landings was akin to a mixture of a spy story and a 'Western', with comic interludes, carried into the field of history. Robert Murphy, the chief American diplomatic representative in North Africa, had been active in preparing the way for the landings by discreet sounding among French officers whom he felt were likely to be in sympathy with, and to give aid to, the project. He relied particularly on General Mast, commander of the troops in the Algiers sector (and previously Chief of Staff to General Juin, the Commander-in-Chief) and General Béthouart who commanded the troops in the Casablanca sector—although that sector as a whole was under the command of Admiral Michelier, a fact that the Americans failed to realise.

Mast had urged that a senior Allied military representative should come secretly to Algiers for back-stage talks, and discussion of plans, with Juin and others. Accordingly General Mark Clark (who had just been appointed Deputy Commander-in-Chief for 'Torch'), flew to Gibraltar with four key staff officers, and the party were carried on by a British submarine, H.M.S. *Seraph* (Lieutenant N. A. A. Jewell), to a rendezvous at a villa on the coast some sixty miles west of Algiers. The submarine arrived off the coast early on October 21 but too late to land Mark Clark's party before daylight, so had to stay submerged all day, while the puzzled and disappointed French party went home. A message from the submarine to Gibraltar, relayed to Algiers over a secret radio chain, brought Murphy and some of the French back to the villa the next night, when Clark's party came ashore in four canvas canoes—one of which upset when they embarked. They had been guided to the meeting place by a lamp, with a white blanket behind, shining through a window.

Mark Clark told Mast, in a broad way, that a large American force was being prepared for despatch to North Africa, and would be supported by British air and sea forces—a statement which was lacking in frankness. Moreover he abstained, in the interests of security, from giving Mast a clear idea of the time and places of the Allied landings. This excess of secrecy in dealing with a man whose help was of key importance was unwise, since it deprived him and his associates of the information and time necessary to plan, and take, co-operative steps. Clark authorised Murphy to inform Mast immediately before the landings of the date, but even then not of the places. That was too late for Mast to notify his associates in Morocco.

The conference was temporarily, and dramatically, interrupted by the appearance on the scene of suspicious French police. Mark Clark and his companions were hurriedly hidden in an empty wine cellar while the police searched the villa. Danger became more acute when one of the British Commando officers who had piloted the party began coughing. Mark Clark passed him a bit of chewing gum as a remedy, but he soon asked for more, saying that it had not got much taste—to which Clark replied: 'That is not surprising, as I have been chewing it for two hours!' After the police at last went away, still suspicious and likely to return, Clark and his party ran into fresh trouble when they tried to re-embark at dusk, for the surf had become heavy, and he had a narrow escape from drowning when his canoe over-turned. At a further attempt shortly before dawn, the others capsized, but all of the party got through the breakers in the end and reached the submarine, safe though soaked. The next day they were transferred to a flying-boat, which carried them back to Gibraltar.

An important issue which came into further discussion at this conference was the choice of the most suitable French leader to rally the French forces in North Africa to the Allied side. While Juin, their Commander-in-Chief, had privately expressed a favourable inclination, he showed a tendency to 'sit on the fence' as long as possible, and a reluctance to take the initiative. His chief subordinate commanders lacked sufficient prestige, and were no less reluctant to take any definite step in disregard or defiance of orders from the Vichy Government. Admiral Darlan, the Commander-in-Chief of its forces as a whole, and potential head of State if the aged Marshal Pétain were to die, had hinted to Leahy in 1941 and more recently to Murphy that he might be willing to break away from the policy of collaboration with Germany and bring the French over to the Allied side if assured of American military aid on a sufficiently large scale. But he had played in with Hitler so long that his hints did not inspire confidence. Moreover he had an anti-British bias, which had naturally been increased by the British action against the French fleet at Oran and elsewhere, after the collapse of France in 1940. This made his attitude all the more doubtful in view of the difficulty of disguising the fact that the British were playing a large part in 'Torch'.

General de Gaulle was ruled out for the opposite reason—that his defiance of Pétain in 1940 and subsequent part in Churchill's moves against Dakar, Syria, and Madagascar would make all French officers who had remained loyal to the Vichy Government unwilling to accept his leadership—even those who were most eager to throw off the German yoke. That was emphasised by Murphy and readily assumed by Roosevelt, who had developed a deep distrust of de Gaulle's judgement and dislike of his arrogance.

Churchill, who had recently dubbed himself 'your lieutenant', bowed to his master's voice, and de Gaulle was given no information of the project until the landings had taken place.

In these circumstances the Americans, from the President downward, readily accepted the view of General Mast and his associates that General Giraud was the most desirable and acceptable candidate for the leadership of the French in North Africa—as Murphy had already conveyed before the conference took place. Giraud, an army commander in May 1940, had been taken prisoner by the Germans, but had managed to escape in April 1942, and reached the unoccupied part of France, where he was allowed to stay, on promising to support Pétain's authority. He took up residence near Lyons. From there, although under surveillance, he got into communication with many officers, both in France itself and in North Africa, who shared his desire to organise a revolt against German domination with American help. Giraud's viewpoint was expressed in a letter to one of his supporters,

General Odic: 'We don't want the Americans to free us; we want them to help us free ourselves, which is not quite the same.' Moreover, in his private negotiations with them he made it one of his conditions that he should be commander-in-chief of Allied troops in French territory wherever French troops were fighting. From a message he received he understood that his conditions were accepted by Roosevelt, but they came as a complete surprise to Eisenhower when Giraud arrived at Gibraltar to meet him on November 7—the eve of the landings.

Giraud had been picked up, at a rendezvous on the south coast of France, by the same British submarine, H.M.S. *Seraph*,* that had carried Mark Clark on his secret mission to the Algerian coast. He was then transferred to a flying-boat, though nearly drowned in doing so, and carried on to Gibraltar. On reaching there, he was staggered at the news that the Allied landings in North Africa were taking place early next morning—as he had been told that they were planned for the following month—and also by the discovery that the command of them was in the hands of Eisenhower, instead of his own. This led to a heated argument, in which he based himself on his higher rank as well as on the assurances he had received, and constantly reiterated that to take anything less than supreme command would be a surrender of his country's prestige and his own. But when talks were resumed in the morning (of the 8th) he reconciled himself to the situation, after explicit assurance that he would be head of the French forces and administration in North Africa—a promise that was soon to be set aside on grounds of expediency and the superior assets of Admiral Darlan.

In bringing the 'Torch' of liberty to French North Africa, the Americans had achieved surprise too fully, throwing their friends and helpers into confusion—more confusion than was caused on the enemy's side. Their French collaborators were caught unready to aid effectively in clearing the way, and under the shock of the sudden invasion most of the French commanders reacted in the way that was natural in such circumstances, and in conformity with their loyalty to legitimate authority, embodied in Marshal Pétain at Vichy. Thus the landings met resistance initially—although less at Algiers than at Oran and Casablanca.

At Casablanca, General Béthouart, the French divisional commander,

---

* Giraud had stipulated that an American ship must be sent to convey him, for political reasons, so his demand was met by putting H.M.S. *Seraph* under nominal command of an American naval officer, Captain Jerauld Wright, and carrying an American flag that could be displayed if necessary. Giraud was accompanied by his son and two young staff officers—one of whom, Captain André Beaufre, had played an influential part in the planning of this dramatic move to swing the French Army into action against the Germans. Both Wright and Beaufre in later years rose to high places in their respective Services, and in the N.A.T.O. command structure.

received a message late in the evening of the 7th that the landing would take place at 2 a.m. on the 8th. He sent off parties of his troops to arrest the German Armistice Commissions, and posted some of his officers to welcome the Americans on the beach at Rabat, fifty miles to the north, as he assumed that they would land there, since it had no coast defence batteries and was the seat of French Government in Morocco.

After these preliminary steps, Béthouart himself went with a battalion to occupy Army headquarters at Rabat, and sent the Army Commander off under escort. Béthouart had also despatched letters to General Noguès, the Resident-General (and overall Commander-in-Chief) in Morocco, and to Admiral Michelier, informing them that the Americans were about to land, that Giraud was coming to take over command of French North Africa as a whole, and that he himself had been appointed by Giraud to take over command of the Army in Morocco. His letter to Noguès and Michelier asked them to back the order he had issued for allowing the Americans to land unopposed, or else to keep out of the way until it was more convenient for them to accept the *fait accompli*.

On receiving the letter, Noguès tried to 'sit on the fence' until the situation was clearer. While Noguès hesitated, Michelier took prompt action. His air and submarine patrols had not spotted the approaching armada before nightfall, so he jumped to the conclusion that Béthouart was deluded or hoaxed. Michelier's assurance that no strong force had been sighted off the coast so impressed Noguès that even when the first reports of the landing reached him, shortly after 5 a.m., he believed that they were no more than Commando raids. He therefore jumped down off the fence, on the anti-American side, and ordered the French forces to resist the landings, while putting Béthouart under arrest on a charge of treason.

Patton's main landing was made at Fedala, fifteen miles north of Casablanca, with subsidiary ones at Mehdia, fifty-five miles farther north, and Safi, 140 miles south of Casablanca. Fedala offered the nearest suitable landing beaches to that city and its strongly defended harbour—the only large and well-equipped one on the Atlantic coast of Morocco. Mehdia was chosen because it was the nearest landing place to the Port Lyautey airfield, the only one in Morocco with a concrete runway. Safi was chosen because a right-wing force operating there might ward off the strong French garrison of the inland city of Marrakesh from intervening at Casablanca, and also because it had a harbour where medium tanks could be disembarked—for the new L.S.T.s (Landing Ships Tank) then being produced were not ready in time for 'Torch'.

As the American armada approached the coast of Morocco on November

6, after a smooth ocean passage, 'heavy seas' were reported there and the forecast for the 8th was that the surf would be so high as to make landings impossible. But Admiral Hewitt's own weather expert predicted that the storm would pass away, and he decided to take the risk of pursuing the plan of landing on the Atlantic coast. On the 7th the sea began to subside, and on the 8th it was calm, with only a moderate ground swell. The surf was slighter than on any morning in the month. Even so, many mishaps and delays arose from inexperience.

But things at least went better than Patton had forecast in a characteristically bombastic 'blood and guts' speech at the final conference before embarkation, when he had caustically told the naval members that their elaborate landing plans would break down 'in the first five minutes' and gone on to declare: 'Never in history has the Navy landed an army at the planned time and place. But if you land us anywhere within fifty miles of Fedala and within one week of D-day, I'll go ahead and win.'

It was fortunate that the confusion and hesitation among the French were such that the landing attack waves were safely ashore before the defenders' fire became serious, and by then the light was good enough to help the American naval gunners in subduing the coastal batteries. But fresh trouble developed in the beachhead, and in extending it, from the inexperience and muddles of the Army's shore parties, so that Patton switched his explosive criticism to the faults of his own force and Service. Both the troops and the boats had been overloaded. Although the advance on Casablanca got going on the second day, and met no serious opposition, it was abruptly halted by the pull on its tail that was caused by lack of equipment—which was piling up on the beaches but failed to come forward to the combat troops. Little progress was made on the third day, and there was an increase of opposition, so that the outlook became gloomy.

The situation would have been more serious if the French naval threat had not been quelled on the first day. This was achieved in a battle off Casablanca that had an old-style flavour. It started just before 7 a.m., when the coast defence battery on Cap El Hank and *Jean Bart* in the harbour—this was the newest French battleship but still uncompleted, and unable to move from her berth—opened fire on Rear-Admiral R. L. Giffen's Covering Group, which comprised the battleship *Massachusetts*, two heavy cruisers and four destroyers. These suffered no hits, although there were several near misses, and their reply was sufficiently effective to silence temporarily both the El Hank battery and *Jean Bart*. But they became so absorbed in this lively action that they neglected their task of keeping the other French ships penned there. By 9 a.m. one light cruiser, seven destroyers and eight submarines had slipped out. The destroyers headed for Fedala, where the American transports were 'sitting ducks'. Fortunately they were headed off and driven to withdraw by a heavy cruiser, a light cruiser and two destroyers which Admiral Hewitt had ordered to intercept them. Then, on his summons, the Covering Group came up to cut off their retreat. Thanks to able seamanship, the skilful use of smokescreens, and the disturbing effect of a relief attack by their submarines, the French managed to survive this overwhelming concentration of heavyweight fire with the loss of only one destroyer, and then made another gallant effort to reach the transport area. In this second engagement, however, another was sunk, and only one of the eight French ships returned to harbour undamaged. There two more sank and others were further crippled by bombing.

But the result was not decisive, as the El Hank batteries and *Jean Bart's* 15-inch guns had come to life again, while the American ships had used up so much of their ammunition that they might not have been able to drive off the French warships based on Dakar if these had come up, as it was feared they might.

Fortunately, the situation at Casablanca, and on the Atlantic coast as a whole, was decisively changed by favourable political developments in Algiers. In the late afternoon General Noguès heard indirectly that the French authorities there, headed by Admiral Darlan, had on the 10th issued an order to stop fighting. Noguès was prompt to act on this unconfirmed report, and ordered his own subordinate commanders to cease active resistance pending an armistice.

Meanwhile, the American landings at Oran had met somewhat stiffer opposition than those of the Western Naval Task Force in the Casablanca area. Yet there was remarkably good joint planning and co-operation between the American military task force and the British naval force which brought it to the scene and delivered it ashore. Moreover its spearhead, the U.S. 1st Infantry Division, commanded by Major-General Terry Allen, was a highly trained formation, and it was backed up by half the 1st Armored Division.

The plan was to capture the port and city of Oran by a double envelopment—two of Terry Allen's regimental combat teams landing on beaches in the Gulf of Arzeu, twenty-four miles to the east, while the third (under Brigadier-General Theodore Roosevelt) landed on beaches at Les Andalouses, fourteen miles to the west of the city. Then a light armoured column was to drive inland from the beachhead at Arzeu, and a smaller one from a further landing point at Mersa Bou Zedjar, thirty miles west of Oran, to capture the airfields south of Oran and close on the city to the rear. To shut it off quickly was the more important because, as estimated, its garrison of 10,000 troops could be almost doubled within twenty-four hours by reinforcement from inland stations.

The operation started well. At nightfall on November 7 the convoy had deceptively passed Oran, heading east, but then doubled back in the dark. The landings began promptly to time (1 a.m.) at Arzeu and only half an hour late at Les Andalouses and Mersa Bou Zedjar. Surprise was complete and no opposition was met on the beaches. Although thirteen coast defence batteries covered this stretch, there was no harassing fire until after daylight, and even then it caused very little damage, thanks to effective naval support and the cloak it provided with smoke-screens. Disembarkation and unloading went smoothly on the whole, although slowed down by the overloading of the troops, who were carrying nearly ninety pounds of equipment apiece. The medium tanks were carried in transports and unloaded on the quay after the harbour at Arzeu was captured.

The only serious reverse was suffered in an attempt to take Oran harbour by direct assault, to forestall sabotage of its apparatus and the ships lying there. Two small British cutters, H.M.S. *Walney* and *Hartland*, carrying 400 American troops, and accompanied by two motor launches, were employed to carry out this daring plan—which the American naval authorities had deprecated as rash. The outcome confirmed their view that it was a 'suicide mission'. Unwisely, it was timed to start two hours after H-hour, just when the French had been aroused by the landings elsewhere. The precaution of displaying a large American flag failed to deter the French from replying with sustained blasts of fire which crippled both cutters, killed half of their crews and troops, while the remainder, mostly wounded, were taken prisoner.

The advance from the beachheads got going by 9 a.m. or earlier, and soon after 11 a.m. Colonel Waters's light armoured column from Arzeu reached Tafaraoui airfield, which was reported an hour later as ready to receive aircraft from Gibraltar. But when the column turned north it was checked short of La Sénia airfield, and so was Colonel Robinett's column from Mersa Bou Zedjar. The converging infantry advances from Arzeu and Les Andalouses also became hung up when they met resistance as they approached Oran.

On the second day little progress was made, as French resistance stiffened and a counterattack on the flank of the Arzeu beachhead dislocated the whole plan of operations through the threat being magnified by lurid reports—which led General Fredenhall to divert forces from other missions. While La Sénia airfield was captured in the afternoon, most of the French aircraft had already flown off, and it could not be used because of persistent shellfire. A concentric attack towards Oran was mounted on the third morning, after some of the islands of resistance on the approach roads had been bypassed during the night. The infantry attacks from east and west again met checks, but helped to fix the attention of the defenders, while advance parties of the two light armoured columns drove into the city from the south without being opposed, apart from occasional sniping, and reached the French military headquarters before midday. The French commanders then agreed to surrender. The American casualties in the three days' fighting on land were under four hundred, and the French even less. These light losses, and particularly the diminishing resistance on the final day, were influenced by the French commanders' awareness that negotiations were proceeding at Algiers.

The landings at Algiers had run a smoother and shorter course, thanks largely to the local commander, General Mast, and his collaborating associates. No serious resistance was met anywhere, except in trying to force an early entry into the harbour, as at Oran.

One transport, U.S.S. *Thomas Stone*, was temporarily disabled at daybreak on the 7th by a torpedo fired by a U-boat when 150 miles short of Algiers, but after that the seaborne approach deeper into the Mediterranean met no further trouble. Although sighted by a few enemy observation planes, no air attack came before the convoy made its southward turn after dark to the landing beaches. One group landed near Cap Matifou, some fifteen miles east of Algiers, another near Cap Sidi Ferruch, ten miles west of the city, and the third group ten miles further west near Castiglione. For political camouflage the landings nearest Algiers were made by the Americans, with an admixture of British Commandos, and the main British one was on the more westerly beaches near Castiglione.

Here the landings began promptly at 1 a.m., and proceeded without mishap despite rough and dangerous beaches. French troops met a short way inland said that they had been instructed to offer no resistance. Blida airfield was reached about 9 a.m. On the eastern side of Algiers the landings were a little late and suffered some confusion, but in the absence of resistance it was possible to straighten out the situation quickly.

The important Maison Blanche airfield was reached soon after 6 a.m. and occupied after a few shots had been fired as token resistance. The advance on Algiers itself, however, met a village strongpoint that refused passage and was then brought to a stop by a threat of attack from three French tanks. The coast battery on Cap Matifou also rejected calls to surrender, and only yielded after being twice bombarded by warships and dive-bombed in the afternoon.

The attempt to rush the port of Algiers fared worse. The British destroyers, *Broke* and *Malcolm*, flying large American flags and carrying an American infantry battalion, were used for this venture—which was planned to enter the harbour three hours after the landings, in the hope that the defenders would have been drawn off, even if their acquiescence had not been secured. Instead, the destroyers came under heavy fire as soon as they approached the entrance. *Malcolm* was badly hit and withdrew. *Broke*, at the fourth try, succeeded in running the gauntlet, and berthed alongside a quay, where her troops disembarked. At first they were allowed to occupy installations unopposed, but about 8 a.m. guns started to shell *Broke*, forcing her to cast off and withdraw. The landing party was hemmed in by French African troops, and surrendered soon after midday, as its ammunition was running low and there were no signs of relief by the main force. The French fire, however, had been directed to keep the landing party in check rather than to destroy it.

In the landings west of Algiers near Cap Sidi Ferruch there was much more delay and confusion, while a number of the landing craft went astray and arrived on the British beaches further west. Components of each battalion were scattered over fifteen miles of coast, while many of the landing craft were wrecked in the surf or delayed by engine trouble. Fortunately, the troops had a friendly or passive reception at first, Mast and some of his officers coming to meet them and clear the way—otherwise these landings would have turned into a costly fiasco. But when, after hasty reorganisation, columns pushed on towards Algiers they encountered resistance in several places. For Mast had by now been relieved of command, his orders for co-operation cancelled, and his troops bidden to oppose the Allied advance.

The Allies' collaborators in Algiers had played their part remarkably well under the difficulties caused by the very short notice they had been given of the landing, and the little they had been told about its objectives. Their own plans to aid such a landing were promptly put into action. Officers were posted along the coast to welcome and guide the Americans, control points seized by organised parties, the telephone service largely blocked, police headquarters and outlying stations occupied, unsympathetic higher officials locked up, and the radio station taken over in readiness for a broadcast by Giraud or on his behalf which it was hoped would be of decisive effect. In sum, the collaborators achieved enough to paralyse opposition by the time that the landings took place, and they kept control of the city until about 7 a.m.—longer than they had reckoned on doing or had regarded as necessary. But the advance from the landing beaches was too slow to match the need.

When the Americans failed to appear by 7 a.m., the limitations of the collaborators' influence on their countrymen became manifest. Moreover, when they broadcast an appeal in the name of Giraud, who had also failed to arrive as expected, this fell so flat as to show that the weight of his name had been overestimated by them. They soon began to lose control of the situation, and were brushed aside or put under arrest.

Meanwhile fateful discussions were proceeding on a higher level. Half an hour after midnight Robert Murphy had gone to see General Juin, broken the news to him that overwhelmingly strong forces were about to land, and urged him to co-operate by prompt instructions that they were not to be resisted. Murphy said that they had come on the invitation of Giraud, to help France in liberating herself. Juin showed no readiness to accept Giraud's leadership or regard his authority as sufficient, and said that the appeal must be submitted to Admiral Darlan—who was, by chance, in Algiers at that moment, having flown there to see his son, who had fallen dangerously ill. Darlan was awakened by a telephone call and asked to come to Juin's villa to receive an urgent message from Murphy. On arrival, when told of the impending stroke, his first reaction was to exclaim angrily: 'I have known for a long time that the British were stupid, but I always believed that the Americans were more intelligent. I begin to believe that you make as many mistakes as they do.'

After some discussion he eventually agreed to send a radio message to Marshal Pétain reporting the situation and asking for authorisation to deal with it freely on the Marshal's behalf. Meanwhile the villa had been surrounded by an armed band of anti-Vichy French, so that Darlan was virtually under guard. But a little later they were driven off by a detachment of *gardes mobiles*, who put Murphy under arrest. Then Darlan and Juin, eyeing one another like suspicious cats, went off to the headquarters in Algiers. From here Juin took steps to regain control, releasing General Koeltz and other officers who had been arrested by Mast and his associates, while putting the latter under arrest in their turn. Darlan, however, sent a further telegram to Marshal Pétain, just before 8 a.m., in which he emphasised that: 'The situation is getting worse and the defences will soon be overwhelmed'—a palpable hint that it would be wise to bow to *force majeure*. Pétain's reply gave the authorisation requested.

Just after 9 a.m. the American chargé d'affaires in Vichy, Pinkney Tuck, had gone to see Pétain and deliver Roosevelt's letter requesting his co-operation. Pétain handed him a reply, already prepared by then, expressing 'bewilderment and sadness' at American 'aggression', and declaring that France would resist attack on her empire even by old friends—'This is the order I give.' But his attitude to Tuck was very pleasant, and he seemed to be far from sad. Indeed, his behaviour conveyed the impression that his formal reply was really meant to allay German suspicions and intervention. But a few hours later Pierre Laval, the Prime Minister, accepted under Hitler's pressure an offer of German air support—and by evening the Axis powers were preparing forces for despatch to Tunisia.

Meanwhile Darlan, on his own responsibility, had issued orders to the French troops and ships in the Algiers area to cease firing. Although this order did not apply to the Oran and Casablanca areas, Darlan authorised Juin to arrange a settlement for the whole of North Africa. Moreover it was agreed early in the evening that control of Algiers should be transferred to the Americans at 8 p.m. and that the Allies should have the use of the harbour from first light the next morning, the 9th.

The afternoon of the 9th saw the arrival of Mark Clark to conduct the fuller negotiations necessary, and of Kenneth Anderson to assume command of the Allied troops for the advance to Tunisia. Giraud also arrived, a little earlier, but found that he was far from welcome among his chief compatriots there, and took refuge with a family who lived in an out of the way place. Mark Clark remarks 'he practically went underground'—although he emerged next morning for Clark's first conference with Darlan, Juin, and their chief subordinates.

Here Clark pressed Darlan to order an immediate cease-fire everywhere in French North Africa, and when he hesitated, arguing that he had sent a summary of the terms to Vichy and must await word from there, Clark began pounding the table and said that he would get Giraud to issue the order in his place. At that, Darlan pointed out Giraud's lack of legal authority or sufficient personal weight. He also declared that such an order 'would result in the immediate occupation of southern France by the Germans'—a forecast that was soon borne out. After some more argument, with an accompaniment of table-pounding, Clark pungently told Darlan that unless he issued the order immediately he would be taken into custody—Clark having taken the precaution of posting an armed guard around the building. Darlan then, after a brief discussion with his staff, accepted this ultimatum—and his order was sent out at 11.20 a.m.

When it was reported to Vichy, Pétain's own reaction was to approve it, but when Laval heard of it en route to Munich, in response to a brusque summons from Hitler, he got on the telephone to Pétain and induced him to disavow it. Early in the afternoon, Clark received the news that Vichy had rejected the armistice. When Darlan was told of this by Clark, he dejectedly said: 'There is nothing I can do but revoke the order I signed this morning.' Thereupon Clark retorted: 'You will do nothing of the kind. There will be no revocation of these orders; and, to make it certain, I shall hold you in custody.' Darlan, who had already hinted at this solution, showed himself very ready to accept it—and sent the reply to Pétain: 'I annul my orders and constitute myself a prisoner'—the annulment being only for Vichy and German ears. Next day, under pressure from Hitler via Laval, Pétain announced that all authority in North Africa had been transferred from Darlan to Noguès, but had already sent Darlan a secret message that the disavowal had been made under German pressure and was contrary to his own wishes. Such double-talk was a subterfuge compelled by the perilous situation in France, but left the situation and French commanders in North Africa, outside Algiers, still confused.

Fortunately, Hitler helped to clarify it and resolve their doubts by ordering his forces to invade the unoccupied part of France that, by the 1940 armistice agreement, had been left under the control of the Vichy Government. On November 8 and 9 Vichy had stalled on the offers of armed support which Hitler pressed on them, making reservations which inflamed his suspicions. On the 10th Laval arrived in Munich to face Hitler and Mussolini, and that afternoon Hitler insisted that the ports and air bases in Tunisia must be made available to the Axis forces. Laval still tried to hedge, saying that France could not agree to the Italians moving in, and that in any case only Pétain could decide. Hitler then lost all patience, and soon after the talk ended gave orders for his forces to drive into the unoccupied part of France at midnight —a move already mounted in readiness—as well as to seize the Tunisian air and sea bases, along with the Italians.

Southern France was speedily overrun by the German mechanised forces while six Italian divisions marched in from the east. German planes had started to arrive on an airfield near Tunis in the afternoon of the 9th, together with an escort of troops to protect them on the ground, but had been confined to the airfield by a ring of French troops. Now, from the 11th onward, the airlift was multiplied, the adjacent French troops disarmed, while tanks, guns, transport vehicles and stores were brought over by sea to Bizerta. By the end of the month 15,000 German troops had arrived, with about 100 tanks, although a large proportion were administrative personnel to organise the base. Some 9,000 Italians had also arrived, largely by road from Tripoli, and were primarily used to cover the southern flank. For a hastily improvised move, at a time when the Axis forces were hard pressed everywhere, that was a fine achievement. But such a scale of force was very small compared with what the Allies had brought to French North Africa, and would have had slight chance of resisting them if the 'Torch' plan had provided for a larger proportion of the Allied expeditionary force to be used for the advance to Tunisia, or if the Allied Command had developed the advance more rapidly than it did.

The German invasion of southern France did more than anything else to help the Allied situation in Africa by the shock it gave to the French commanders there. On the morning of the 11th, before the news came, there had been another see-saw in Algiers. The first sign was when Clark went to see Darlan, and pressed him to take two urgent steps—to order the French fleet at Toulon to come to a North African port, and to order the Governor of Tunisia, Admiral Esteva, to resist the Germans' entry. Darlan was at first evasive, arguing that his orders might not be obeyed in view of the broadcast announcement that he had been dismissed from command of the French forces—and, when further pressed, he refused to comply with Clark's demands. Clark marched out of the house, slamming the door to relieve his feelings. But in the afternoon he had a telephone message asking him to see Darlan again, and Darlan now agreed to comply with Clark's wishes, in view of developments in France—although his message to the commander of the fleet at Toulon was worded as urgent advice rather than as an order. Another favourable turn was that General Noguès, Darlan's Vichy-nominated successor, agreed to come to Algiers for a conference next day.

But in the early hours of the 12th Clark had a fresh jolt on hearing that Darlan's order for resistance in Tunisia had been revoked. Summoning Darlan and Juin to his hotel, it soon became apparent that the change was due to Juin, who argued that it was not a revocation but only a suspension of the previous order pending the arrival of Noguès, who was now his legitimate superior. Such scruples about legality, while characteristic of the French military code, appeared to Clark as merely legalistic quibbles. Although they bowed to his insistence that the order to Tunisia must be reissued immediately, without waiting for the arrival of Noguès, his suspicion was renewed by their reluctance to accept Giraud's participation in the conference. Clark was so exasperated at their procrastination that he spoke of putting all the French leaders under arrest, and locking them up aboard a ship in the harbour, unless they came to a satisfactory decision within twenty-four hours.

Meanwhile, Darlan's position in relation to the other French leaders in Africa had been strengthened by the receipt of a second clandestine message from Pétain reaffirming his confidence in Darlan and emphasising that he himself was in *accord intime* with President Roosevelt, although he could not speak his mind openly because of the Germans' presence. This helped Darlan, who had a shrewder sense of realities than many of his compatriots, to secure the agreement of Noguès and the others for a working agreement with the Allies, including the recognition of Giraud. Their discussions at a further conference on the 13th were expedited by a fresh threat by Clark that he would lock up the lot. That afternoon it was settled, and promptly endorsed by Eisenhower who had just flown over from Gibraltar. Under its terms, Darlan was to be High Commissioner and Commander-in-Chief of Naval Forces; Giraud to be Commander-in-Chief of Ground and Air Forces; Juin, Commander of the Eastern Sector; Noguès, Commander of the Western Sector, as well as Resident-General of French Morocco. Active co-operation with the Allies in liberating Tunisia was to begin immediately.

Eisenhower endorsed the agreement all the more readily because he had come to realise, like Clark, that Darlan was the only man who could bring the French round to the Allied side, and also because he remembered Churchill's remark to him just before he left London: 'If I could meet Darlan, much as I hate him, I would cheerfully crawl on my hands and knees for a mile if by doing so I could get him to bring that fleet of his into the circle of the Allied forces.' Eisenhower's decision was no less promptly endorsed by Roosevelt and Churchill.

But such a 'deal with Darlan', who had so long been presented in the press as a sinister pro-Nazi figure, aroused a storm of protest in Britain and America—a worse storm than either Churchill or Roosevelt had foreseen. In Britain it was the greater, since de Gaulle was there, and his supporters did their utmost to increase the outburst of popular indignation. Roosevelt sought to calm the tumult by a public statement of explanation in which he adopted a phrase from Churchill's private cable to him, saying that the arrangement with Darlan 'is only a temporary expedient, justified solely by the stress of battle'. Moreover, in an off-the-record press conference, he described it as an application of an old proverb of the Orthodox Church: 'My children, it is permitted you in time of grave danger to walk with the devil until you have crossed the bridge.'

Roosevelt's way of explaining away the arrangement as 'only a temporary expedient' naturally came as a shock to Darlan, who felt that he had been tricked. In a letter of protest to Mark Clark he bitterly remarked that both public statement and private word appeared to show that he was regarded as 'only a lemon which the Americans will drop after they have squeezed it dry'. Roosevelt's statement was still more hotly resented by the French commanders who had supported Darlan in reaching an agreement with the Allies. Eisenhower, very perturbed, cabled to Washington emphasising that 'existing French sentiment does not even remotely resemble prior calculation, and it is of utmost importance that no precipitate action be taken which will upset such equilibrium as we have been able to establish'. General Smuts, who flew to Algiers on his way back from London to South Africa, cabled to Churchill: 'As regards Darlan, statements published have had unsettling effect on local French leaders, and it would be dangerous to go further on these lines. Noguès has threatened to resign, and as he controls the Moroccan population the results of such a step may be far-reaching.'

Meanwhile, Darlan had made a definite and detailed agreement with Clark for co-operative action. He also induced the French leaders in West Africa to follow his lead, and make the key port of Dakar, together with the air bases, available to the Allies. But, on Christmas Eve, he was assassinated by a fanatical young man, Bonnier de la Chapelle, who belonged to the Royalist and Gaullist circle, which had been pressing for Darlan's removal from power. That accelerated removal helped to solve the Allies' awkward political problem, and to clear the way for de Gaulle's advent, while the Allies had already reaped the benefit of their 'deal with Darlan'. Churchill's comments in his memoirs: 'Darlan's murder, however criminal, relieved the Allies of their embarrassment in working with him, and at the same time left them with all the advantages he had been able to bestow during the vital hours of the Allied landings.' His assassin was promptly tried by court-martial on Giraud's orders, and quickly executed. On the following day the French leaders agreed to choose Giraud as High Commissioner in succession to Darlan. He 'filled the gap'—for a short time.

If the Allies had not succeeded in enlisting Darlan's help their problem would have been much tougher than it turned out. For there were nearly 120,000 French troops in North Africa—about 55,000 in Morocco, 50,000 in Algeria, and 15,000 in Tunisia. Although widely spread, they could have provided formidable opposition if they had continued to resist the Allies.

The only important respect in which Darlan's aid and authority failed to achieve the desired effect was over bringing the main French fleet across from Toulon to North Africa. Its commander, Admiral de Laborde, hesitated to respond to Darlan's summons without confirming word from Pétain, and a special emissary sent by Darlan to convince him was picked up by the Germans. Laborde's hesitation was prolonged, and his anxiety lulled, by the Germans' shrewdness in halting on the outskirts of the naval base and allowing it to remain an unoccupied zone garrisoned by French troops. Meanwhile they prepared a plan for a coup to seize the fleet intact, and launched it on November 27, after blocking the harbour exits with a minefield. But although delay had forfeited the chance of breaking out, the French managed to carry out their prepared plan for scuttling the fleet quickly enough to frustrate the German attempt to capture it—thus fulfilling the assurance that Darlan had given in his initial conference with Clark at Algiers on November 10: 'In no circumstances will our fleet fall into German hands.' The Allies' disappointment that it had not come to North Africa was outweighed by their relief that the danger of it being used against them had vanished with its sinking.

Another cause of relief during this critical period, and especially the first few days, was that the Spanish had abstained from any intervention and that Hitler had not attempted to strike back through Spain against the western gateway into the Mediterranean. The Spanish Army could have made the harbour and airfield at Gibraltar unusable by artillery fire from Algeçiras, and could also have cut communications between Patton's force and the Allied forces in Algeria, as the railway from Casablanca to Oran ran close to the border of Spanish Morocco—as close as twenty miles. When 'Torch' was being planned, the British had said that if Franco were to intervene it would be impossible to preserve the use of Gibraltar,* while Eisenhower's planning staff reckoned that a force of five divisions would be necessary to occupy Spanish Morocco and that the task would take three and a half months. Fortunately Franco was content to stay quiet, as a 'non-belligerent' ally of the Axis—and the more contentedly because the Americans were both buying Spanish products and allowing him to obtain oil from the Caribbean. Moreover, the Axis archives show that Hitler, after his earlier experience of Franco's skill in evading his desires for a move through Spain against Gibraltar, did not really consider attempting such a counterstroke in November 1942. The idea was only revived, and then by Mussolini, the following April—when the Axis forces in Tunisia were hard pressed and an early Allied invasion of Italy was feared. Even then Hitler turned down Mussolini's plea, both because he feared that a move through Spain would be fiercely and stubbornly resisted by his 'non-belligerent' ally, and because he remained confident that the Axis forces could maintain their hold on Tunisia. That confidence of his was bolstered by the remarkable success of the very slender Axis forces sent to Tunisia by the end of November in holding up the Allied advance at that time.

* It was no new conclusion. I had emphasised this point in numerous articles, lectures, and private discussions after the Spanish Civil War broke out in 1936, when discussing the danger that might develop if Spain came to be dominated by a Fascist régime, and if this should decide to co-operate actively with the Axis powers.

CHAPTER 22

THE RACE FOR TUNIS

The advance on Tunis and Bizerta started with a seaborne move, but one of very short extent—to the port of Bougie, about a hundred miles east of Algiers and only a quarter of the distance to Bizerta. This was a diminution of the original plan which, assuming full and prompt French co-operation, was to use parachute troops and seaborne Commandos to seize the airfields at Bône, Bizerta, and Tunis on successive days—November 11, 12, and 13— while a floating reserve of the force landed at Algiers was to sail for, and seize, the port of Bougie and the Djidjelli airfield forty miles beyond the forward base. But in the state of uncertainty after the landing at Algiers, this plan was considered too hazardous, and the more distant moves were dropped. Instead, it was decided on the 9th to occupy Bougie and the airfield, and then rush a force to a railhead at Souk Ahras close to the Tunisian border, while a second seaborne and airborne force occupied Bône.

On the early evening of the 10th two well-protected convoys sailed from Algiers, carrying the leading brigade group (the 36th) of the British 78th Division (Major-General Vyvyan Evelegh) and the stores for the expedition. It arrived off Bougie early next morning, but lost time by landing on nearby beaches, in heavy surf, from fear of a hostile reception—although in the event it proved a friendly one. Because of heavy surf an intended landing close to Djidjelli was not attempted, and the airfield was not occupied in time to provide effective fighter protection until two days later, so that several ships were destroyed in air raids. Early on the 12th, however, a Commando force slipped into the port of Bône and a parachute detachment dropped on the airfield, both being well received by the French there.

By the 13th the brigade group at Bougie was moving forward, while other elements of the division were advancing overland from Algiers, quickly followed by Blade Force, an armoured column just landed, which was composed of the 17th/21st Lancers and attached troops, under Colonel

* For maps, see pp. 280, 404, 414.

R. A. Hull—it was the leading contingent of the 6th Armoured Division.*
To pave the way it was planned that on the 15th a British parachute battalion
would be dropped ahead at Souk el Arba eighty miles from Tunis inside the
Tunisian border, and an American parachute battalion near Tebessa to cover
the southern flank and secure a forward airfield there. The American drop
was carried out as planned—and two days later this battalion, under Colonel
E. D. Raff, made an eighty miles bound south-eastward to secure the airfield
at Gafsa, barely seventy miles from the Gulf of Gabes and the bottleneck
approach from Tripoli. The British drop was delayed a day because of
weather conditions, and the leading ground troops came up so fast that they
also reached Souk el Arba on the 16th. By then, too, the small Tunisian
port of Tabarka, on the road to Bizerta, was reached by another column
advancing along the coast road.

Next day, the 17th, General Anderson gave orders for the 78th Division
'to advance on Tunis and destroy the Axis forces' after completing its
forward concentration. That pause to concentrate, however desirable it
seemed, was unfortunate in view of the slenderness of the Axis forces that
had so far arrived—an understrength parachute regiment of two battalions
at Tunis, which had been flown over from Italy on the 11th, and two battalions at Bizerta (one of parachute engineers, and one of infantry). On the
16th General Nehring—the former Commander of the Afrika Korps, who
had been badly wounded in the Alam Halfa battle and just recovered—
arrived with a solitary staff officer to command this nucleus, some 3,000
troops of what was entitled the '90th Corps'. Even at the end of the month it
had only the strength of a division.

The Germans, without waiting to concentrate, quickly thrust to the westward, and by that boldness disguised their weakness. The French troops in
Tunisia, although much more numerous, fell back before them to avoid a
premature clash before Allied reinforcements arrived. On the 17th a German
parachute battalion (of some 300 men only) under Captain Knoche pushed
out along the Tunis–Algiers road, and the French group posted there withdrew to the road-centre of Medjez el Bab (thirty-five miles west of Tunis),
with its important bridge across the Medjerda River. Here the French were
reinforced on the night of the 18th by elements of Blade Force, including a
British parachute battalion and an American field artillery battalion. (The
17th/21st Lancers and their tanks had not yet arrived; the leading squadron
reached Souk el Arba on the 18th, but was not sent forward.)

* In the 17th/21st Lancers, and other armoured regiments of this division, two troops of
each squadron had the new, and fast, Crusader III tank armed with the powerful 6-pounder gun,
while the other two troops were equipped with the 2-pounder armed Valentine which, although
slower, was far more reliable and also better armoured.

At 4 a.m. the French commander in Tunisia, General Barré, was called there to meet a German envoy who presented an ultimatum from Nehring that French troops must withdraw to a line near the border of Tunisia. Barré tried to parley, but the Germans realised that it was merely an attempt to gain time, and early morning reconnaissance spotted the presence of Allied troops. So at 9 a.m. they broke off parleys, and a quarter of an hour later opened fire. An hour and a half later German dive-bombers came on the scene to add punch to the bluff. Following up the bombing attacks, which shook the defenders badly, the paratroopers made two small ground attacks, and that air of vigorous effect created an exaggerated impression of their strength. The opposing commanders felt that they could not hold out unless further reinforcements came to the rescue—and General Anderson's instructions curbed such aid pending the completion of the Allied concentration for the planned advance on Tunis.

After dark Captain Knoche sent small parties to swim across the river, and these very effectively simulated an attack with growing strength. The Allied troops fell back from the bridge, leaving it intact. Just before midnight the local British commander called the French commander to his command post and insisted that an immediate withdrawal should be made to a more secure position on the high ground eight miles back. This was done, and the Germans occupied Medjez el Bab. It was a striking example of bluff achieved by boldness by a small detachment less than a tenth of the size of the force in possession.

Farther north, Major Witzig's parachute engineer battalion from Bizerta, with some tanks, had pushed west along the coast-road, and met the leading battalion of the 36th Infantry Brigade Group, the 6th Royal West Kents, at Jebel Abiod. But although the Germans overran part of the battalion it held on until the rest of the brigade came up to its relief.

Meantime smaller German parties, sent south, had secured the key towns on the approach from Tripoli—Sousse, Sfax, and Gabes. Some fifty paratroopers, carried by air, bluffed the French garrison into evacuating Gabes. They were reinforced on the 20th by two Italian battalions marching from Tripoli, which arrived just in time to foil an American move on Gabes by Colonel Raff's paratroopers. On the 22nd a small German armoured column drove the French out of the central road-junction at Sbeitla, and installed an Italian detachment there before returning to Tunis—but this was promptly expelled by another detachment of Raff's battalion.

Nevertheless, Nehring's skeleton force had not only preserved their bridgeheads at Tunis and Bizerta, but extended these into a very large bridgehead embracing most of the northern half of Tunisia.

Anderson's planned offensive to capture Tunis did not start until the 25th. During the interval the slender German strength had been trebled, although its close combat component comprised only two small parachute regiments (of two battalions apiece), a battalion of parachute engineers, three infantry draft-holding battalions, and two companies of a panzer battalion (the 190th) with thirty tanks. These included a number of the new model Panzer IV with the long 75-mm. gun, an important asset. Thus the extreme disparity between the Axis and Allied forces had diminished through Anderson's lengthy pause near the border of Tunisia to complete the process of concentration.

He himself on the 21st expressed doubt whether his strength was sufficient to gain that objective. So he was hurriedly reinforced with more American units on Eisenhower's orders, particularly Combat Command B of the 1st Armored Division, which came all the way from Oran, 700 miles back—the wheeled and half-track vehicles by road, and the tanks by rail.* Only part of this, however, arrived in time for the start of the operation.

It was a three-pronged offensive, the 36th Infantry Brigade Group on the left near the coast, the much larger Blade Force in the centre, and the 11th Infantry Brigade Group on the right along the main highway—each reinforced with American armoured and artillery units.

The left prong, on the hilly coastal road, started a day late and advanced only six miles on each of the first two days, in a cautious way—Witzig's small battalion of parachute engineers falling back before it. Then on the 28th it pushed on twice as far, but ran into an ambush that Witzig had laid in a pass near Djefna station, and the leading battalion was badly mauled. A larger attack on the 30th failed against a strengthened defence, and the attack was then abandoned. That repulse, in turn, led to the failure of an amphibious move by a mixed Anglo-American Commando which landed on the coast north of Djefna early next morning, and blocked the road behind, east of Mateur, but was driven to withdraw three days later as no sign of relief had come and its supplies were running low.

The centre prong was formed by Blade Force, which had been further strengthened by the inclusion of an American light tank battalion (the 1st Battalion, 1st Armored Regiment, equipped with Stuarts), so that it now had well over a hundred tanks. It thrust forward thirty miles on the 25th to the Chouigui pass, after breaking through an outpost line held by a small

---

* American armoured divisions at this period of the war included two armoured regiments, each comprising one light and four medium battalions, an armoured infantry regiment of three battalions, and three armoured field artillery battalions. It had an establishment of 390 tanks—158 light and 232 medium tanks. Operationally, it was distributed in two Combat Commands, A and B, and a third was later added.

Axis detachment. Next morning, however, a check came from a German detachment, a panzer company of ten tanks followed by two foot-fighting companies, which struck southward from Mateur. Eight of these tanks were knocked out, most by the American 37-mm. anti-tank guns, but their sacrifice in creating this flank threat led the British higher command to break off Blade Force's thrust, and distribute this force to cover the flank of the right prong.

Both sides were groping in 'the fog of war' but such caution at a crucial moment was in unwise contrast to the Germans' boldness—and all the more because on the previous afternoon a small detachment of Blade Force had by chance given the German higher command a bad fright. Hull had ordered Lieutenant-Colonel John K. Waters, commanding the American light tank battalion, to reconnoitre the bridges across the Medjerda River near Tebourba and Djedeida. Company C, under Major Rudolph Barlow, was sent on this mission and thus happened to arrive on the edge of the Djedeida airfield, newly brought into use. Seeing and seizing the opportunity, Barlow swept over the airfield with his seventeen tanks and destroyed some twenty aircraft—in reports it was magnified to forty. This deep penetration, also magnified in the reports that reached Nehring, came as such a shock that he pulled back his forces for a close-in defence of Tunis.

The Allied right prong, on the main highway, had met an early check in attacking Medjez el Bab,* and small counterattacks produced a disorganised retirement. But after nightfall on the 25th Nehring—shaken by the Djedeida raid—ordered the defenders to withdraw, fearing that they might be overwhelmed by a renewed attack. Following them up, the Allied column occupied Tebourba, twenty miles further on, in the early hours of the 27th. But after a short advance next day it was abruptly checked at Djedeida, twelve miles from Tunis, by a mixed battalion group. A renewed assault on the 29th was also repulsed. General Evelegh then advised a pause until further reinforcements came up and closer fighter protection had been provided against the German dive-bombers, which had harassed Allied troops increasingly and frayed their nerves.

This recommendation was accepted by Anderson, and by Eisenhower. He visited the forward area on those two days, and was greeted by American officers with 'the constant plaint, "Where is this bloody Air Force of ours? Why do we see nothing but Heinies?".' In his memoirs he remarks: 'Every conversation along the roadside brought out astounding exaggerations' about the damage, but it was nonetheless ominous to hear such

---

* Medjez el Bab was held by a German parachute battalion, an Italian anti-tank company, and two 88 mm. guns, supported by a company of the 190th Panzer Battalion, with 17 tanks.

comments as: 'Our troops will surely have to retreat; humans cannot exist in these conditions.'*

Meanwhile Field-Marshal Kesselring, who visited Tunis at the same time, was reproaching Nehring for being too cautious and defensive. He brushed aside arguments about the much larger strength of the Allied forces, and the fact that the inflow of Axis reinforcements was being badly hindered by Allied bombing of the airfields. Criticising the decision to withdraw from Medjez el Bab, he ordered him to regain the lost ground, as far as Tebourba at least. So, on December 1, a counterthrust was delivered by three panzer companies† with some forty tanks and a few supporting elements, including a field battery of three guns and two companies of anti-tank guns. The counterthrust was aimed, not direct at the force which had attacked Djedeida, but from the north towards the Chouigui pass, on the flank, with the intention of swinging round onto its rear near Tebourba. The Germans, in two converging columns, first hit Blade Force, which suffered from being widely distributed in its flank protective role, part of it being overrun and destroyed. Then, in the afternoon, the Germans pushed towards Tebourba but were checked by artillery fire and bombing before they reached their objective and got astride the main road.

But their continued pressure produced such a close threat to this artery that the Allies' spearhead at Djedeida was pulled back to a position nearer Tebourba. On the 3rd the pressure was increased to strangling pitch, and became concentric as Nehring threw in all the other German detachments that were within reach, leaving only a tiny handful on guard in the city of Tunis. That night the Allies' spearhead force was squeezed out of Tebourba, and barely managed to escape—by using a dirt track along the river bank, which entailed the abandonment of much equipment and transport. The Germans in their counterstroke took more than a thousand prisoners, and their 'bag' also included more than fifty tanks.

It deserves mention that the recent German reinforcements included five of the new fifty-six ton Tiger tanks, mounting a long 88-mm. gun. These monsters were a 'secret weapon', but Hitler had decided to send a few to Tunis for test in combat, and two of them were attached to the Djedeida combat group in this fight for Tebourba.

In the days that followed, the Allied commanders planned an early renewal of their offensive, with increased strength. But the prospect was soon

* Eisenhower: *Crusade in Europe*, p. 120.

† The leading elements of the 10th Panzer Division had just arrived in Tunisia, and included two companies of a fresh panzer battalion—with 32 Panzer IIIs and two of the new model Panzer IVs. These two companies were immediately used for the counterthrust along with one company of the panzer battalion that had arrived earlier.

diminished by Nehring's early action to extend his gains. He now planned to use his small armoured force to recapture Medjez el Bab by a wide out-flanking move south of the Medjerda River. Here Combat Command B of the U.S. 1st Armored Division had just been deployed, with a view both to the renewed advance and to keeping it separate from the British, so that it could fight as an integrated team. An advanced detachment was posted at Jebel el Guessa, a piece of high ground south-west of Tebourba which overlooked the flat country further south. As a preliminary to their own out-flanking move, the Germans attacked this observation point early on December 6, and overran its defenders, who had become disorganised in a hasty attempt to withdraw. Reinforcements had been sent, but were slow in starting, and when they arrived on the scene suffered a costly repulse.

This fresh German stroke, and threat, caused the newly arrived commander of the British 5th Corps, Lieutenant-General Allfrey, to order a withdrawal of his troops north of the river, from their position near Tebourba to one near Hill 290 (which the British had named 'Longstop Hill') closer to Medjez el Bab. Moreover, he advised a longer withdrawal, to a line west of Medjez el Bab. This proposal was endorsed by Anderson but turned down by Eisenhower. Longstop Hill, however, was evacuated.

Writing on the 7th to a friend, General Handy, Eisenhower remarked: 'I think the best way to describe our operations to date is that they have violated every recognised principle of war, are in conflict with all operational and logistic methods laid down in text-books, and will be condemned in their entirety by all Leavenworth and War College classes for the next twenty-five years.'

Resuming their flank thrust on December 10, with a force including about thirty medium and two Tiger tanks, the Germans were checked two miles short of Medjez el Bab by a well-posted French battery, became temporarily bogged when they tried to move off the road to outflank it, and were then led to withdraw by an American threat to their own rear from a detachment of Combat Command B. But they scored an indirect and un-foreseen success when Combat Command B started to withdraw after dark from its exposed position, became confused, reversed course on a false rumour of German threat, and turned off along a muddy track near the river, where many of its remaining tanks and other vehicles became stuck, and were abandoned. This disaster was temporarily crippling, while very damaging to the prospect of an early resumption of the Allied push for Tunis. For the moment, Combat Command B had only forty-four tanks left fit for action—barely a quarter of its full strength. The two German counterstrokes had all too effectively upset the Allies' plan and prospects.

Meanwhile Colonel-General Jurgen von Arnim had been sent by Hitler to take supreme command of the Axis forces, which were rechristened the 5th Panzer Army. He took over from Nehring on the 9th and, with the arrival of further reinforcements, proceeded to expand the two perimeters covering Tunis and Bizerta into a general bridgehead, formed by a hundred-mile chain of defence posts, and stretching from the coast some twenty miles west of Bizerta to Enfidaville on the east coast. It was divided into three sectors, the northern one held by the improvised Division von Broich (named after its commander), the central one (from west of Chouigui to just beyond Pont-du-Fahs) by the 10th Panzer Division, which had been arriving in driblets, and the southern sector by the Italian Superga Division. The Allied Intelligence estimated the Axis forces in mid-December as about 25,000 fighting troops and 10,000 administrative personnel, with eighty tanks—an estimate which was in excess of the mark. The Allies' effective fighting troops numbered close on 40,000—some 20,000 British, 12,000 American, and 7,000 French—and their total strength was much larger, as their administrative organisation was more lavish.

Delays in the build-up, partly due to bad weather, led Anderson to postpone the renewal of the offensive. But on the 16th he decided that it should start on the 24th, so as to utilise a full moon for an infantry night assault. It was to be delivered by the British 78th Division and 6th Armoured Divisions, together with part of the U.S. 1st Infantry Division.

To gain room for deployment, preliminary attacks were made to regain Longstop Hill and also Hill 466 on the more northerly line of approach to Tebourba. Both suffered from confusion in bad weather and developed into protracted see-saw battles, so that the main attack had to be postponed. By the 25th the Germans had completely regained their original positions—and, very naturally, now gave 'Longstop Hill' the name 'Christmas Hill'.

Already, on Christmas Eve, Eisenhower and Anderson had reluctantly decided to abandon the intended offensive in view of these setbacks and the torrential rain, which was turning the battleground into a morass. The Allies had lost 'the race for Tunis'.

Yet, by the irony of luck, this failure turned out one of the biggest blessings in disguise that could have happened. For without such a failure Hitler and Mussolini would not have had the time or encouragement to pour very large reinforcements into Tunisia and build up the defence of that bridgehead to a strength of over a quarter of a million men—who had to fight with an enemy-dominated sea at their back, and if defeated would be trapped. When the Axis forces were eventually overwhelmed, in May, the south of Europe was left almost bare, so that the follow-up Allied invasion of

Sicily in July had an easy run. But for the Allied failure in December which led to that huge 'bag' in May, it is all too probable that the Allied re-entry into Europe would have been repelled. What Churchill was fond of calling the 'soft under-belly' was so mountainous as to be very hard country for an invading force, and only became soft when there was a lack of defenders.

CHAPTER 23

THE TIDE TURNS IN THE PACIFIC

Japan's offensive aims in the Pacific, to establish what she called 'The Greater East Asia Co-Prosperity Sphere', had been virtually achieved within four months.* By that time Malaya and the Dutch East Indies had been completely conquered, as well as Hong Kong; so had almost the entire Philippines and the southern part of Burma. Within another month the surrender of the island-fortress of Corregidor brought the fall of America's last foothold in the Philippines. A week later the British had been driven out of Burma, back into India, and China was thus cut off from her allies. This vast run of conquest had cost the Japanese only about 15,000 men, 380 aircraft, and four destroyers.

After such a series of easy triumphs the Japanese were, naturally, reluctant to change over to the defensive—as their strategic plan ordained. They feared that such a change might bring a gradual decline of fighting spirit, while giving their Western opponents, economically much stronger, a breathing space for recovery. The Japanese Navy, in particular, was anxious to eliminate the two possible bases for an American come-back in the Pacific—Hawaii and Australia. As they pointed out, the U.S. Navy's carrier force could still operate from Hawaii, while Australia was obviously being turned into a springboard, as well as a stronghold.

The Japanese Army, with its mind still focused on China and Man-churia, was unwilling to release the troops required for such expeditions, which in the case of an expedition to invade Australia would have to be large. It had already declined to co-operate in a plan of the Combined Fleet Staff to take Ceylon.

The Navy, however, hoped that by a further successful stroke in either direction it might overcome the Army chiefs' objection and induce them to provide the troops required for one or other of these expeditions, but was itself divided in mind about the best direction. Admiral Yamamoto and the Combined Fleet Staff favoured a plan to take Midway Island (1,100 miles

* For map, see pp. 200–1.

west of Pearl Harbor)—as a bait to draw the U.S. Pacific Fleet to action, and crush it. The Naval Staff, however, preferred a thrust through the Solomon Islands to take New Caledonia, Fiji, and Samoa—and, by capturing this island chain, block the sea-routes between America and Australia. A weighty argument for the latter plan, of isolating Australia, was that the Japanese had already gone a long way towards completing the ring. For by the end of March they had advanced from Rabaul into the Solomon Islands as well as into the northern coast of New Guinea.

The debate between the alternative naval plans was interrupted, and diverted, by the American air raid on Tokyo, of April 18, 1942.

THE TOKYO RAID

This air strike at the Japanese capital, the heart of Japan's homeland, was inspired by the idea of retaliation for Pearl Harbor, and planning for it had begun in January. As the distance from any surviving American base was too far, the raid must necessarily be made from naval carriers. But as the Japanese were known to have a picket boat patrol operating 500 miles out from the mainland, the strike aircraft would have to be launched from a distance of about 550 miles, involving an out and back flight of at least 1,100 miles—which was too far for naval carrier planes. Moreover the U.S. Navy's few, and precious, carriers would be endangered if they had to wait in the area until the raiding planes returned. So it was decided to use U.S. Army Air Force bombers, of longer range, and also that they should fly westward after bombing Tokyo to land on Chinese airfields.

That entailed a flight of more than 2,000 miles, and the ability to take off from carriers. So the B.25 Mitchell was selected. These bombers, with extra fuel tanks fitted, could carry a 2,000 lb. bomb load for 2,400 miles. The pilots, led by Lieutenant-Colonel James H. Doolittle, practised short take-offs and long overwater flights. Only sixteen planes were employed, as they were too large to be stowed below deck, while they had to be allowed sufficient space for the take-off.

On April 2 the carrier selected for the task, *Hornet*, sailed from San Francisco with its escort of cruisers and destroyers. On the 13th it was joined by Task Force 16, organised round the carrier *Enterprise*, which was to give air support—as the *Hornet*'s own planes were stowed below deck. Early on the 18th the carrier force was sighted by a Japanese patrol boat while still more than 650 miles from Tokyo. The naval commander, Vice-Admiral William F. Halsey, conferred with Doolittle, and they agreed that it would be better to launch the bombers immediately despite the extra distance involved. It proved a wise and fortunate decision.

Taking off in a heavy sea between 0815 and 0924, the bombers reached Japan within four hours, catching the defences by surprise, and dropped their bombs (including incendiaries), on Tokyo, Nagoya, and Kobe. They then flew on to China, aided by a tail wind. Unfortunately, by a misunderstanding, Chuchow airfield was not ready to receive them, so that the crews had to make a crash-landing or drop by parachute. Out of the eighty-two man total, seventy returned—three who did not were executed by the Japanese for bombing civilian targets. The two carriers escaped unhurt, and reached Pearl Harbor on the 25th.

Another piece of good fortune was that, despite the patrol boat's warning, the Japanese had expected the raid to come a day later than it did, on the 19th—when, as they reckoned, the carriers would be close enough to launch their naval bombers. By then the air forces would have been ready and Admiral Nagumo's carriers would have reached their planned position for a counterstroke.

The prime result of the raid was the fillip it gave to American morale, which had been badly shaken by Pearl Harbor. But it also forced the Japanese to keep four Army fighter groups at home for the defence of Tokyo and other cities, while another resultant diversion was the despatch of a punitive expedition of fifty-three battalions to drive through Chekiang Province, where the American bombers had landed. A still more important effect, inherently causing a diversion of strength, was the decision to forestall further raids by undertaking the Midway operation as well as the thrust to cut Australia off from America. The dual effort was detrimental to concentration of effort and strength.

Under the revised Japanese plan the first move, itself dual, was to be an advance deeper into the Solomon Islands to seize Tulagi as a seaplane base to cover a further leap south-eastward, coupled with the capture of Port Moresby on the south coast of New Guinea, which would bring Queensland within range of Japanese bombers. Then the Combined Fleet under Yamamoto was to carry out the occupation of Midway Island and key points in the Western Aleutians. After the desired destruction of the U.S. Pacific Fleet, the third move would be a resumption of the advance in the south-east to block the sea-routes from America to Australia.

The first of these moves led to the Battle of the Coral Sea, the second to the Battle of Midway, and the third to the prolonged and intense struggle for Guadalcanal, the large island close to Tulagi.

An ironical, and indirect, effect of this diverse Japanese plan was that it-helped to cement a split in American planning and command arrangements.

At the beginning of April the United States had assumed responsibility for the whole Pacific area, except Sumatra, while the British would remain responsible for Sumatra and the Indian Ocean area. China was a separate theatre of war, under American tutelage. The American sphere was divided in two—the South-west Pacific area under General MacArthur, whose headquarters were now established in Australia, and the Pacific Ocean area under Admiral Chester W. Nimitz. Both were strong and forceful men, likely to clash. The Japanese plan provided ample call on, and scope for, the activity of each. Moreover the borderline between their respective spheres came in the Solomon Islands, where the Japanese amphibious threat required the conjoint use of MacArthur's ground forces and Nimitz's naval forces. Thus they had to develop a working arrangement.

THE BATTLE OF THE CORAL SEA

The Japanese ground and air forces for the first move assembled at Rabaul in New Britain, and the naval forces at Truk in the Caroline Islands, a thousand miles to the north. Behind the amphibious groups destined for the two invasions lay a carrier striking force ready to beat off any American intervention. It comprised the carriers *Zuikaku* and *Shokaku*, with an escort of cruisers and destroyers, and carried 125 naval aircraft (42 fighters and 83 bombers). A further 150 aircraft at Rabaul could aid it.

American Intelligence, the Allies' chief advantage, had discovered the main threads of the Japanese plan, and Admiral Nimitz sent all his available forces southward—the carriers *Yorktown* and *Lexington* from Pearl Harbor, with 141 aircraft (42 fighters, 99 bombers), and two groups of cruisers to escort them. (The two other American carriers, *Enterprise* and *Hornet*, returning from their part in the Tokyo raid, were also ordered to hurry down to the Coral Sea, but arrived too late for the battle.)

On May 3 the Japanese landed on Tulagi and took that island unopposed— as the small Australian garrison, forewarned, had been withdrawn. At that moment the *Lexington* was refuelling at sea while the *Yorktown* under Rear-Admiral Fletcher was farther away from the scene. But the next day it launched a number of strikes when about 100 miles distant from Tulagi. These had little effect beyond sinking a Japanese destroyer. The *Yorktown* was fortunate in escaping retaliation. For the two Japanese carriers had been sent to deliver a handful of fighter planes to Rabaul—sent off the scene merely to save an extra ferrying mission. It was the start of a series of mistakes or misunderstandings on both sides from which the Americans eventually profited on balance.

Admiral Takagi's carrier group now came south, passing to the east of the Solomons and round into the Coral Sea, hoping to take in rear the American carrier force. Meanwhile the *Lexington* had joined the *Yorktown* and the two were steering north to intercept the Japanese invasion force that was on the way to Port Moresby. On May 6—the black day of Corregidor's surrender—the opposing carrier groups searched for one another without making contact, although at one time they were only seventy miles apart.

Early on the 7th the Japanese searching planes reported that they had spotted a carrier and a cruiser, whereupon Takagi promptly ordered an all-out bombing attack on the ships, and speedily sank both. But, actually, they were only a tanker and escorting destroyer, so that time and effort were wasted. That evening Tugaki tried another and lesser strike, but the result was that twenty of the twenty-seven planes he employed were lost. Meanwhile Fletcher's carrier aircraft, likewise led astray by a false report, expended their effort in an attack upon the close-covering force of the Port Moresby invasion. In this stroke they sank the light carrier *Shoho*, and did so in ten minutes—one of the quickest sinkings on record in the entire war. A more important effect was that the Japanese were led to postpone the invasion and order their force to turn back. It was an ironical benefit from the mistake of attacking the wrong ship. It was, also, one of several blind shots that day.

On the morning of May 8 the two opposing carrier forces at last came to grips. The two sides were closely matched, the Japanese having 121 aircraft and the Americans 122, while their escorts were almost equal in strength—four heavy cruisers and six destroyers on the Japanese side, five heavy cruisers and seven destroyers on the American side. The Japanese, however, were moving in a belt of cloud while the Americans had to operate under a clear sky. The primary consequence of this was that the carrier *Zuikaku* escaped attention. The *Shokaku*, however, suffered three bomb-hits and had to be withdrawn from the battle. On the other side, the *Lexington* suffered two torpedo-hits and two bomb-hits, and subsequent internal explosions compelled the abandonment of this much cherished ship—which sailors called the 'Lady Lex'. The nimbler *Yorktown* escaped with only one bomb hit.

In the afternoon, Nimitz ordered the carrier force to withdraw from the Coral Sea—and the more readily as the threat to Port Moresby had vanished for the time being. The Japanese also retired from the scene, in the mistaken belief that both the American carriers had been sunk.

In absolute losses the Americans came off slightly better in aircraft, seventy-four compared with over eighty, while their loss in men was only

The Battle of Midway

Sequence of events of June 4, 1942

A 0600 HRS — Japanese planes attack Midway; Midway bombers attack Japanese carriers
B 0820 HRS — US carriers sighted by Japanese planes
C 1026 HRS — Akagi, Kaga and Soryu hit by US dive-bombers (sink later)
D 1400 HRS — Yorktown bombed by Japanese planes (sinks later)
E 1700 HRS — Hiryu bombed (sinks later)

US CARRIERS : ENTERPRISE
YORKTOWN & HORNET

JAP. SUBMARINES ARRIVE
TOO LATE TO DETECT
US CARRIERS

Oahu
PEARL HARBOR
Hawaii

MIDWAY
Kure

To Dutch Harbor (Aleutian Is)

Miles
Kilometres
0 ... 1000
0 ... 1600

0900 HRS. JUNE 3,
JAP. TRANSPORTS SIGHTED
BY US RECCE. PLANES

To Attu and Kiska

ALEUTIAN INVASION FORCE
ALEUTIAN CARRIER FORCE

ALEUTIAN COVERING FORCE

From Northern Japan

FIRST CARRIER FORCE
(Nagumo)

MAIN BATTLE FLEET
(Yamamoto)

COVERING FORCE
[Kondo]

MIDWAY
INVASION FORCE

From Southern Japan

From Saipan

543 compared with over a thousand, but they had lost a fleet carrier whereas the Japanese had lost only a light carrier. More important, the Americans had thwarted their enemy's strategic object, the capture of Port Moresby in New Guinea. And now by a superiority in technical achievement they managed to repair the *Yorktown* in time for the next stage of the Pacific conflict, whereas neither of the two Japanese carriers in the Coral Sea fight could be got ready for use in the second and more decisive fight.

The Battle of the Coral Sea was the first in history fought out between fleets that never came in sight of one another, and at ranges that had been extended, from the battleship's extreme limit of about twenty miles, to a hundred miles and more. A greater repetition was soon to follow.

THE BATTLE OF MIDWAY

Imperial General Headquarters in Japan had already set this next stage going by its order of May 5. The plan produced by the Combined Fleet staff was extraordinarily comprehensive and elaborate, but lacking in flexibility. Almost the entire Navy was to be used in the operation. The total of some 200 ships included 8 carriers, 11 battleships, 22 cruisers, 65 destroyers, 21 submarines. They were assisted by more than 600 aircraft. Admiral Nimitz could scrape together only 76 ships, and of these a third, belonging to the North Pacific Force, never came into the battle.

For the main, the Midway operation, the Japanese employed (1) an advanced submarine force, patrolling in three cordons, and intended to cripple American naval countermoves; (2) an invasion force under Admiral Kondo of twelve escorted transports, carrying 5,000 troops, with close support by four heavy cruisers, and more distant cover from a force comprising two battleships, one light carrier and a further four heavy cruisers; (3) Nagumo's First Carrier Force of four fleet carriers—carrying over 250 planes—escorted by two battleships, two heavy cruisers and a destroyer screen; (4) the main battle fleet under Yamamoto, comprising three battleships, with a destroyer screen, and one light carrier. One of the battleships was the recently built giant, the *Yamato*, of 70,000 tons and mounting nine 18-inch guns.

For the Aleutians operation the Japanese allotted (1) an invasion force of three escorted transports, carrying 2,400 troops, with a support group of two heavy cruisers; (2) a carrier force of two light carriers; (3) a covering force of four older battleships.

The battle was to open in the Aleutians, with air strikes against Dutch

Harbor on June 3, followed by landings at three points on the 6th. Meanwhile, on the 4th, Nagumo's carrier planes were to attack the airfield on Midway, and next day Kurè Atoll (sixty miles to the west) was to be occupied for a seaplane base. On the 6th, cruisers would bombard Midway, and the troops be landed, the invasion being covered by Kondo's battleships.

The Japanese expectation was that there would be no American ships in the Midway area until after the landing, and their hope was that the U.S. Pacific Fleet would hurry northward as soon as news came of the opening air strike in the Aleutians. That would enable them to trap it between their two carrier forces. But in pursuing this strategic aim, the destruction of the American carriers, the Japanese handicapped themselves by their tactical arrangements. Because of the favourable moon conditions of early June, Yamamoto was unwilling to wait until the *Zuikaku* had replaced her aircraft losses in the Coral Sea and could reinforce the other carriers. As for the eight available carriers, two were sent to the Aleutians and two more were accompanying battleship groups. At the same time, fleet movements were tied to the speed of slow troop transports. Moreover, it is hard to see the point of a diversionary move to the Aleutians if the Japanese main object was the destruction of the American carriers, and not merely the capture of Midway. Worst of all, by committing themselves to the capture of a fixed point at a fixed time, the Japanese forfeited strategic flexibility.

On the American side, Admiral Nimitz's main worry was the Japanese superiority of force. Since the Pearl Harbor disaster he had no battleships left, and after the Coral Sea battle only two carriers fit for action, the *Enterprise* and the *Hornet*. But by an astonishing effort they were increased to three through the repair of the *Yorktown* in two days instead of an estimated ninety.

Nimitz's one great, and offsetting, advantage was the superiority of his means and supply of information. The three American carriers, with their 233 planes, were stationed well to the north of Midway, so as to be out of sight of Japanese reconnoitring planes, while they could count on getting early word of Japanese movements from their long-range Catalinas based in Midway. Thus they hoped to make a flank attack on the Japanese forces. On June 3, the day after the carriers were in position, air reconnaissance sighted the slow-moving Japanese transports 600 miles west of Midway. Gaps in the search patterns flown by Japanese aircraft allowed the American carriers to approach unseen, from the north-east. They were also helped by the belief of Yamamoto and Nagumo that the U.S. Pacific Fleet would not be at sea.

Early on June 4, Nagumo launched a strike by 108 of his aircraft against Midway, while a further wave of similar size was being prepared to attack any warships sighted. The first wave did much damage to installations on Midway, with little loss to itself, but reported to Nagumo that there was need for a second attack. Since his own carriers were being bombed by planes from Midway, he felt that there was still need to neutralise the island's airfields, so ordered his second wave to change from torpedoes to bombs for this purpose, as there was still no sign of the American carriers.

Shortly afterwards, a group of American ships was reported about 200 miles away, although it was at first thought to consist only of cruisers and destroyers. But at 0820 came a rather more precise report saying that the group included a carrier. This was an awkward moment for Nagumo, as most of his torpedo-bombers were now equipped with bombs, and most of his fighters were on patrol. He had, also, to recover the aircraft returning from the first strike at Midway.

Nevertheless, the change of course north-eastward which Nagumo made on receiving the news helped him to avoid the first wave of dive-bombers despatched against him from the American carriers. And when three successive waves of torpedo-bombers—relatively slow machines—attacked the Japanese carriers between 0930 and 1024, thirty-five of the forty-one used were shot down by the Japanese fighters or anti-aircraft guns. At that moment the Japanese felt that they had won the battle.

But two minutes later thirty-seven American dive-bombers from the *Enterprise* (under Lieutenant-Commander Clarence W. McClusky) swooped down from 19,000 feet, so unexpectedly that they met no opposition. The Japanese fighters that had just shot down the third wave of torpedo-bombers had no chance to climb and counterattack. The carrier *Akagi*, Nagumo's flagship, was hit by bombs which caught its planes changing their own projectiles and exploded many of the torpedoes, compelling the crew to abandon ship. The carrier *Kaga* suffered bomb-hits that destroyed her bridge and set her on fire from stem to stern; she eventually sank in the evening. The carrier *Soryu* suffered three hits with half-ton bombs from the *Yorktown's* dive-bombers, which now arrived on the scene, and was abandoned within twenty minutes.

The only still intact fleet carrier, the *Hiryu*, struck back at the *Yorktown* and hit her so badly in the afternoon as to cause her abandonment—she was weakened by the damage, hastily repaired, that she had suffered in the Coral Sea battles. But twenty-four American dive-bombers, including ten from the *Yorktown*, caught the *Hiryu* in the late afternoon and hit her so severely that she had to be abandoned in the early hours of the 5th, and sank at 0900 hours.

This battle of the Fourth of June saw the most extraordinarily quick change of fortune known in naval history, and also showed the 'chanciness' of battles fought out in the new style by long-range sea-air action.

Admiral Yamamoto's first reaction to the news of the disaster to his carrier force was to bring up his battleships, while bringing back his two light carriers from the Aleutians—still in the hope of fighting a sea-battle more in the old style to restore the prospect. But the subsequent news of the loss of the *Hiryu*, and Nagumo's gloomy reports, led to a change of mind, and early on the 5th Yamamoto decided to suspend the attack on Midway. He still hoped to draw the Americans into a trap, by withdrawing westward, but was foiled by the fine combination of boldness with caution shown by Admiral Raymond A. Spruance, who commanded the two American carriers *Enterprise* and *Hornet* in this crucial battle.

Meantime, the Japanese attack on the Aleutian Islands in the North Pacific had been delivered as planned early on June 3, when the two light carriers allotted for the operation launched twenty-three bombers, with twelve fighters, against Dutch Harbor. It was too small a force for serious effect except by luck, and did little damage, as cloud obscured the ground. A repetition next day, in clearer weather, achieved some hits but nothing drastic. Then on June 5 the carriers were called southward to help in the main operation. On the 7th, however, the small seaborne force of Japanese troops landed on, and captured unopposed, two of the three islands—Kiska and Attu—which had been assigned as objectives. Japanese propaganda made the most of this minor achievement, to offset the crucial failure at Midway. Superficially, the capture of these points looked an important gain, as the Aleutian chain of islands stretching across the North Pacific lay close to the shortest route between San Francisco and Tokyo. But in reality these bleak and rocky islands, often covered in fog or battered by storms, were quite unsuitable as air or naval bases for a trans-Pacific advance either way.

In sum, the operations of June 1942 were a crushing defeat for the Japanese. They had lost in the Midway battle itself four fleet carriers and some 330 aircraft, most of which went down with the carriers, as well as a heavy cruiser—whereas the Americans lost only one carrier and about 150 aircraft. The dive-bombers had been the key weapon on the American side—in contrast, over 90 per cent of the torpedo-bombers had been shot down, while the large B.17 bombers of the Army had proved quite ineffective against ships.

Beside the basic strategic errors earlier mentioned, the Japanese also suffered from other handicapping faults of various kinds. Among 'command' faults was Yamamoto's virtual isolation, on the bridge of the battleship *Yamato*, Nagumo's loss of nerve, and the naval tradition that led Yamaguchi and other leaders to go down with their ships instead of seeking to recover the initiative. Nimitz, by remaining on shore, was able to keep an overall grip on the strategic situation, in contrast to Yamamoto.

Japanese troubles were multiplied by a string of tactical errors—the failure to fly sufficient search planes to spot the American carriers; lack of fighter cover at high altitude; poor fire precautions; striking with the planes of all four carriers, which meant that they had to recover and rearm their aircraft at the same time, so that there was a period when their carrier force had no striking power; steering towards the enemy when the changes were taking place, which gave the American planes the chance to locate Nagumo's force more easily and to hit it before it could hit back or even defend itself with its fighters. Most of these faults could be traced to complacent over-confidence.

Once the Japanese had lost these four fleet-carriers, and their well-trained aircrews, their continued preponderance in battleships and cruisers counted for little. These ships could only venture out in areas that could be covered by their own land-based aircraft—and the Japanese defeat in the long struggle for Guadalcanal was principally due to lack of air control. The Battle of Midway gave the Americans an invaluable breathing space until, at the end of the year, their new 'Essex' class fleet carriers began to become available. Thus it can reasonably be said that Midway was the turning point that spelt the ultimate doom of Japan.

THE SOUTH-WEST PACIFIC AFTER MIDWAY

Even so, although the outcome of the Midway battle severely handi-capped—and, indeed, curbed—the Japanese advance in the South-west Pacific, it did not halt it. While the Japanese could no longer use their fleet to press their advance, they still chose to continue it, and in a two-pronged way—in New Guinea, by overland attack across the Papuan Peninsula in the east of that vast island; and in the Solomons by a process of hopping from island to island, establishing airfields along the chain to cover successive short hops.

NEW GUINEA AND PAPUA

When the Japanese entered the war in December 1941, most of Aus-tralia's operational forces were fighting with the British Eighth Army in North Africa—although they were to be recalled when the emergency developed. In New Guinea, so menacingly close to Australia itself, the only

The Tide Turns in the Pacific
August 1942 / Nov 1944

considerable force was one of brigade size posted at Port Moresby, the capital of Papua, on the south coast. The very small Australian garrisons on the north coast, as well as in the Bismarck Archipelago and the Solomons, were withdrawn as soon as the Japanese approached. But it was considered essential to hold on to Port Moresby, because Japanese air attacks from there could have reached Queensland itself, on the Australian mainland. The Australian people were, naturally, sensitive to such a threat.

Early in March 1942, the Japanese, from Rabaul, had landed at Lae on the north coast of New Guinea, close to the Papuan Peninsula. But, as already related, their seaborne expeditionary force to capture Port Moresby was turned back in consequence of the otherwise indecisive Battle of the Coral Sea in May. Meanwhile General Douglas MacArthur had been appointed Allied Commander-in-Chief of the South-west Pacific area. And after the Battle of Midway early in June, the Allied position became much more secure, directly as well as indirectly, since most of the Australian troops had by now returned home, and new divisions were being formed, while the United States had placed two divisions and eight air groups in Australia. In Papua, too, Australia's strength was increased to more than the size of a division—two brigades at Port Moresby, and a third at Milne Bay on the eastern tip of the peninsula, while two battalions were pushing forward over the Kokoda trail to Buna, on the north coast, with the aim of establishing an airbase there to provide cover for the planned amphibious advance by the Allies westward along the coast of New Guinea.

But on July 21 this move was forestalled, and the apparently fading Japanese threat revived, when the Japanese landed near Buna—with some 2,000 men—as part of their renewed attempt to capture Port Moresby, this time by overland attack. The Allies had a further shock when, on the 29th, the Japanese took Kokoda, nearly half way across the peninsula—and by mid-August, with a force built up to a strength of over 13,000 men, they were pressing the Australians back along the jungle track. But although the peninsula here was little more than a hundred miles wide, the trail had to cross the Owen Stanley Mountains, at a point 8,500 feet high, and the growing difficulties of supply across such difficult terrain—naturally worse for the attacking side—were multiplied by Allied air attacks. Within a month the Japanese advance was brought to a halt some thirty miles short of its objective. Meantime, a smaller Japanese force (of 1,200 men, reinforced to 2,000) had landed in Milne Bay on August 25, and succeeded in reaching the edge of the airstrip there after five days' fierce fighting, but was then counterattacked by the Australians and driven to re-embark.

By mid-September MacArthur had concentrated in Papua the bulk of the 6th and 7th Australian Divisions, and an American regiment, ready to take the offensive. On the 23rd General Sir Thomas Blamey, the Australian Commander-in-Chief of the Allied Land Forces, South-west Pacific, arrived at Port Moresby to take control of the operations. His forces in their turn met fierce resistance as they strove to fight their way back to Kokoda, and on to Buna, but their difficulties of supply were eased by increasing use of air transport. By the end of October the Japanese were dislodged from the last of the three successive positions they had constructed near Templeton's Crossing, at the top of the range, and on November 2 the Australians reoccupied Kokoda, reopening the airfield there. The Japanese tried to make a fresh stand on the Kumusi River, but their defence was overcome with the aid of bridging material dropped by air, and the flank threat of fresh Australian and American troops who were brought forward by air to the north coast.

Nevertheless the Japanese managed to make a prolonged final stand around Buna throughout December, and it was not until further Allied reinforcements had arrived, by sea and air, that the last pocket of Japanese resistance on the coast was liquidated, on January 21, 1943. In the six months' campaign they had lost over 12,000 men. The Australian battle-casualties were 5,700 and the American 2,800—a total of 8,500—while they had suffered three times as many from sickness in the tropical damp-heat and malarial jungles. They had proved, however, that they could successfully fight the Japanese even in such appalling jungle conditions, and that air-power in all its varied forms provided a decisive advantage.

GUADALCANAL

The Guadalcanal campaign developed from the mutual, and natural, desire of General MacArthur and Admiral Nimitz to exploit the Midway victory by a speedy change-over from the defensive to the counteroffensive in the Pacific. Their desire was backed by their respective chiefs in Washington, General Marshall and Admiral King, in so far as such an offensive could be reconciled with the grand strategy, agreed with the British, of 'beat Germany first'. For any early counteroffensive the only feasible area was the South-west Pacific, and on that all were agreed. But a conflict of opinion arose, also quite naturally, as to who should direct and command the counteroffensive. Now that enemy pressure on the Hawaiian Islands, in the Central Pacific, had been not only relieved but removed, the Navy became all the more eager to play its full part in what basically had to be an amphibious operation. It was only with reluctance that Admiral King had accepted the policy of tackling Germany first and building up American strength in Britain for that purpose. British arguments against an early cross-Channel attack, in 1942, had caused Marshall to veer round towards the idea of giving the Pacific priority, and King was delighted to welcome such a change of view, even if it were no more than temporary—and unlikely to be endorsed by President Roosevelt as a definite change of policy.

But agreement about a changeover to the offensive in the South-west Pacific immediately sharpened the argument as to who should be in charge of it, and in the last part of June the debate became passionate. The outcome was a compromise, expressed in the Joint Chiefs of Staff directive of July 2, inspired by Marshall. The offensive was to be carried out in three stages, the first being the occupation of the Santa Cruz islands and the eastern Solomons, especially Tulagi and Guadalcanal. For this purpose the boundary between the zones was shifted, so that this area came under Nimitz, who would therefore conduct the first stage of the offensive. The second stage would be the capture of the rest of the Solomons, and of the New Guinea coast as far as the Huon Peninsula, just beyond Lae, while the third stage would be the capture of Rabaul, the main Japanese base in the South-west Pacific, and the rest of the Bismarck Archipelago—these two stages falling to MacArthur's direction under the redistribution of zones.

The plan under this compromise did not please MacArthur who, immediately after the Midway victory, advocated a speedy and large-scale attack on Rabaul, confidently predicting that he could quickly capture it, with the rest of the Bismarcks, and drive the Japanese back to Truk (in the 700-miles-distant Caroline Islands). But he was brought to recognise that he could not hope to obtain the force he considered necessary—a marine division and two carriers, in addition to the three infantry divisions he already had. So the compromise three-stage plan was adopted—and took much longer to complete than any of the leaders had expected.

The Allies' plan, for capturing the eastern Solomons, was forestalled—as it had been in Papua. On July 5 reconnaissance planes reported that the Japanese had moved some forces from Tulagi to the larger nearby island of Guadalcanal (ninety miles long and twenty-five miles wide), and were building an airstrip at Lunga Point (this later came to be called 'Henderson Field'). The obvious danger of Japanese bombers operating from there caused an immediate reconsideration of American strategy, and Guadalcanal itself became the primary objective. With its backbone of wooded mountains, heavy rainfall, and unhealthy climate it was not a favourable objective for any campaign.

The overall strategic direction of the operation, under Nimitz, was entrusted to Vice-Admiral Robert L. Ghormley, the area C.-in-C., while Rear-Admiral Fletcher was in tactical command of it—he also controlled the three covering carrier groups built around the *Enterprise*, *Saratoga*, and *Wasp* respectively. Land-based air support came from Port Moresby, Queensland, and various island airstrips. The landing force, commanded by Major-General Alexander A. Vandegrift, comprised the 1st Marine Division and a regiment of the 2nd, totalling 19,000 Marines carried in nineteen transports, with escorts. No sign of the enemy was seen as the armada approached, and early on August 7 the air and naval bombardment opened, while the landings began at 0900 hours. By evening 11,000 Marines were ashore, and the airfield was occupied next morning; it was found to be nearly completed. The 2,200 Japanese on Guadalcanal, who were largely construction workers, had mostly fled into the jungle. On Tulagi, the Japanese garrison of 1,500 troops had put up a tougher resistance, and it was not until the second evening that they were overcome and wiped out, by the 6,000 Marines who had landed there.

Japanese reaction was prompt—and, ironically, all the quicker because reports had led the Japanese to believe that the American landing force was only a fraction of its actual numbers. Thus they did not pause to prepare an adequate response, but sent off a series of reinforcing driblets, repeatedly increased, so that what the two sides had conceived as a swift stroke and counterstroke developed into a protracted campaign.

The Japanese naval escorts were stronger, however, and their successive advances produced a series of momentous naval clashes. The first of these, and the worst for the Americans, was the Battle of Savo Island, off the north-west coast of Guadalcanal. On the evening of August 7 Vice-Admiral Mikawa, the Japanese Commander-in-Chief at Rabaul, assembled a force of five heavy cruisers, with two light cruisers, and set off for Guadalcanal. Slipping undetected next day through what was called 'the Slot', the narrow waters between the two chains of the Solomons, he approached Savo Island in the evening—just after Fletcher had withdrawn the American carriers because their fuel and fighter strength were running short. Although the Allied cruiser and destroyer force had taken up precautionary dispositions for the night, co-operation and watch-keeping were poor. In the early hours of the morning Mikawa took by surprise in turn its southerly and northerly groups, and within an hour was steaming back through the Slot, leaving behind four Allied heavy cruisers sunk or sinking, and one badly damaged— five out of five—while his own were almost undamaged.

The Japanese profited greatly from their superior skill at night-fighting, helped by their superior optical instruments, and especially their 24-inch 'long lance' torpedoes. It was one of the worst defeats that the U.S. Navy suffered at sea in the war. Fortunately for the Allies, Mikawa did not complete his mission by destroying the mass of transport and supply ships lying defenceless in Lunga Roads—being unaware that the Allied carriers had been withdrawn, and thus expecting early counterattack from the air if he did not quickly regain the relative shelter of the Slot. Moreover, he did not know that the American landing on Guadalcanal was on any such large scale as it actually was. A commander should be judged in the light of the information he has at the moment he makes his decisions.

But all that remained of the Allied naval forces withdrew southward that afternoon to avoid further attack, although less than half the Marines' supplies of food and ammunition had been unloaded by then. Troop rations were reduced to two meals a day, and for the next two weeks the Marines were isolated—without naval support and also without air cover until Henderson Field was brought into use on the 20th with the arrival of the first squadrons of Marine aircraft. Even then, such air cover was narrowly limited.

The Japanese forfeited the opportunity largely because they still greatly underestimated the strength of the Marine force landed on Guadalcanal— estimating it at 2,000 men, and assuming that a force of 6,000 would be sufficient to overcome them and regain the island. They sent off two advanced detachments, totalling 1,500 men, carried in destroyers, which landed east and west of Lunga Point on August 18; these attacked without waiting for the follow-up convoy, and were promptly wiped out by the Marines. The follow-up convoy—of only 2,000 men—sailed from Rabaul on the 19th. While small in itself, it was given strong naval aid—being intended as a bait to draw the U.S. fleet into a trap, as had been the idea at Midway. The advance was led by the light carrier *Ryujo*, itself part of the bait, while behind came two battleships and three cruisers under Admiral Kondo, and behind them the fleet carriers *Zuikaku* and *Shokaku* under Admiral Nagumo.

This baited plan led to what was called the Battle of the Eastern Solomons, but not to the achievement of the trap that the Japanese intended. For Admiral Ghormley received timely warning of their approach from 'Coast-watchers'—an organisation composed mostly of Royal Australian Navy Intelligence officers and local planters. He concentrated three naval task forces south-east of Guadalcanal, built round the carriers *Enterprise*, *Saratoga*, and *Wasp*. The *Ryujo* was sighted on the morning of the 24th, and sunk in the afternoon by aircraft from the American carriers. Meanwhile the two Japanese fleet carriers had also been sighted, so that when the expected attacks came from them the American carriers had their full fighter strength in the air to meet them, and took heavy toll, knocking out over seventy of eighty enemy planes employed, and losing only seventeen of their own. The *Enterprise* was the only ship that suffered any serious damage. After this indecisive battle the Japanese fleet retired during the night, and so did the American.

After this ineffectual naval effort there was a lull, except on land, where the weak Japanese forces made unsuccessful efforts to reach Henderson Field, being beaten off by the Marines, although they so 'fought to the death' that almost all of them were killed. But they were replaced by a series of small detachments brought along by destroyers—in such regular succession that the process came to be called by the Marines the 'Tokyo Express'. Thereby the Japanese ground strength on Guadalcanal was steadily increased, a further 6,000 men being shuttled there by early September. On the night of September 13/14 this force fiercely attacked the Marines' position—which came to be called 'Bloody Ridge'—but all its attacks were repelled, and its loss was over 1,200 men.

Meanwhile, however, the U.S. Navy in that area was badly depleted by the loss of the carriers *Saratoga* and *Wasp* to Japanese submarine attacks—the former badly damaged and the latter sunk. As the *Enterprise* was still under repair, this left only the *Hornet* to provide air cover.

After the failure of the earlier Japanese attempts to retake Guadalcanal, Imperial General Headquarters issued a new directive on September 18 that gave this campaign priority to the one in New Guinea. But the Japanese still greatly underestimated the size of the Marine force there, putting it as no more than 7,500, and on this calculation reckoned that the despatch of a division would suffice, in co-operation with the temporary use of their Combined Fleet. The preliminary seaborne move of the first reinforcing contingent led to another naval battle off the coast of Guadalcanal, on October 11/12. In this fight, called the Battle of Cape Esperance, the respective losses were not heavy but on balance favourable to the Americans—which came as a moral tonic. During the battle, however, the Japanese managed to land reinforcements that brought their total of troops up to 22,000. At the same time the Americans brought their strength up to 23,000—with 4,500 more on Tulagi.

Even so, mid-October was the most critical period of the campaign for them, particularly when a bombardment from two Japanese battleships ploughed up Henderson Field, set fuel stocks on fire, and reduced the number of their planes there from ninety to forty-two—while they also forced the U.S. Army's heavy bombers to fly back to the New Hebrides. Repeated

Japanese bombing attacks were another strain, while the humid heat and inadequate diet were taking a heavy toll.

On October 24 the Japanese land offensive developed, having been delayed by torrential rain and the dense jungle. The main attack came up from the south, but the Marines were well-posted in their defensive position and their artillery was well handled. The Japanese were beaten off, their losses running into thousands compared with a few hundred on the American side, and by the 26th they were driven to retreat, leaving behind about 2,000 dead.

Meanwhile the Combined Fleet under Yamamoto had advanced with two fleet carriers, two light carriers, four battleships, fourteen cruisers, and forty-four destroyers, and cruised to the north-east of the Solomons, awaiting the expected news that Henderson Field had been captured by the Army. On the American side, the naval strength was barely half, despite the arrival of the new battleship *South Dakota* and several cruisers. In battleships, there was only one against four. But the carrier *Hornet* had now been reinforced by the repaired *Enterprise*, and that was more important in modern naval terms. Fresh vigour also came with the appointment of Admiral Halsey to replace the overtired Ghormley. The two fleets clashed on October 26 in what was called the Battle of the Santa Cruz Islands, a battle once again dominated by air action on either side. The *Hornet* was sunk and the *Enterprise* damaged, while on the other side the *Shokaku* was badly damaged and also the light carrier *Zuiho*, before the two fleets retired from the scene on the 27th. But in planes lost the Japanese suffered much the worse—seventy of them failed to return, and in the ten-day period culminating in this battle they lost 200— to add to the 300 they had lost since the last week of August. Moreover the Americans soon received a reinforcement of over 200 planes, as well as the rest of the 2nd Marine Division and part of the Americal Division.

Nevertheless the Japanese were also reinforced sufficiently to resume their efforts—impelled by pride, and also gulled by absurdly optimistic reports of the damage they had inflicted. These efforts led to the two clashes known as the 'Naval Battle of Guadalcanal'. The first took place in the early hours of Friday November 13, and although it lasted barely half an hour, the Americans had two cruisers sunk while the Japanese battleship *Hiei* was so badly crippled that it had to be scuttled next day—the first Japanese battleship lost in the war.

The second part of this naval battle came on the night of the 14th/15th, and with roles reversed, when the Japanese tried to bring down a reinforcement of 11,000 troops in a convoy with a large destroyer escort under the indomitable Rear-Admiral Tanaka, covered by Admiral Kondo's heavier ships. Seven of the transports were sunk in the approach, and although the other four reached Guadalcanal they were smashed by air attack in the morning, so that only 4,000 of the troops were landed, and very few of the urgently needed supplies.

In the accompanying naval battle, the American destroyers suffered badly, but then Kondo's remaining battleship, the *Kirishima*, was crippled when, at midnight, the radar-controlled guns of the U.S. battleship *Washington* opened fire on it at a range of 8,400 yards, and hit it so devastatingly that it was put out of action within seven minutes, and soon had to be scuttled.

Meanwhile on land the Marines and the other American troops, having now the advantage in supplies, had gone over to the offensive, and were expanding their perimeter. By the end of the month the American air strength on the island had risen to 188, and the Japanese no longer dared to ship either reinforcements or supplies by slow convoy. In December they were reduced to sending driblets of both in submarines.

The Japanese Navy had suffered so heavily that its chiefs urged the abandonment of Guadalcanal, but the Army chiefs, who had now assembled 50,000 troops at Rabaul, were still hoping to send them to reinforce the 25,000 now on the island. Meanwhile, however, the Americans had built up their strength on Guadalcanal to over 50,000 by January 7, 1943, which were now well-supplied, while the Japanese, who had been reduced to one-third of normal rations, were so weakened by hunger and malaria that they could not hope to take the offensive—tenaciously as they still fought on the defensive.

So on January 4 Imperial G.H.Q. reluctantly faced realities, and gave the order for them to be gradually evacuated. Unaware of this decision, the Americans pushed forward cautiously, so that the Japanese were able to take away all their troops in three moves, starting on the night of February 1 and completed on the night of February 7, losing only one destroyer in the process.

On balance, however, the prolonged struggle for Guadalcanal was a very serious defeat for Japan. She had lost some 25,000 men, including 9,000 from hunger and disease, while American losses were much smaller. Worse still she had lost at least 600 planes, with their trained crews. At the same time America's strength in all spheres was continually increasing, as her mobilisation of manpower and industry got into its stride.

BURMA MAY 1942–MAY 1943—THE RIPOSTE MISCARRIES

By May 1942, with the British withdrawal from Burma into India, the Japanese had achieved the planned limit of their expansion in South-east

Asia, so they changed over to the defensive and sought to consolidate their conquests. Meanwhile the British made plans for a come-back when the next dry season came, in November 1942. None of them proved feasible—because of logistical difficulties. And the only one even attempted, the very limited Arakan offensive, resulted in a disastrous failure.*

The crucial area logistically, Assam and Bengal, had never been regarded or planned as a military base area. Airfields, depots, roads, railways, and pipelines all had to be built, ports enlarged, and the whole region reorganised.

First of the major difficulties facing the India Command was shipping, as most of its needs had to come from overseas. But all other theatres of war had priority, and little shipping was left for India, even when threatened with invasion, after providing for the Atlantic and Arctic convoys, the Mediterranean and Pacific theatres. The amount allotted for India was only about one-third of what was necessary for the build-up of the area as the springboard for an offensive.

Internal transport was also a major difficulty. The road and rail systems of north-east India were old and haphazard. They required great improvement before the supplies coming from Calcutta and the other ports could be carried to the front line. Shortages of all kinds hampered the progress of the work. So did the monsoons, which caused landslides and carried away bridges. Japanese air raids also contributed, while labour troubles and political unrest were worse hindrances—particularly the widespread disorder and risks that followed the failure of the Cripps mission in the late summer of 1942, when the Indian Congress called for a civil disobedience campaign. This was fomented by pro-Japanese elements as well as by the worsening economic situation in India. The worst handicap of all was the lack of locomotives—Wavell had begged for at least 185, but was given four!

Yet the logistical problem had been vastly multiplied by the decision that India was to be built up as a base, to hold thirty-four divisions and 100 air squadrons. Over a million men were employed in building the 220 new airfields, thus greatly reducing the labour force available for other projects—of which road-building was the primary need. Moreover the supply problem was increased by the need to feed 400,000 civilian refugees from Burma.

Although the Indian Command now comprised a large number of divisions, most of them were newly formed ones produced by the wartime expansion of the Indian Army; they lacked equipment and training, as well as experienced officers and N.C.O.s. The few that had some battle experience were exhausted and depleted not only by the Burma campaign but by the ravages of malaria, while they had lost most of their equipment in the

* For map, see p. 514.

retreat. Only three of some fifteen divisions nominally available were in any respect fit for operations in the near future.

Administrative problems were accentuated by Command problems, especially with the Chinese forces which had withdrawn into India, with the 10th U.S. Army Air Force, and with the prickly General Stilwell.

Another crucial factor was the need for air superiority—to protect India itself, to ensure continual supplies to China, and to provide the air cover essential for the success of any attempt to reconquer Burma. Fortunately, as soon as the monsoon had come, in May 1942, the Japanese had sent a large number of their aircraft to help the South-west Pacific campaigns, and had given the remainder a period of rest. That enabled the Allies to build up their own air strength in comparative peace. By September, 1942 there were thirty-one British and Indian squadrons in India. Of these, however, six were unfit for operations, nine were kept for the defence of Ceylon, and five were employed for transport and reconnaissance duties—leaving only seven fighter and four bomber squadrons for operations in north-east India. But the flow of aircraft, from both Britain and the U.S.A., was increasing monthly, and by February 1943 there would be fifty-two squadrons. Moreover the aircraft themselves were being replaced by newer types—Mitchells, Hurricanes, Liberators, Beaufighters. Most of them could go straight to the new airfields in Assam and Bengal, as the possibility of a seaborne invasion of India had become slight after the naval battles of the Coral Sea and Midway.

In April 1942 Wavell had reorganised the India Command. The Central Command H.Q., now at Agra, was responsible for training and supply, while there were three regional Army Commands: the North-western, the Southern, and the Eastern, which was the operational one.

Planning for the reconquest of Burma entailed co-operation with the Chinese armies, both those now in Assam and those in the Yunnan province of China. The Chinese plan, of October 1942, was for a converging advance on Burma by fifteen Chinese divisions, so-called, from Yunnan and three from Assam, together with some ten British or Indian divisions. The role of the latter, in the Chinese plan, was not only to invade northern Burma but to launch a seaborne attack on Rangoon. Wavell agreed to the plan in principle, although dubious whether what he considered the two essential requirements were obtainable—sufficiently powerful air forces to dominate the sky over Burma; and a strong British fleet, with four or five carriers, to dominate the Indian Ocean and cover the Rangoon attack. The second requirement was, in fact, impossible—in view of naval commitments elsewhere. Chiang Kai-Shek—regarding these essential conditions as

Wavell's quibbles and as a sign that the British were not going to make a serious effort, angrily abandoned his part in the operation, at the end of 1942.

THE ARAKAN OFFENSIVE, DECEMBER 1942–MAY 1943

Wavell nevertheless decided to carry out a limited offensive to recover the Arakan coastal region by a hundred-mile advance down the Mayu Peninsula, combined with a seaborne invasion of Akyab island, at the tip of the next peninsula, to recapture the airfields there—from which Japanese squadrons could attack most of north-east India. If the Allied squadrons could be re-established there they could cover all of north and central Burma. This important part of the plan, however, was dropped because of the lack of landing craft.

Even so, Wavell persisted with the overland advance into Arakan rather than do nothing. The 14th Indian Division started to advance in December 1942, but moved so slowly that the commander of the Japanese 15th Army, General Iida, was able to send reinforcements thither and halt the British advance by the end of January—while he sent still more in February. Yet Wavell insisted that the advance must be continued, despite the arguments and protests of General Noel Irwin, the Commander of the Eastern Army, who warned him that the troops were badly depleted, and their morale affected, by malaria. Thus the Japanese were able to strike against the 14th Division's rear, and reached Htizwe on the Mayu River by March 18, thereby uncovering its flank and causing it to retreat. The 14th Indian Division was now replaced by the 26th, but the Japanese counterstroke continued, over the Mayu, reaching the coast at Indin early in April. The Japanese then pushed on northward, with the aim of capturing the line Maungdaw–Buthidaung by May, when the monsoon season was due, and thus dislocate any British plans for a renewed advance into Burma during the next dry season—from November 1943 to May 1944.

On April 14 Lieutenant-General W. J. Slim, 15th Indian Corps, took over command of the forces in Arakan, and was appalled to find how badly their physical and moral state had suffered from the ravages of malaria and the battle-losses due to frontal attacks on Japanese positions. While hoping to hold the Maungdaw–Buthidaung line, between the sea and the Mayu River, he planned to withdraw farther if necessary to a line running inland from Cox's Bazar, a further fifty miles northward and just over the frontier. Here the country was comparatively open, and thus more suited to the British advantage in artillery and tanks than the jungles and swamps of the Mayu

Peninsula, while the Japanese communications up the coast would be more stretched and thus more vulnerable.

But neither plan came into effect. For the Japanese drove the British to abandon Buthidaung after dark on May 6, and that flanking threat led to the abandonment of Maungdaw, on the coast. And the Japanese then decided to stop on the newly captured line, as the monsoon was due. In sum, the British attempt to recapture Akyab and its airfields—by an overland advance and without seaborne aid—had proved a complete, and dismal, failure. The Japanese had shown their skill in flanking moves and infiltrations through the jungle, while the British had damped the spirit of their troops by costly frontal attacks and blundering disregard for the indirect approach. By May 1943 they were back on the line they had held the previous autumn.

THE CHINDITS

The only glimmer of light in this darkly clouded phase of the war came, at the northern end of the Burmese theatre, from the first 'Chindit' operation—a name taken by its initiator, Orde Wingate, from a mythical beast, the Chinthe, half lion and half eagle, of which statues are numerous in Burmese pagodas. His imagination was caught by the way this griffin-like beast symbolised the close ground-and-air co-operation needed in such operations and by such forces. The fact that the first operations were carried out across and beyond the Chindwin River, in northern Burma, may have helped to engrave the name on the minds of the public.

In the autumn of 1938 Orde Wingate, then a captain on leave from Palestine, had met, and made a strong impression on, a number of influential people—as he had earlier that year on General Wavell, then the Commander in Palestine, and Brigadier John Evetts, who was in charge of the northern area.* But on returning to Palestine in December he found that his political activities in Zionist circles had made him such an object of suspicion in British official quarters that Wavell's successor, General Haining —who had originally approved the 'S.N.S.' organisation—had decided to remove him from control of it and appoint him to an innocuous job at his

---

* He came to see me several times to discuss the training of the 'S.N.S.'—'Special Night Squads'—that he had been allowed to organise in the spring, from young and picked members of the 'underground' Jewish defence force, the Hagana, to tackle the Arab armed bands which had been causing much trouble in Palestine. He told me how he had been applying my tactical ideas in such guerrilla-type operations, and gave me a set of his papers on the subject. He also emphasised with evident pride, at that time, that he was a distant cousin of T. E. Lawrence— although he later tended to disparage Lawrence when he himself became famous. At Wingate's request I wrote to Winston Churchill about him, to effect an introduction.

own headquarters. Then, in May 1938, he was sent home at Haining's request, and given a minor staff post in Anti-Aircraft Command.

But in the autumn of 1940 he was rescued from this backwater and sent to organise a guerrilla campaign in Ethiopia against the Italian control of East Africa. The appointment, suggested by Leo Amery, who had joined the Cabinet, was clinched by Wavell's prompt acceptance of the proposal. The successful conclusion of this East African Campaign in May 1941 was followed by another slump in Wingate's personal fortunes, and to a state of depression that caused him to attempt suicide during a bout of malaria. But when convalescing at home he was rescued by a call to fresh opportunity, this time arising from the British disasters in the Far East. The opportunity was once again provided by Wavell, who had himself been removed from the Middle East Command in June, after the failure of the summer offensive there, and sent to India. At the end of the year Wavell found himself caught up in a greater crisis when the Japanese invaded Malaya and Burma successively. In February 1942, when the situation even in Burma was looking bleak, Wavell asked for Wingate to be sent to him with a view to developing guerrilla operations there.

After his arrival Wingate urged the creation of what were called 'Long Range Penetration Groups' trained to operate in the Burmese jungle and strike at the Japanese communications as well as against the Japanese outposts. He argued that the force must be sufficiently large to strike with strong effect, while small enough to evade the enemy. Brigade size was considered suitable, and the 77th Indian Brigade was reorganised for the purpose. These 'Chindits' must be better jungle fighters than the Japanese, and they needed to comprise experts in such kinds of fighting, particularly experts in demolition and radio communication. They must also develop ground-and-air co-operation, as they would be dependent on supply by air; for that reason a small R.A.F. section was attached to each column. Within the column, pack-animals would provide the transport.

Wingate pressed for an early operation, both to restore British morale by demonstrating their power to upset the enemy's morale, and as a test of the working of such Long-Range Penetration Groups. Wavell preferred that they should be used immediately before, and during, a British general offensive, but decided in response to Wingate's desire that an earlier experiment was worth risking because of the experience and the information that could be gained.

The Brigade comprised seven columns, and for the planned operation was divided into two groups—a Northern Group of five columns, totalling 2,200 men with 850 mules, and a Southern Group of two columns, totalling

1,000 men with 250 mules. The two groups crossed the Chindwin River on the night of February 14, 1943, assisted by diverting actions on the part of the regular forces. Moving on eastward, the groups split up into their pre-arranged columns, and then carried out a series of attacks on Japanese outposts, as well as to cut railway lines, blow up bridges and create ambushes on the roads. In mid-March the columns crossed the Irrawaddy, a hundred miles east of the Chindwin. By then, however, the Japanese had awoken to the threat and deployed a large part of two divisions, of their five in Burma, to counter it. Under the counterpressure and other difficulties the columns were forced to withdraw, and by mid-April were back in India, having lost one-third of their strength and left behind most of their equipment.

The operation had little strategic effect, and Japanese casualties had been slight, but it did show that British and Indian troops could operate in the jungle, and it had provided useful experience in air supply, as well as the need for air superiority.

It also led General Mutagachi, Commander of the Japanese 15th Army, to recognise that he could not regard the Chindwin as a secure barrier, and that to forestall a British counteroffensive he would have to continue his own advance. Thereby it led to the Japanese advance across the Indian frontier in 1944, and the crucial battle of Imphal.

FUTURE PLANNING

A serious British offensive in the dry season of 1942–43 had been annulled by the combination of administrative difficulties and lack of resources. The main plan for the next dry season, of 1943–44, as decided at the Casablanca conference of January 1943, was intended to be a seaborne assault on Rangoon, called 'Operation Anakim', following British and Chinese offensives in the north of Burma and the capture of key points on the coast. Those aims meant that air superiority had to be gained, and a strong naval force assembled, with ample landing craft—as well as the solution of the administrative and overland transport problems.

The difficulties of meeting all these requirements were, clearly, so great that in the spring of 1943 Wavell was inclined to turn away from Burma, and to favour a move against Sumatra as an indirect way of approach to the defeat of the Japanese. His talks with Churchill and the Chiefs of Staff on a visit to London in April convinced them that 'Operation Anakim' must be deferred or discarded, and in its place the Sumatra move was chosen—a move code-named 'Culverin'. This indirect move became attractive to Churchill, but it had to be abandoned in its turn for the same reasons that

'Anakim' had been given up, and also because of American insistence on the importance of reopening the land route of supply to China as soon as possible. Hence southern operations were shelved, although planning for them continued. If anything at all was to be done in this theatre of war, it would have to be in the north of Burma.

CHAPTER 24

THE BATTLE OF THE ATLANTIC

The most critical period in the Battle of the Atlantic was during the second half of 1942 and the first half of 1943, but its long and fluctuating course was co-existent with the whole six years' course of the war. Indeed, it can be said to have started before the war itself, as the first ocean-going U-boats sailed from Germany to their war stations in the Atlantic on August 19, 1939. By the end of that month, on the eve of the German invasion of Poland, seventeen were out in the Atlantic, while some fourteen coastal-type U-boats were out in the North Sea.

Despite their late start in rearming themselves with submarines, the Germans had a total strength of fifty-six (although ten were not fully operational) on the outbreak of war, which was only one less than that of the British Navy. Of these, thirty were 'North Sea Ducks', unsuitable for the Atlantic.

The first score achieved was the sinking of the outward-bound liner *Athenia* on the evening of September 3, the same day that Britain declared war, two days after the German invasion of Poland. It was actually torpedoed without warning, contrary to Hitler's specific order that submarine warfare was to be conducted only in accordance with the Hague Conventions; the U-boat commander justified his action by asserting his belief that the liner was an armed merchant cruiser. During the next few days several more ships were sunk.

Then on the 17th a more important success was gained when the aircraft-carrier *Courageous* was sunk by *U.29* off the Western Approaches to the British Isles. Three days earlier the aircraft-carrier *Ark Royal* had had a narrow escape from *U.39*—which, however, was promptly counterattacked and sunk by the escorting destroyers. The manifest risks led to the fleet aircraft-carriers being withdrawn from submarine-hunting.

U-boat attacks against merchant-shipping also had considerable success. A total of forty-one Allied and neutral ships, amounting to 154,000 tons, were sunk in the opening month, September, and by the end of the year the losses reached 114 ships, and over 420,000 tons. Moreover in mid-October the *U.47* under Lieutenant Prien had penetrated the fleet anchorage at Scapa Flow and sunk the battleship *Royal Oak*, causing the temporary abandonment of this main base until the defences were improved.

It is significant, however, that in November and December, merchant shipping losses were less than half what they had been the first two months, and more shipping had been lost to mines than to U-boats. Moreover, nine U-boats had been sunk—a sixth of the total strength. Air attacks on shipping had been a nuisance, but no worse.

During this early part of the war, the German Navy placed great hopes in its surface warships, and not only in its U-boats, but such hopes were not borne out by experience. On the outbreak of war the pocket-battleship *Admiral Graf Spee* was in position in mid-Atlantic, and her sister-ship *Deutschland* (later renamed *Lützow*) in the North Atlantic—although Hitler did not allow them to start attacks on British shipping until September 26. Neither of them achieved much—and the *Graf Spee*, cornered in the mouth of the River Plate, was driven to scuttle herself in December. The new battle-cruisers *Gneisenau* and *Scharnhorst* made a brief sortie in November, but after sinking an armed merchant cruiser in the Iceland-Faeroes channel bolted for home. Allied ships were already sailing in convoy, after their experience in 1917–18, and although escorts were inadequate—and all too many ships still had none—they proved a remarkably effective deterrent.

After the fall of France in June 1940 the danger to Britain's shipping routes became much more severe. All ships passing south of Ireland were now exposed to German submarine, surface, and air attack. Except at great hazard, the only remaining route in and out was round the north of Ireland—the North-Western Approaches. Even that route could be reached, reported on, and bombed by the first of the German long-range aircraft, the four-engined Focke-Wulf 'Kondor' (the F.W. 200), operating from Stavanger in Norway and Merignac near Bordeaux. In November 1940 these long-range bombers sank eighteen ships, of 66,000 tons. Moreover the U-boats' toll had risen greatly—to a total sixty-three ships, amounting to over 350,000 tons, in the month of October.

The threat had become so serious that a large number of British warships were pulled back from anti-invasion duties and sent to the North-Western Approaches. Even so, surface and air escorts were perilously weak.

In June, the first month of the changed strategic situation, U-boat sinkings had bounded up to fifty-eight ships of 284,000 tons, and although falling a little in July, they averaged over 250,000 tons during the months that followed.

On the east coast route, minelaying by air had caused more damage than

The Battle of the Atlantic

Axis, or Axis occupied
at Nov. 1942

Convoy Routes

Main U-boat operational areas

Sept 1939/July 1942

Aug 1942/May 1945

Limit of Allied air cover

Sept 1939/July 1942

Aug 1942/May 1945

Copyright © Cassell & Co.Ltd 1970

SIERRA
LEONE

Freetown

Equator

Ascension

SOUTH ATLANTIC

OCEAN

BRAZIL

Rio de Janeiro

Montevideo

DEC 14,1939
BATTLE OF
THE RIVER PLATE

To Middle East and Far East

Cape
Town

U-boats in the later months of 1939, and after the German invasion of Norway and the Low Countries in the spring of 1940 its menacing pressure was intensified.

Moreover in the autumn the pocket-battleship *Admiral Scheer* slipped out undetected into the North Atlantic, and on November 5 attacked a convoy homeward-bound from Halifax, Nova Scotia, sinking five merchant ships and the sole escort, the armed merchant cruiser *Jervis Bay*—which sacrificed herself in gaining time for the rest of the convoy to escape. The *Scheer*'s sudden appearance on this vital convoy route temporarily disorganised the entire flow of shipping across the Atlantic, causing other convoys to be held up for two weeks, until it was known that the *Scheer* had gone on into the South Atlantic. Here she found fewer targets, but raised her toll to sixteen ships, of 99,000 tons, by the time she returned safely to Kiel on April 1 after a 'cruise' of over 46,000 miles. The cruiser *Admiral Hipper* also broke out into the Atlantic at the end of November, but at dawn on Christmas Day had a rude shock when she attacked a convoy which she soon found to be strongly escorted, as it was a troop convoy bound for the Middle East. The escorting cruisers drove off the *Hipper*, and trouble in her own machinery led her to make for Brest. From here in February she made a second sortie, and was somewhat more successful, sinking seven ships in an unescorted group steaming up the African coast, but her own fuel was running low and her captain thus decided to return to Brest. In mid-March the German Naval Staff ordered her to return home for a more thorough refit, and she got back to Kiel just before the *Scheer*. The *Hipper*'s low endurance had shown that, apart from mechanical defects, her type was not suited for commerce raiding.

Next to the U-boats and minelaying, the Germans' most effective weapon in the war at sea proved to be disguised merchant ships converted for raiding purposes, which they had been sending out on long cruises since April 1940. By the end of that year the first 'wave' of six had sunk fifty-four merchantmen, totalling 366,000 tons—largely in distant seas. Their presence, or possible presence, caused as much worry and dislocation as the sinkings they achieved, while the threat was multiplied by the masterly way in which the Germans kept them refuelled and supplied at secret rendezvous. The raiders were skilfully handled and their targets well-chosen—only one of them had been brought to action, and that had escaped serious damage. Yet their captains, with one exception, had behaved humanely, allowing the crews of the ships attacked time to take to the boats, and treating their prisoners decently.

In face of the manifold threat, above all that of U-boats in the Atlantic approaches to Britain, the Royal Navy's escort resources were heavily strained, and overstrained. From the French Atlantic ports—Brest, Lorient, and La Pallice near La Rochelle—U-boats were able to cruise as far as 25° West, whereas during the summer of 1940 the British could only provide escorts up to about 15° West, some 200 miles west of Ireland, and outward bound convoys then had to disperse, or steam on unescorted. Even in October, close escort was only extended to about 19° West—about 400 miles west of Ireland. Moreover, the usual escort was merely one armed merchant cruiser, and it was not until the end of the year that the average could be increased to two vessels. Only convoys to the Middle East were given more powerful protection.

Here it should be mentioned that Halifax in Nova Scotia was the main Western terminal for the Atlantic convoys, and that homeward-bound convoys—carrying supplies of food, oil, and munitions—were escorted by Canadian destroyers for the first 300–400 miles, after which the ocean escort took over, until the convoy reached the better-protected area of the Western Approaches.

Valuable aid towards meeting the escort problem came from the advent of the corvettes in the spring of 1940. These small vessels, of a mere 925 tons, were exhausting for the crews in rough weather, and suffered the handicap of not being fast enough to overtake, or even to keep up with, a U-boat on the surface, but they did most gallant work in escorting convoys in all weathers.

A larger aid came from the agreement which Churchill negotiated with President Roosevelt, in September, after two months' persuasive efforts, whereby fifty of the U.S. Navy's old and surplus destroyers from World War I were obtained in exchange for a ninety-nine year lease of eight British bases on the far side of the Atlantic. Although these destroyers were obsolescent, and had to be fitted with the Asdic submarine-detecting device before they could be brought into use, they were soon able to make an important contribution to the escort problem and the anti-submarine campaign. Moreover the double transfer enabled the United States to prepare bases for the protection of its own seabound and coastal shipping, while taking the first of the steps which involved that great neutral country in the Battle of the Atlantic.

The coming of winter, and bad weather, naturally brought an increase of the difficulties of convoy, and convoy escorts, but also a diminution of German submarine activity. By July 1940 German figures show that U-boat strength had been increased 50 per cent since the start of the war, that twenty-seven had been destroyed, and fifty-one remained. By the following February the effective total fell to twenty-one. But with the French bases the Germans could keep more U-boats at sea out of a reduced smaller total strength, and could also use their smaller coastal-type U-boats on the ocean routes.

On the other hand, the Italian Navy's contribution to the struggle proved negligible. Although their submarines had begun to operate in the Atlantic from August on, and by November no less than twenty-six were out on the ocean, they achieved virtually nothing.

Although the pressure of the U-boat campaign diminished during the winter, mainly due to bad weather, it was renewed early in 1941, and at the same time multiplied by Admiral Dönitz's introduction of 'wolf-pack' tactics—by several U-boats working together, instead of individually. These new tactics had been introduced in October 1940, and were developed in the months that followed.

The way they operated was that, when the existence of a convoy had been approximately established, U-boat Command H.Q. ashore would warn the nearest U-boat group, which would send a submarine to find and shadow the convoy and 'home' the others onto it by wireless. When they were assembled on the scene, they would launch night attacks on the surface, preferably up-wind of the convoy, and continue these for several nights. During daylight the U-boats would withdraw well clear of the convoy and its escort. Attacking on the surface, they had an advantage in speed over most of the escorts. Night surface attacks had been made in World War I, and Dönitz himself had described in a book before the second war how he would do them.

These new tactics took the British unawares, as they had been thinking mainly of submerged attack, and pinned their faith to the Asdic device, the underwater detecting device, which had a range of about 1,500 yards. The Asdic could not detect U-boats that were operating on the surface like torpedo-boats near the convoy, and when these submarines were employed at night, escorts were virtually blindfolded. This German exploitation of the value of night attacks by surfaced U-boats thus nullified the British preparation for submarine warfare, and threw it off balance.

The best chance of countering the new tactics lay in early location of the shadowing U-boat, the 'contact-keeper', and driving it away. If the escort could make the U-boats dive, these would be handicapped, their periscopes being useless at night. A very important countermeasure to night attacks was the illumination of the sea. At first this was dependent on star-shell and rocket flares, but these were superseded by a more efficient illuminant known as 'snowflake', which went far towards turning darkness into daylight, while a powerful searchlight, called the Leigh Light after its inventor, was fitted in aircraft that were employed in convoy escorts and anti-submarine patrols. Still more important was the development of radar to supplement visual sighting. Along with new instrumental devices came more thorough training for escort vessels and escort groups and a marked improvement in the intelligence organisation.

But all the improvements took time, and it was fortunate that the small number of U-boats at this period restricted the activity of the new 'wolf-packs'. Before the war Admiral Dönitz had estimated that if the British adopted a world-wide convoy system Germany would need 300 U-boats for decisive results, whereas in the spring of 1941 she had an operational strength of only a tenth of that scale.

That was the more fortunate because the commerce raids by other war-ships, and by aircraft, reached a new peak in March. The pocket-battleship *Scheer* and the battlecruisers *Scharnhorst* and *Gneisenau* sank or captured seventeen ships, the long-range bombers sank forty-one, and the U-boats the same number—from all causes a total of 139 ships, and over half a million tons of shipping, destroyed.

After reaching Brest on March 22, however, the battlecruisers were im-mobilised there, by damaging British air attacks on the port during April.

Just after the middle of May the new German battleship *Bismarck*, accom-panied by the new cruiser *Prinz Eugen*, sailed out into the Atlantic to multiply the threat. British Intelligence worked well and warning of their presence in the Kattegat was received in London early on May 21, while later the same day they were spotted by Coastal Command aircraft near Bergen. The battlecruiser *Hood* and the battleship *Prince of Wales*, under Vice-Admiral L. Holland, at once sailed from Scapa Flow to intercept their expected passage round the north of Iceland, and next evening, after air reconnaissance had shown they were no longer in the Bergen area, the main fleet (under Admiral Tovey), also sailed from Scapa in the same direction. On the evening of the 23rd the two German ships were sighted, by the cruisers *Norfolk* and *Suffolk*, in the Denmark Strait—between the west of Iceland and the edge of the icefields east of Greenland. By that time Admiral Holland's force was close to the southerly end of the Strait.

On paper, this force had a big advantage, as the 42,000-ton *Hood* was nominally the largest ship in either Navy, and mounted eight 15-inch guns, while it was accompanied by the new battleship *Prince of Wales* (35,000 tons and ten 14-inch guns). But the *Hood*, built in 1920, before the Washington Treaty, had never been thoroughly modernised—the coming of war in 1939 had forestalled the Board of Admiralty's decision in March that year to give her better armour-protection, horizontal and vertical—and the *Prince of Wales* was so new that her armament had not been fully tested.* The German ships, although supposed to conform to the treaty limitations—35,000 tons for battleships and 10,000 for heavy cruisers—actually displaced about 42,000 tons and 15,000 tons respectively, which enabled them to be given heavier armour-protection than appeared. Moreover their disadvantage in main armament—eight 15-inch guns in the *Bismarck* and eight 8-inch guns in the *Prinz Eugen*—was offset not only by defects in the guns of the *Prince of Wales* and superior range-finding equipment on the German side, but by the way the British ships came into action.

The Germans were sighted (in the twilight) at 5.35 a.m., an hour before sunrise, and at 5.52 all four ships opened fire—at a range of about 25,000 yards (fourteen miles). On the British side the *Hood* was leading, and both the German ships concentrated their fire on her. Besides being the flagship, she was the most vulnerable, and particularly vulnerable to plunging fire—a reason for seeking to close the range as soon as possible. The approach was nearly end-on, so the British could not bring their after turrets to bear, whereas the Germans could use their entire broadsides. Their second or third salvo took effect, and such effect that at 6 a.m. the *Hood* blew up, and sank within a few minutes—only three of her crew of over 1,400 surviving. That was all too grimly reminiscent of the fate of the British battlecruisers at Jutland a quarter of a century earlier.

The *Prince of Wales*, on which both German ships were now able to concentrate, also suffered from damaging hits from the *Bismarck*, as well as three from the *Prinz Eugen*, within a few minutes. So, at 6.13 a.m. the captain of the *Prince of Wales* wisely decided to break off the fight, and turned away under cover of a smokescreen. The range was now down to 14,600 yards. Rear-Admiral Wake-Walker, commanding the two cruisers—and now the whole force since Holland's death—confirmed the decision, and decided merely to keep touch with the enemy until the main fleet under Tovey arrived on the scene. This was now about 300 miles away, and the prospects of catching the Germans were not good, since the visibility became worse during the morning. It was thus a relief to Tovey when he heard in the early afternoon that the *Bismarck* had altered course and dropped its speed to about 24 knots.

For in the brief morning action the *Prince of Wales* had made two hits on the *Bismarck*, and one of these had caused an oil leak which reduced its fuel endurance, and led the German admiral, Lütjens, to make for a western

* There were, in fact, still some Clydeside workers on board.

French port, abandoning his raid into the Atlantic—and the alternative of turning back to Germany before the several British forces now converging towards the scene could intercept him.

That afternoon Tovey detached the 2nd Cruiser Squadron under Admiral Curteis and the aircraft-carrier *Victorious*—which had been about to start for the Mediterranean with a cargo of fighters—to proceed to a position within 100 miles of the *Bismarck* and near enough to launch the *Victorious*'s nine torpedo-bombers. These took off soon after 10 p.m., in very bad weather, and had difficulty in finding the *Bismarck*, but eventually delivered successive attacks on her soon after midnight. One hit was achieved, but did no serious damage to the heavily armoured battleship. Moreover she managed to give her pursuers the slip early on the 25th, and the rest of that day was spent in fruitless efforts to find her again.

Not until 10.30 a.m. on the 26th was she spotted and reported, by a patrolling Catalina aircraft of Coastal Command, about 700 miles distant from Brest. Tovey's widely spread fleet was by then badly placed to catch her before she reached shelter, and was also running short of fuel. But Admiral Somerville's Force H, coming up from Gibraltar, was now close enough to intercept the *Bismarck*. Moreover this force included the large carrier *Ark Royal*. The first strike miscarried, but a second one, around 9 p.m., was more successful. Two of the thirteen torpedoes released reached their mark. Although one hit was on the *Bismarck*'s armour belt and had little effect, the other, right aft, damaged her propellor, wrecked her steering gear, and jammed the rudders. That proved decisive.

While Captain Vian's destroyers held the ring, as well as making further torpedo attacks during the night, the battleships *King George V* and *Rodney* arrived on the scene, and pounded the crippled *Bismarck* with armour-piercing shell from their heavy guns for $1\frac{1}{2}$ hours. By 10.15 she was a flaming shambles. On Tovey's order the British battleships then withdrew, before U-boats or the Luftwaffe's heavy bombers arrived to endanger them, leaving the cruisers to finish off the sinking ship. The *Dorsetshire* did this, with three torpedoes, and the *Bismarck* disappeared under the waves at 10.36.

Before the end came she had suffered, and survived, at least eight, and possibly twelve, torpedo hits, and many more heavy shell hits. That was a remarkable tribute to her designers.

The *Prinz Eugen* had left the *Bismarck* on the 24th, to refuel in mid-Atlantic, but after doing so she had developed engine defects, so her Captain had decided to abandon his excursion and make for Brest. Although her approach to that port was detected, she reached it safely on June 1.

However, in the end these dramatic events of May 1941 marked the climax, and final defeat, of the German plans and efforts to win the Battle of the Atlantic with surface ships.

The U-boat campaign continued for a much longer time, and became a grave menace, although it ran a fluctuating course.

In May U-boat sinkings rose sharply and in June again reached the high figure of over 300,000 tons—to be exact, sixty-one ships of 310,000 tons. That was as many ships as there were in a single large convoy. It was remarkable that sailors were not deterred from manning them, and there was never a shortage of crews.

A number of important counteracting factors came into play, however, that spring. On March 11 the United States Lend-Lease Bill became law, and in that same month the American 'Atlantic Fleet Support Group', of destroyers and flying-boats, was formed. In April, the American 'Security Zone', patrolled by U.S. Navy forces, was extended eastward from 60° to 26° West.

Also in March, American air bases were opened on the east coast of Greenland, and installations in Bermuda, while in May the U.S. Navy took over the leased base at Argentia in the south-east of Newfoundland. Early in July U.S. Marines relieved the British garrison at Reykjavik in Iceland, and from then on U.S. naval forces protected American shipping to and from Iceland. American 'neutrality' in the Atlantic was becoming markedly less neutral. The refitting of British ships in American yards had already been approved in April, while the building of warships and merchant-ships on Lend-Lease account had started.

Meanwhile Canada was becoming more strongly a relief to Britain in the Atlantic struggle. A Canadian Escort Force was created in June, and based on St John's, Newfoundland. The Royal Canadian Navy now took the responsibility for ocean anti-submarine escort eastwards to a rendezvous south of Iceland. Thus the British Admiralty's plans for continuous escort became possible.

In the summer of 1941, Canadian and British escorts met and handed over their convoys to one another at the Mid-Ocean Meeting Point in about 35° West. The Iceland escorts and the Western Approaches escorts met, and handed over at the Eastern Ocean Meeting Point in about 18° West.

From July onwards, too, a close escort group accompanied Gibraltar convoys the whole way there, and continuous escort, down the West African coast, was also given to the Sierra Leone convoys.

Convoys now could be provided with an average of five escort vessels. A convoy of forty-five ships had a perimeter of over thirty miles to protect.

Even so, each escort vessel's Asdic would only sweep an arc of a mile—so there were still wide gaps through which a U-boat could penetrate without being detected.

As to air cover, the addition of Lend-Lease Catalina flying-boats from the spring onward extended such cover to some 700 miles from the British Isles (forcing the U-boats away from Western Approaches) 600 miles from Canada, and 400 miles to the south of Iceland. But a gap about 300 miles wide remained in mid-Atlantic, and the very long-range American Liberators, which could have covered it, were not regularly available until the end of March 1943, and by mid-April only forty-one were in service.

Meanwhile, the number of U-boats was increasing. By July 1941, sixty-five were operational and in October eighty. The total U-boat strength on September 1 was 198—while forty-seven had been lost so far. In sum, new U-boats were entering service much faster than they were being sunk. Moreover U-boats were being made stronger. Their welded pressure hulls were proving more difficult to break than the British plated and riveted hulls and a depth-charge had to explode much closer than before for a kill.

During September four convoys suffered heavy losses—all of these lacking adequate air cover.

That month, however, following an August meeting between Roosevelt and Churchill, co-operation between the two navies was increased still more by the President's approval of the well-planned American 'Western Hemisphere Defence Plan Number 4'. Under this the U.S. Navy was permitted to escort convoys of non-American ships, and started to provide escorts for certain Atlantic convoys eastwards as far as the Mid-Ocean Meeting Point, while this Meeting Point was moved eastwards to about 22° West.

This helped to ease the British problem of providing adequate escorts between the British Isles and the Mid-Ocean Meeting Point. By the end of the year they had been increased to eight groups, each of three destroyers and about six corvettes. A further eleven groups, each of five destroyers, were nominally in reserve to reinforce the escort of any convoy that might be in trouble, or to deal with the U-boat concentrations, but were largely occupied with routine tasks.

In October U-boat sinkings fell to thirty-two ships of 156,000 tons. Significantly no ships were sunk within 400 miles of a Coastal Command base. That showed the reluctance of U-boats to enter zones covered by long-range reconnaissance and bomber aircraft, although the drop was also due in part to the despatch of U-boats to the Mediterranean to support Rommel's operations in North Africa.

In November, U-boat sinkings fell again—to little more than a third of the October total—and in December they were smaller still in the North Atlantic. But the heavy losses in the Far East that followed Japan's entry into the war raised the total sinkings from all causes to 282 ships of nearly 600,000 tons.

In the West, the German long-range bombers had become a greater menace than U-boats during the second half of 1941, especially to the Gibraltar convoys. This led to a realisation of the need for fighters in close support of any convoy, and thus to the introduction of the first escort carrier, H.M.S. *Audacity*, with catapult-launched fighters, in June. She played a key part in the successful defence of a homeward-bound Gibraltar convoy in December, although herself sunk in the nine-day fight.

At the end of that year the total of operational U-boats was eighty-six, and about 150 more were in training or running trials. But as fifty were now in the Mediterranean or its approaches, only thirty-six were left for use in the North Atlantic. A sweep for supply ships there in June had resulted in nine being intercepted, and to the withdrawal of U-boats from the South Atlantic. During the nine months April to December 1941 the total German and Italian submarine sinkings had been 328 ships of 1,576,000 tons, but only one-third of these had been sailing in convoy. Moreover twenty of the thirty submarines lost had been destroyed by convoy escorts. It was clear that stronger escorting, and evasive routing, had temporarily gained the upper hand over the U-boats.

It may be useful to give here a summary of the escort situation at the beginning of 1942. The three great operational bases of the Western Approaches Command under Admiral Sir Percy Noble were Liverpool, Greenock and Londonderry, and controlled twenty-five escort groups—totalling about seventy destroyers and ninety-five smaller craft.

They were in four categories: (i) short-endurance destroyers for Middle East and Arctic convoys on the first part of their passage, and for the liners when they started bringing American troops across; (ii) long-distance destroyers and corvettes for the North Atlantic convoys, from the Western Ocean Meeting Point to Britain, and for the Gibraltar convoys; (iii) long-range sloops, destroyers, and cutters for the Sierre Leone convoys on the main part of their journey; (iv) anti-aircraft groups to back up escort of convoys within reach of German bombers, and for the Arctic and Gibraltar convoys.

There were also the equivalent of two groups at Gibraltar for local escort, and the Freetown Escort Force of one destroyer flotilla and about two dozen corvettes. The Newfoundland Escort Force, provided mainly by the Canadian

Navy, had fourteen destroyers and about forty corvettes, as well as a score of other vessels for local escort.

But the improving prospect in the Battle of the Atlantic suffered bad handicaps in the early part of 1942. One was a lack of aircraft. On taking over Coastal Command in the previous summer, Sir Philip Joubert de la Ferté had assessed its needs as approximately 800 aircraft of all types, and particularly emphasised the importance of long-range bombers. But in the New Year, Coastal Command's bombers were transferred to Bomber Command, and all the new ones allotted to it, for the air offensive against Germany. The clash of priorities became intense. Moreover the Fleet Air Arm was having difficulties in obtaining fighters for the thirty-one new escort carriers that had been ordered.

Another handicap was that the new frigates that were being built in America for the British were not entering service as fast as was hoped—largely because priority was being given to the landing-craft needed for a cross-Channel operation, which the Americans still hoped to launch in 1943, if not in 1942. This priority contributed greatly to the continuing weakness of British Atlantic efforts, and to the further heavy shipping losses.

A third handicap came in the early months of 1942 from America's own maritime troubles—troubles which came not only in the Pacific, from the Pearl Harbor disaster, but also in the Atlantic, from the extension of U-boat activities and America's own consequent shipping losses.

Admiral Dönitz and his staff estimated in May 1942 that to defeat Britain their sinkings must average 700,000 tons a month. They knew that in 1941 these had not reached such an average—although they did not know that the monthly average had actually been no more than 180,000 tons. But they had thought that America's entry into the war would give them increased freedom of action in the Western Atlantic, and more opportunity of finding unescorted targets.

Only a small number of U-boats could be sent to operate off the American coast, but these achieved disproportionately large results. For the American admirals were slow, and reluctant, to start convoys—as the British admirals had been in the First World War. The Americans were also slow to take other precautions. Lighted channel markers and the unrestricted use of ship's radio gave the U-boats all the help they wanted. Coastal resorts, such as Miami, continued to illuminate their sea-fronts at night with miles of neon-lighted beaches—against which the shipping was clearly silhouetted. The U-boats lay submerged offshore during the day, and moved in to attack, with guns or torpedoes, on the surface at night time.

Although there were never more than about a dozen U-boats operating off the American coast, they sank nearly half a million tons of shipping by the beginning of April—and 57 per cent consisted of tankers.

The reaction on Britain's situation was serious. The United States Navy was having to withdraw its escort vessels and aircraft to its own coastal waters, and British merchant ships, after surviving the crossing of the Atlantic, became an easy prey in American waters.

Admiral Dönitz was so encouraged by the results that he wanted to send every U-boat he could to the American seaboard. Fortunately for the Allies, Hitler's 'intuition' came to their aid at this critical moment. At his conference on January 22 he announced his conviction that Norway was 'the zone of destiny' and insisted that every surface warship and U-boat available should be sent thither to ward off an Allied invasion. Three days later Dönitz received a completely unexpected order to despatch an initial batch of eight U-boats to cover the sea-approaches to that country. The new battleship *Tirpitz* was also moved to Norway in January, and was followed by the *Scheer*, *Prinz Eugen*, *Hipper*, and *Lützow*.

There was something in his foresight, as in April Churchill did tell the British Chiefs of Staff to examine the feasibility of a landing in Norway, with the aim of relieving German pressure on the Arctic convoys—but their doubts were reinforced by the Americans, and the project never matured.

Another piece of good fortune for the Allies was that the severe winter of 1941-2 delayed U-boat training in the Baltic, with the effect that only sixty-nine submarines in all were made ready for operations in the first half of 1942. Of these, twenty-six were eventually sent to northern Norway, two to the Mediterranean, and twelve replaced losses, so that the net gain in the Atlantic was only twenty-nine.

Even as it was, Axis submarine sinkings increased monthly—in February to nearly 500,000 tons, in March to over 500,000 tons; in April there was a drop to 430,000 tons, but in May 600,000 tons and in June sinkings reached the ominous figure of 700,000 tons. By the end of June the toll for the half-year was over 3 million tons out of 4,147,406 tons sunk from all causes—of which nearly 90 per cent was in the Atlantic and Arctic. It was not until July that the monthly loss from submarines fell to just under 500,000 tons, thanks to an all-round improvement in anti-submarine methods, and the American adoption of convoy.

The improvement in the summer of 1942 proved illusory. By August the advent of freshly built U-boats had raised the total strength to over 300, and of the total about half was operational. It comprised groups off Greenland, off the Canadian coast, off the Azores, off North-west Africa, in or near the Caribbean, and off Brazil. Sinkings by U-boats in August went above the 500,000 tons mark again. In the next few months they made a particularly large bag near Trinidad, where many ships were still travelling independently. A more dubious action, politically and in terms of grand strategy, was the sinking of five Brazilian ships in mid-August, which led to a prompt declaration of war by Brazil. The use of Brazilian bases enabled the Allies to exercise much stronger control of the whole South Atlantic, and drive out surface raiders from then on.

That, however, mattered less than it would have earlier, as the place of the German armed merchant ship for commerce raiding in the far oceans was being taken over by new and larger U-boats—the so-called 'U-cruisers' of 1,600 tons, whose radius of action was 30,000 miles.

U-boats were now able to dive much deeper, to depths of 600 feet, or even more in emergency—an advantage that was soon offset, however, by the fact that depth-charges were being set to explode at greater depths—as well as being produced in greater quantity. The U-boats were also benefiting from the way that the new U-tankers could refuel them on the oceans, and from increasingly efficient wireless Intelligence. Moreover the Germans were now able to read many of the British ciphered convoy control signals again, as they had done up to August 1940.

On the other side, the new 10-centimetre radar set—which the U-boats could not intercept—was paramount among all the achievements of British scientists. When it came into full use in aircraft early in 1943, in conjunction with the Leigh Light, it restored the Allied initiative by night or in low visibility, and defeated the U-boats' radar search receivers working on $1\frac{1}{2}$ metres.

Dönitz's war diary for this period shows how worried he was about the effect of this new British location device, as well as about the increased number of British aircraft in the Eastern Atlantic.

Throughout the campaign Dönitz had shown himself a very able strategist, always probing for the soft spots and concentrating to strike when the defence was weak. He had held the initiative from the outset, and the Allied anti-submarine forces were always a stage behind.

In the second half of 1942 his plan focused on the air escort gap south of Greenland, aiming to locate Allied convoys before they reached it, to concentrate against them while they traversed it, and to withdraw when air cover was resumed.

Moreover by the autumn Dönitz had sufficient U-boats to allow a 'pack' to strike on its own initiative whenever opportunity offered.

Thus U-boat pressure increased from July on, and in November sinkings rose to 119 ships of 729,000 tons. A large proportion, however, were caught by U-boats when sailing independently, out of convoy, off South Africa or South America.

The call for escorts was increased by the naval requirements of 'Operation Torch', the American–British landings in North-west Africa, which was carried out that autumn. The Gibraltar, Sierre Leone, and Arctic convoys had to be temporarily suspended. There was also fresh demand for escorts to the troopship convoys carrying American troops from Iceland to Britain. These fast convoys had at least four destroyers to escort three troopships.

An exception to the demand for escort was provided by the conversion of the two giant 80,000-ton liners *Queen Mary* and *Queen Elizabeth* into troopships, with a carrying capacity of 15,000 men and more—the major part of a division. Their speed, over 28 knots, was too high for any destroyers to accompany them except at the start and finish of their voyages, so it was on speed alone, combined with zigzagging and ever-changing routes, that such giant liners depended for their safety. The hazardous policy succeeded so well that no submarine ever managed to intercept them on their many transatlantic journeys from August onward.

In general, the provision of naval escorts and air cover did not, and could not, keep up with the increasing menace from the output of U-boats. Of these an average of about seventeen had entered the service each month, and at the end of 1942 there were 212 operational, out of a total of 393—compared with ninety-one operational, out of 249, at the start of the year. The number destroyed was eighty-seven German, and twenty-two Italian—a total quite insufficient to offset the construction rate.

During the year Axis submarines had sunk, in all waters, 1,160 ships totalling 6,266,000 tons—while the enemy's other weapons had raised the total loss to 1,664 ships and over 7,790,000 tons.

Although about 7 million tons of new Allied shipping was put into service, even that left a further deficit of nearly a million tons to the adverse balance shown in each year's accounts since the outbreak of war. British imports during the year fell below 34 million tons—one-third less than the figure in 1939. In particular, stocks of commercial bunker fuel in Britain had fallen precariously low—only 300,000 tons, compared with a monthly consumption of 130,000 tons. Although it could be eked out from the Navy's reserve stocks, that was a course to be avoided save in grave emergency.

Thus when the Allied Conference assembled at Casablanca, on the Moroccan coast, in January 1943, to settle the next steps in Allied strategy, it was faced with a very disturbing balance-sheet of mercantile tonnage.

Until the U-boat menace was overcome, and the Battle of the Atlantic won, an effective invasion of Europe was not practicable. That battle had become as crucial as the Battle of Britain in 1940. The issue depended, basically, on which side could endure the longer, materially and psychologically.

The course of the struggle was affected by changes of command. In November, Admiral Sir Percy Noble was appointed head of the British Naval Mission in Washington, and thus became the First Sea Lord's representative on the American side of the Combined Chiefs of Staff organisation. During his twenty months' tenure as C.-in-C. of the Western Approaches he had done much to improve the anti-submarine measures, and to keep up morale among the escort and aircraft crews by the understanding he showed of their problems and the close personal touch he established. His successor, fortunately, was well chosen. This was Admiral Sir Max Horton, who had been an outstanding submarine commander in World War I, and in command of Britain's home-based submarines since early 1940. He brought an expert knowledge of submarines, and submariners, to the anti-submarine campaign, coupled with driving energy and imagination. This combination of qualities made him a fit man to match Dönitz.

Horton's plan was to develop a more powerful and concentrated counter-attack on the U-boats. The corvettes and other small craft had not got the speed sufficient to follow through in their fights with U-boats, for if they pursued them far they could not catch up with the convoys they were escorting. More destroyers and frigates were needed, working separately, to come to the aid of convoy escorts and, after making contact with the U-boats, hunt them to the death. Support groups for this purpose had already begun to be formed in September, but Horton at once developed them intensively, and even reduced the strength of the close-escort groups in order to do so. He aimed to surprise the enemy in mid-Atlantic with a co-ordinated counterattack by several of the new support groups and carrier-borne aircraft, working in co-operation with the escorts and with very long-range aircraft. He emphasised that the support groups should not waste time searching widely for the U-boats—the mistake in the past. The place to find them was near the convoys, and the support groups should work closely with the convoy escort groups. Each of these while in the Greenland air gap was to be reinforced by a support group, and whenever possible by aircraft. He reckoned that the U-boats, accustomed to being attacked from the direction of the convoy, would be thrown off balance when the support groups came in attacking from all quarters.

On the German side Hitler was enraged by the ineffective result of a New Year's Eve attack on an Arctic convoy by the *Hipper*, *Lützow* and six destroyers, emerging from Altenfiord, and this had important effects. In his disgust he expressed his 'firm and unalterable resolve' to pay off his big ships. This brought about the resignation of Grand Admiral Raeder a month later, and his replacement, as Naval Commander-in-Chief, by Dönitz—who at the same time retained his title and office as Commander, U-boats. Dönitz had a better knack of handling Hitler, and in the end obtained Hitler's agreement to the retention of the *Tirpitz*, *Lützow*, and *Scharnhorst* in Norway as 'a fairly powerful task force'.

There was a lull in the Atlantic during December and January, when U-boat sinkings fell to barely 200,000 tons. That was largely due to stormy weather. But the respite was offset by the dispersing effect and havoc caused to the merchant ships in convoy, especially the more weakly powered ones.

In February the U-boat sinkings were almost doubled, while in March they amounted to 108 ships of 627,000 tons—thus approaching once again the peak figures of June and November 1942. Most worryingly, nearly two-thirds were sunk in convoy. In the middle of March thirty-eight U-boats were concentrated on two homeward-bound convoys, which happened to be close together, and sank twenty-one ships of 141,000 tons, for a loss of only one U-boat, before air cover was resumed on the 20th. This was one of the biggest convoy battles of the whole war.

In retrospect, the Admiralty recorded that 'the Germans never came so near to disrupting communication between the New World and the Old as in the first twenty days of March, 1943'. Moreover, the Naval Staff was brought to the point of wondering whether convoy could continue to be regarded, and used, as an effective system of defence.

But in the last eleven days of March—the last third of that fateful month— a great change came over the scene. Only fifteen ships were sunk in the North Atlantic compared with 107 in the first two-thirds. In April the month's toll was halved, and in May it was much less still. Max Horton's co-ordinated counteroffensive had come into effect—and fulfilled its desired effect in a remarkably short time.

The Americans, at the most critical time in March, had asked to withdraw from the North Atlantic escort system, taking responsibility for the South Atlantic routes, particularly to the Mediterranean. They also had the Pacific much in mind. However, the practical effect was not great. The U.S. Government put the first support group carrier under British Command and provided the vital V.L.R. (very long range) Liberators. So from April 1, Britain and Canada had taken complete charge of all convoys between the American continent and Britain.

During the spring of 1943, the U-boats met defeat in a series of convoy battles, and suffered heavy losses in them. In mid-May Dönitz perceptively reported to Hitler: 'We are facing the greatest crisis in submarine warfare, since the enemy, by means of new location devices . . . makes fighting impossible, and is causing us heavy losses.' For U-boat losses in May had more than doubled, rising to 30 per cent of those at sea—a rate of loss that could not be borne for long. Hence on May 23 Dönitz withdrew his U-boats from the North Atlantic until he had new weapons to use.

By July, more Allied merchant ships were being built than were being sunk. That was the crux of the matter and the proof that the U-boat offensive had been defeated.

Yet, looking back, it is evident that Britain had herself narrowly escaped defeat in March. It is also evident that the primary cause of her danger was the lack of long-range aircraft for the protection of convoys. From January to May, only two ships were sunk in convoy, in the Atlantic, while an air escort was present. Once adequate air cover of this kind was provided for convoys, particularly by the long-range Liberators, it became increasingly difficult for U-boats to operate in 'wolf-packs'. They might now at any moment suddenly find an aircraft over them, directing a support group to their position.

But radar, on the new 10-cm. wavelength that the U-boats could not intercept, was certainly a very important factor, as Dönitz realised and emphasised. New weapons such as the 'Hedgehog', an anti-submarine rocket device, and heavier depth-charges, also contributed. So did the analytical work of the Western Approaches Tactical Unit set up early in 1942 to evolve the best tactical system for dealing with U-boats, and Professor P. M. S. Blackett's operational analysis of convoy deployment. Moreover a new cipher, for shipping control, introduced at the end of May 1943, deprived the Germans of their most valuable source of Intelligence.

Probably the most important factors in the victory, however, was the improvement in training standards of the escorts and aircraft, and the increased co-operation between sailors and airmen.

Among individuals, the outstanding part in the defeat of the U-boats was played by Admiral Sir Max Horton, as already emphasised. Much was also due to Air Marshal Sir John Slessor, who became Commander-in-Chief of Coastal Command in February 1943, the crucial period of the battle. Among the fine band of escort group commanders, two deserve special mention for their exploits—Captain F. J. Walker, from 1941 on, and Commander P. W. (later Vice Admiral Sir Peter) Gretton in 1942–3.

No convoys were attacked in the North Atlantic during the month of

June 1943, while July was very costly for the U-boats, particularly in the Bay of Biscay, where Coastal Command's air patrols had a rich harvest. Of eighty-six U-boats which tried to cross the Bay that month, fifty-five were sighted, seventeen were sunk (all save one by aircraft), and six forced to turn back. Their only outward route had become a narrow line in the Bay of Biscay, hugging the Spanish coast, as Dönitz gloomily reported to Hitler. The anti-submarine patrols, however, paid a considerable price for their successes, fourteen planes being lost.

During the three months June to August 1943, the German U-boats sank no more than fifty-eight Allied merchant ships in all waters excluding the Mediterranean, and nearly half of them were off South Africa and in the Indian Ocean. They gained that very moderate result at a cost of seventy-nine U-boats—of which no less than fifty-eight were sunk by aircraft.

In the hope of regaining the upper hand, Dönitz pressed Hitler for more long-range air reconnaissance in the Atlantic and stronger air cover on the transit routes—and did get a more sympathetic hearing than Raeder had for his arguments towards overcoming Göring's unwillingness to provide air co-operation. Dönitz also obtained approval to increase U-boat production from thirty to forty a month, and to give priority to new types of submarine which would be capable of higher speed when submerged. But the very promising 'Walter' type submarine, driven by a combination of diesel fuel and hydrogen peroxide, suffered so many 'teething' troubles that none was ready for service before the war ended in 1945. A new and important development, however, came with the fitting of the 'Schnorkel' air intake and diesel exhaust mast, a device of pre-1940 Dutch origin, that enabled submarines to charge their batteries while remaining at periscope depth. Thirty of them were fitted with it by the middle of 1944.

Two other new German devices of the mid-1943 period were the 'homing' torpedo, acoustically guided to ships' propellers, and the glider bomb. But during September and October, the first two months of the renewed U-boat campaign, the Allies lost only nine merchant ships—out of the 2,468 which sailed in sixty-four North Atlantic convoys—whereas twenty-five U-boats were sunk. After that further heavy defeat Dönitz gave up working the U-boats in large mobile groups.

On October 8 Britain took over two air bases in the Azores, by agreement with Portugal, and from then onward air cover could be provided over the whole North Atlantic.

In the first three months of 1944 the U-boats suffered still worse losses. Only three merchant ships were sunk—out of 3,360 which crossed the North Atlantic, in 105 convoys—whereas thirty-six U-boats were lost.

Dönitz now cancelled all further operations against convoys, telling Hitler that they could not be renewed until the new types of U-boat and new defensive devices were available, and better air reconnaissance provided.

At the end of March, 1944, Dönitz was ordered to form a group of forty U-boats for inshore operations in the event of an Allied invasion of Western Europe. By the end of May he had concentrated seventy in Biscay ports, and only three remained in the North Atlantic, while these were merely kept on the task of weather reporting.

The German abandonment of the U-boat campaign in the North Atlantic was a relief to Coastal Command, whose aircraft, of No. 19 Group, had sunk fifty U-boats and damaged fifty-six (out of 2,425 passages in and out from the Biscay bases) by May 1944, during forty-one months of anti-submarine operations. No. 19 Group had lost 350 aircraft in the Bay during that period. Its losses would probably have been less, and its effect even greater, if Coastal Command had been allotted a larger scale of aircraft, more appropriate to the key importance of its task.

Among other events of the period were two damaging attacks on the *Tirpitz* at her moorings in northern Norway—by three midget-submarines in September, 1943, and by the Fleet Air Arm in March 1944—which preceded her eventual sinking by R.A.F. heavy bombers in November that year. She had only once fired her main armament in earnest (in a raid on Spitzbergen), but the amount of damage she survived was testimony to the design and strength of German naval construction. Moreover, her mere existence as a 'ship in being', and threat in the offing, had a great influence on Britain's maritime strategy, while absorbing a remarkably large amount of her naval strength.

The threat of the *Scharnhorst* had been brought to an end in the previous December, when she was intercepted and sunk by a strong force from the British Home Fleet, when herself attempting to intercept an Arctic convoy.

During the first half of 1944, Britain's chief trouble in home waters came from the small motor torpedo-boats, called 'E-boats', which the Germans had developed. Although their number was never more than about three dozen, they could be switched rapidly from one convoy route to another and, by choosing suitable opportunities, became a harassing nuisance.

The U-boats that had been concentrated in the western ports of France to oppose an Allied cross-Channel move proved of little effect, although they benefited from having been fitted with the Schnorkel device by the time the Normandy invasion came in June, and were thus less vulnerable to air attack.

When the American Third Army, breaking out from Normandy, arrived close to these western ports—Brest, Lorient, and St Nazaire—in mid-August, most of the U-boats were moved to Norway. And from then shipping to and from Britain could again use the old, and normal, route round the south of Ireland, as well as the route round the north coast.

From the later part of August onward, a stream of U-boats started to come out from Norway, and Germany, by passing round the north of Scotland and Ireland, and positioned themselves close inshore, at busy corners —as far south as Portland Bill on the south coast of England. But they achieved little by this inshore campaign—although, thanks to constant submergence and use of their Schnorkels they suffered fewer losses than before. During the four months September–December 1944, they sank only fourteen ships in British coastal waters.

THE ARCTIC CONVOYS

British convoys to North Russia were started at the end of September, 1941. Ice blocked Archangel in the winter, so Murmansk was used, Russia's only important ice-free port. The Germans' failure to capture that port by a strong overland move was a strange strategic omission as it lost them the chance to strangle this northern supply-route when it was most vulnerable.

As the Germans came to realise the large scale on which British, and then also American, ships were carrying aid to Russia by this route, they hastened to reinforce their naval and air strength in Norway, and developed a series of powerful attacks on the Allies' Arctic convoys in March, April, and May, 1942. The worst hit was eastbound convoy PQ 17, sailing at the end of June. The Admiralty, believing that the convoy and its escort were about to be overwhelmed by German warships, ordered the convoy to scatter in the Barents Sea on July 4. The helpless merchant ships were attacked by aircraft and U-boats, only thirteen out of thirty-six surviving. Of the aircraft which this convoy was carrying eighty-seven were delivered, but 210 lost; of the tanks 164 were delivered, but 430 lost: of non-fighting vehicles 896 were delivered, but 3,350 lost—along with two-thirds of the other cargo, some 99,316 tons.

After that disaster, the next convoy to Russia was not despatched until September. It was given a much stronger escort and Admiral Raeder, warned by radio intelligence, cautiously held back his larger warships— which might have overwhelmed the escorts. As it was, twenty-seven of PQ 18's forty merchant ships got safely through to Archangel, while the German aircraft and U-boats suffered badly. Never again did the Germans deploy such great air strength in the far north.

After another interval, a few smaller convoys were sent in the winter. But the Russians, while repeatedly pressing for more convoys to be run, gave no help in protecting them on the long ocean passage and only a little at the receiving end. From March 1943 onward the C.-in-C., Home Fleet, Admiral Tovey, was unwilling to risk further convoys as the daylight lengthened. The critical situation in the Atlantic decided the argument, and the Arctic escorts were diverted to the Atlantic, where they played a great part in the decisive defeat of the U-boats that spring.

By November, when the Arctic convoys were resumed, much stronger escorts were available, and included the new escort carriers. These inflicted heavy loss on the weakening Luftwaffe as well as on the U-boats, while bringing huge cargoes safely through to Russia.

In the forty outward Arctic convoys from 1941 on, 811 ships sailed, of which fifty-eight were sunk and thirty-three turned back for one reason or another, while 720 came safely through—and delivered about four million tons of cargo to Russia. The deliveries included 5,000 tanks and over 7,000 aircraft. In delivering that large-scale aid the Allies had lost eighteen warships and ninety-eight merchant ships, including those on the homeward convoys, while the Germans had lost the battlecruiser *Scharnhorst*, three destroyers, and thirty-eight U-boats in trying to stop it.

THE LAST PHASE

During the early months of 1945 the size of the U-boat fleet was still increasing—through new production and reduced losses, thanks to the Schnorkel device as well as to the suspension of long-range operations in the Atlantic. In January, thirty new boats were put into service, compared with the recent monthly average of eighteen. Some of them were of the new and improved models with longer cruising range and higher speed when submerged—the ocean-going Type XXI of 1,600 tons, and the coastal Type XXIII of 230 tons (of which about two-thirds were of the larger type). In March, the U-boat fleet reached its peak strength, a total of 463.

It was not until March that the bombing campaign began to have a serious effect on production. Fortunately for the Allies the air minelaying in the Baltic, although it did little material damage compared with the effort, had an important effect—more than was realised by their naval chiefs—in hindering U-boat trials and training, and thus the operational advent of the new submarine types in large numbers. If the new types had ever got to sea in strength they might have revived the U-boat menace as dangerously as in 1943.

But once the Allied armies crossed the Rhine in March, closing on Berlin in conjunction with the Russian advance from the east, all forms of pressure could be, and were, intensified—with crippling effect.

During the last few weeks of the war, the U-boats' activity was mainly off the east and north-east coasts of Britain. Although they achieved little, it is significant that none of the new types was ever sunk in these waters.

After Germany's capitulation in May, 159 U-boats surrendered, but a further 203 were scuttled by their crews. That was characteristic of the U-boat crews' stubborn pride and unshaken morale.

During the 5½ years of war, the Germans had built and commissioned 1,157 U-boats and fifteen ex-foreign submarines were taken over by them: 789 (including 3 ex-foreign) had been lost. They had also commissioned some 700 midget submarines. By far the largest proportion of those sunk *at sea*—500 out of 632—were destroyed by British or British-controlled forces. On the other side, submarines—German, Italian, and Japanese—sank 2,828 ships, totalling nearly 15 million tons. Much the greatest proportion of that huge total was sunk by the Germans—whose U-boats also sank 175 Allied warships, most of them British. Of the Allied losses to U-boats, 61 per cent of the total was made up of ships sailing independently of convoys, 9 per cent was of stragglers from convoys, and only 30 per cent came from ships in convoy—and very few were lost in convoy when air-cover was available.

The Germans' possession of the French naval bases on the Bay of Biscay, for four years, and Eire's refusal to allow the Allies use of her western and southern coastlines, even though she herself depended largely upon the supplies the convoys brought her, contributed immensely to the Allied losses in the Atlantic. And it was largely the Allies' hold on Northern Ireland and Iceland that kept open the one remaining route to Britain.

INDEX

SUBJECT INDEX

GENERAL INDEX

A6M. *See* Zero
Aa, River, 80
Aachen, 561, 646, 655; entanglement of U.S. First Army around, 560, 564–5, 649; air raids on, 600
Aalborg, 100
Aandalsnes, 62
A.B.D.A. Command, 227–8
Abbeville, 75
Abuyog, Philippines, 628
Abyssinia, *see* Ethiopia
'Acrobat, Operation', 267
Acroma, 196, 275
Adachi, Lieut.-General H., 615, 687
Adak Island, 500
Addis Ababa, 125
Addu Attol, 237
Adige, River, 674
Adlertag (Eagle Day), 99
Admiral Graf Spee, the, 371
Admiral Hipper, the, 374, 384, 387
Admiral Scheer, the, 374, 377, 384
Admiralty Islands, 509, 613
Adriatic, Allied failure to use amphibious power in, 474–5
Agedabia, 198, 267
Agheila, bottleneck, 116–17; Rommel's advance to, 119, 172
'A-Go, Operation', 618
Agordat, 126
Agra, Central Command H.Q. at, 364
Aire–St Omer–Graveline canal, 75, 80
Aisne, River, 72, 80–1, 84
Aitape, New Guinea, 615, 687
Akagi, the, 351
Akyab Island, 365–6, 515–16, 634
Alagir, 255
Alam Halfa, Battle of, 291–7, 335
Alam Nayil Ridge, 293
Alamein, Eighth Army driven back to, 266; Auchinlek decides to stand at, 278; Rommel pauses near, 281, 296; defensive position at, 281; 'First' battle of, 281–3, 296; July battle of, 284–90; final battle of, 297–304; comparative strength of armies at, 298–9; Martel on reasons for success at, 489
Alaska, 500
Alban Hills, 528-9, 536
Albania, 135; oil of, 24
Albert Canal, German capture of bridges over, 68–9; scratch German forces to line, 559–60; British secure crossing over, 559; British failure to secure bridges over, 565–7

Aleutian Islands, Japanese attack, 345, 349–350, 352; American expedition to regain, 500–1
Alexander, General (later Field-Marshal) Sir Harold, in Burma, 235–6; appointed C.-in-C. Middle East, 266, 290; acts on Auchinleck's plan, 291–2; fixes date for Alamein attack, 297–8; Deputy C.-in-C. to Eisenhower, 402; commands 18th Army Group in Tunisia, 402, 415, 420; on rout of Allied forces, 405; lucky placing of forces by, 406; plans for 'final' Tunisian offensive, 423–4; fresh plan of, 426–8; completes conquest of Tunisia, 430–1, 435; on number of prisoners taken, 431; commands 15th Army Group in invasion of Sicily, 439; reports on Sicilian campaign, 442,445; in Italy,450; gives object for Calabrian landings, 457, 467; optimism of, about landings in Italy, 458; visits Salerno bridgehead, 464; four-phase directive of, 471; on slow advance, 473; plans Anzio landing, 527; endorses destruction of Cassino monastery, 530; calls off Cassino offensive, 532; and 1944 spring offensive in Italy, 532–3, 535; opposes 'Anvil' operation, 537–8; loses divisions and air support to 'Dragoon', 538; follow-up plan of, 539–40, 542; Supreme Commander, Mediterranean, 541; mentioned, 295, 463, 528
Alexandria, tank convoy arrives at, 176; Rommel fails to reach, 266; British Fleet leaves, 283
Alexandropolis, 133
Algeria, project for landing in, 310, 313–17; landings in, 323–6; French forces in, 332; advance on Tunisia through, 334. *See also* 'Torch, Operation'; North-West Africa
Algiers, Allied landing at, 313–16, 320, 325–6; assault forces for, 317; secret meeting with French near, 318–19; French resistance at, 320, 323, 325–6; cease-fire at, 323, 327–8; confusion among French in, 327–30; planning of 'Husky' in, 439; convoys embark from, 441, 460
Allen, Major-General Terry, 323, 409, 415–416
Allenstein, 667
Allfrey, Lieut.-General C. W., 340, 423, 467
Alps, German infiltration through, into Italy, 451–2
Alsace, 560
Altenfiord, 388
Altmark, the, 55–6

Berg, 652
Bergen, 51, 56–7, 61
Bergius hydrogenation plants, 610
Berlin, reprisal raid on, 102; road to, through
Ruhr, 565; bombers to raid (1918), 589;
air raids on, 596, 601, 603, 608; 'Battle of',
602; Russian offensive aimed at, 664;
Russians approach, 667–8; Germans speed
Western Allies towards, 679; Russians in,
680–1
Bermuda, U.S. installations in, 380
Besançon, 85
Bessarabia, Russia aims at, 14; Russian
troops in, 143, 165; Hitler promises return
of, to Rumania, 150; German troops com-
pelled to hold to ground in, 575; Germans
cut off in salient in S., 584–5
Béthouart, Major-General E., 317, 320–1
Beveland Peninsula, Germans allowed to
escape through, 565
Bevin, Ernest, 694
Biak Island, 616, 618
Biala, River, 30
Bialystok, 31, 580–1
Biferno, River, 468, 471
Biggin Hill sector station, 95, 101
Bilin River, 234
Billancourt, 597
Bir Berraneb, 195
Bir el Gubi, 186, 195–6
Bir Gibni, 187
Bir Hacheim, 269, 272–3, 275
Bir Sheferzen, 190
Bir Waid, 176
Birmingham, air raids on, 108
Biscay, Bay of, U-boats destroyed in, 390–1;
U-boat concentration in, 391; German
bases in, 394
Bismarck, the, 377–9
Bismarck Archipelago, U.S. plan to capture,
357, 502; Japanese Navy gives priority to,
501; Japanese forces in, 502; classed non-
essential to Japanese plans, 506; capture of,
508–9, 613; Japanese aircraft withdrawn
from, 513; mopping-up operations in, 688
Bismarck Sea, Battle of, 503
Bitburg, 565
Bizerta, need for quick capture of, 313n., 315;
Allied advance on, 334; airfield at, 334;
German troops at, 335–6, 427; capture of,
430; convoys for Sicily pass near, 440; em-
barkation point for invasion convoys, 441,
460, 466
Black Sea, German drive near, 247, 253;
Russians lose naval base on, 249; 'danger
area' between Carpathians and, 573;
threat to German armies on, 574–5. See
also Crimea; Kerch
Blackett, Prof. P. M. S., 389
Blamey, General Sir Thomas, 356, 687–8
Blaskowitz, General J., 29–30
Blida airfield, 325
'Blitz', the, 105–8
Blücher, the, 61
Blumentritt, General G., on Hitler's attitude to
Britain (1940), 83; on difficulty of getting
information out of Britain, 548; on obtain-
ing use of reserve panzer corps, 549; on

Hitler's decision of no withdrawal, 550–1;
on Kluge and plot to kill Hitler, 551; on
Germany's lack of defences (1944), 558n.;
on Allied mistakes in advance to Germany,
565–6; commands 15th Army, 649
Bobruisk, 163, 580
Bochum, 600
Bock, Field-Marshal F. von, army group of,
28, 38, 75, 77; to complete encirclement of
Allied troops, 81; commands army group
in Russia, 132, 148–9, 159, 161, 166–8;
urges continued offensive, 168–9; resigns
through illness, 169, 244; takes Rund-
stedt's place, 245; successful counter-
offensive of, 248
Bologna, 540–2, 671–3
Bond, Lieut.-General L. V., 231
Bône, 313–14, 334
Bonin Islands, 630
Bonomi, Ivanoe, 537
Bor-Komorowski, General, 583
Bordeaux, French Government in, 85
Boris, King of Bulgaria, 133–4
Borneo, 203, 688–9
Bougainville Island, 502–3, 505; Japanese
force in, 507; campaign in, 507–9; mopping-
up operations in, 687–8
Bougie, 334
Boulogne, 75; mobile radar station at, cap-
tured by Germans, 94
Bradley, General Omar, in Tunisia, 402;
takes command of 2nd Corps, 424,
427; commands 12th Army Group in
'Overlord', 561; in disagreement with
Montgomery on strategy, 561–3; opposed
to airborne attack, 564; confident that
enemy is beaten, 639; receives news of
Ardennes attack, 642, 655; proves identity
to cautious G.I.s, 645; seeks to exploit
Rhine crossing, 677–8
Brandenberger, General E., 653
Brandenburg, 667–8
Brauchitsch, General Walther von, in Polish
campaign, 29; opposed to invasion of
France, 35–7; opposed to Manstein's plan,
39–40; and Hitler's order for standstill of
panzer forces, 81–2; opposed to Hitler's
Russian strategy, 166–7; urges continued
offensive, 168; asks to be relieved of com-
mand, 169; Hitler's scapegoat, 244
Braun, Eva, 680–1
Brazil, 385
Bremen, air raids on, 598, 603
Breslau, 667–8
Brest, German commerce-raiders in, 374–5,
377, 379, 596; air raid damage to port, 377;
U.S. Army arrives at, 392; Germans hold
out in, 557
Brest-Litovsk, 31, 161–2, 580–1
'Brevity, Operation', 174, 176–7
Briansk, 241, 490–1, 493
Briggs, Major-General Raymond, 418–19
Brighton, 89
Brindisi, 456, 466–7
Bristol, air attacks on, 107–8
Britain, guarantees integrity of Poland, 3,
11–15, 704; appeasement policy of, 6–7,
10–11; suddenly reverses policy, 7, 11, 15;

French in North Africa—*contd.*
rally forces to Allied side, 319–20; resistance from, 320–3
Freyberg, Lieut.-General Sir Bernard, in Crete, 135–6; in Tunisia, 417, 426; in Italy, 529–30, 532
Friedman, Colonel William F., 209
Friessner, General, 148, 581–2, 587
Fromm, General Friedrich, 36
Frusci, General, 126
Fuka, 279, 303–6

Gabes, 336, 415, 417, 419; bottleneck at, 309, 335, 416; Gulf of, 335; 21st Panzer Division sent to, 398
Gabr Saleh, 187–8
Gaeta, 464, 470; Gulf of, 456
Gaffey, Major-General Hugh J., 657
Gafsa, Tunisia, airfield at, 335; Rommel attacks near, 401–3; occupied by Germans, 405; captured by Americans, 413, 415
Galal, 305
Galatz, 584–5; Gap, 573, 575
Gallabat, 112, 121, 125
Galland, General Adolf, 92
Gällivare iron-mines, 45, 52–5, 57
'Galvanic, Operation', 511
Gambut, 276
Gamelin, General M., plans invasion of Belgium, 35, 41, 70; Plan 'D' of, 41; plans operation in Scandinavia, 54–5, 58–9; on crossing of Meuse, 73; removed from command, 74, 76
Gangaw, 635
Garigliano, River, 469–70, 472, 527, 532
Gatehouse, Major-General A. H., 291
Gaulle, General Charles de, interested in tanks, 21; not told of North-west African landings, 319; and Darlan's appointment and murder, 331–2
Gazala, Rommel withdraws to line of, 196–7; Eighth Army driven back to, 266, 268; Battle of, 269–75, 311; fortification of, 269, 271
Gazzera, General P., 127
Gehlen, Major-General R., 663
Gela, 441, 443
Gelsenkirchen, raid on, 608
Gemas, 228
'Generals' Plot', 479, 551–2, 582, 649
Genoa, 671
Georges, General A., 17, 70, 73
Germany, invades Poland, 3, 16, 28–9, 705; needs *lebensraum*, 7–8; economic difficulties of, 10; makes pact with Russia, 13–14, 206, 705; gains Czecho-Slovakian armaments, 22–3; lacks raw materials for war, 23–4, 150, 611; opposition to Hitler in, 35*n.*, 36, 40, 713; mass of troops and people of, put trust in Hitler, 36; gets iron from Sweden, 45, 52–5; occupies Norway, 45, 51–6, 58–63, 706; occupies Denmark, 51; plan to drop mines into rivers of, 57; invades Holland and Belgium, 66–9, 707; invades France, 65, 69–72, 707; prepares to invade Britain, 87–90; air attacks of, on Britain, 90–108; fails to make use of captured knowledge of radar, 94–5; pact between Yugo-Slavia and, 132–4; bombing of, 102, 142, 231, 393, 589–612; invades Russia, 141, 157–70; importance of Rumanian oil to, 143–4, 147, 149, 585; signs new treaty with Russia, 147; exploitation of Russia planned by, 150; Japan's alliance with, 205–6; exhausting effect of Russian campaign on, 241, 247; needs oil of Caucasus, 245, 248; has limited reserve of men and machines, 257, 485; possible actions of, to frustrate 'Torch', 313, 315; occupies Southern France, 329–30; air offensive over, deprives Coastal Command of aircraft, 383; bombing of, affects U-boat construction, 393; Hitler runs down resources of, to supply Italy, 450; secrecy as to shrinkage of assets of, 485; seeks frontier on Dnieper, 488; Rommel in, at time of invasion, 550; nothing to stop Allies driving into (1944), 558, 566; Allies approach frontier of, 560; improves defences of frontier, 560; causes of Allied failure to defeat, in 1944, 561–7; increases commitments in Finland, 578; Rumania and Bulgaria declare war on, 585; Finland at war with, 587; strategic air offensive against, 589–612; bombs London (1914–1918), 589; improved air defences of, 596–598; bombing of, fails to prevent increased output, 599, 605; air attacks on oil targets in, 605–8; air attacks on communications in, 607; assessment of results of bombing, 610–12; evacuation of population from towns of east, 666; collapse in, 677–81; people of, want Allies to reach Berlin before Russians, 679; surrender of, 680–1
Gerow, General Leonard, 652
Ghazal, 305
Ghormley, Vice-Admiral Robert L., 358–9, 361
Gibraltar, Germans plan operation against, 145, 150; fears of German seizure of, 313; 'Torch' assault forces pass through Straits of, 317; Mark Clark carried to Algiers from, 318; Giraud at, 320; Spain takes no action against, 333
Gibraltar convoys, 380, 382, 386
Gibson, Wing Commander Guy, 600
'Gideon Force', 125
Giffard, General Sir George, 515
Giffen, Rear-Admiral R. L., 322
Gilbert Islands, 506, 510–11, 513, 613
Giraud, General Henri, chosen as leader of French in N. Africa, 319–21; Algiers broadcast in favour of, 326–7; leadership of, not accepted by French, 327–8, 330; Commander-in-Chief of Ground and Air Forces, 331; High Commissioner, 332
Givet, 657
Glaire, bridge over Meuse at, 71
Gleiwitz, 667
Gneisenau, the, 371, 377, 596
Gniezno, 667
Godwin-Austen, Lieut.-General A. R., 124, 184, 196, 268
Golikov, General P. I., 263, 480–1
Gondar, 125, 127
'Goodwood, Operation', 556

BOOKS REFERRED TO IN THE TEXT

Where British and American publishers are given, the first mentioned is the edition from which I have taken any quotations, and the page numbers of any reference may be valid for that edition only. I would like to thank the authors, publishers and other copyright holders concerned for permission to make quotations from some of these works.

Bradley, Omar N.: *A Soldier's Story of the Allied Campaigns from Tunis to the Elbe*. London, Eyre & Spottiswoode, 1951; New York, H. Holt & Co., 1951.

Butcher, Captain Harry C.: *My Three Years with Eisenhower*. New York, Simon & Schuster, 1946; London, Heinemann, 1946.

Churchill, Winston S.: *The War Speeches of Winston S. Churchill* (compiled by Charles Eade, 3 vols). London, Cassell, 1952; Boston, Houghton Mifflin, 1953.

Churchill, Winston S.: *The Second World War* (6 vols). London, Cassell, 1948–54: Boston, Houghton, Mifflin, 1948–54.
    Vol. I: *The Gathering Storm* (9th edition, 1967).
    Vol. II: *Their Finest Hour* (9th edition, 1967).
    Vol. III: *The Grand Alliance* (5th edition, 1968).
    Vol. IV: *The Hinge of Fate* (4th edition, 2nd impression, 1968).
    Vol. V: *Closing the Ring* (4th edition, 2nd impression, 1968).
    Vol. VI: *Triumph and Tragedy* (2nd edition, 1954).

Clark, General Mark: *Calculated Risk*. London, Harrap, 1951; New York, Harper, 1950.

Cunningham, Admiral Lord: *A Sailor's Odyssey*. London, Hutchinson, 1951.

Douhet, Giulio: *The Command of the Air*. London, Faber, 1943; New York, Coward-McCann, 1942.

Eisenhower, Dwight D.: *Crusade in Europe*. New York, Doubleday, 1948; London, Heinemann, 1949.

Feiling, Keith: *The Life of Neville Chamberlain*. London, Macmillan, 1946.

Halder, General Franz: *Diaries*. Privately printed. Copyright © Infantry Journal Inc. (U.S.A.), 1950.

Kippenberger, Major-General Sir Howard: *Infantry Brigadier*. London (and New York), Oxford University Press, 1949.

Liddell Hart, Captain B. H.: *The Defence of Britain*. London, Faber, 1939.
    The Other Side of the Hill. London, Cassell, 1951.
    (See my list of books, following the Index. *The Other Side of the Hill* in its 1951 edition has not been published in the United States. The considerably smaller 1948 edition was published in New York by Morrow in 1948 as *The German Generals Talk*.)
    The Tanks: The History of the Royal Tank Regiment and its Predecessors etc. (2 vols). London, Cassell, 1959; New York, Praeger, 1959.

Linklater, Eric: *The Campaign in Italy*. London, H.M.S.O., 1951.

Martel, Lieut.-General Sir Gifford: *An Outspoken Soldier*. London, Sifton Praed, 1949.

North, John: *North-West Europe 1944-5. The Achievements of 21st Army Group*. London, H.M.S.O., 1953.

Rommel, Field-Marshal Erwin: *The Rommel Papers* (ed. B. H. Liddell Hart). London, Collins, 1953; New York, Harcourt, Brace, 1953.

Schmidt, H. W.: *With Rommel in the Desert*. London, Harrap, 1951.

Seaton, Lieut.-Colonel Albert: *The Russo-German War, 1941-1945*. London, Arthur Barker, 1970; New York, Praeger, 1970.

Tedder, Marshal of the Royal Air Force Lord: *With Prejudice*. London, Cassell, 1966; Boston, Little, Brown, 1967.

Westphal, General Siegfried: *The German Army in the West*. London, Cassell, 1951.

OFFICIAL HISTORIES
Great Britain

Roskill, Captain S. W.: *The War at Sea*. Vol. I. London, H.M.S.O., 1954.

Ehrman, John: *Grand Strategy*. Vol. V. London, H.M.S.O., 1956.

Woodburn Kirby, Major-General S.: *The War Against Japan*. Vol. I. London. H.M.S.O., 1957.

Playfair, Major-General I.S.O., and others: *The Mediterranean and the Middle East*. Vol. III. London, H.M.S.O., 1960.

Webster, Sir Charles, and Frankland, Noble: *The Strategic Air Offensive Against Germany, 1939-1945*.
  Vol. I: *Preparation*. London, H.M.S.O., 1961.
  Vol. II: *Endeavour*. London, H.M.S.O., 1961.
  Vol. III: *Victory*. London, H.M.S.O., 1961.

United States

United States Army in World War II

Cole, H. M.: *The European Theater of Operations: The Lorraine Campaign*. Washington D.C., Historical Division, Department of the Army, 1950.

Matloff, Maurice, and Snell, Edwin M.: *The War Department: Strategic Planning for Coalition Warfare, 1941-1942*. Washington, D.C., Office of the Chief of Military History, Department of the Army, 1953.

Howe, George F.: *The Mediterranean Theater of Operations: Northwest Africa: Seizing the Initiative in the West*. Washington, D.C., Office of the Chief of Military History, Department of the Army, 1957.

History of United States Naval Operations in World War II

Morison, S. E.: Vol. IX: *Sicily–Salerno–Anzio, January 1943–June 1944*. Boston. Little, Brown, 1954.

DESPATCHES

Supplement to The London Gazette, 3 February 1948.
  Despatch submitted . . . by . . . Field-Marshal the Viscount Alexander of Tunis, K.G., G.C.B., G.C.M.G., C.S.I., D.S.O., M.C.

Supplement to The London Gazette, 25 April 1950.
  Despatch submitted . . . by Admiral of the Fleet Sir Andrew B. Cunningham, G.C.B., D.S.O.